#1 New York Times *bestselling author Nora Roberts writing as J. D. Robb presents her newest novel in the "sexy and suspenseful"* (Publishers Weekly) *series. It is the year 2059, a future where technology and humanity collide, and a new computer virus has become the latest form of terrorism . . .*

DIVIDED IN DEATH

Reva Ewing was a former member of the Secret Service, and then a security specialist for Roarke Enterprises—until she was found standing over the dead bodies of her husband, renowned artist Blair Bissel, and her best friend. But Lieutenant Eve Dallas believes there was more to the killings than jealous rage—all of Bissel's computer files were deliberately corrupted. To Roarke, it's the computer attack that poses the real threat. He and Reva have been under a Code Red government contract to develop a program that would shield against techno-terrorists. But this deadly new breed of hackers isn't afraid to kill to protect their secret—and it's up to Lieutenant Eve Dallas to shut them down before the nightmare can spread to the whole country.

"Any 'In Death' book should be at the top of any reading list. Eve, Roarke, and the rest of the cast will enchant you, and the murder plots will enthrall you." —*Grand Forks Herald*

Nora Roberts

HOT ICE
SACRED SINS
BRAZEN VIRTUE
SWEET REVENGE
PUBLIC SECRETS
GENUINE LIES
CARNAL INNOCENCE
DIVINE EVIL
HONEST ILLUSIONS
PRIVATE SCANDALS
HIDDEN RICHES
TRUE BETRAYALS
MONTANA SKY
SANCTUARY
HOMEPORT
THE REEF
RIVER'S END
CAROLINA MOON
THE VILLA
MIDNIGHT BAYOU
THREE FATES
BIRTHRIGHT
NORTHERN LIGHTS
BLUE SMOKE
ANGELS FALL
HIGH NOON
TRIBUTE

Series

Born In Trilogy
BORN IN FIRE
BORN IN ICE
BORN IN SHAME

Dream Trilogy
DARING TO DREAM
HOLDING THE DREAM
FINDING THE DREAM

Chesapeake Bay Saga
SEA SWEPT
RISING TIDES
INNER HARBOR
CHESAPEAKE BLUE

Gallaghers of Ardmore Trilogy
JEWELS OF THE SUN
TEARS OF THE MOON
HEART OF THE SEA

Three Sisters Island Trilogy
DANCE UPON THE AIR
HEAVEN AND EARTH
FACE THE FIRE

Key Trilogy
KEY OF LIGHT
KEY OF KNOWLEDGE
KEY OF VALOR

In the Garden Trilogy
BLUE DAHLIA
BLACK ROSE
RED LILY

Circle Trilogy
MORRIGAN'S CROSS
DANCE OF THE GODS
VALLEY OF SILENCE

Sign of Seven Trilogy
BLOOD BROTHERS
THE HOLLOW

Nora Roberts & J. D. Robb

REMEMBER WHEN

J. D. Robb

NAKED IN DEATH
GLORY IN DEATH
IMMORTAL IN DEATH
RAPTURE IN DEATH
CEREMONY IN DEATH
VENGEANCE IN DEATH
HOLIDAY IN DEATH
CONSPIRACY IN DEATH
LOYALTY IN DEATH
WITNESS IN DEATH
JUDGMENT IN DEATH
BETRAYAL IN DEATH
SEDUCTION IN DEATH
REUNION IN DEATH
PURITY IN DEATH
PORTRAIT IN DEATH
IMITATION IN DEATH
DIVIDED IN DEATH
VISIONS IN DEATH
SURVIVOR IN DEATH
ORIGIN IN DEATH
MEMORY IN DEATH
BORN IN DEATH
INNOCENT IN DEATH
CREATION IN DEATH
STRANGERS IN DEATH

Anthologies

FROM THE HEART

A LITTLE MAGIC

A LITTLE FATE

Moon Shadows

(*with Jill Gregory, Ruth Ryan Langan, and Marianne Willman*)

The Once Upon Series

(*with Jill Gregory, Ruth Ryan Langan, and Marianne Willman*)

ONCE UPON A CASTLE

ONCE UPON A STAR

ONCE UPON A DREAM

ONCE UPON A ROSE

ONCE UPON A KISS

ONCE UPON A MIDNIGHT

***

SILENT NIGHT

(*with Susan Plunkett, Dee Holmes, and Claire Cross*)

OUT OF THIS WORLD

(*with Laurell K. Hamilton, Susan Krinard, and Maggie Shayne*)

BUMP IN THE NIGHT

(*with Mary Blayney, Ruth Ryan Langan, and Mary Kay McComas*)

DEAD OF NIGHT

(*with Mary Blayney, Ruth Ryan Langan, and Mary Kay McComas*)

THREE IN DEATH

Also available . . .

THE OFFICIAL NORA ROBERTS COMPANION

(*edited by Denise Little and Laura Hayden*)

Divided in Death

J. D. Robb

DIVIDED IN DEATH

A Berkley Book / published by arrangement with
the author

PRINTING HISTORY
G. P. Putnam's Son's hardcover edition / January 2004
Berkley mass-market edition / September 2004

Cover art by Tony Greco.
Cover design by Rich Hasselberger.

For information address: The Berkley Publishing Group,
a division of Penguin Group (USA) Inc.,
375 Hudson Street, New York, New York 10014.

ISBN: 978-0-425-19795-0

BERKLEY®
Berkley Books are published by The Berkley Publishing Group,
a division of Penguin Group (USA) Inc.,
375 Hudson Street, New York, New York 10014.
BERKLEY and the "B" design
are trademarks belonging to Penguin Group (USA) Inc.

PRINTED IN THE UNITED STATES OF AMERICA

10 9 8 7 6 5

Sigh no more, ladies, sigh no more,
Men were deceivers ever.

—WILLIAM SHAKESPEARE

Marriage is a desperate thing.

—JOHN SELDEN

Prologue

Killing was too good for him.

Death was an end, even a release. He'd go to hell, there was no question in her mind, and there he would suffer eternal torment. She wanted that for him—eventually. But for the time being, she wanted him to suffer where she could watch.

Lying, cheating son of a *bitch!* She wanted him to snivel and beg and plead and slither on his belly like the gutter rat he was. She wanted him to bleed from the ears, to scream like a girl. She wanted to twist his adulterous dick into knots while he shrieked for the mercy she'd never give.

She wanted to pound her fists into his beautiful liar's face until it was a pulpy, pustulated mass of blood and bone.

Then and only then, the dickless, faceless bastard could die. A slow, withering, agonizing death.

Nobody, *nobody* cheated on Reva Ewing.

She had to pull over and stop the car in the breakdown lane of the Queensboro Bridge until she calmed down enough to trust herself to continue. Because someone *had* cheated on Reva Ewing. The man she'd loved, the man she'd married, the man she'd believed in utterly was, even now, making love to another woman.

Touching another woman, tasting her, using that skilled deceiver's mouth, those clever cheating hands, to drive another woman wild.

And not just any other woman. A friend. Someone else she'd loved and trusted, believed in, counted on.

It wasn't just infuriating. It wasn't just painful to know her husband and her friend were having an affair, and right under her oblivious nose. It was *embarrassing* to discover herself a cliché. The deceived wife, the clueless dolt who accepted and believed the adulterer every time he said he had to work late, or had a dinner meeting with a client, or was zipping out of town for a few days to nail down, or hand deliver, a commission.

Worse, Reva thought now as traffic whizzed by her car, that she of all people had been so easily duped. She was a goddamn security expert. She'd spent five years in the Secret Service and had guarded a president before going into the private sector. Where were her instincts, her eyes, her ears?

How could Blair have been coming home to her, night after night, fresh from another woman and she not *know?*

Because she'd loved him, Reva admitted. Because she'd been happy, deliriously happy to believe a man like Blair—with his sophistication and amazing looks—had loved and wanted her.

He was so handsome, so talented, so smart. The elegant bohemian with his dark silky hair and emerald green eyes. She'd been sunk, she thought now, the minute he'd turned those eyes on her, the instant he'd sent her that killer smile. And six months later, they'd been married and living in the big, secluded house in Queens.

Two years, she thought, two years she'd given him everything she had, shared every piece of herself with him, and had loved him with every cell of her body. And all the while he'd been playing her for a fool.

Well, now he'd pay. She dashed the tears from her cheeks, dug deep again for her anger. Now, Blair Bissel was going to find out just what she was made of.

She pulled back into traffic, and drove at a rapid clip to Manhattan's Upper East Side.

* * *

The husband-stealing bitch, as Reva now thought of her former friend, Felicity Kade, lived in a lovely converted brownstone near the north corner of Central Park. Instead of reminding herself of all the time she'd spent inside, at parties, casual evenings, at Felicity's famed Sunday brunches, Reva concentrated on the security.

It was good. Felicity collected art and guarded that collection like a dog guarded his meaty bone. The fact was, Reva had met her three years before when she'd helped design and install Felicity's security system.

It would take an expert to gain entrance, and even then, there were backups and fail-safes that would foil all but the crème de la crème of burglars.

But when a woman made her living, her very good living, looking for chinks in security, she could always find one. She'd come armed, with two jammers, a beefed-up personal palm computer, an illegal police master code, and a stunner she intended to slap right against Blair's cheating balls.

After that, well, she wasn't quite sure what she'd do. She'd just play the rest by ear.

She hefted her bag of tools, shoved the stunner in her back pocket, and marched through the balmy September evening toward the front entrance.

She keyed in the first jammer as she walked, knowing she'd have thirty seconds only once she'd locked it on the exterior panel. Numbers began to flash on her handheld, and her heart began to race as she counted off the time.

Three seconds before the alarm was set to trip, the first code scanned onto her jammer. She let out the breath she'd held, glanced up at the dark windows.

"Just keep doing what you're doing up there, you pair of slime," she muttered as she set the second jammer. "I only need a few more minutes here. Then we'll *really* party."

She heard the whiz of a car on the street behind her, and cursed softly as it braked. A quick look back and she spotted a cab at the curb, and the laughing couple in evening clothes who climbed out. Reva edged closer to the door, deeper in the shadows. With a minidrill she removed the side of the palm plate, noting that Felicity's house droid kept even the screws spotless.

Interfacing her PPC with a hair-thin wire, she keyed in a bypass code, waited the sweaty seconds for it to clear. Meticulously, she replaced the panel, then used the second jammer on the voice box.

It took longer to clone, a full two minutes, but she felt a frisson of excitement work through her fury when the last voice entry played back.

August Rembrandt.

Reva's lips twisted in a sneer as her false friend's voice murmured the password. Reva had only to key in the cloned security numbers, then use her tools to lift the last, manual lock.

She slipped inside, closed the door, and out of habit reset the security.

Prepared for the house droid to appear, to request her business, she held her stunner at the ready. He'd recognize her, of course, and that would give her just enough time to fry his circuits and clear her way.

But the house stayed silent, and no droid stepped into the foyer. So, they'd shut him down for the night, she thought grimly. So they could have a little more privacy.

She could smell the roses Felicity always kept on the table in the foyer—pink roses, replaced weekly. There was a low light burning beside the vase, but Reva didn't need it. She knew her way, and walked directly to the stairs to climb to the second floor. To the bedroom.

When she reached the landing she saw all she needed to bring her rage back in full force. Tossed carelessly over the rail was Blair's light leather jacket. It was the one she'd given him for his birthday the previous spring. The one he'd hooked carelessly with his fingers over his shoulder just that morning when he'd kissed his loving wife good-bye, and told her how much he'd miss her, told her as he'd nuzzled her neck how much he hated having to take even this quick out-of-town trip.

Reva lifted the jacket, brought it to her face. She could

smell him on it, and the scent of him nearly tore her grief through her anger.

To stave it off, she took one of her tools out of her bag and quietly shred the leather to ribbons. Then, tossing it on the floor, she ground her heel into it before stepping away.

Face hot with temper, she set her bag down, took the stunner back out of her pocket. As she approached the bedroom she saw the flicker of light. Candles, she could even smell them now, some spicy female perfume. And she could hear the low notes of music—something classic, like the roses, like the scent of the candles.

It was all so Felicity, she thought furiously. All so female and fragile and perfect. She'd have preferred something modern, something *today* and gutsy for this altercation.

Give her Mavis Freestone kicking some serious musical ass, she thought.

But then it was easy to tune out the music with the buzzing of temper and the ring of betrayal in her head. She toed the door wider with her foot, eased in.

She could see the two figures huddled together under the silk and lace of the coverlet. They'd fallen asleep, she thought bitterly. All cozy and warm and loose from sex.

Their clothes were tossed over a chair, messily, as if they'd been in a hurry to start. Seeing them, the tangle of clothes, broke her heart in hundreds of pieces.

Bracing against it, she strode to the bed, gripped the stunner in her hand. "Wake-up call, you piss-buckets."

And whipped the silk and lace cover away.

The blood. Oh my God, the blood. The sight of it all over flesh, all over the sheets, made her head spin. The sudden smell of it, of death, mixed with the scents of flowers and candles, made her gag and stumble back.

"Blair? *Blair?*"

She screamed once, shocking herself into action. Sucking in air to scream again, she lunged forward.

Something, someone, slipped out of the shadows. She caught the movement, and another smell—harsh, medicinal. It filled her throat, her lungs.

She turned, to flee or defend she wasn't sure, and fought to swim through air that had gone to water around her. But the power had drained out of her limbs, numbing them seconds before her eyes rolled back in her head.

And she collapsed in a heap beside the dead who had betrayed her.

Chapter 1

Lieutenant Eve Dallas, one of New York's top cops, sprawled naked with the blood beating in her ears and her heart pounding like an airjack. She managed to wheeze in a breath, then gave it up.

Who needed air when the system was revving from the aftermath of truly spectacular sex?

Beneath her, her husband lay warm and hard and still. The only movement was the knock of his heart against hers. Until he lifted one of those amazing hands and cruised it along her spine, from nape to butt.

"You want me to move," she mumbled, "you're out of luck."

"I'd say my luck's in."

She smiled in the dark. She loved hearing his voice, the way Ireland shimmered through it. "Pretty good welcome home, especially since you were gone less than forty-eight hours."

"It certainly put a nice cap on a short trip to Florence."

"I didn't ask, did you stop off in Ireland to see your—" She hesitated just a beat. It was still so odd to think of Roarke with family. "Your family?"

"I did, yes. Had a nice few hours." He continued to stroke that hand, up and down, up and down her back so that her heartbeat slowed and her eyes began to droop. "It's very strange, isn't it?"

"I guess it will be, for a while yet."

"And how's the new detective?"

Eve snuggled in, thinking of her former aide and how she was handling her recent promotion. "Peabody's good. Still finding her rhythm. We had a family dispute gone sour. Two brothers mixing it up over inherited property. Knocked the shit out of each other before one of them takes a header down the steps and breaks his stupid neck. So the other brother tries to mock it up like a bungled burglary. Tosses all this stuff they were fighting over in a blanket, hauls it out to his car, shoves it in the trunk. Like we're not going to look there."

The derision in her tone had him chuckling. Eve rolled off and stretched.

"Anyway, it was pretty much connect the big, pulsing red dots, so I put Peabody on as primary. After she started breathing again, she did fine. Sweepers were already sucking up evidence, but she takes this jerk in the kitchen, sits down with him all sympathetic—used all that family business she knows so well. Had him babbling out a confession in about ten minutes. Got him on Man Two."

"Good for her."

"It'll help build her confidence." She stretched again. "We could use a few more walks in the meadow like that one after the summer we put in."

"You might take a few days off. We could walk in a real meadow."

"Give me a couple of weeks with her. I want to make sure she finds her feet before I let her solo."

"That's a date, then. Oh, your . . . enthusiastic welcome, while much appreciated, drove this right out of my mind." He got out of bed, calling for the lights at ten percent.

In their subtle glow, she could watch him step off the wide platform where the bed stood, move toward the small bag he'd taken with him. Watching him move, graceful as some lean, elegant cat, gave her such pleasure.

Was that kind of grace innate, she wondered, or had he learned it dodging cops and picking pockets as a child on the streets of Dublin? However it had come to him, it had served him well, as that clever boy, and as the clever man who'd built an empire out of guts and guile and a wily kind of genius.

When he turned, and she saw his face in that shadowed light, it blew straight through her. The staggering love, the breathless wonder that he should be hers—that anything so beautiful should be hers.

He looked like a work of art, one carved by some brilliant sorcerer. The keen bones of his face, the generous mouth that was sensual magic. Those eyes, that wild Celtic blue, that could still make her throat ache when they looked at her. And that miraculous canvas was framed by black silk that swept nearly to his shoulders, and continually made her fingers itch to touch it.

They'd been married more than a year, and there were times, unexpected times, when just looking at him could stop her heart.

He came back to sit beside her, cupped her chin in his hand, brushed his thumb over the little dent in its center. "Darling Eve, so still and quiet in the dark." He touched his lips to her brow. "I've brought you a present."

She blinked, and immediately edged back. It made him smile, this habitual reaction of hers to gifts. Just as the uneasy look she gave the long, narrow box in his hand made him grin.

"It won't bite you," he promised.

"You weren't even gone two days. There has to be some sort of time requirement for bringing back presents."

"I missed you after two minutes."

"You're saying that to soften me up."

"Doesn't make it less true. Open the box, Eve, then say: 'Thank you, Roarke.' "

She rolled her eyes, but she opened the box.

It was a bracelet, a kind of cuff with a pattern of minute diamond shapes etched into the gold to give it sparkle. In the center was a stone—and as it was bloodred, she assumed it was a ruby—big as her thumb and smooth to the touch.

It looked old, and important, in that priceless antique way that made her stomach jitter.

"Roarke—"

"You forgot the thank-you part."

"Roarke," she said again. "You're going to tell me this once belonged to some Italian countess or—"

"Princess," he supplied, and took the bracelet from her to slip it onto her wrist. "Sixteenth century. Now it belongs to a queen."

"Oh, please."

"Okay, that was laying it on a bit thick. Looks good on you, though."

"It'd look good on a tree stump." She wasn't much on glitters, despite the fact that the man heaped them on her at every opportunity. But this one had . . . something, she thought, as she lifted her arm and turned her wrist so the stone and etching caught and scattered light. "What if I lose it, or break it?"

"That would be a shame. But until you do, I enjoy seeing it on you. If it makes you feel any better, my aunt Sinead seemed equally flustered by the necklace I bought her."

"She struck me as a sensible woman."

He tugged a lock of Eve's hair. "The women in my life are sensible enough to indulge me, as giving them gifts brings me such pleasure."

"That's a slick way to box it in. It's beautiful." And she had to admit, at least privately, that she liked the way it slid fluidly over her skin. "I can't wear this to work."

"I don't suppose so. Then again, I like the way it looks on you now. When you're wearing nothing else."

"Don't get any ideas, ace. I'm on shift in—six hours," she calculated after a glance at the time.

Because she recognized the gleam in his eye, she narrowed her own. But the token protest she intended to give was interrupted by the bedside 'link.

"That's your signal." She nodded toward the 'link, then rolled off the bed. "At least when somebody calls *you* at two in the morning, nobody's dead."

She wandered off into the bathroom as she heard him block video, and answer.

She took her time, then as an afterthought snagged the robe off the back of the door in case he'd reinstated the video on the 'link.

She was belting it as she went back in, and saw he was up and at his closet. "Who was it?"

"Caro."

"You've got to go now? At two in the morning?" His tone, just the way he'd said his admin's name, had the skin on her neck prickling. "What is it?"

"Eve." He pulled out a shirt to go with the trousers he'd hastily put on. "I need a favor. A very large favor."

Not from his wife, she thought. But from his cop. "What is it?"

"One of my employees." He dragged on the shirt, but his eyes stayed on Eve. "She's in trouble. Considerable trouble. Someone is dead, after all."

"One of your employees kill someone, Roarke?"

"No." Since she continued to stand where she was, he moved to her closet, took out clothes. "She's confused and panicked, and Caro says somewhat incoherent. These are not traits one associates with Reva. She works in Security. Design and installation, primarily. She's solid as stone. She was with the Secret Service for a number of years, and isn't a woman who shakes easily."

"You're not telling me what happened."

"She found her husband and her friend in bed at the friend's apartment. Dead. Already dead, Eve."

"And finding two dead bodies, she contacted your administrative assistant instead of the police."

"No." He pushed the clothes he'd chosen into Eve's hands. "She contacted her mother."

Eve stared at him, cursed softly, then began to dress. "I have to call this in."

"I'm asking you to wait, until you see for yourself, until you talk to Reva." He laid his hands on hers, held them there until she looked back at him again. "Eve, I'm asking you, please, wait that long. You don't have to call in what you haven't seen with your own eyes. I know this woman. I've known her mother more than a dozen years, and trust her to the level I trust very few. They need your help. I need it."

She picked up her weapon harness, strapped it on. "Then let's get there. Fast."

It was a clear night with the heaviness that had dogged the summer of 2059 lightening toward the crispness of the coming fall. Traffic was light, and the short drive required little skill or concentration on Roarke's part. He judged by his wife's silence that she'd closed in. She asked no questions as she wanted no more information, nothing that would influence her from her own impressions of what she would see and hear and *feel*.

Her narrow, angular face was set, the long golden brown eyes cop flat. Unreadable even to him. The wide mouth that had been hot and soft against his only a short time before was firm and tight-lipped.

He parked on the street, in an illegal spot, and flicked the ON DUTY light in her vehicle before she could do so herself.

She said nothing, but stepped onto the sidewalk and stood, tall and lanky, her shaggy brown hair still mussed from love-making.

He crossed to her, gently combed his own fingers through her hair to order it, as well as he could. "Thank you for this."

"You don't want to thank me yet. Prime digs," she commented with a nod toward the brownstone. Before she could mount the steps, the door opened.

There was Caro, her shiny white hair like a silvery halo around her head. Without that, Eve might not have recognized Roarke's dignified and efficient admin in the pale woman wearing a smart red jacket over blue cotton pajamas.

"Thank God. Thank God. Thank you for coming so

quickly." She reached out with a visibly trembling hand and gripped Roarke's. "I didn't know quite what to do."

"You did just right," Roarke told her, and drew her in.

Eve heard her stifle a sob, let go with a sigh. "Reva—she's not well, not well at all. I have her in the living area. I didn't go upstairs."

Caro eased away from Roarke, straightened her shoulders. "I didn't think I should. I haven't touched anything, Lieutenant, except a glass out of the kitchen. I got Reva a glass of water, but I only touched the glass, and the bottle. Oh, and the handle of the friggie. I—"

"It's all right. Why don't you go sit with your daughter? Roarke, stay with them."

"You'll be all right with Reva for a few minutes, won't you?" he asked Caro. "I'll go with the lieutenant." Ignoring the flash of irritation over Eve's face, he gave Caro's shoulder a comforting rub. "I won't be long."

"She said—Reva said it was horrible. And now she just sits there, and doesn't say anything at all."

"Keep her quiet," Eve advised. "Keep her down here." She started upstairs. She glanced at the leather jacket, ripped to shreds and tossed into a heap on the floor. "Did she tell you which room?"

"No. Just that Reva found them in the bed."

Eve glanced at the room on the right, another on the left. Then she scented the blood. She continued down the hall, stopped at the doorway.

The two bodies were turned on their sides, facing each other. As if they were telling secrets. Blood stained the sheets, the pillows, the lacy cover that was tangled on the floor.

It stained the hilt and blade of the knife jabbed viciously into the mattress.

She saw a black bag near the door, a high-end stunner on the floor near the left side of the bed, a disordered pile of clothes heaped on a chair. Candles, still lit and wafting fragrance. Music still playing in soft, sexy notes.

"This is no walk in the meadow," she murmured. "Double homicide. I have to call it in."

"Will you stand as primary?"

"I'll stand," she agreed. "But if your friend did this, that's not going to be a favor."

"She didn't."

He stepped back while Eve drew out her communicator.

"I need you to take Caro in another room," she told him when she was finished. "Not the kitchen," she added with another glance at the knife. "There must be a den or a library or something like that down there. Try not to touch anything. I need to question—what was it? Reva?"

"Reva Ewing, yes."

"I need to question her, and I don't want you or her mother around when I do. You want to help her," she said before he could speak, "let's keep this as much by the book as we can from this point. You said she's security."

"Yes."

"Since she's one of yours I don't have to ask if she's good."

"She is. Very good."

"And he was her husband?"

Roarke looked back at the bed. "He was. Blair Bissel, an artist of some debatable talent. Works—worked in metal. That's one of his, I believe." He gestured toward a tall, seemingly jumbled series of metal tubes and blocks that stood in the corner of the room.

"And people pay for that?" She shook her head. "Takes all kinds. I'm going to ask you more about her later, but I want to get to her first, then take a closer look at the scene here. How long have they had marital problems?" Eve asked as she started down the hall again.

"I wasn't aware they had any."

"Well, they're over now. Keep Caro tucked away," she ordered, then walked to the living area to get her first look at Reva Ewing.

Caro sat with her arm around a woman in her early thirties. She had dark hair, cut short in a style nearly as careless as Eve's. She looked to have a small, compact body, the athletic sort that showed off well in the black T-shirt and jeans she wore.

Her skin was icy white, her eyes a kind of sooty gray that was nearly black with shock. Her lips were colorless, a bit on the thin side. As Eve stepped closer, those eyes flicked up, stared blindly. They were red-rimmed and puffy, and showed none of the sharp intelligence Eve assumed she owned.

"Ms. Ewing, I'm Lieutenant Dallas."

She continued to stare, but there was a faint movement of her head, as much shudder as nod.

"I need to ask you some questions. Your mother's going to go with Roarke while we talk."

"Oh, couldn't I stay with her?" Caro's arm tightened on Reva's shoulders. "I won't interfere, I promise, but—"

"Caro." Roarke moved to stand beside her, reached down and took her hand. "It's better this way." Gently, he drew Caro to her feet. "Better for Reva. You can trust Eve."

"Yes, I know. It's just . . ." She looked back as Roarke led her from the room. "I'll be right here. Reva, I'm right here."

"Ms. Ewing." Eve sat across from her, set her recorder on the table between them. And saw Reva's gaze fix on it. "I'm going to record this. I'm going to read you your rights, then ask you some questions. Do you understand?"

"Blair's dead. I saw. They're dead. Blair and Felicity."

"Ms. Ewing, you have the right to remain silent." Eve walked through the revised Miranda, and Reva closed her eyes.

"Oh God, oh God. It's real. It's not some horrible dream. It's real."

"Tell me what happened here tonight."

"I don't know." A tear dribbled down her cheek. "I don't know what happened."

"Was your husband sexually involved with Felicity?"

"I don't understand it. I don't understand. I thought he loved me." Her eyes locked on Eve's. "I didn't believe it at first. How could I? Blair and Felicity. My husband and my friend. But then I could see it, could see all the signs I missed, all the clues, all the mistakes—those little mistakes they both made."

"How long have you known?"

"Just tonight. Just tonight." Her breath shuddered in and out as she used a balled fist to wipe at the tears on her cheeks. "He was supposed to be out of town until tomorrow. A client, a new commission. But he was here, with her. I came, and I saw . . ."

"You came here tonight to confront them?"

"I was so angry. They'd made a fool out of me, and I was so angry. They broke my heart, and I was so sad. Then they were dead. All that blood. All the blood."

"Did you kill them, Reva?"

"No!" Her whole body jerked at the question. "No, no, no! I wanted to hurt them. I wanted them to *pay*. But I didn't . . . I couldn't have. I don't know what happened."

"Tell me what you do know."

"I drove over. We have a house in Queens. Blair wanted a house, and he didn't want to live in Manhattan where we both worked. Someplace private and away, that's what he said. Someplace just ours."

Her voice broke on the words so that she covered her face with her hands. "I'm sorry. It all seems impossible. It seems I'll wake up any minute and none of this will have happened."

There was some blood on her shirt. None on her hands, on her arms, her face. Eve noted it down among her observations and waited for Reva to compose herself and go on.

"I was furious, and I knew just what I wanted to do. I'd designed the security here, so I knew how to get in. I broke in."

She dashed a tear off her cheek. "I didn't want to give them time to prepare, so I broke in, and I went upstairs, to her bedroom."

"Did you have a weapon?"

"No . . . Well, I had a stunner. My SS issue, reconfigured. It won't go over minimum power, so I can carry it with a civilian license. I was . . ." She heaved a breath. "I was going to give him a jolt with it. On the balls."

"And did you?"

"No." She covered her face with her hands. "I can't remember clearly. It's like this smear over my brain."

"You tear up the leather jacket?"

"Yeah." She sighed now. "I saw it hanging over the rail. I gave him that goddamn jacket, and seeing it just made me crazy. I took out my minidrill and went to work on it. Petty, I know it was petty, but I was so angry."

"Doesn't seem petty to me," Eve said, keeping her tone mild and just a little sympathetic. "Husband's cheating on you with your pal, you'd want to get some of your own back."

"That's the way I felt. Then I saw them in the bed, together. And I saw them—dead. The blood. I've never seen so much blood. She screamed—no, no, I screamed. I must've screamed."

She rubbed a hand over her throat, as if she could still feel the sound ripping through it. "Then I passed out—I think. I smelled something. The blood, but something. Something else, and I passed out. I don't know how long."

She reached for the glass of water, drank deeply. "I woke up, and I felt fuzzy and sick and strange. Then I saw them, on the bed. I saw them again and I crawled out. I couldn't seem to stand up, so I crawled out to the bathroom and got sick. I called my mother. I don't know why exactly. I should've called the police, but I called Mom. I wasn't thinking straight."

"Did you come here tonight with the intention of killing your husband and your friend?"

"No. I came here with the intention of pitching a royal fit. Lieutenant, I'm going to be sick again. I need to—"

She clutched her stomach, then sprang up and ran. Eve was on her heels when Reva flung open a door and dived into a powder room. Dropping to her knees, she was hideously ill.

"Burns," she managed, and gratefully took the damp cloth Eve offered. "Burns my throat."

"You take any illegals tonight, Reva?"

"I don't do illegals." She mopped the cloth over her face. "Believe me, you're raised by Caro, screened by the Secret Service, then Roarke, you don't screw around." Exhaustion in every line of her body, she leaned back against the wall. "Lieutenant, I've never killed anyone. I carried a weapon when I stood for the President, and once took a hit for her. I've got a temper, and when I'm riding on it, I can be rash. Whoever did that to Blair, to Felicity, wasn't rash. They had to be crazy. Fucking out of their minds. I couldn't have done it. I couldn't have."

Eve crouched down so they were eye-to-eye. "Why do you sound like you're trying to convince yourself of that, Reva, as much as me?"

Her lips trembled, her eyes swam with fresh tears. "Because I can't remember. I just can't remember." She covered her face with her hands, and wept.

Eve left her long enough to get Caro. "I want you to sit with her," Eve instructed. "I'm going to put a guard with you momentarily. That's procedure."

"Are you arresting her?"

"I haven't made that determination. She's cooperating, and that's going to help. It'd be best if you bring her in here, keep her in this room until I come back."

"All right. Thank you."

"I've got to get my field kit out of the car."

"I'll get it." Roarke walked out with her. "What do you think?"

"I'm not thinking anything until I secure and examine the scene."

"Lieutenant, you're always thinking."

"Let me do my job. You want to help? Direct my partner and the CSU upstairs when they arrive. Until then, you need to back off or you'll just muck up the works."

"Tell me one thing. Should I advise Reva to contact a lawyer?"

"You put me in a hell of a fix." She snatched the field kit from him. "I'm a cop. Let me go be a cop. You figure out the rest. Goddamn it to hell and back again."

She stomped upstairs. Breaking open the kit, she yanked out a can of Seal-It and coated her hands and boots. Then, fixing a recorder on her lapel, she reentered the crime scene and got to work.

She'd progressed to the bodies themselves when she heard

the creak of a floorboard. She whirled, ready to snap at the intruder, and bit back the oath when she spotted Peabody.

She was going to have to get used to her former aide's lack of clomping. The new detective no longer wore the hard-soled cop shoes of uniform, but cushy airsneaks that were all but soundless. And just, in Eve's opinion, a little spooky.

She had them, apparently, in every color of the rainbow, including the mustard yellow she wore now to match her jacket. Despite them, and the straight-legged black pants and scoop-necked top, she managed to look pressed and polished and coplike.

Her square face was sober and concerned, and framed by her standard 'do, the straight bowl cut that seemed to suit her dark hair.

"It's insult on injury to buy it naked," Peabody said. "And embarrassing on top of it to buy it naked with another woman's husband, or a woman not your wife."

"Is that what we've got? Dispatch wasn't big on details."

"I didn't give them details. Dead guy is Roarke's admin's son-in-law, and right at the moment, her daughter's prime suspect."

Peabody looked at the bed. "Looks like a messy situation just got messier."

"Take the scene first, then I'll fill you in on the players. "Stunner." She lifted the sealed weapon. "Suspect claims—"

"Holy wow!"

"What? What?" Eve's free hand slammed onto the butt of her weapon.

"That." Reaching out, Peabody danced her fingers delicately over the bracelet on Eve's wrist. "It's mag. I mean mondo mag, Dallas."

Mortified, Eve shoved the cuff under the sleeve of her jacket. She'd forgotten she was wearing the bracelet. "Maybe we could concentrate on the scene of the crime rather than my accessories."

"Sure, but that is *some* ultimate accessory. Is that big fat red stone a ruby?"

"Peabody."

"Okay, okay." But she was going to get a closer look, when Dallas wasn't paying attention. "Where were you?"

"Just playing around with evidence, amusing myself at a crime scene."

Peabody rolled her eyes. "Jeez, beat me with a stick."

"First chance," Eve agreed. "To continue. The suspect claims that she brought a stunner with her, a reconfigured one that meets civilian licensee requirements. This is not a reconfigured stunner, but a military issue with full capabilities."

"Uh-huh."

"Succinct, as always."

"That's inscrutable detective-speak."

"Said weapon, which I've already tested for prints, has suspect's, and only suspect's, prints all over it. As does the murder weapon." Eve gestured to another sealed bag, and the bloody knife within. "The carry bag over there holds electronic jammers and burglar tools, also loaded with Reva Ewing's prints."

"Is she security savvy?"

"Works in that capacity for Roarke Enterprises, and is a former member of the Secret Service."

"From the setup, it appears that the suspect broke in, found her husband noodling strange, and hacked away."

But she moved closer to the bed, the bodies. "No defensive wounds on either vic, no signs of struggle. Somebody starts hacking away, most people tend to object, at least a little."

"Hard to when you're stunned first."

With a fingertip, Eve indicated the small red dots between Blair's shoulder blades, the matching ones between Felicity's breasts.

"Him on the back, her on the front," Peabody noted.

"Yeah. I'd say they were in the middle of noodling strange. Killer walks in behind, zaps him first, shoves him aside and zaps her before she can more than peep. They were unconscious, or at least incapacitated when the hacking began."

"Serious overkill," Peabody commented. "There must be a dozen wounds on each of them."

"Eighteen for him, fourteen for her."

"Ouch."

"I'll say. No heart wounds, which is interesting. Makes more blood if you don't hit the heart."

She studied the way it spread over the sheets, the light spatter on the shade of the lamp beside the bed. Nasty work, she thought. Very nasty, very messy.

"Also interesting that none of the holes in them struck the points where the stunner left the burn marks. Suspect has some blood on her clothes—not much, considering, but some. Hands and arms are clean."

"She'd have to wash up after something like this."

"You'd think. You'd think if she did, she'd have gotten rid of the shirt, too. But people dumb down a lot of times after they hack a couple people to death."

"Her mother's here," Peabody pointed out.

"Yeah. So maybe her mother washed her up some, but Caro strikes me as more careful than that. Time of death is one-twelve A.M. We'll have EDD check the security, see if we can determine when she bypassed and entered. I need you to check the kitchen, see if the murder weapon came from the premises, or if it was brought on scene."

She paused a moment. "You see what's left of the leather bomber jacket on the floor down there?"

"Yeah. Looked like nice material."

"I want it tagged, too. Ewing says she tore it up with her minidrill. Let's see if that matches."

"Huh. Why'd she use a drill if she had a knife? Ripping away with a knife's got to be more satisfying and efficient."

"Yeah, there's a question. We'll also run both vics, see if we can find anyone who'd want them dead besides the betrayed wife."

Hissing a breath out between her teeth, Peabody looked back at the bodies. "If it's what it looks like, she'll make diminished capacity in a walk."

"Let's find out what it is, not what it looks like."

Chapter 2

"No. No. I didn't wash her hands or face."

Caro sat, eyes level, face composed. But her hands were knotted together in her lap, as if she used them as a rope to anchor her body to the chair.

"I tried to touch as little as possible, and just keep her calm until you got here."

"Caro." Eve kept her gaze focused on the woman's face, and tried to ignore the fact—and the small kernel of resentment in her belly—that Roarke remained in the room. At Caro's request. "There's a master bath upstairs, off the main bedroom. There are indications, though the sink was wiped down, that someone washed blood away."

"I didn't go upstairs. I give you my word."

Because she did, because Eve believed her, she realized Caro didn't understand the implications of her statement. But from the change in Roarke's posture, the subtle shifting to alert, Eve knew he did.

Because he remained silent, that kernel of resentment shrank a bit.

"There's blood on Reva's clothes," Eve said.

"Yes, I know. I saw . . ." And the understanding dawned in

her eyes, followed instantly by a barely controlled panic. "Lieutenant, if Reva—if she used the washroom, it would've been while she was in shock. Not to try to cover anything up. You have to believe that. She was in shock."

Sick, certainly, Eve thought. Her prints were on the bowl and rim of the toilet. Just as they'd be if she'd held on while being violently ill. But not in the master bath. The evidence of her illness was in the bath down the hall from the bedroom.

While the blood traces were in the master bath.

"How did you enter the premises, Caro?"

"How did I . . . oh." She brushed a hand over her face like a woman brushing absently at a cobweb. "The door, the front door was unlocked. It was open a little."

"Open?"

"Yes. Yes, the lock light was green, then I saw it wasn't quite closed, so I just pushed it open and came in."

"And what was the situation when you entered?"

"Reva was sitting on the floor, in the foyer. Sitting there, in a ball, shaking. She was barely coherent."

"But she'd been coherent enough when she contacted you for you to understand Blair and Felicity were dead, and she—your daughter—was in trouble."

"Yes. That is, I understood she needed me, and that Blair—Blair and Felicity—were dead. She said: 'Mom. Mom, they're dead. Someone's killed them.' She was crying, and her voice was hollow and strange. She said she didn't know what to do, what she should do. I asked where she was, and she told me. I can't remember exactly what she said, or I said. But it's on my 'link at home. You'll hear for yourself." Her voice tightened a little.

"Yes, we will."

"I realize that Reva, then I, should have contacted the police immediately."

Caro smoothed a hand over the knees of her pajama pants, then simply stared at them as if she'd just realized what she was wearing.

Her cheeks went a little pink, then she sighed. "I can only tell you that both of us, both of us were . . . we weren't thinking clearly, and only thought to contact the person we each trusted most."

"Were you aware that your son-in-law was unfaithful?"

"No. No, I was not." The words snapped out, with anger just behind them. "And before you ask, I knew Felicity quite well, or thought I did," Caro amended. "I considered her one of Reva's closest friends, almost a sister. She was often in my home, as I was often in hers."

"Was she, Felicity, involved with other men?"

"She had a very active social life, and leaned toward artists." Her mouth went grim as her thoughts veered, obviously, to her son-in-law. "She used to joke that she wasn't ready to settle on any one style or era—in men or in her art collection. She was, I thought, a clever woman, with a great deal of style and humor. Reva is often so serious and focused on her work. I thought . . . I believed Felicity was a good friend for her, someone who brought out her more frivolous side."

"Who was Felicity seeing now?"

"I'm not sure. There was a man a few weeks ago. We were all here for one of her Sunday brunches. He was a painter, I think." She closed her eyes as if to focus. "Yes, a painter. His name was Fredo. She introduced him as Fredo, and he struck me as very dramatic, very foreign and intense. But a few weeks before that, there was another. Thin and pale and brooding. And before that . . ."

She shrugged a shoulder. "She enjoyed men, and from all appearance didn't develop relationships with any beyond the surface."

"Is there anyone else who might have had the access codes for this residence?"

"I don't know of anyone. Felicity was very strict about her security. She wouldn't employ any staff and kept only droids for domestic work. She used to say people couldn't be trusted because they always trusted the wrong people. I remember once I told her I found that very sad, and she laughed, and reminded me if it wasn't true, my daughter wouldn't have a job."

Eve saw Peabody come to the doorway, and rose. "Thank you. I'll need to talk to you again, and I need your permission, on record, to take your home 'links in for examination."

"You have it, and whatever else you need to clear this up. I want you to know how much I appreciate you handling this personally. I know you'll find the truth. Can I go to Reva now?"

"It would be better if you waited here, for a little while longer." She shot a glance at Roarke, so that he understood she meant for him to do the same.

In the hallway, she nodded a go-ahead to Peabody.

"Sweepers got blood out of the bathroom drain upstairs, and Ewing's print on the bowl, though it had been wiped pretty carefully. The murder weapon doesn't match the kitchen cutlery here. There's a pretty fancy set, and nothing appears to be missing."

She consulted her notes. "Reactivated the house droid. It was shut down at twenty-one-thirty. Prior to that time, it records that Felicity was at home with a companion. She'd programmed the droid not to give names or details. We'll need to take it in to override."

"See to it, then. Any blood traces in the second bath upstairs?"

"None. Just Ewing's prints on the toilet."

"Okay. Let's give Ewing a second pass."

They moved together into the living area where a uniform baby-sat Reva. The minute Eve stepped in, Reva surged to her feet.

"Lieutenant. I'd like to speak with you. Privately."

Eve gestured for the uniform to leave the room, and spoke without looking at Peabody. "This is my partner, Detective Peabody. What would you like to speak with us about, Ms. Ewing?"

Reva hesitated, then, when Eve sat, let out a resigned breath. "It's just that my head's clearing up, and I've realized what sort of jam I'm in. And the sort of jam I've put my mother in. She only came because I was hysterical. I don't want any of the mess that's on me to rub off on her."

"Don't worry about your mother. No one's looking to hurt her in this."

"Okay." Reva gave a short nod. "Okay, then."

"You said when you pulled back the covers, you saw the bodies, the blood."

"Yes. I saw they were dead. I knew they were dead. Had to be."

"Where was the knife?"

"The knife?"

"The murder weapon. Where was it?"

"I don't know. I didn't see a knife. Just Blair and Felicity."

"Peabody, would you show Ms. Ewing the weapon we've taken into evidence."

Peabody drew out the sealed knife, walked over to show it to Reva. "Do you recognize this knife, Ms. Ewing?"

Reva stared at the smeared blade, the smeared handle, then lifted her gaze, full of stunned confusion, to Eve's. "It's Blair's. It's one of the set he bought last year, when he decided we should both take cooking classes. I told him to go right ahead, but I'd stick with the AutoChef or take-out. He actually took the classes, and did some cooking now and then. This looks like one of his kitchen knives."

"Did you bring it with you tonight, Reva? Were you so angry that you put it in your bag, maybe to threaten them, to scare them?"

"No." She took a step back from it. "No, I didn't bring it."

This time Eve held out an evidence bag. "Is this your stunner?"

"No." Reva's fingers curled into her palms. "That's a recent military model. Mine's over six years old, a reconfigured Secret Service make. That doesn't belong to me. I've never seen it before."

"Both this and the knife were used on the victims. Both this and the knife have your fingerprints on them."

"This is crazy."

"The violence of the stabbings would have resulted in considerable blood spatter. On your hands, your arms, your face, as well as your clothes."

Dully now, Reva looked down at her hands, rubbed them gently together. "I know there's blood on my shirt. I don't know . . . Maybe I touched something up there. I don't remember. But I didn't kill them. I never touched that knife, that stunner. There's no blood on my hands."

"There's blood in the bathroom drain, and your fingerprints are on the sink."

"You think I washed my hands? You think I tried to clean up, cover up, then called my mother?"

Eve could tell that Reva's head was clearing, and her temper was coming back along with her coherency. Those dark eyes were hot, and her teeth clamped together as her color came up. "What the hell do you think I am? You think I'd rip my husband and my friend to pieces, to goddamn pieces because they made a fool out of me? And if I did, I wouldn't have the fucking sense to get rid of the murder weapon and cover myself? For God's sake, they were *dead*. They were dead when I got here."

She pushed out of her chair as she spat out the words, and the anger so alive on her face pushed her to whirl around the room. "What the hell is going on? What the hell *is* this?"

"Why did you come here tonight, Reva?"

"To confront them, to shout and yell and maybe to knee Blair in the balls. To slap Felicity in that gorgeous, lying face. To break something and create one hell of an ugly scene."

"Why tonight?"

"Because I only found *out* tonight, goddamn it."

"How? How did you find out?"

Reva stopped, stared at Eve as if trying to understand some odd, half-remembered language. "The package. Oh Jesus, the photographs and the receipts. There was a package delivered to my house. I was already in bed. It was early, just after eleven, but I was bored and went to bed. I heard the bell from the gate. It irritated me. I couldn't think who'd be coming by at eleven, but I went down. There was a package left at the gate. I went out and got it."

"Did you see anyone?"

"No. Just the package, and being a suspicious sort, I ran a

scanner over it. I didn't expect a boomer," she said with a wry smile, "but, it's habit. I got the all-clear and brought it in. I thought it was from Blair. An I-already-miss-you present. He did that sort of thing—silly, romantic . . ."

She trailed off, struggled as her eyes went shiny with tears. "I just figured it was from him, and I opened it up. There were photographs, a lot of surveillance-type shots of Blair with Felicity. Intimate, unmistakable sort of photos of the two of them, and copies of receipts from hotels and restaurants. Shit."

She pressed her fingers to her lips. "Receipts for jewelry and lingerie he'd bought—and not for me. All from an account I didn't know he had. And there were two discs—one of 'link calls between them, one of e-mail text they'd exchanged. Love calls, love letters—very intimate and graphic."

"There was nothing to indicate who'd send these things to you."

"No, and I didn't look or even wonder at the time. I was too shocked and angry and hurt. The last transmission on the disc was the two of them talking about how they were going to have two days together, right here in her place while I thought he was out of town. They laughed at me," she murmured. "Had a good laugh over how oblivious I was to what was going on right under my nose. Some security expert who couldn't even keep tabs on her own husband."

She sat again, heavily. "This doesn't make sense. It's just crazy. Who would kill them, and set me up to take the fall?"

"Where's the package?" Eve asked her.

"In my ride. I brought it with me in case I softened up on the way over, though there wasn't much chance of it. It's in the passenger seat where I could see it."

"Peabody."

Reva waited until Peabody walked outside to retrieve the package. "It doesn't make me look any less guilty. I get proof my husband's diddling my best friend, find out they have a rendezvous tonight, and I come over here, armed and ready. I walked right into this. I don't know how or why I was set up. I don't know why you'd believe me when I tell you I was set up. But that's the truth."

"I'm going to have to take you in. I'm going to have to charge you. The charge is going to be Murder in the First, two counts." She watched Reva's color drain. "I don't know you," Eve continued, "but I know your mother, and I know Roarke. Neither of them are pushovers. They both believe in you, so here's what I'm going to tell you. Off record. Get a lawyer. Get a damn good fleet of lawyers. And don't lie to me. Don't lie to me about anything I might ask you. Those lawyers are good enough, they'll have you out on bond first thing in the morning. Stay clean, stay straight, and stay available to me. You hide something, I'll find it, and that'll piss me off."

"I've got nothing to hide."

"You might think of something. If and when you do, think again. I want you to volunteer for a Truth Test, third level. It's hell, it's intrusive, and it can be painful, but if you've got nothing to hide and you're being straight with me, you'll pass it. A third level will weigh heavy on your side."

She closed her eyes, breathed deep. "I can handle third level."

Eve smiled thinly. "Don't go in with a chip on your shoulder. I've been there, and it's going to flatten you. I can get a warrant to search your house, your office, your vehicles, everything. But if you give me permission to do so, on record, that's going to weigh, too."

"I'm putting a hell of a lot in your hands, Dallas."

"It's in them anyway."

She took Reva in, booked her. Due to the hour she could opt, without breaking procedure, to continue their interview until morning. But she still had work, and she still had Roarke.

She walked through the bull pen in Homicide where the scatter of detectives on graveyard shift yawned their way through the last couple of hours of work. As she expected, Roarke waited in her office.

"I need to speak with you," he began.

"Figured. Don't speak until I have coffee." She went directly to the AutoChef, programmed a double serving, strong and black.

He stood where he was, only turned to stare out of her miserly window at the fitful predawn traffic. As she drank, she could all but see impatience and outrage snaking out of his skin like lightning bolts.

"I arranged it so Caro could have fifteen minutes with her. That's the best I can do. Then you need to take Caro out of here, take her home, settle her down. You'll know how."

"She's out of her mind with worry."

"I expect she is."

"You expect?" He turned around then, slowly. Slowly enough for her to understand his temper was on its shortest, thinnest leash. "You've just booked her only child for two first-degree murders. You have her daughter in a cage."

"And did you think because you're fond of them, and I of you, I'd just let her waltz into the night when I have her prints all over a murder weapon? When I have her on the scene of a double murder and the victims just happen to be her husband and her pal, both naked in bed? When she fucking admits she broke in after learning he was sticking it to her good pal Felicity?"

She took a deep gulp of the coffee, gestured toward him with the cup. "Hey, maybe I should've pulled the religious cop routine, and nudged her out the door with the advice to go forth and sin no more."

"She didn't kill anyone. It's obvious Reva was set up, and that whoever killed them marked her for it, planned it out and left her twisting in the wind."

"I happen to agree with you."

"And locking her up only gives whoever did this time and opportunity to—what?"

"I said I agree with you, about the setup. But not with what you didn't quite finish saying there." She drank more coffee, slower this time, letting it slide deliciously into her system. "I'm not giving whoever did this the time and opportunity to get away. I'm giving them the time and opportunity to think they'll get away—and keeping Reva safe in the meantime. And following the pesky little letter of the law while I'm at it. I'm doing my job, so get off my back."

He sat because he was suddenly tired, and because he, too, was sick with worry over the mother, the daughter. Both of whom he considered his responsibility. "You believed her."

"Yeah, I believed her. And I believe my own eyes."

"I'm sorry. I seem to be a little dull this morning. What did your own eyes tell you?"

"That it was too staged. The scene. Like a vid set. Viciously murdered naked couple, knife—from the prime suspect's own kitchen, sticking out of the mattress. Blood in the bathroom drain, suspect's print on the sink—one little spot she just happened to miss on the wipe-down. Her prints all over the weapons, just in case the investigating officer needs to be led by the fucking nose."

"And you certainly don't. Should I apologize for doubting you?"

"You get a free one, seeing as it's five in the morning and we've put in a long night." She felt generous enough to give him the coffee, and program another mug for herself. "Classy frame job for the most part, though. Whoever did it had to know your girl—what she does for a living, how she reacts. Had to be dead sure she'd rush over to her pal's house with blood in her eye. That she'd bypass security. Might have figured she'd just beat on the door first, but that she wouldn't turn around and slink off home when nobody answered. But they missed a few."

"Which were?"

"If she'd walked in with a big, nasty knife in her hand, she wouldn't have dug into her bag of tricks for a minidrill to go at the jacket. If she washed up, why'd she use the other upstairs bath to get sick? Why leave her prints there? How come there's no blood in her hair? Spatter hits the lamp, some of the wall, and to do what she did, she'd have been right on top of them, but there's no spatter in her hair. She wash that, too? Then why didn't the sweepers find any of her hair in the bathroom drains?

"You're very thorough."

"That's why they pay me the big bucks. Whoever did this *knows* her, Roarke, and the victims. Wanted one or the other of them dead, maybe both. Or maybe just wants Reva Ewing doing life in a cage. That's a puzzler."

She sat on the corner of her desk sipping her coffee. "I'm going to turn her life inside out, and do the same job on the victims. At least one of them is the key. Whoever did it surveilled the vics, got the photos, the discs. Good quality. And they got into the house as slick as Reva did, so security's no problem for them. Had a military-style stunner. I need it analyzed yet, but I'm betting it's no black-market knockoff. They think the cop's going to step into that scene and gobble all that shit right up, then go eat a fricking doughnut."

"Not my cop."

"Not any cop in this division or that cop deserves a boot up the ass," Eve said with feeling. "When something looks that perfect on the surface, it never is down below. Whoever set this up was just a little too creative. Maybe he figured she'd run. That when she woke up, she'd panic and run. But she didn't. I'm having the medicals go over her, see if she was knocked out, or given a dose of something that knocked her out. She doesn't strike me as the fainting type."

"I wouldn't think so."

Still sipping, she looked at him over the rim of her mug. "You're going to get in my face on this again?"

"I am, yes." He touched her arm, ran his hand down it, then let her go. "Both Caro and Reva are important to me. I'll ask you to let me help. If you refuse, I'll go around you. I'll be sorry for it, but I'll do it. Caro isn't just an employee to me, Eve. She's asked me for help, and she's never asked me for anything before. Not once in all the years she's been with me. I can't step aside on this, not even for you."

She took another contemplative sip. "If you could step aside on this, even for me, you wouldn't be the man I fell for in the first place, would you?"

He set his coffee down, stepped over to frame her face in his hands. "Remember this moment, won't you, the next time you're furious with me? And I'll do the same." He lowered his head to press his lips to her forehead.

"I'll send you my files on both Caro and Reva, which contain considerable personal data. And I'll get you more."

"That's a good start."

"Caro asked me to do so." He eased back. "I would've done it anyway, but it's easier all around that she asked. You'll find, in your dealings with her, she is scrupulous."

"How'd she get that way working for you?"

He grinned now. "A paradox, isn't it? You'll call Feeney in?"

"I'm going to need ace EDD men, so yeah, it'll be Feeney—and he'll bring in McNab."

"I could help with the electronics."

"If Feeney wants you, he can have you. I'll clear it with the commander. But you know it's going to be touchy, your connection to the suspect. If I don't convince Commander Whitney this is a frame, he's not going to go along, even unofficially."

"My money's on you."

"Let's take it a step at a time. Get Caro home."

"I will. I'm going to clear my calendar as much as possible until this is finished."

"You paying for the lawyers?"

"She won't let me." A shadow of annoyance rippled over his face. "Neither of them will budge in that particular area."

"One more. Did you and Reva ever tango?"

"Do you mean were we ever lovers? No."

"Good. Slightly less sticky that way. Clear out," she ordered. "I've got to round up my partner and drive to Queens."

"Could I ask a question first?"

"Make it snappy."

"If you'd walked into that scene tonight, and there'd been no connection, would you have looked at it the same way?"

"There was no connection when I walked onto the scene," she told him. "That's how I could see it for what it was. I couldn't take you in with me, not literally, not in my head. You'd've done the same."

"I like to think so."

"You would have. You know how to be cold when you have to be. I mean that in a good way."

"I believe you do," he said with a half laugh.

"I did let you in a minute after I stepped out of it."

"Did you?"

"I thought: If Roarke had set this up, nobody would've seen the frame. Whoever did it should've taken lessons."

This time he did laugh, and she was pleased to see some of the worry warm out of his eyes. "Well now, that is high praise."

"Just calling them as I see them, and another reason I've agreed to use you. I want to find out the how and why of a classy frame, I might as well make use of somebody who'd know the hows and whys. Start thinking about what Reva's working on for you—or what she has been working on, or will be."

"I already am."

"See, just one more reason. You're going to want a bodyguard for Caro, just in case. She'd prefer private to a cop."

"It's already done."

"And the reasons just keep on ticking. Beat it."

"Since you ask so nice." He kissed her first, a soft touch of mouth to mouth. "Get something decent to eat," he called out as he left.

And though her gaze went to the ceiling tile where she was currently hiding her candy stash, she didn't think that was quite what he had in mind.

Chapter 3

She was expecting a midlevel suburban house. The Ewing-Bissel place was several steps up from mid. It was a very contemporary streamlined white box on box behind a recycled-stone riot fence. Lots of one-way glass and sharp angles.

The entrance area was that same recycled stone, tinted a strong red. There were ornamental trees and shrubs growing out of large pots and several odd metal sculptures she attributed to Blair Bissel.

But it struck her as cold, and more pretentious than gingerbread and gilt.

"Ewing knows her security," Peabody commented after they'd dealt with the layers of it just to get through the riot wall. "Fancy digs, too, if you go for this kind of thing."

"You don't?"

"Uh-uh." Peabody grimaced as they walked over the red stone lawn. "This kind of design makes me think of a prison, and I can't quite figure out if it keeps people in or keeps them out. And the art."

She stopped to study a squat metal shape with eight

spindly legs and an elongated triangular head, lined with sparkling teeth.

"We've got a lot of artists in the family," Peabody went on. "A couple who work primarily in metals, and some of the stuff's odd. But it's . . . interesting odd and usually kind of fun or poignant."

"Poignant metal."

"Yeah, really. But this, I guess it's a cross between a watchdog and a spider. It's creepy, and a little mean. And what about that?"

She pointed to another sculpture. This, Eve saw when she wandered closer, was of two figures, closely entwined. Male and female, which was obvious when you saw the exaggerated length of the penis painted royal purple. It was honed to a knife-point at the end, and an inch away from penetrating the female figure.

She was, Eve noted, bowed back in either passion or terror, the long gleaming tendrils of her hair streaming back.

They were faceless, just form and feeling. And after a moment she decided that feeling wasn't romantic, or even sexual. It was violent.

"I'd say he was probably talented, and even talent can be sick."

Because it made her uncomfortable, she turned away from the figures and approached the door. Even with the codes and clearance Reva had provided, it took some time and some trouble to access entry.

The door opened into a kind of atrium with tinted sky windows three floors up, and slick ocean-blue tiles for the floor.

There was a fountain in the center of the space, burbling as the half-man, half-fish figures that circled it vomited violently into the pool.

The walls were mirrored, tossing back their reflections dozens of times. Rooms fanned off from this center, through wide, doorless rectangles.

"This doesn't fit her," Eve said. "I'd say he picked the place and the decor, and she went along."

Peabody looked up, studied the nightmarish bird sculptures hanging high in the air. They looked like they were circling over a meal. "Would you?"

"I don't fit where I live either."

"That's not true."

Eve shrugged, cautiously circled the fountain. "I didn't when I moved into it. Okay, it's not like this. It's beautiful, and it's livable, and it's, well, it's warm. But it was Roarke's place. It's still more his than mine, and that's okay."

"She really loved him." The place gave Peabody the creeps, which she didn't bother to hide. "If she could live here because he wanted it, she had to really love him."

"That's my take," Eve agreed.

"I'll find the kitchen, verify the murder weapon was taken from here."

Eve nodded, and using the blueprint Reva had drawn for her, started upstairs.

She'd been sleeping, Eve thought. Heard the gate bell. Got up, checked the security screen. Saw the package.

She paused by a sheer window that looked down over a stone-and-metal garden. Nothing living, she mused. Nothing real.

Got up, she continued, went down and out to retrieve the package. Took a scanner, checked the contents for explosives. Careful, cautious woman.

Brought the package back inside.

Eve entered the master bedroom and saw the first signs of life in the house. There were more mirrors, silvery panels of them on one wall, more forming a double door. The bed, wide as a canyon, was unmade, with a nightshirt tossed into a tangle over in one corner. One closet door was open—Reva's closet, Eve noted after a glance.

She'd opened the package, sat on the bed when her legs gave out from under her, Eve imagined. Looked at the photographs again and again while her brain tried to compute the meaning. Studied the receipts. Went to the data center across the room, loaded the discs.

Some pacing, Eve was sure. That's what she'd've done. Paced, cursed, shed a few tears of rage. Tossed something breakable.

And she noted, with some satisfaction, the shards of glass in the far corner.

Okay, then it's time for action. Dress, gather the tools. Work out the plan in your head in between rages and more curses.

It took, what, an hour, an hour tops, from the time she opened the package until she headed out.

Eve turned to the bedroom 'link, and replayed the transmissions for the last twenty-four hours.

There was one from Felicity that was timed in at fourteen hundred.

Hi, Reev. I know you're at work, but I hate to bother you there. Just wanted to let you know I've got a hot date tonight. Hoping we can get together Friday or Saturday. I'll spill all the dirty deets. Be a good girl while Blair's away. Or if you're not, tell me *everything. Ciao!*

Eve froze the visual and took a hard look at Felicity Kade. The wealthy, stylish bombshell type, Eve mused. Blonde and rosy, with ice-edged cheekbones and a full, seductive mouth. Eyes so deeply blue they were nearly purple, with a tiny black mole at the outside tip of the left.

Eve was willing to bet she'd paid plenty for the face.

She'd been covering herself with the transmission. *Don't call me tonight, I've got a hot one. It just happens to be your husband, but what you don't know won't hurt me.*

Or so she'd believed when she'd placed the bubbling call.

And there was a look in those eyes, a kind of live-wire excitement that told Eve Blair Bissel had likely been with her already, just out of range of the 'link.

And when he'd called home, at seventeen-twenty, Eve noted, he'd been very careful to have nothing but his own face on screen. His eyes, cat-green, were heavy. The smile, curve of that handsome mouth, was weary, like his voice.

She could see why Reva had fallen for him, more so on the transmission than in the ID still Eve had studied. You added that lazy animation to the face, that slow, sexy voice, and you got a powerful punch.

Hey, baby. I was hoping you'd be home by now. Should've called your pocket 'link. Pretty fuzzy with the travel and time change. I'm going to shut down, so you won't be able to reach me. I've just got to catch some serious z's. I'll try you again as soon as I surface.

Miss me, baby. You know I'm missing you.

Covered his ass, too, and gave himself a clear night to play with his bed pal.

Still, it was careless. Reckless. At least it would've been if she'd trusted him less. What if she'd tracked the transmission as Eve would do. What if she'd gotten a wild hare and decided to transport herself to where he'd said he'd be?

What if . . . a dozen things that often happened to blow up the secret affair and leave the cheating spouse with his or her ass in the sling.

Instead he'd ended up dead. Because someone else had been tracking, someone else had been watching and waiting for the right time and place.

But why?

"Matching set of cooking tools," Peabody reported as she walked in. "Missing the bread knife."

"Would that be a bread knife in our evidence bag?"

"Yes, sir, it would. I also checked the log on the AutoChef. It looks like Reva Ewing had a single serving of chicken piccata and a garden salad at nineteen-thirty last night. Prior to that, there was a double serving of wheat waffles and a pot of coffee at seven-thirty yesterday morning."

"So they had breakfast together before he left on his fake business trip and she went to work."

"Security logs also show Reva Ewing entering, alone, at eighteen-twelve. And the gate bell sounding, as per her statement, just after twenty-three hundred. Her leaving to retrieve the package and returning with it to the house after a scan also checks."

"You've been busy."

Peabody grinned. "We detectives do what we can."

"You're not going to be able to milk that much longer."

"I figure I've got at least a month to mention my detective status at least three times a day. After that, I'm weaning myself."

"So noted. I want to take the security discs and the 'links to EDD. If Reva's being set up, whoever's doing it knows as much about security as she does."

"You said if. Do you have doubts?"

"There's always room for doubts."

"Okay, so I was thinking—and it doesn't really gel for me, but since there's room . . . What if she set it up to look like a setup? It'd be cold, and it'd be risky. But it'd be smart, too."

"Yeah, it would." Eve began to go through the desk drawers methodically.

"You already thought of it."

"Peabody, we lieutenants are always thinking."

"But you don't buy it."

"Look at it this way. If she did it, it's a dunk. The case fell whole into our laps. Nothing to do but file the reports and wait for it to come to trial. But if she's telling the truth, we've got a real, live mystery on our hands. I just fucking love a mystery."

She took all the discs into evidence for viewing at Central, added memo cubes, a PPC, and what appeared to be a broken address book.

"Pick a dresser," Eve invited.

They searched the bedroom, moving from the contents of the dressers to the contents of the closet. They turned up nothing of interest but what Peabody referred to as monkey-sex underwear.

They split up on the home offices, with Eve taking Blair's.

He had, she noted, the better end of the deal there. His was twice the size of hers, and with a view of the stone garden—the garden she assumed he'd wanted. There was also a long leather couch, the color of light coffee, with a mirrored wall behind it, and an entertainment center loaded with the latest toys.

It was, she thought, more a man-as-boy playroom than

workspace. And when she called up his data unit, she found it wasn't working at all.

She gave it a quick slap with the heel of her hand, which was her usual way of dealing with recalcitrant machines. "I said, 'Computer, on,' " she repeated, and once again read in her name, rank, and badge number for override of standard passcodes.

The screen stayed blank, the unit silent.

Interesting, she thought, as she circled around it as she might a sleeping animal. What did he have in there he didn't want his wife to see?

Still watching the unit, she pulled out her communicator and tagged Feeney at EDD.

His hound-dog face had been sun-kissed by his recent vacation in Bimini. He'd only been back a couple of days, and Eve was hoping it would fade soon. It was . . . disconcerting to see Feeney with a tan.

She wanted his hair to grow back, too. He'd shorn his wiry ginger-and-gray mop painfully short while he'd been gone. It looked like he was wearing a snug, fuzzy helmet.

When you added the post-holiday sparkle to his droopy brown eyes, it was a study in mixed signals, and made her head hurt.

"Hey, kid."

"Hey. Did you get my request?"

"First thing. Already cleared the time and manpower for you."

"I got more. Dead guy's home unit. He must have it seriously passcoded. I can't get it on."

"Dallas, there are times you can't get your AutoChef on."

"That's a dirty lie." She poked the data unit with a finger. "I need a pickup for this, and for a houseful of 'links and data centers. A boatload of security discs I need studied and analyzed."

"I'll send out a team for pickup."

She waited a beat. "Just like that? I don't even get a token bitch?"

"I'm in too good a mood to bitch. The wife made me pancakes this morning. Can't do enough for me. I'm a fricking hero with my whole family. You flipped me that Bimini deal, Dallas, and I figure I'm going to reap the rewards for the next six months. I owe you."

"Feeney, you look sort of scary when you smile like that. So cut it out."

His grin only widened. "Can't help it. I'm a happy man."

"I've got enough EDD work on this one to keep you and a full team buried for days."

"Sounds good." He almost sang it. "I'm ready for a real challenge. Guy gets soft sitting on the beach sucking coconut juice all day."

This had to stop, was all she could think. And now. "Case is a slam," she said and showed her teeth. "And I've already booked the suspect on two counts in the first. I'm using departmental time and money to pick the case apart from the inside out."

"Sounds like fun," he said with a lilt in his voice. "Glad you called me in."

"I could learn to hate you like this, Feeney." She rattled off the address, and cut transmission as he began to hum.

"Do a favor for a friend," she muttered, "and it bites you on the ass. Peabody!" She shouted it. "Tag all electronics for EDD pickup. Arrange for two droids to guard the premises and seal it after EDD has come and gone. And move it. We need to go check Bissel's gallery and studio."

"If we're partners now, how come I have to do all the tagging?" Peabody shouted back. "And are we ever going to eat? We've already been on the clock six hours, and my blood sugar's dropping. I can feel it."

"Just move your ass," Eve shot back, but she smiled. At least she still worked with somebody who knew how to bitch.

Because she appreciated it, and she remembered she hadn't eaten since the night before herself, she double-parked in front of a 24/7 and let Peabody make the dash in for some to-go food.

They were both going to need to go off the clock for a couple of hours, get some sleep. But she wanted to get a look at Blair's workspace and get all the electronics and security discs in evidence first.

Because the only why she could think of equaled security. The only why made Reva the real target. The killings took her out, deliberately. Unless there was a personal reason to target her, and she'd explore that angle, it was professional.

Any professional motive against Reva brushed a little too close for comfort to Roarke. So she intended to move fast, and get as much locked in to Central as she could before moving on to the next stage.

Peabody hurried out again, carrying an enormous take-out bag.

"Got hoagies." With a grunt, she dropped back in the seat.

"What, for the whole squad?"

"And other provisions."

"Because we're going on safari?"

With some dignity, Peabody pulled out a tidily wrapped hoagie and passed it to Eve. "Drinks, and a bag of soy chips, and a bag of dried apricots—"

"Dried apricots, in case the rumor of the coming Armageddon is true."

"And some damn cookies." Peabody's face closed in on a scowl that was edging toward pout. "I'm hungry, and when you're on a roll like this, I might not see food again until I'm a withered sack of bones. You don't have to eat, you know." She made a fuss out of unwrapping her own sandwich. "Nobody's holding a blaster to your head."

Eve peeked inside her sandwich and saw something that was pretending to have come from a pig. It was good enough. "In the event of Armageddon, I hope those cookies have some form of chocolate in them."

"Maybe." Slightly mollified when Eve drove one-handed and bit into her sandwich, Peabody opened a tube of Pepsi and stuck it in the drink slot.

By the time Eve got to the Flatiron Building, Peabody had mowed her way through the hoagie and a good portion of chips. As a result, both her mood and her energy were up again.

"This is my favorite New York building," she said. "When I first moved here, I took a day and went around taking pictures of the places I used to read about. This was one of the top on my list. It's so *yesterday,* you know. But here it is, still standing. The oldest remaining skyscraper in the city."

Eve hadn't known that. Then again she didn't collect that sort of trivia. She supposed she'd admired its unique triangular style now and then, in an absent sort of way.

But for her, buildings simply were. People lived or worked in them, and they took up space, gave the city shape.

She decided against trying Broadway for parking, as this section always had a party going on. Instead she turned onto Twenty-third and crammed her unit into a loading zone.

The next drop-off or pickup was going to bitch, but she flipped up her ON DUTY sign, and climbed out.

"Bissel rented space on the top floor."

"Jesus, that's got to be prime."

Eve nodded as they walked toward an entrance door. "I glanced through his financials, and he could afford it. Apparently that metal crap he built went for big bucks. And he had his own gallery, bought and sold art."

"His connection to Felicity Kade?"

"Apparently. She was a client, according to Reva. So she bought from both Blair and Reva, and she's the one who persuaded Reva to come to the art showing where Reva met Blair."

"Cozy."

With appreciation, Eve glanced at Peabody as they crossed the lobby. "That's right. Too cozy for my liking, too. So why do you figure Felicity puts her lover and her friend together?"

"Maybe they weren't lovers yet. Or maybe she didn't know they'd get serious about each other."

"Maybe." Eve bypassed the security desk and used the code Reva had given her to access the elevator to the top floor.

Instead of the doors opening, the computer gave a warning buzz.

> YOU ARE NOT CLEARED FOR THIS ELEVATOR. PLEASE RETURN TO THE SECURITY AND/OR INFORMATION DESK FOR INSTRUCTIONS ON HOW TO ACCESS THE PUBLIC ENTRANCE OF BISSEL GALLERY. THIS ELEVATOR IS FOR PRIVATE USE ONLY.

"Maybe she gave you the wrong code," Peabody suggested.

"I don't think so."

Eve walked to the main security station. "Who used that elevator last?"

The young, prim woman in black curled her lip. "I beg your pardon?"

"Don't bother," Eve told her and slapped down her badge. "Just answer the question."

"I'll need to verify your identification." With her nose still in the air, she scanned Eve's badge, then slid over a palm plate. When Eve's ID was verified, she tucked the palm plate away again. "Is this about what happened to Mr. Bissel?"

Eve merely smiled. "I beg your pardon?"

The woman sniffed, then turned to her log book. "Mr. Bissel himself was the last to use that elevator. It goes directly to his studio. His employees and clients use the one to the right. That will go to the gallery."

"You have the code for the studio elevator."

"Of course. It's required that all tenants file their security and passcodes with us."

"What is it?"

"I'm not permitted to give out that data, not without proper authorization."

Eve wondered if stuffing her badge up the woman's snooty nose would qualify as proper authorization. Instead, she shoved her own memo book onto the desk, tapped the screen. "Is this it?"

Once again, the woman turned to her data unit, keyed in a complex series of numbers. She glanced at her screen, then Eve's. "If you have it, why are you bothering to ask me?"

"It doesn't work."

"Of *course* it works. You just didn't do it properly."

"Why don't you show me how to do it properly?"

Heaving a sigh, the woman gestured to a coworker. "Watch the station," she snapped, then clipped her way over to the elevators on hair-thin heels.

She coded in, and when she got the same result as Eve, coded in again. "I don't understand it. This is the proper code. It's *registered.* Building security checks all passcodes twice a week."

"When was the last check?"

"Two days ago."

"How long will it take maintenance to bypass?"

"I have no idea."

"Is there access from the gallery to the studio?"

Obviously aggrieved, she marched back to her station, called up the diagram for the top level. "There is. There's a security door between them. I have the passcode for that."

"Which, I imagine, is about as much good as the one you have for the elevator. Give it to me anyway."

Eve pulled out her pocket 'link as she walked to the gallery elevator. "I need you at the Flatiron Building," she said the minute Roarke answered. "Bissel Gallery, top floor. The security code for the direct elevator to his studio has been changed, so I can't access it. I'm going to try to get through the door between the gallery and the studio, but I'm figuring I'll find the same block."

"Leave it be. If someone tampered with it, using the original code could add another block. I'm on my way."

"What could Bissel have in his studio he didn't want his wife to see?" Peabody wondered.

"Doesn't make sense." Eve shook her head. "Nothing in his file to indicate he's that security savvy. It takes savvy to alter a code without building security sniffing it out. And a guy who risks an affair with his wife's friend, all but under her nose? Why'd he do that? For the sex, sure, but also for the thrill. Look what I can get away with. Why does a man who goes for the thrill take such extensive precautions with his home office unit, his art studio? What does one have to do with the other?"

She stepped off the elevator, into a space filled with sculpture, paintings, both static and animated. In the midst of the softly lighted room, a woman sat on the floor, sobbing her heart out.

"Man," Eve said under her breath. "I hate when this happens. You take her."

Pleased to have a concrete assignment, Peabody approached the woman, crouched in front of her. "Miss."

"We're closed." She wailed into her own hands. "Due to a *de-de-death*."

"I'm Detective Peabody." Under the circumstances, she tried not to display too much glee in being able to say just that. "This is my partner, Lieutenant Dallas. We're investigating the deaths of Blair Bissel and Felicity Kade."

"Blair!" She all but screamed it, and threw herself facedown on the floor. "No, no, no, he can't be dead. I can't *stand* it."

"I'm sorry, this is a difficult time for you."

"I don't think I can go on! All the light, all the air's gone out of the world."

"Oh, Jesus Christ." Since enough was enough, Eve stalked over, took the woman by one arm, and hauled her back to a sitting position. "I want your name, your connection with Blair Bissel, and the reason you're here."

"Ch-ch-ch—"

"Suck it in," Eve snapped. "Spit it out."

"Chloe McCoy. I run the gallery. And I'm here, I'm here, because . . ." She crossed her arms over her heart, as if she were trying to hold it inside her. "We *loved* each other."

Barely old enough to buy a drink in a legit bar, Eve gauged. Her face was ravaged, swollen and splotchy, with huge brown eyes still busily pumping out the tears. Her hair was ink-black and tumbled over her shoulders, over a pair of young and perky breasts shown off in a snug black shirt.

"You had an intimate relationship with Bissel."

"We were in love!" She threw out her arms, then wrapped them tightly around her own body. "We were soulmates. Destined for each other from our first breaths. We were—"

"Did you fuck him, Chloe?"

The crudeness did what Eve had hoped, and the tears magically dried up. "How *dare* you? How dare you demean something so beautiful?" She threw up her chin, and though it trembled, it stayed so high it nearly pointed at the ceiling. "Yes, we were lovers. Now that he's dead, my soul is dead, too. How could she do it? That horrible, horrible woman? How could she turn out the light on someone so good, so true, so perfect."

"So good and true he was sleeping with her friend and one of his employees?" Eve said pleasantly.

"His marriage was over." Chloe turned her head away, stared at the wall. "It was just a matter of time until it was legally ended, and we'd be together in the sunlight, instead of in shadows."

"How old are you?"

"I'm twenty-one, but age means nothing." She closed her hand over a heart-shaped pendant around her throat. "I'm as old as time now, as old as grief."

"When's the last time you saw Blair?"

"Yesterday morning. We met here." She brushed her free hand over her brow while she stroked the little gold heart. "To say a sweet good-bye before he had to go on his trip."

"That would be his trip uptown where he snuggled in with Felicity Kade for a couple days?"

"That isn't true." Her puffy eyes took on a mutinous expression. "I don't know what happened, what that horrible woman made it appear, but Blair certainly wasn't involved that way with Ms. Kade. She was a client, and no more."

"Uh-huh" was the kindest response Eve could think of. "How long have you worked here?"

"Eight months. The most vital eight months of my life. I only started to live when—"

"Did his wife come here?"

"Rarely." Chloe pressed her lips together. "She pretended an interest in his work, in public. But in private she was critical, and was draining his energies. Of course, she had no problem spending the money he made from the sweat of his soul."

"Is that so? He tell you that?"

"He told me everything." She beat her breast, her hand fisted around the locket. Heart tapped against heart. "There were no secrets between us."

"So you have the passcode into his studio."

She opened her mouth, firmed it again before speaking. "No. An artist such as Blair needs his privacy. I would never intrude. Naturally, he would open the door when he wanted to share something with me."

"Right. So you wouldn't know if he ever had visitors in there."

"He worked alone. It was necessary for his creativity."

Dupe, Eve thought. Foolish, gullible, and probably no more than a casual toy for Bissel. She started to turn as the elevator opened again, and Chloe flung her arms around Eve's legs.

"Please, please! You must let me see him. You must let me say goodbye to my heart. Let me *go* to him. Let me touch his face one last time! You must. You must give me that much."

Eve saw Roarke quirk a brow in a kind of amused horror. Bending, Eve peeled Chloe off her shins.

"Peabody, deal with this."

"Sure. Come on, Chloe." Putting her back into it, Peabody hefted the weeping girl. "Let's go splash some water on your face. Blair would want you to be strong. I've got some questions I need to ask you. He'd want you to help us, so we can see justice is done."

"I will! I will be strong, for Blair. No matter how hard it is."

"I know you will," Peabody replied, and led Chloe through an archway.

"Second, much younger side dish," Eve said before Roarke could ask.

"Ah."

"Yeah. Ah. I don't think she knows anything, but Peabody'll coax it out of her if she does."

"I wonder if it'll be easier on Reva, knowing what a complete bastard the man was. Her lawyer got her out on bail. She has to wear a bracelet, but she's out. She'll stay with Caro until this is cleared up."

He studied the wide double doorway taking up most of a wall, and, strolling over, gave it a light tap. "Steel, reinforced, I'd wager. Odd to go to all that for a space such as this."

"So I'm thinking."

"Hmm." He wandered to the security panel. "Feeney contacted me shortly before you did. In fact, I was on the point of heading down to Central when you gave me this interesting assignment."

Taking a case of slim tools from his pocket, Roarke selected one, removed the plate. "He appears to have had a very fine time with his family in Bimini."

"He has a tan. He smiles all the time. I'm not entirely sure they didn't replace him with a droid."

Roarke made not entirely sympathetic mouth noises before taking a small electronic unit out of another pocket.

"What's that?"

"Oh, just a little something I've been toying with. A good time to try it out in the field, so to speak." He interfaced it with the pad, waited through a series of beeps, and brushed Eve gently back when she tried to stare at it over his shoulder.

"Don't crowd me, Lieutenant."

"What's it doing?"

"All manner of things you wouldn't understand, and you'd just get testy if I tried to explain. Simplest to say it's mating—as machines do. And seducing Bissel's unit into revealing all sorts of secrets. And isn't this interesting?"

"What? Damn it. Can you get in or not?"

"I don't know why I tolerate the insults." He glanced over his shoulder, directly into her annoyed eyes. "Maybe it's the sex. How lowering that would be. Then again, I'm as weak and vulnerable as the next man."

"Are you trying to piss me off?"

"Darling, it's no effort at all. Now what I've learned here, through my delightful new toy, is exactly when this passcode was changed. And I think you'll find it as interesting as I do that it was done at nearly the same time someone was jamming a kitchen knife in Blair Bissel's ribs."

Her eyes flickered, narrowed. "No mistake?"

"None. He could hardly have done this himself."

"Hardly."

"Nor could his equally dead mistress, or his wife. Or, for that matter, his killer."

"But I'll bet you whoever locked this up knew he was dead, or dying. Knew his wife was in the frame. This has to be another stage of the whole bloody mess. Get me inside."

Chapter 4

It didn't take him long. Such things rarely did. He had thief's hands—quick, agile, and sneaky—but since he used them for her, and on her, with cheerful regularity, it was tough to criticize.

And when he was done, the heavy doors slid back with barely a sound into wall pockets to reveal Blair Bissel's studio.

He'd given himself a lot of space here, too. And it looked like he needed it. There was metal everywhere, in long beams, short stacks, in piles of cubes and balls. The floor and the walls were covered in some sort of fireproof, reflective material that did double duty and mirrored back vague ghosts of the equipment and works-in-progress.

Tools that made Eve think of medieval torture devices lay on a long metal table. Tools that cut and snipped and bent, she assumed. And three large tanks fixed into rolling stands were in various positions around the room. From the attachments and hoses on each, she deduced they were filled with some sort of flammable gas and provided the heat used to weld or melt or whatever the hell people who made weird things out of metal did with fire.

Another wall was covered with sketches. Some looked to

have been done by hand, others computer generated. Since one matched the strange twists and spikes of a piece in the center of the room, she decided they were ideas or blueprints for his art.

He may have spent his off time diddling anything female, but it appeared he took his vocation seriously.

She skirted around the centered sculpture, and only then noted that there was a form of a hand, fingers spread as if desperately reaching, plunging out of the twist of metal.

She glanced back at the sketch, read the notation at the bottom.

ESCAPE FROM HELL

"Who buys this shit?" she wondered.

"Collectors," Roarke supplied, eyeing a tall, obviously female form that was, apparently, giving birth to something not completely human. "Corporations and businesses that want to be seen as patrons of the arts."

"Don't tell me you have some of this?"

"Actually, I don't. His work doesn't . . . speak to me."

"That's something, anyway." Turning her back on the sculpture, she walked to the data station set up at the far end of the room.

She glanced at the stack of beams. "How does he get the stuff in and out? No way some of this fits on the elevator."

"There's another lift to the roof. There." He gestured to the east wall. "Installed at his own expense. "It's triple the size of the standard freight elevator. There's a copter pad on the roof, and he has pieces and equipment airlifted."

She just looked at him. "Don't tell me you own this place."

"Partially." He spoke absently as he wandered, studying metal forms. "It's a conglomerate sort of thing."

"You know, it gets embarrassing after a point."

He lifted his eyebrows, all innocence. "Really? I can't imagine why."

"You wouldn't. Which reminds me." She shoved back her jacket sleeve and held out her arm so the bracelet glittered.

"Take this thing, will you? I forgot I was wearing it when we headed out to the scene. Peabody keeps staring at it, and pretends she's not staring at it. It's freaking me out, and if I stuff it in my pocket or something, I'll probably lose it."

"You know," he began as she unclasped it, "people tend to wear jewelry so other people will notice it. Admire it, even covet it."

"Which is why people who hang baubles all over themselves end up getting mugged."

"That's a downside," he agreed and slipped the bracelet into his pocket. "But life's full of risks. I'll consider holding this for you my little way of saving some poor, foolish street thief from ending up with your boot stomped on his throat."

"Birds of a feather," she murmured and made him grin.

She went to work on the computer, with the same results she'd gotten from Bissel's home unit. "Why is an artist so damn careful and paranoid about his data?"

"Let me have a go at it, and let's find out."

She stepped back, did a walk through the studio to get a sense of Bissel's style, and to give those magic hands of Roarke's time to work.

There was a red-and-white bath off the main floor, complete with jet tub, drying tube, and the same sort of fancy towels Roarke favored. A bedroom had been set up as well. Small, she noted, but with all the comforts. Bissel had liked his comforts.

The gel mattress was thick and cushy, the cover slick and black and sexy. One wall was mirrored, and she thought of the entrance to his house, the master bed and bath.

Liked to look at himself, and to watch himself with women. Egoist, narcissist. Pampered and confident. There was a mini data and communication center near the bed, as blocked as the others.

Chewing it over, she moved to a narrow three-drawer chest and began riffling. Spare underwear, extra work clothes.

And ah, a locked bottom drawer. Roarke wasn't the only one who could handle such things, she thought, as she pulled out a pocketknife.

She attacked the old-fashioned lock, hacking happily away, and gave a grunt of satisfaction as it gave. She jerked open the drawer. And even her cynical, seen-it-all-and-then-some eyes popped wide.

"Holy jumping Jesus."

She pawed through satin restraints, velvet whips, leather strap-ons, the connoisseur's collection of dildos. There were vials of the illegal substance known as Rabbit, a bag she identified as Zeus, another of Erotica. There were gel balls, butt plugs, blindfolds, numerous battery-operated toys and devices, cock and nipple rings of all description.

And more. A great deal more she wasn't entirely sure she could identify.

It appeared Bissel not only took his work seriously, but his games as well.

"The unit's not blocked, Lieutenant. It's . . ." Roarke trailed off as he stepped in and saw what Eve was examining. "Well, well, well, what have we here?"

"The goodie drawer of all goodie drawers. This dildo not only throbs, vibrates, expands, and comes equipped with hands-free feature, it sings a choice of five popular tunes."

He crouched beside her. "You couldn't have tried it out that quickly."

"Pervert. I turned it on to see. He's got some illegals sprinkled through here, too."

"So I see. Oh, look, what fun. His and her VR. Maybe we could—" He started to reach for the matching goggles, and had his hand slapped away.

"No."

"You're so strict." He walked his fingers along her knee. "Maybe you could be strict with me later." Wiggling those eyebrows, he held up a pair of restraints. "We already have these."

A quick check proved the restraints were indeed her own, lifted right off her person without her feeling a thing. She snatched them back. "Cut that *out*. And don't touch anything in there. I mean it. I have to log this crap. Even the mother of all goodie drawers is no reason for a guy to passcode his computers, lock the drawer in an already secured area. He—"

"I said the unit wasn't blocked." He patted her knee and rose, resisting—though it was difficult—palming a couple of the goodies just for the fun of it. "It's fried."

"What the hell do you mean 'fried'?"

"Fried, toasted, whacked, zapped, dead."

"I know what fried means, I meant—damn it." She sprang up, kicked the drawer closed. "When? Can you tell when? When and how?"

"I imagine so, given the right tools and a bit of time, but I can tell you this much just from this cursory exam: It was professionally and expertly fried."

"What does that mean?"

"Simply, the main board was destroyed so that all data was corrupted. My first guess would be a very insidious worm, with specificity for this purpose. Likely contained on a disc, inserted into the drive, used to infect, then removed when the task was complete."

"Can you tell if data was removed first?"

"Trickier, but we can certainly try."

"How about retrieving anything? Digging in and finding what data was on there, uncorrupting?"

"Trickier yet."

"It's there. It's always there, no matter what. I know that from Feeney."

"Well, that may not be quite true. Eve, there's a group of techno-terrorists. They call themselves the Doomsday Group."

"I know who they are. Glorified hackers, like to infiltrate systems, upload what they can, screw with the data. They've got some good, twisted brains and plenty of financial backing."

"A bit more than glorified," he corrected. "They're responsible for downing a number of private shuttles by skewing data in air traffic control. They helped themselves to several works of art, and deliberately damaged others at the Louvre by shutting down their security. They killed twenty-six employees of a research lab in Prague by sabotaging their system, shutting down the air supply, and sealing all doors."

"I said they were twisted. I know they're dangerous. What does it have to do with a fried unit in a dead man's art studio?"

"They've been working on a worm of just this nature for the past few years. Potent, portable. Its design is not simply to corrupt data or hijack it, but to eliminate it, and on a large scale. To network, to proliferate."

"How large a scale?"

"Theoretically, a disc could be slipped into a drive on a networking unit—even a network with fail-safes and blocks, with virus detectors and bug zappers—and download the entire data bank from that network, then corrupt the units. An office, a building, a corporation. A country."

"Not possible. Even midlevel security detects intrusive viruses and bugs and shuts down before infection. You can't download without detection from CompuGuard. Home units like this, okay, you might get it off and down before the security dropped on you. Small operations networks, maybe. Maybe even with the CompuGuard shields in place. But nothing over that."

"Theoretically," he repeated. "And this faction is reputed to have some particularly brilliant minds on board this project. The intel indicates the worm is near completion, and could work."

"How do you know about this?"

"I have connections." He gave an easy shrug. "And it happens Roarke Industries is under government contract, a Code Red contract, to develop and create an exterminator program and shield against this potential threat."

She sat on the side of the bed. "You're working for the government. Ours?"

"Well, if by that you mean the U.S., yes. Actually, it's also a conglomeration sort of thing. The U.S., the Euro Community, Russia, a few other concerned areas. Roarke Industries Securecomp arm has the contract, and R and D is working on it."

"And Reva Ewing works in R and D, for Roarke Industries Securecomp arm."

"She does. Eve, I said Code Red, that's highest clearance.

This isn't something she'd have chatted about with her husband over dinner, I can promise you."

"Because you didn't chat with me about it over dinner?"

Irritation sparked, then was controlled. "Because she's a pro, Eve. She wouldn't hold the position she does if there was any doubt of that. She doesn't leak data."

"Maybe not." Coincidence, to her mind, was just a link between points. "But it's certainly possible someone else doesn't have the same confidence in her that you do. It sure adds an interesting angle."

She pushed off the bed, circled the room. "Check this out, will you?" she said absently with a gesture toward the mini data center. "Techno-terrorists. What does a philandering metal sculptor have in common with techno-terrorists besides his wife's position? Why, if they found some use for him, do they kill him, his mistress, and frame his wife? Of course, with the wife in a cage on two counts in the first, this could put a crimp into the research and development of the extermination program and shields."

She looked toward Roarke for confirmation.

"Somewhat. But not an insurmountable crimp. She's heading this, and a couple of other sensitive projects, but there's a very competent team as well. All data on the project would remain locked in-house. None of it is taken outside."

"Are you sure of that? Dead sure?"

"I would have been. This is fried as well, same method." Because he had the same cynical take on coincidence as Eve, anger began to rise through his concern. "Do you speculate that Bissel somehow got his hands on data pertaining to the programs, and was killed for it?"

"It's a good place to start. Did he, or Felicity, ever visit Reva at work?"

"Not that I'm aware of, but I'll find out. They'd never have been admitted into the lab—not this lab—but there are visitors' areas, so I'll see about that. I'll also have a look, personally, at the security of the project, and the personnel assigned."

She knew that icy, controlled tone of voice. "No point in getting pissed off until you know you've got a leak."

"Just getting a jump on it. You'll want to talk to Reva again, and press her on how her husband might have known something of this project."

"Like I said, it's a place to start."

"She might talk to me more freely."

"Her boss? The man who hired her, pays her, and trusted her with the responsibility of a Code Red? Why should she?"

"Because I've known her since she was in bloody university," he said with some impatience. "And if she lies to me, I'll know it."

"You're on EDD duty on this," she reminded him. "You wanted the gig, and you've got it. It looks to me as if we're going to make some use of you in that area. I've got to call for a pickup here of all electronics. And I want the gallery and the studio swept. So that's going to take a little time. I'll give you ten minutes with her, then she's mine."

"I appreciate it."

"No, you don't. You're still pissed off."

"At least I'm polite about it."

"If she leaked it—" She held up a hand to stop his automatic denial. "If she leaked it, how much of the fallout lands on you?"

He wanted a cigarette, and denied himself that small weakness out of principle. "She's mine, so it's my responsibility. We'll take a hit, a hard one. There are a number of other contracts pending. If this blows up in my face, I'd estimate seventy percent of them—and that's optimistic—will cancel."

She couldn't estimate the real value of seventy percent of pending contracts. Millions? Billions? But more, she knew, would be the damage to his pride, and his rep. So she kept her face sober. "Does that mean we won't be able to afford live-in help?"

Appreciating her, he angled his head, then gave her a quick poke with his finger in the belly. "We'll muddle through somehow. I've a bit put by for a rainy day."

"Yeah, a couple of continents, I imagine. Just like I imagine your rep will stand the hit, if it comes. It will," she repeated when he said nothing. "And I'd make book you'll fast-talk your way into keeping the bulk of those pendings."

The first gush of anger cooled. "That's considerable faith in me, Lieutenant."

"Considerable faith in that Irish guile of yours, ace."

She pulled out her communicator and called for an EDD pickup. She stepped into the studio from the bedroom area as Peabody stepped in from the gallery.

"Got the interview—the really long, rambling, theatrical interview with McCoy. Due to which, I just took a departmentally approved blocker for the amazing headache."

"Where is she?"

"I let her go. She's planning to lay prostrate in bed in her apartment, and permit herself to be swept away by the rising tide of her grief. That's a direct quote. I did a standard run on her while she was babbling," she added, and brightened considerably when Roarke stepped out. "She's twenty-one, as advertised. Still working on her art and theater degrees, big surprise there. Employed here for the last eight months. No criminal. Born in Topeka." She tried and failed to stifle a yawn. "Sorry. Was Farm Queen her senior year of high school, another shocker. Moved here at eighteen to attend Columbia, partial scholarship. She comes up as clean and green as a Kansas wheat field."

"Do a second-level run on her anyway."

"On her?"

"I'll fill you in on the way. You come in your own transpo?" she asked Roarke.

"I did. I'll follow you over."

"Good enough. Since you're civilian consultant for EDD, contact Feeney and bring him up to date."

"Yes, sir." He winked at Peabody as they stepped into the elevator. "You look tired, Detective."

"I'm whipped. It's what . . . fourteen hundred. Twelve hours on the clock, on no sleep to speak of. I don't know how she does it."

"Just focus," Eve ordered. "I'll give you an hour's personal in the crib at Central after this."

"A whole hour." Peabody gave up and yawned again. "Boy, that ought to set me up."

By the time they were double-parked in front of Caro's building, Peabody's droopy eyes were back on alert.

"Techno-terrorists, Code Reds, government alliances. Jeez, Dallas, it sort of rocks. It's like spy stuff."

"It's like murder stuff, seeing as there are two bodies in the morgue."

Even as she got out of the car, the doorman, spiffy in hunter green with gold braid, marched over. "Ma'am, I'm sorry, but you can't leave your vehicle there. Public parking is available two blocks west, on . . ."

He trailed off, snapped to attention like a new army recruit faced with a five-star general when Roarke strolled up to join them. "Sir! I wasn't told you were expected. I was just informing this woman that her vehicle is in violation of the parking code."

"This is my wife, Jerry."

"Oh, I beg your pardon, Mrs.—"

"Lieutenant." She ground it out between her teeth. "Dallas, and that makes this a police vehicle. That means it stays where I put it."

"Of course, Lieutenant. I'll make certain it's not disturbed."

He hustled to the door, opened it with some flourish. "Just call down if you need anything," he said. "I'm on the door until four."

"We're fine. Nice to see you again, Jerry."

"Always a pleasure, sir."

Roarke walked directly to the automated security panel that was flanked by two tall urns filled with burnished gold fall flowers. "Why don't I do it, and save time?" Without waiting for the go-ahead, he placed his palm on the plate, and was immediately cleared.

GOOD AFTERNOON, SIR! the computer said, with the same

delighted enthusiasm as Jerry the doorman. WELCOME BACK. WHAT CAN I DO FOR YOU?

"Inform Ms. Ewing that I'm here, along with Lieutenant Dallas and Detective Peabody. And clear the elevator."

YES, SIR. ENJOY YOUR VISIT.

"Now, wasn't that better than having a pissing match with a machine?" Roarke asked as he led the way to a trio of silver elevator doors.

"No. I like having pissing matches with machines. It gets my blood moving."

He patted her on the shoulder, nudged her into the car ahead of him. "Well, next time, then. Eighteenth floor," he requested.

"I guess this is one of your buildings."

He smiled over at Peabody. "It is, yes."

"Sweet. So, if I ever have any money to invest, would you maybe give me some pointers?"

"I'd be delighted to."

"Yeah, like cops have investment funds." Eve shook her head.

"You just start out saving a little bit of each payday check," Peabody explained. "Then you find the right place to put it, so you can increase the pot. Right?"

"Exactly so," Roarke agreed. "Just let me know when you're ready, and I'll find you a rainbow to bury that pot under."

He gestured when the doors opened on eighteen. "Ladies."

"We're on duty. That makes us cops, not ladies." But Eve stalked out and to the door of the east corner apartment.

It opened before she could bother with the buzzer.

"Is there some news? Has there been a development?" Caro caught herself, drew a breath. "I'm so sorry. Please come in. Why don't we sit in the living area?"

She stepped back to welcome them into the spacious apartment with a river view. Twin sofas done in strong blue were grouped into a conversation area accented with pretty lamps with jeweled shades and glossy tables.

In what Eve considered a female trait, she'd arranged plump and colorful pillows on the sofas.

There were fresh flowers in vases, attractive little dust catchers, and books—the sort with pages—grouped on shelves.

She'd changed, Eve noted, into what she imagined Caro considered around-the-house attire. Both the shirt and pants were bronze; both were meticulously tailored.

"What can I get you?"

"Coffee would be lovely," Roarke said before Eve could reject the offer. "If it's not too much trouble."

"Of course not. I'll just be a minute. Please, sit down. Be comfortable."

Eve waited until Caro had walked through a doorway. "This isn't a social call, Roarke."

"She needs something to do, something normal. She needs a moment to settle."

"This is really beautiful," Peabody said into the silence. "This place. Simple, classy elegance. Just right, you know. Like her."

"Caro is a woman of quiet and unquestionable taste. She's built a life that reflects her own style and desires, and she's done it on her own. Something you'd respect," he said to Eve.

"I do respect her. I like her." *Am intimidated by her,* she thought. "And you know I can't let that get in the way of the job."

"No. But you might add it into the equation."

"If you get overprotective and defensive, this isn't going to work."

"I'm only asking for you to go gently with her."

"And here I was planning on smacking her around."

"Eve—"

"Please, don't quarrel over me." Caro stepped back in, carrying a tray. "This is a very difficult situation we find ourselves in. I don't need or expect special handling."

"Let me take that." Roarke took the tray from her. "You should sit down, Caro. You look worn out."

"Not very flattering, but certainly true. I'm a little worn at the edges." She made herself smile as she sat. "But I'm perfectly capable of handling the tough stuff, Lieutenant. I'm not fragile."

"No, I've never thought of you as fragile. Formidable."

"Formidable." Now her smile warmed. "I'm not sure that's flattering either. You take yours black, as Roarke does. And you, Detective?"

"I'll have it light, thanks."

"I need to speak with your daughter," Eve began.

"She's resting. I browbeat her into taking a soother a couple hours ago." As she poured, Caro pressed her lips together. "She's grieving for him. Part of me is angry that she could grieve for him, under the circumstances. She's not fragile either. I didn't raise a fragile child. But she's damaged by this—by all of it. And afraid. We're both afraid."

She passed the coffee around, then a plate of thin golden cookies.

"You must have some questions you need to ask me. Couldn't you interview me first, give her just a little more time to rest?"

"Tell me what you thought of Blair Bissel."

"What I thought of him, before this morning?" Caro lifted her cup. It was a pretty floral pattern. "I liked him, because my daughter loved him. Because by all appearances he loved her. I never felt as much for him as I'd hoped to feel for my daughter's choice of mate, which sounds . . . convenient under the circumstances, but doesn't make it less true."

"Why? Why didn't you like him as much as you'd hoped to?"

"That's a good question, and difficult to answer with specifics. I'd imagined when she married that I'd love her husband, much as I might've loved a son. But I didn't. I found him pleasant and amusing, considerate and intelligent. But . . . cool. On some inner level, cool and distant."

She set her cup down again, without drinking. "It was my

hope that I'd have grandchildren, when they were ready. And my secret hope, one I never shared with Reva, that when the grandchildren came I'd find that love for Blair."

"And his work?"

"It's necessary to be honest now, isn't it?" There was, for just an instant, a twinkle in her eyes. "I could never be honest before. Preposterous, occasionally offensive, and very often unseemly. Art should often be surprising, and even unseemly, I suppose. But I'm more traditional in my tastes. He did very well, though."

"Reva strikes me as an urbanite. What's she doing in a house in Queens?"

"He wanted it. A big house, in his own style. I admit it broke my heart a little to have her move even that far away. We've always been very close. Her father hasn't been part of our lives since she was twelve."

"Why?"

"He preferred other women." She said it without any trace of bitterness. Without, Eve noticed, any trace of anything. "It seems my daughter was attracted to the same kind of man."

"She lived farther away from you at one time, during her time with the Secret Service."

"Yes. She needed to spread her wings. I was very proud of her, and extremely relieved when she retired and moved back, went into R and D. Safe, I thought." Caro's lips trembled. "So much safer for my girl."

"Did Reva ever talk about her work with you?"

"Hmm? Oh, from time to time. We were often involved, in our different ways, in the same projects."

"Has she discussed with you the project she's involved with now?"

Caro picked up her cup again, but Eve had seen the quick widening of her pupils. "I imagine Reva's involved in a number of projects at the moment."

"You know the one I'm talking about, Caro."

This time there was a faint line of confusion between her eyebrows, and a quick glance at Roarke. "I'm not at liberty to discuss any of the projects in development through Roarke Industries. Even with you, Lieutenant."

"It's all right, Caro. The lieutenant is aware of the Code Red."

"I see." But it was clear to Eve that she didn't. "I'm privy to certain details on any project with this level of sensitivity. As Roarke's admin, I assist in meetings and review contracts, evaluate personnel. These are part of my duties. So yes, I'm aware of the project Reva's heading."

"And the two of you have discussed it."

"Reva and I? No. We wouldn't speak of this, any details of it. With Code Red, all data—verbal, electronic, holographic—all files, all notes, all intel remains top level. I've discussed this with no one, until now, but Roarke himself. In the office. This is global security, Lieutenant," she said with brisk disapproval in her tone. "It isn't coffee talk."

"I'm not bringing it up to juice up the cookies."

"They're great cookies," Peabody piped up, and earned a scowl from Eve. "I bet you get them from a bakery."

Caro smiled a little. "Yes, I do."

"We always had fresh cookies in the house when I was a kid. Now that we're grown up, my mom still has them around. Habit," Peabody said, and took another bite. "You probably always had them around when Reva was a kid."

"I did."

"I guess especially when you're raising a kid on your own, you tend to be close, and a mom gets to be even more protective."

"Probably." The stiffness in Caro's voice, in her body language, relaxed. "Though I've tried, always, to give her room. Independence."

"Still worry, like you said. Like when she was with the Secret Service. Probably worried some too, like moms do, when she got serious about Blair."

"Yes, a bit. Still, she was a grown woman."

"My mom always said we can get as old as we want, she's still our mom. Did you run Bissel, Ms. Ewing?"

Caro started to speak, then flushed and stared hard at the window. "I . . . she's my only child. Yes. I'm ashamed to say I did. I know I asked you specifically not to," she said to Roarke. "Made a point of it, even an issue of it with you."

"I did two levels anyway."

"Well, of course. Of course you did." Her hand fluttered to her face, then fell back into her lap. "She was an employee, after all." She sighed now. "I knew you would do that much. You have to protect yourself, your holdings."

"I wasn't only thinking of myself, Caro, or my holdings."

She reached out, touched his hand. "No, I know that. But I also knew, because I asked—well, demanded, really—you wouldn't go deeper than that. And I swore to myself I wouldn't. I absolutely would not interfere in such an underhanded way with my daughter's life. Then I did. Another full level. And I used your resources to do it. I'm terribly sorry."

"Caro." He picked up her hand, kissed her fingers gently. "I was perfectly aware of what you did. I had no problem with it."

"Oh." She let out a shaky laugh. "How foolish of me. Remarkably."

"How could you do that, Mom?" Reva stepped into the room. Her eyes were ravaged, her hair disordered from sleep. "How could you go behind my back that way?"

Chapter 5

Roarke got to his feet and moved so smoothly, so subtly between mother and daughter, Eve wondered if anyone noticed that he'd placed himself as Caro's shield.

"For that matter, Reva, so did I, go behind your back, as it were."

"You're not my mother." She bit the words off as she stepped forward, and Roarke simply shifted his body without seeming to move at all.

"Which would mean, all in all, I had less of a right." He spoke easily, drawing his cigarette case out of his pocket. The gesture, Eve noted, distracted Reva. If only for a moment. "Do you mind, Caro?" he asked, very pleasant.

"No." Flustered, she looked around, then rose. "I'll get an ashtray."

"Thanks. Of course you could say I did the basic run on Blair as your employer. And that would be true." He lit the cigarette. "True enough, but not fully true. You're a friend of mine, as is your mother, so that was another factor."

Color was riding high in Reva's cheeks, a full temper strike at the flashpoint, made no less volatile by the fact she was bundled into a petal-pink robe and wearing thick gray socks. "If I can't be trusted to—"

"You I trust, and always have, Reva. Him I didn't know, so why should I have trusted him? Still, I didn't go beyond two levels out of respect for your mother."

"But not for me, not out of respect for me. Either of you," she said with a furious look at her mother as Caro came back with a small crystal dish. "You were spying on him, checking up on him, and all the while you were making wedding plans, pretending to be happy for me."

"Reva, I was happy for you," Caro began.

"You didn't like him, you *never* liked him," Reva spat out. "If you think I didn't know you—"

"Sorry. If you want to get into a family spat, it'll have to wait." Eve made a show of getting out her recorder when Reva whipped around toward her. "Homicide investigations take precedence. You've already been read your rights—"

"You agreed to give me ten minutes," Roarke reminded her. "I'll take it now."

Eve shrugged. "A deal's a deal."

"Caro, is there somewhere private I could have a few moments with Reva?"

"Yes. You could use my office. I'll just show you—"

"I know where it is." Turning her back on Caro, Reva stalked away. The ensuing silence was punctuated by the violent slamming of a door.

"I'm very sorry." Caro sat again, folded her hands in her lap. "She's understandably upset."

"Sure." Eve glanced at her wrist unit. Ten minutes was all Roarke was going to get.

In Caro's office, with its streamlined D and C center on top of an antique rosewood desk, Reva stood as rigid as a blindfolded prisoner awaiting execution. "I'm so angry with her, with you. With every fucking thing."

"Well, there's a bulletin. Why don't you sit down, Reva?"

"I don't want to sit down. I'm not going to sit down. I want to punch something, kick something. *Break* something."

"Do what you need to do." His tone was bored, a verbal shrug that caused embarrassed color to rise up and join the flush of Reva's temper. "That's between you and Caro, as these are her things. When you've finished your tantrum, you can sit down and we'll talk like reasonable adults."

"I've always hated that about you."

"What's that?" he asked and took a slow drag on his cigarette.

"That control of yours. That ice you use instead of blood in your veins."

"Ah, that. The lieutenant can tell you there are times when even my astonishing control and marvelously even temper fails. No one snaps our composure quite like someone we love."

"I didn't say you had an even temper, marvelous or otherwise," she said dryly. "There's no one scarier, or meaner. Or kinder." Her breath hitched, forcing her to take a gulp of air, or sob. "I know you have to fire me, and that you're going to try to do it gently. I'm not angry about that. I can't blame you for that. If it makes things easier, less messy, I'll resign."

He took another drag, then tapped the cigarette out in the little crystal dish he'd brought in with him. "Why would I need to fire you?"

"I've been charged with murder, for God's sake. I'm out on bail, the kind of bail that's going to require me to sell my house and nearly everything else I own. I'm wearing this."

She shot out a hand, her fingers fisted tight below the dull silver tracking bracelet on her wrist.

"I suppose it's too much to ask for them to make those things even remotely stylish."

At the comment, she could only stare at him. "They know if I walk outside to go to the corner deli. They know I'm upset right now because they can read my pulse rate. It's just a prison without the cage."

"I know it, Reva. I'm sorry for it. But the cage could be worse, a great deal worse. You're not to sell your house, or anything else. I'll lend you the money. Shut up," he ordered even as she opened her mouth. "You'll take it because I'm telling you to take it. It's an investment for me. And when this is cleared up and you're exonerated, I'll have it back. Then you'll work off what I consider a fair interest on the loan."

She did sit down, dropping onto the little love seat beside him. "You have to fire me."

"You're telling me how to run my own business now?" His tone was cold, deliberately so. "However valued an employee you are, I don't take orders from you."

She leaned forward, elbows on knees, and covered her face with her hands. "If this is for friendship—"

"Partially, of course. The friendship and affection I have for you and for Caro. It's also a matter of you being a very important part of Securecomp. And aside from that, I believe you're innocent, and trust my wife to prove it."

"She's almost as scary as you."

"And she can be more so, in certain areas."

"How could I be so *stupid!*" Her voice was wavering again, tears shimmering in it. "How could I be such a fool?"

"You weren't stupid. You loved him. Love's supposed to make us fools, or what's the point of it? Pull yourself together now. We don't have much time, for believe me, when my cop says ten minutes, she means ten. The extermination program and shield, Reva, the Code Red."

"Yeah." She sniffled, wiped her hands over her face to dry it. "We're close, nearly there. All the data's on the secured unit in my office—double passcoded and blocked. Backup copies in the vault, encrypted. The latest was hand-delivered to your office yesterday. Also encrypted. Tokimoto can take it over. He's the best choice. I can brief him on the areas he doesn't know, or you can. Probably best if you bump LaSalle up to second-in-command on that. She's as smart as Tokimoto, just not as creative."

"Did you ever mention the project to your husband?"

She rubbed her eyes, then blinked them. "Why would I?"

"Think carefully, Reva. Any mention of it, however casual?"

"No. I might've said something like I had a hot one and that was why I was putting in some extra hours. But nothing specific. It's Code Red."

"Did he ask you about it?"

"He can't ask me about what he doesn't know," she responded in a tone tight with impatience. "He was an artist, Roarke. His only interest in my work pertained to how I'd design and implement security for our house, and his work."

"My wife's a cop, and couldn't be less interested in my business. But occasionally, for form anyway, she asks about it. How was your day, what are you working on, that sort of thing."

"Sure, okay, sure. I'm not getting this."

"Did he, or anyone else, ask you about this project, Reva?"

She leaned back. Her face was pale again, her voice thin and weary. "I guess he might have. What's so hot about this one, something like that. I'd've told him I couldn't talk about it. He might've teased me about it. He sometimes did that. Top secret, hush-hush. My wife, the secret agent or something."

Her lip trembled so that she sank her teeth into it, biting back some control. "He got off on espionage, loved spy vids and games. But if he said anything it was just joking. You know how it is. Friends might do the same now and then, but they weren't really interested."

"Felicity, for instance?"

"Yeah." And now those teary eyes opened, went hot. "She was all about art, fashion, socializing. Sneaky bitch. She'd say things like how could I stand being holed up in some lab all day, fiddling with codes and machines. And what was so damn interesting about that? But I never discussed details, not even on the minor projects. It would violate the confidentiality contract."

"All right."

"You're thinking Blair's dead and I'm in this fix because of the Code Red? That's just not possible. He didn't know anything, and nobody without clearance knew I was on it."

"It may be very possible, Reva."

Her head jerked around. Before she could speak, there was a brisk knock on the door. "Time's up," Eve called out.

She opened the door just as Reva was getting slowly to her

feet. Reading Reva's expression, Eve nodded at Roarke. "I take it you laid the groundwork."

"He knew she was working on a top-level project, but the details weren't discussed."

"This can't have anything to do with what happened to Blair," Reva insisted. "If this was a terrorist hit, why wouldn't they come after me, or you?" she said to Roarke. "Or any active member of the team?"

"Let's try to find out," Eve suggested. "Come back in here so we can lay this all out once, for everyone."

"What does killing Blair accomplish?" Reva hurried out behind Eve. "It doesn't affect the project."

"Got you booked on a double homicide, didn't it? Sit down. When's the last time either of you were in Bissel's studio?"

"Months for me," Caro responded. "I was there last spring. April? Yes, I'm sure it was April. He wanted to show me the fountain he was working on for Reva's birthday."

"I was there last month," Reva said. "Early August. I went there after work to meet him. We were going to a dinner party at Felicity's. He cleared me, and I went up, waited a few minutes while he finished changing."

"Cleared you?" Eve prompted.

"Yeah. He was a maniac about his studio security. Nobody, but nobody, got the passcode."

"You gave me the passcode."

Reva flushed, cleared her throat. "I accessed it—on that same visit. I just couldn't resist. And it seemed like the perfect time to field test a new security scanner we were working on. So I accessed the code, tested it, and got clearance. Then I reset the security, and called up to Blair. I didn't tell him because it would've pissed him off."

"Did you ever go up there when he wasn't around?"

"What for?"

"Poke around, see what he was up to."

"I never spied on him." She sent a long look toward Caro. "I never spied on him. Maybe I should have, maybe if I had

I'd've known about him and Felicity long ago. But I respected his space and his privacy, and expected the same from him."

"Did you know about him and Chloe McCoy?"

"Who?"

"Chloe McCoy, Reva. The pretty young thing who works in his gallery?"

"The little drama queen?" She laughed. "Oh, please. Blair couldn't possibly have . . ." She trailed off as the cool, direct gaze had her belly trembling. "No. She's hardly more than a child. She's still in *college*, for God's sake." She curled herself into a ball and rocked. "Oh God. Oh God."

"Baby. Reva." Caro moved quickly to sit beside her daughter, wrap her arms around her. "Don't cry. Don't cry over him."

"I don't know if it's over him, or over me. First Felicity, and now that—that brainless little coed. How many others?"

"It only takes one."

Reva turned her face into her mother's neck. "Like mother, like daughter," Reva murmured. "If what you're saying is true, Lieutenant, maybe it was some jealous boyfriend who killed them. Somebody who knew they were being cheated on."

"That doesn't explain why you were lured there at exactly the right time. It doesn't explain why the passcodes on the elevator to the studio were changed at nearly the same time Blair Bissel and Felicity Kade were being murdered. It doesn't explain why the computers at your home, at Bissel's gallery and studio, and at Felicity Kade's home—Feeney just verified"—she said to Roarke—"have all been infected with an as yet unidentified worm that has corrupted all data thereon."

"A worm?" She pushed away from Caro. "All those computers, in all those locations? Corrupted. You're sure?"

"I've examined two of them myself," Roarke told her. "There's every indication they were infected with the Doomsday worm. We'll test to be certain, but I know what to look for."

"It can't be done by remote. We know it has to be done on site." Reva sprang up to pace. "It's a flaw in the system. It has to be uploaded directly into one of the units in a network to infect the network. It requires an operator."

"That's right."

"If the units were infected with the Doomsday, it means someone got through the security. At my house, at the gallery, the studio, at Felicity's. I can check those systems. I designed and installed all of them. I can run scans to see if they were compromised, and when."

"If you run the scans, the results are inadmissible," Eve told her.

"I'll run them." Roarke waited until she'd stopped pacing long enough to look at him. "You'll trust me for that."

"Damn right. Lieutenant." Reva came back, sat on the edge of the sofa. "If this is—if what happened has something to do with the project, it means Blair was set up, too. It was all staged, all put together so I'd go running over there, so it would look to me, to everyone, as if Blair and Felicity had been lovers. He's dead because of what he was to me. They're both dead because of me."

"You can believe that if you want. Me, I'd rather deal with the truth."

"But there's no proof that he was ever unfaithful. It could all be faked. The photographs, the receipts, the discs. He could've been kidnapped and taken to Felicity's. He might've been . . ."

She was running down as the facts, the time lines, the sheer weight of her fantasy began to bear down. "It doesn't make any sense that way. I know it. But it doesn't make sense any other way either."

"It makes sense if Bissel was not only unfaithful with Felicity Kade and Chloe McCoy, but if the terrorists believed he had intel. More sense yet if they had reason to believe it."

"Because they think I talk to him? But—"

"No. Because he talked to them."

She jerked back as if Eve had struck her. "That's not possible." The words came out in a croak. "You're saying that Blair had knowledge of, had contact with this radical terrorist group? That he fed them information? That's ludicrous."

"I'm saying it's a possibility I'm going to explore. I'm saying person or persons unknown went to a lot of trouble to kill Bissel and Kade and point the finger at you. And if this had been taken as the classic crime of passion it appeared to be, those units wouldn't have been given more than a cursory look."

She waited, just a beat, as she watched the possibilities hit home with Reva. "It would be assumed that you, with your knowledge of computers and your temper, destroyed them out of spite. That the changes in security at Bissel's gallery would be considered a glitch."

"I can't—I can't believe this of him."

"What you believe or don't believe is up to you. But if you look deeper, if you start tugging on all the threads, you start to see there's a lot more here than a couple of murders and a suspect served up to the cops on a shiny, silver platter."

Reva got up, walked to the wide window that looked out over the river. "I can't . . . You want me to believe this, to accept it, and if I do, it means everything was a lie. Right from the beginning, it was a lie. He never loved me. Or he loved me so little, he was seduced by whatever these people offered him. Money, or power, or just the thrill of playing techno-espionage for real instead of on VR. You want me to believe he used me, exploited everything I've worked for, the trust and respect I've earned in my field."

"If you look at it straight, it's about him. It's not about you."

Reva only stared out the window. "I loved him, Lieutenant. Maybe from where you're sitting that's weak of me, and stupid of me, but I loved him, the way I've never loved anyone else. If I accept all this, I have to let go of that, and everything it means to me. I'm not sure prison's any worse."

"You don't have to believe anything, or accept anything. That's your choice. But unless you want to find out if prison's any worse, you'll cooperate. You'll submit to Truth Testing, level three, tomorrow at oh eight hundred. You'll agree to full psychiatric eval by the departmental psychiatrist, and you'll instruct your attorneys to clear all of your records. All of them, and those of your husband. If there are any sealed records—either yours or his—you will authorize us to break them."

"I don't have any sealeds," Reva replied softly.

"You were Secret Service. You'll have sealeds."

She turned back, and her eyes were dazed like a woman living in a dream. "You're right. Sorry. I'll authorize."

"And yours," Eve said to Caro.

"Why hers?" The earlier resentment was forgotten as she leaped to her mother's defense. "She's not part of this."

"She's connected to you, to the victim, and to the project."

"If you think she might be in danger, she should have protection."

"I've seen to it, Reva," Roarke stated, and earned a quick, surprised look from Caro.

"You might have mentioned it," she mumbled, then sighed. "But I won't argue. And I'll take care of the authorization immediately."

"Good. Meanwhile, both of you think, go back over any conversations you might have had with either victim, or anyone else for that matter, about work. Particularly this Code Red. I'll be in touch."

Eve started for the door, but Roarke lingered another moment. "Get some rest, both of you. Take tomorrow if you need it, but I expect you both back to work the following day." He glanced over at Eve. "Any problem with that, Lieutenant?"

"Not for me. That's your deal."

"Thank you, Lieutenant. Detective"—Caro opened the door—"I hope you get some rest yourselves."

"We'll get to it."

Eve waited until they were in the elevator and heading down before she spoke to Peabody. "That was a good hunch about Caro running Bissel. How'd you come to it?"

"She strikes me as a thorough woman *and* a thorough mom. She didn't much like Bissel."

"I got that part."

"So, she doesn't much like him, but she loves her daughter

and wants her daughter to have what she wants. Still, she'd want to be sure he was what he said he was. She had to look."

"And she looked deep enough that you'd figure he was straight." Eve nodded. "Good catch, even if you did lead up to it with cookies."

"Hey, they were really good cookies."

"It earned you the rest of the day. Go home, get some sleep."

"Seriously?"

"And report to my home office at seven hundred. Sharp."

"With bells on."

She looked down at Peabody's colorful airsneaks. "It wouldn't surprise me."

"I can put in a couple more hours if you want to keep pushing."

"Neither of us is going to do the investigation much good if we're asleep on our feet. Let's hit it fresh in the morning."

"Take my car," Roarke offered, and Peabody's eyes all but popped out of her head and onto her shoes.

"Really? What is this, be nice to Peabody day?"

"If it's not it should be. You'll save me from having to have it picked up, as I'd like to ride with the lieutenant."

"Well, any little thing I can do."

He gave her the code, and watched with amusement as she sauntered off. Then indulged herself with a little boogie dance around the hot red sportster.

"You know she's not going to drive back to her place, not right away." Watching Peabody's happy dance, Eve fisted her hands on her hips. "She's going to take it out on the freeway or the turnpike, open up that ridiculous engine, and end up somewhere in New Jersey, explaining to some traffic droid that she's a cop, and on some bogus assignment. Then she'll carom back to the city, get pulled over again, and give them the same story."

"Carom?"

"That's the sound that toy of yours makes. *Ca-rom.* Then when McNab gets off shift, he'll talk her into letting *him* take it out, and they'll get pulled over again, have to flash their badges. And if any of the traffic droids interface, you're going to get tagged and have to explain why a vehicle registered to you is being used by a couple of idiotic city detectives."

"Sounds like fun for everyone. In you go, Lieutenant. I'll drive."

She didn't argue. Lack of sleep had dulled her reflexes, and traffic was starting to heat up.

"You were hard on her," he commented as he nudged the police unit away from the curb.

"If you've got a problem with my technique, file a damn complaint."

"I don't. She needed you to be hard on her. And when she gets her feet under her again, she'll respect that. She'll also push back."

Eve stretched out as best she could, and shut her eyes. "That doesn't worry me."

"It wouldn't. I think you'll like her better when she starts to push."

"I didn't say I didn't like her."

"No, but you think she's weak and she's not." He skimmed a hand, lightly, over Eve's hair. "You think she's foolish, and she isn't. What she is, is shaken, on every level, and grieving for a man she knows, at the core, isn't worthy of that grief. So she grieves instead for the illusion. And that, I think, might be even more wrenching."

"If you ended up naked and dead with another woman, I'd do the rumba on your corpse."

"You can't do the rumba."

"I'd take lessons first."

He laughed, rubbed a hand over her thigh. "You might very well, not that you'll ever get the chance. But you'd also grieve."

"Wouldn't give you the satisfaction," she mumbled, half asleep. "You cheating fuckwit putz."

"You'd weep in the dark and call my name."

"Call your name all right: How are things in hell, you dickless bastard? and I'd laugh and laugh. That's how I'd call your name."

"Christ Jesus, Eve, I love you."

"Yeah, yeah." And she smirked in her sleep. "Then I'd put all your precious shoes in the recycler, take your fancy suits and burn them in a celebrational fire, and kick Summerset out of *my* house on his bony ass. After which I'd have a party where we'd drink all your expensive wine and whiskey. And after *that* I'd hire two, no three, of the top LCs in the business to come over and pleasure me."

When she noticed the car was stopped, she blinked her eyes open and saw he was staring at her. "What?"

"It just occurs to me that you've given this matter a great deal of thought."

"No, not really." She rolled some of the stiffness out of her shoulders and yawned. "It all just came to me in one big lump. Where'd I leave off?"

"Being pleasured by three LCs. I assume you'd need three in order to be pleasured in the style to which you've become accustomed in the last couple years."

"Yeah, you'd think that. Okay, after the orgy, I'd start on your toys. First, I'd . . ." She broke off, narrowed her eyes as she focused out the car window. "Funny, that doesn't look like Central."

"You can work from home, and plan my memorial from here as well. After we both get some sleep."

He got out, came around, and opened her door because she hadn't budged. "I haven't updated my report, or checked in with the commander."

"Which can be done from here, as well." He simply reached in, gathered her up, and slung her over his shoulder.

"You think this is all macho and sexy, right?"

"I think it's expedient."

She decided to play possum when he walked in the house. At least that way she wouldn't have to speak to Summerset. But when she heard the irritating sound of his voice she wished she could screw up her ears as handily as she could her eyes.

"Is she injured?"

"No." Roarke shifted his balance as he started up the stairs. "Just tired."

"You look tired yourself."

"I am. Hold any transmissions that aren't emergencies for the next few hours, will you? And anything that's not priority for an hour beyond that."

"I will."

"I'll need to speak with you about several matters after that. Put up full security, and stay in the house until I do."

"Very well."

Because she'd opened one eye, she saw Summerset's concerned frown before Roarke turned at the top of the stairs.

"He in on this Code Red?"

"He knows a great deal about a great deal. Anyone looking at me would look at him." He booted the door closed behind him, then walked over to dump her on the bed.

"I guess you do look tired." She angled her head as she studied his face. "You hardly ever do."

"Been a long day, all around. Boots off."

"I can get my own boots off." She brushed his hands away. "Deal with your own."

"Ah yes, a pair of my precious shoes, soon doomed to the recycler."

She had to admit, he had a great smirk. "If you don't watch your step, pal."

She stripped off the boots, the jacket, her weapon harness, then crawled into bed.

"You'd sleep better without the clothes."

"You get ideas when I'm naked."

"Darling Eve, I get ideas when you're wearing riot armor. All I'm after is a bit of sleep, I promise you."

She wiggled out of the jeans, the shirt, then gave him a mock scowl when he slid in beside her, drew her against him. "Don't even think about engaging thrusters."

"Quiet." He kissed the top of her head, snuggled her in. "Go to sleep."

Because she was warm, comfortable, and her head was perfectly pillowed on his shoulder, she did. A moment after he felt her float off, he followed.

How could things have gone so wrong? How could it have fallen apart when it was all so perfect, so meticulously planned? And executed, he reminded himself as he huddled in the dark.

He'd done everything right. Absolutely everything. And now he was hiding behind locked doors and shaded windows, in fear for his life.

His *life*.

There'd been a mistake. That had to be it. Something had gone wrong, somewhere. But it made no sense.

He calmed himself with slow sips of whiskey.

He hadn't made a mistake. He'd gone into the brownstone at exactly the right time. His skin sealed, his clothes protected by the thin, clear lab suit, and his hair covered with a zero-contamination skullcap. There would be no trace of him inside the house.

He'd checked the house droid to verify it had been shut down for the night. Then he'd gone upstairs. God, how his heart had pounded. He'd been afraid, *almost* afraid, he amended, that they'd be able to hear the wild beat of it over the music, over their own moans as they fucked.

He'd had the stunner in his hand, the knife in the sheath on his belt. He'd liked the way the sheath had bumped against his thigh. Anticipation.

He'd moved quickly, just as planned. Just as he'd practiced. One shot between the shoulder blades, and the first half of the target was done. Maybe, just maybe he'd hesitated a fraction of a second then. Maybe, just maybe he'd watched Felicity's eyes, and had caught the shock in them an instant before he'd rammed the stunner between those beautiful breasts.

But he hadn't hesitated after that. He *hadn't*.

The knife now, drawing steel out of leather with a sexy little swish.

Then the killing. His first kills.

He had to admit he'd liked it. More, much more than he'd expected. The feel of the knife driving into flesh, and the warm wash of blood.

So primal. So *basic.*

And so, well, easy, he mused, as the whiskey soothed his nerves. So easy once you got started.

He'd set the stage then, and he'd been very, very careful. So careful, so precise, he'd been barely finished when Reva had arrived, when his alarm had beeped quietly to signal she'd begun to disengage the security.

But he'd stayed calm, he'd stayed cool. Silent as a shadow, he thought with some pride, as he'd waited for her to come into the room.

Had he grinned when she'd marched to the bed, spewing temper? Maybe he had, but it hadn't affected his performance.

One quick spray of the anesthetic, and she'd been out.

He'd added a few touches there. Genius, really. Dragging her into the bath to get her fingerprint on the sink, smearing a bit of blood on her shirt. And he thought the knife stabbed into the mattress spoke for itself.

It was so Reva, after all.

He'd left the front door ajar, just as planned, when he left. She should've been out long enough for security to find her on the routine check. All right, all right, maybe that had been a small miscalculation. He hadn't sprayed enough, or he'd wasted a little time with the extra touches.

But even that shouldn't matter. She was charged. Blair Bissel and Felicity Kade were dead, and she was the only suspect.

He should've been away by now. His accounts bursting with fresh money. Instead, he was a marked man.

He had to get away. He had to protect himself.

He wasn't even safe here. Not completely safe. But he could fix that. He could fix that, he realized, and sat up as the clouds of fear and self-pity began to clear. And solve some of the financial squeeze at the same time.

Then he'd deal with the rest.

A little more time to think, and he'd deal with it all.

Steadier, he rose to pour more whiskey, and to plan his next steps.

Chapter 6

Eve was alone when she woke, and a quick check showed her she'd slept a half hour longer than she'd intended.

Too groggy to curse, she crawled out of bed, stumbled to the Auto-Chef, and got coffee. She carried it with her to the shower, called for water on full at a hundred and one, then glugged down caffeine while the hot water pounded on her.

She was halfway through with the oversized mug when she realized she was still wearing her underwear.

Now she did curse. After downing the rest of the coffee, she peeled off the tank and panties and tossed them into a sopping heap in the corner of the shower.

Dead philandering husband and mistress, she thought. Both connected to the art world. Possible connection to techno-terrorists. Super computer worm. Security compromised in several areas. Preplanned frame on security expert in charge of developing extermination program and shield.

What was the point of the frame? Somebody else would step up to the plate. No one was indispensable.

She worried it, juggled it, twisted it around, and didn't like any of the patterns that formed. Why was something so neat and slick so sloppy once you chipped off the shine?

Even if the case was treated as a straight crime of passion, even if Reva Ewing was charged, tried, convicted, and spent the rest of her life in a cage, what did it accomplish?

She was on her second cup of coffee and another mental run-through when Roarke walked into the bedroom.

"Somebody want you to take a major hit bad enough to kill two people and frame an employee?" she asked.

"There are all kinds of people in the world."

"Yeah, that's what's wrong with the world. There are people in it. But there are easier ways to screw with you than double murder. I don't think you're it."

"Darling, I'm shattered. I was so sure I was it for you."

"But you could be it, on some level. Roarke Industries could, or more specifically Securecomp. We'll have to play with that some. But first I want a closer look at the victims."

"I started the runs for you. I was up," he said when she frowned at him. "Now that we both are, I'm thinking seriously about food."

"You'll have to have it in my office."

"Naturally."

"You're pretty agreeable."

"No, actually, just hungry."

Because he was, he ordered up steaks in her office. "You can have a look at the life and times of Blair Bissel while you eat. Computer, data on screen one."

"Any sealeds?"

"No. At least none that show."

"What do you mean, none that show?"

"Just that it's all very, very tidy. See for yourself."

She cut into her steak as she read the data on screen.

BISSEL, BLAIR. CAUCASIAN. HEIGHT: SIX FEET, ONE INCH. WEIGHT: ONE HUNDRED AND NINETY-SIX POUNDS. HAIR: BROWN. EYES: GREEN. DOB . . . MARCH 3, 2023, CLEVELAND, OHIO. PARENTS: MARCUS BISSEL AND RITA HASS, DIVORCED 2030. ONE BROTHER, CARTER. DOB: DECEMBER 12, 2025. OCCUPATION: SCULPTOR.

RESIDES: 21981 SERENITY LANE, QUEENS, NEW YORK.

"Serenity Lane." Eve shook her head as she chewed. "What twink comes up with that stuff?"

"I imagine you'd prefer Kick-Ass Drive."

"Who wouldn't?"

Because he'd gone deep, she was treated to educational history from Bissel's formal play group at age three right through his two years abroad at an art school in Paris.

She read through his medical—the broken tibia at age twelve, the standard sight checks and adjustments at ages fifteen, twenty, twenty-five, and so on. He'd had some face and body work—ass, chin, nose.

He'd been a registered Republican, and had a gross worth of one million, eight hundred thousand and some change.

There was no criminal record, not even a whiff as a juvenile.

He'd paid his taxes in a timely fashion, lived well, but within his means.

Reva was his only marriage.

His parents were still living. His father remained in Cleveland with wife number two, and his mother in Boca Raton with husband number three. His brother—no marriage on record, no children registered—had *entrepreneur* listed as profession, a sure tip-off to the less polite: no gainful employment. His work history was varied as he'd moved from job to job and place to place. He was currently listed as residing in Jamaica, as part owner of a tiki bar.

His criminal record was equally varied. Petty ante stuff, Eve noted. A little graft, a bit of grift, a touch of larceny. He'd served eighteen months in an Ohio state pen for his part in selling seniors nonexistent time-shares.

His gross worth was just over twelve thousand, which included his part in the tiki bar.

"I wonder if the younger brother has some issues with the fact big brother got the bucks and the glory. No violent crimes on record, but it's different with family. People get worked up when it's family. Add money and it gets messy."

"So little brother comes up from Jamaica, kills big brother and frames sister-in-law."

"Reaching," she admitted with a purse of her lips, "but not that far if you speculate Carter Bissel knew about the project. Maybe he was approached, offered money for any information he could get. Maybe he gets some, maybe he doesn't. But he's slick enough to figure out his brother's diddling on the side. Maybe a spot of blackmail, family fight. Threats." She shrugged.

"Yes, I see the picture." While he ate, Roarke turned it over in his mind. "He may have been a conduit. A liaison. Sibling rivalry turns deadly, and he and whoever recruited him decided to eliminate the loose ends."

"Makes the most sense so far. We'll want to chat with little bro Carter."

"That's handy as we don't spend nearly enough time in tiki bars."

Since it was there, she picked up the glass of cabernet and sipped while she studied her husband's face. "You're thinking something else."

"No, just thinking. Have a look at Felicity Kade. Kade data, on screen two."

She got the picture quickly enough of the only child of well-to-do parents. Extensive education, extensive travel. Homes in New York City, the Hamptons, and Tuscany. A socialite who earned some pin money as an art broker. Not that she needed extra to buy her pins, Eve thought, with a net worth—mostly inherited and through trust funds—of five million plus.

Never married, though there was one brief cohabitation on record in her twenties. At thirty, she lived alone, lived well—or had.

She'd had considerable body work, but had apparently been happy enough with her face. There was no unusual or unexpected medical data, and no criminal. No sealeds.

"Spends a lot," Eve commented. "Clothes, salons, jewelry, art, travel. Lots of travel. And isn't it interesting that she's been to Jamaica four times in the last eighteen months."

"Yes, it's very interesting."

"Could be she was cheating on the cheating husband with the cheating husband's feckless brother."

"Keep it in the family."

"Or maybe she did the recruiting, looking for a fall guy should the situation call for one."

He speared an artichoke heart. "It's Reva who's taking the fall."

"Yeah. Just let me play with it." She picked up her wine again, sipping at it as she rose to pace. "First trip a year and a half ago. Feels him out, maybe. Could use him to double-team Reva or Blair. Or both. She likes money. She likes risks. You don't sleep with your friend's husband if you don't like risk, or if you have a conscience. Playing with global techno-terrorists might appeal to her. She likes travel, and with all the people she meets—through traveling, through her social position, through the art world . . . yeah, she could've been approached."

"So, how did she end up dead?"

"I'm getting there. Maybe little brother was jealous. That's a time-honored motive for hacking your lover to bits."

"Or learning how to rumba."

"Har-har. Maybe he wanted a bigger cut, or maybe she double-crossed him. And maybe this is all bullshit, but it's something to explore."

She gestured with the glass toward the wall screen. "I'll tell you something else I think. They're just too damn clean."

"Ah. I was hoping you'd feel that way." He leaned back in the chair with his wine. "Just so very smooth aren't they, our Mr. Bissel and Ms. Kade. Just so completely what one would expect. Educated, law-abiding, financially cozy. Not the least little smudge. It all fits so exactly—"

"That it doesn't fit at all. They're liars and cheats, and liars and cheats generally have a smudge or two."

He sipped, smiling at her over the rich red in a crystal glass. "Enough skill, enough money, all matter of smudges can be erased."

"You'd know. We're going to take this deeper, because I'm just not buying. Meanwhile, I want to see Reva."

"Screen three."

The data flashed on, and the 'link from Roarke's adjoining office beeped.

"I need to take that."

She nodded absently, and read as he went into his own office.

EWING, REVA. CAUCASIAN. HAIR: BROWN. EYES: GRAY. HEIGHT: FIVE FEET, FOUR INCHES. WEIGHT: ONE HUNDRED AND EIGHTEEN POUNDS. DOB: MAY 15, 2027. PARENTS: BRYCE GRUBER AND CAROLINE EWING, DIVORCED 2040. RESIDES: 21981 SERENITY LANE, QUEENS, NEW YORK. OCCUPATION: ELECTRONIC SECURITY EXPERT. EMPLOYED: SECURECOMP, ROARKE INDUSTRIES. MARRIED: OCTOBER 12, 2057, BLAIR BISSEL. NO CHILDREN REGISTERED.

EDUCATION: KENNEDY PRIMARY, NEW YORK. LINCOLN HIGH SCHOOL—FAST TRACK—NEW YORK. GEORGETOWN UNIVERSITY, EAST WASHINGTON, WITH DEGREES IN COMPUTER SCIENCE, ELECTRONIC CRIMINOLOGY, AND LAW.

JOINED SECRET SERVICE, JANUARY 2051. ASSIGNED TO PRESIDENT ANNE B. FOSTER, 2053–55. COMPLETE SERVICE RECORD IN ATTACHED FILE, INCLUDING SEALED RECORDS, OPENED BY AUTHORIZATION OF EWING, REVA.

Good as her word, then, Eve decided, and opted to read the service record later.

RESIGNED FROM SECRET SERVICE, JANUARY 2056. RELOCATED TO NEW YORK CITY. EMPLOYED SECURECOMP, ROARKE INDUSTRIES, JANUARY 2056 TO PRESENT.

NO CRIMINAL RECORD. MISDEMEANOR TRUANCY CHARGE, MISDEMEANOR UNDERAGE ALCOHOL CONSUMPTION CHARGE, BOTH EXPUNGED FROM JUVENILE RECORD IN COMPLIANCE WITH COURT ORDER. COMMUNITY SERVICE COMPLETED.

The medical included a broken index finger at age eight, a hairline fracture of the left ankle at age twelve, broken collarbone, thirteen. Doctor's and social worker's reports ascertained that the injuries, and the numerous subsequent injuries, were the result of various sports and recreational activities that included ice hockey, softball, martial arts training, parasailing, basketball, and skiing.

But the most serious injury had come as an adult, and on the job. Reva had done what every SS agent vows to do. She'd taken a hit for the President.

A full-body blast that had lain her up for three months, and had required treatment in one of the top clinics in the world. She'd been paralyzed from the waist down for six weeks.

Remembering how hideous it had been when McNab had taken a similar hit earlier that summer, and how slim his chances had been if the nerves hadn't regenerated on their own, she had a good idea of the pain, the fear, and the work Reva had gone through to recover.

She remembered the assassination attempt as well. The suicidal fanatic who'd charged at the President, and had taken out three civilians and two agents before he'd been stopped. She now recalled seeing Reva's image on the media. But she'd looked very different then.

Longer hair, Eve recalled. Dark blonde, with a fuller, softer face.

Eve glanced over her shoulder as Roarke came back. "I remember her now. Remember hearing about her when she took that hit. Lots of buzz. She took the guy out, didn't she? Took him down while she used herself to shield Foster."

"They didn't think she'd live. Then they didn't think she'd walk again. She proved them wrong."

"You didn't hear much about her after the first few days."

"That's the way she wanted it." He glanced over at the image of Reva, still on screen. "She didn't like the attention. She'll get it again now. They'll make the connection quickly, and the buzz will start again. Heroic woman charged in double murder and so on."

"She'll deal."

"She will, yes. She'll bury herself in work, like someone else I know."

"How far will this set back the project?"

"Half a day. That was Tokimoto. Reva's already briefed

him, though she plans to be back at it herself as soon as she's done with Truth Testing. If two people are dead for the purposes of scrapping this project, it was severely misdirected."

"You'd think anybody smart enough to pull this off would be smart enough to know that. Desperation move?" she speculated. "Trouble in the rank and file? Carter Bissel. I really want to talk to Carter Bissel."

"Are we going to Jamaica?"

"Don't grab your beach towel yet. I'll start by chatting up the local authorities. I've got to write my report, shoot a copy to Whitney. And I've got to follow through with the standard investigative routine. Check with the ME, the lab, the sweepers, EDD. Media's going to start jumping by morning. You're probably going to want to formulate an official statement as her employer."

"I'm already working on that."

"I want her under wraps, Roarke. No statements from her, so if she goes back to work, I need her tucked up tight."

"I can promise you, she knows how to stonewall the media."

"Just make sure of it. If you don't have something else going, you could start digging deeper on Bissel and Kade."

"I've cleared the table for this." He picked up his wineglass again. "I'll get my shovel."

"You're okay, you know." She stepped to him, gave him a light bite on the bottom lip. "For a slick-talking, sticky-fingered civilian."

"You're okay yourself. For a mean-tempered, single-minded cop."

"Aren't we the pair? Give a yell if you find something interesting."

She sat at her desk to sort through her notes, the statements, preliminary findings. Then began to write up a report for her files, and her commander's.

Halfway through, she pulled out the crime scene stills and studied them yet again. Had they been conscious when the stabbing started?

Unlikely, she thought, given the time frame. Whoever

killed them had wanted them dead and hadn't cared about causing pain. That left out rage, in her opinion. It had been too cold-blooded, too premeditated for rage.

It was meant to *look* like rage.

Front door was open. She frowned as she rechecked her notes. Caro's statement asserted the front door was open when she arrived. Yet in Reva's, *she* stated she'd reset the locks and the security. And Eve was inclined to believe she had. It would be habit, routine, training, the sort of thing she'd do automatically even when in a temper.

Whoever had killed them, and incapacitated Reva, had gone back out the front door, leaving the locks open. Why not? What would it matter?

In fact . . .

She got up, went to the doorway. "Fancy security system like Kade's"—she began—". . . if it's shut down, and an egress is left open, how long before the company'd do a routine check of the premises?"

"That would depend on the client's request. It's individualized." He glanced up from his own work. "You're wanting me to check."

"You could get the answer faster, seeing as you own the world."

"I only own specific parts of the world. Open Securecomp," he ordered his computer. "Authorization Roarke."

WORKING . . . SECURECOMP OPEN ON AUTHORIZATION ROARKE.

"Access client file for Kade, Felicity, residential account, NYC."

WORKING . . . KADE, FELICITY, ACCESSED. DO YOU WANT THE DATA ON SCREEN OR ON AUDIO?

"On screen. Detail client's profile for house security."

PROFILE DISPLAYED.

"Let's see, then . . . sixty minutes on the street-level doors and windows. The instructions are to monitor for motion, and to relay any questions to her house droid after a sixty-minute period."

"Is that standard?"

"It's rather long, actually. I'd have to assume she trusted the system, and didn't care to be disturbed should there be a glitch."

"Sixty minutes. Okay. Okay, thanks." She wandered back, running it around her head.

Had they figured Reva would be out at least an hour, or if not out, disoriented? Security company activates house droid, house droid reports security has been compromised, and the company automatically reports same to the police and sends over a team.

But Reva's a tough customer. She surfaces quicker, and even though she's sick, scared, confused, she makes a call. So that part of the plan—if it was part of the plan—didn't work, because Caro, rushing the few blocks with a coat thrown over her pajamas, closed the door before the sixty was up.

She added the detail to her report.

What was left on scene?

The kitchen knife from the Bissel-Ewing house. How long had it been missing? Unlikely they'd be able to determine.

Military-issue stunner. Used by military personnel, Special Forces, certain city crisis-response teams. Who else?

"Computer, what weaponry is issued to United States Secret Service agents, specifically those on presidential detail.

WORKING . . . ALL AGENTS ARE ISSUED AN M3 STUNNER AND A NEURON BLASTER, BOTH HANDHELD MODELS. AGENTS MAY CHOOSE BETWEEN A 4000 BLASTER AND A 5200, AS SUITS THEIR PERSONAL PREFERENCE.

"An M3," Eve murmured. "I was under the impression SS agents carried A-1s."

PRIOR TO DECEMBER 5, 2055, A-1 STUNNERS WERE STANDARD ISSUE FOR SECRET SERVICE. THE CHANGE TO THE

MORE POWERFUL M3 WENT INTO EFFECT AT THIS TIME. THE ATTEMPT ON THE LIFE OF THEN PRESIDENT ANNE B. FOSTER, ON AUGUST 8, 2055, THE LOSS OF TWO AGENTS AND CIVILIAN CASUALTIES DURING THIS ASSASSINATION ATTEMPT RESULTED IN THE UPGRADE OF WEAPONRY.

"Is that so?"

THIS IS ACCURATE DATA.

"Right." Eve tipped back in her chair. Whoever had used and planted the M3 had assumed Reva had one. She hadn't left the SS until January. But she'd never gone back to active duty either. It was a simple matter to check to see if she'd ever been issued that style weapon.

Another detail for her report. When she'd compiled everything she wanted, she dumped it all into a file, saved it.

"Computer, analyze all data in case file HE-45209-2. Using known data, run a probability scan on Ewing, Reva, as perpetrator."

WORKING . . .

"Take your time," Eve murmured and rose to get more coffee.

She wandered back to her desk. Sat, sipped, played idly with the stuffed cat Roarke had given her since Galahad appeared to be spending the evening with Summerset.

Which just went to show, she thought, the cat's lousy judge of character.

PROBABILITY SCAN COMPLETE. PROBABILITY THAT EWING, REVA, IS PERPETRATOR IN THE MURDERS OF BISSEL, BLAIR, AND KADE, FELICITY, IS SEVENTY-SEVEN POINT SIX PERCENT.

"That's interesting. That's pretty interesting for something that, on the surface, looked like a walk. She passes level three tomorrow, that's going to drop another twenty points, easy. Then her lawyers are going to kick my ass."

"You don't sound overly concerned about that."

She turned her head to look at Roarke, lounging against the doorjamb between their offices. "I can take my licks."

"I'll owe you for it. Yes, yes," he said, reading her face. "Doing your job, and so on and so forth. But you'll be taking some of those licks to help a friend of mine. So I'll owe you for it. The media loves to slap down anyone who's at the top of their game, as you are."

"And gee"—she held up the stuffed cat as if speaking to it—"the media worries me almost as much as a bunch of pussy lawyers."

"I beg your pardon, but my lawyers are not pussies."

Eve set the stuffed cat aside and gave Roarke a steely stare. "I figured she'd lawyered up with some of your suits. If they're worth half of what you pay them, they'll have the charges dropped within another twenty-four. It'd be better if they didn't."

"Why is that?"

"As long as whoever's running this show thinks she's in the squeeze, she's safe and he won't be as likely to blow. If he's not already in the wind, and Reva shakes this loose, he'll blow. Or they will."

"They."

"There's got to be a team working on this. Someone for the murder, someone for the setup, someone for the hit on the security and data units at the gallery and studio. And somebody, I betcha, pushing all the buttons."

"It's so nice when we agree. I need to move this to the unregistered."

"Why?"

"Come with me, and I'll show you."

"I'm working here."

"You'll want to see this, Lieutenant."

"Better be good."

The equipment unregistered with, and undetectable by, CompuGuard was in a secured room.

The wide wall of windows was screened against prying eyes

but let in the view of New York, with all its spires and spears rising into the night sky.

The black, U-shaped console was slick and studded with dozens of controls. It reminded Eve, always, of some sort of futuristic spacecraft. So much so, she wouldn't have batted an eye if the entire thing had floated up from the floor, then zoomed off, to wink away in some time warp.

He got a brandy from the fully stocked bar behind a wall panel, and because he intended for her to sleep shortly, poured her another glass of wine.

"I'm on coffee now."

"Then it won't hurt you to dilute some of the caffeine. And look what else I have." He held up a candy bar.

Greed shot into her eyes before she could disguise it. "You have candy in here? I've never seen candy in here."

"I'm just full of surprises." Watching her, he waved the wrapped bar from side to side. "You can have the candy if you sit on my lap."

"That sounds like something perverted old men say to young, stupid girls."

"I'm not old, and you're not stupid." He sat, patted his knee. "It's Belgian chocolate."

"Just because I'm sitting on your lap and eating your candy doesn't mean you can cop a feel," she said as she folded into his lap.

"I'll just have to live in hope that you'll change your mind. Which you may when you see what I've found for you."

"Put up, or shut up."

"That's my line." He nipped her ear, passed her the candy bar, then inserted a disc. Reaching over, he laid a palm on the console. "Roarke. Open operations."

It hummed, more like a powerful animal waking than a machine booting up. Lights flashed on.

"Upload data."

"If you've got data on the disc"—she swallowed a bite of candy—"why do you need the unregistered? You're already on record."

"It's not what I have, but what I intend to do with it. Digging around, I ran into a couple of blocks. Nothing unusual initially. Standard privacy blocks, all very usual and law-abiding. But when I nudged them a bit, I got this. Computer, display last task from disc on screen one."

SCREEN ONE ON. DISPLAY UP.

Eve frowned at the snowy-white screen and blurred black letters.

RESTRICTED DATA
ACCESSED DENIED

"That's it? Access denied? You run into a wall and I have to come in here and sit on your lap?"

"No, you're sitting on my lap because you wanted my candy."

Rather than admit that was true, she took another bite of chocolate. "Why's the display fuzzy?"

"Because, fortunately, I engaged filters before digging around. If I hadn't, I'd have set off an alarm, and my little excavation would have sent up all manner of flags. So, we do it in here. Computer, redo last task."

ACKNOWLEDGED.

The screen flashed off, then on again, clear.

TASK COMPLETE.

"So?"

"You have no faith whatsoever. Just for that, sit over there and be quiet."

She shrugged, moved off his lap, and onto a chair. She finished off her candy bar, sipped lazily at her wine.

It wasn't exactly a hardship to watch him work. She liked the way he rolled his sleeves up to the elbow, tied his hair back—like a man preparing to do some serious physical labor.

He used both manual and verbal commands, so she could watch his quick fingers fly over keys, hear his voice—more Irish as he concentrated—flow out.

"Access denied? I'll show you access denied, bloody wanker."

Smiling a little, she closed her eyes, telling herself she was just going to rest them while she walked mentally through the investigation to date.

The next thing she knew, he was shaking her gently by the shoulder. "Eve."

"What!" Her eyes popped open. "I wasn't sleeping. I was thinking."

"Yes, I could hear you thinking."

"If that's some smart-ass way of saying I was snoring, bite me."

"I'd be more than happy to bite you later, but I really believe you'll want to see this."

She rubbed her eyes, and focused on his face. "Since you've got that big I'm-the-cat's-ass grin on your face, I guess you got into whatever you wanted to get into."

"Have a look." He gestured toward the screen.

Reading, Eve got slowly to her feet.

HOMELAND SECURITY ORGANIZATION
REDSTAR ACCESS ONLY!

"Jesus Christ, Roarke, you hacked into the HSO?"

"I have." He toasted himself with a brandy. "By God, I have, and it took considerable doing. You were . . . thinking for over an hour."

She knew she was goggling, but she couldn't stop. "You can't hack into the HSO."

"Well, I hate to disagree, but as you can plainly see—"

"I don't mean you can't. I mean you *can't*."

"Relax, Lieutenant, we're shielded." He leaned over and kissed the tip of her nose. "Right and tight."

"Roarke—"

"Ssh, you haven't seen it yet. Computer, employ passcode.

Now, you'll see the file I dug for is encrypted, for obvious reasons. You'd think a gang like the HSO would employ more complex encryptions. Then again, I don't suppose they counted on anyone actually getting through to this point. It was a bloody battle."

"I think you've lost your mind. You may be able to get off on an insanity defense. They'll still torture you, brainwash you, and lock you in a cage for the rest of your life, but they might not beat you to death if they know you're insane. This is the HSO. The antiterrorist organization that employs methods every bit as dirty as the terrorists they were initially formed to seek out and destroy. Roarke—"

"Yes, yes." He waved away her concerns. "Ah, here we are. Take a look."

She hissed out a breath, turned back to the screen, and stared at the ID photo and the personnel file of Bissel, Blair, level-two operative.

"Goddamn! Goddamn!" She was grinning now, as wildly as Roarke. "We got us a freaking spook!"

Chapter 7

"You have a dead spook," Roarke pointed out. "I wonder if that's redundant."

"It makes sense. Don't you see?" She punched him lightly on the shoulder. "Who gets through security slicker than a spook?"

"Well, foregoing modesty, I must point out that I—"

"You don't have any modesty to forego. Bissel was HSO, so it jibes for him to have all those blocks on his studio, for him to hook up with a security expert, and for him to be dead."

"Assassinated by another spook, national or foreign."

"Exactly. They knew about Bissel and Kade, and when the time was right they let Reva know. Set her up to take the fall."

"Why? What's the point in framing an innocent woman?"

Frowning, she studied the screen. He looked like an ordinary man, she thought. Good-looking, if you went for the smooth type, but ordinary. That would, she imagined, be part of the point. Spooks needed to blend in to stay spooks.

"Not sure there has to be a point, but if there is, it could be as simple as not wanting anyone looking too closely at Bissel, taking it on the surface. A philandering husband whacked by his crazed wife in the heat of passion. Homicide comes in, takes a look at the mess, hauls Reva off, and that's the end of that."

"That's simple enough, but it would've been simpler yet to stage a burglary gone wrong and leave Reva out of it."

"Yeah." She looked back at Roarke. "And that tells me she was already in it."

"The Code Red."

"The Code Red, and other things she's been working on over the past couple of years." Jamming her hands in her pocket she began to pace. "This current isn't your only government or sensitive project."

"Hardly." Roarke studied Bissel's ID image. "He married her because of her work. Because of *what* she was rather than who."

"Or because of what *you* are. They'll have a file on you."

"Yes, I'm sure they do." And he intended to take a look at it before he was done.

"What's *level two* mean? *Level-two operative*."

"I have no idea."

"Let's take a look at his dossier. See when he was recruited." Thumbs hooked in pockets, she read the data on screen. "Nine years ago, so he wasn't a rookie. Based in Rome a couple of years, and in Paris, in Bonn. Got around. I'd say his artistic profession would make good cover. Spoke four languages—and that'd be a plus. We know he's good with the ladies, and that couldn't hurt."

"Eve, look at his recruiter."

"Where?"

With a keystroke, he highlighted a name.

"Felicity Kade? Son of a bitch. She brought him in." She held up her hand for silence and paced out her thoughts. "She'd've been a kind of trainer to him, seems to me. A lot of times trainers and trainees develop a close relationship. They worked together, and they were lovers. Probably lovers, on and off, all along. They're a type."

"Which type is that?" he wondered.

"Slick, upper-class, social animals. Vain—"

"Why vain?"

"Lots of mirrors, lots of fancy duds, lots of money spent on body and face work, salons."

Amused, he studied his fingernails. "One could claim those attributes are simply natural elements of a comfortable lifestyle."

"Yeah, if they add up to you. You've got a big trunkful of vanity yourself, but it's not the same as these two. You don't throw mirrors onto the walls every damn place so you can check yourself out every time you move, like Bissel."

Thoughtfully, she glanced back at Roarke and decided if she looked as good as he did, she'd probably spend half the day staring at herself.

Weird.

"All those mirrors, reflective surfaces," she continued when he just smiled at her, "you could argue that was as much lack of confidence as vanity."

"That would be my take, but it sounds like a question for Mira."

"Yeah." She would get to that, and soon. "Anyway, they're a type. Like the artsy scene, and showing themselves off. Even if it's cover, they have to be into it. And on another level, it must take a certain type to go into covert work, on the long haul. You live a lie, you set up an identity, a persona that's part reality, part fantasy. How else could you make it work?"

"I'll agree that Bissel and Kade appear to be more suited than Bissel and Reva—at least on the surface."

"Okay, but they need Reva. They need, want, or have been assigned to infiltrate Securecomp. Felicity approaches Reva first, makes pals. Maybe feels her out. But for whatever reason Reva's not a good candidate for the HSO."

"She's worked for the government," Roarke pointed out. "Nearly died for it. She's loyal, and the administration she was attached to had no great affection for the HSO, as I recall."

"Politics." Eve blew out a breath. "Makes me screwy. But if we take it down to 'she's not a candidate for covert,' it doesn't mean she's not a good resource for the HSO. So they bring in Bissel. Romance, sex. But the marriage, that says they expected her to be of long-term use."

"And disposable."

She turned back to him. "It's tough to see a friend get kicked around this way. I'm sorry."

"I wonder if it'll be easier on her, or harder, knowing all this."

"Whichever, she'll have to cope. She doesn't have a lot of options." She nodded toward the wall screens. "These two were using her as an information source, and it's probable they planted various devices in the home, in her data unit, her vehicles, maybe on her person. She was their plant, an unwitting mole, and odds are they tapped her for plenty. No point in keeping up the charade of marriage and friendship if it wasn't paying off."

"Agreed." And the fact that it must have been paying off was, he imagined, going to cause him considerable annoyance. "But what point is there in eliminating two operatives? If it was an in-house assassination, it seems wasteful. Outside, it seems like overkill. Messy, Eve, either way."

"Messy, but it had the potential of taking out three key players." She drummed her fingers on her hips. "There's more. Has to be more. Maybe Bissel and Kade screwed up. Maybe they tried playing both sides. Maybe they blew their cover. We need to pick our way through their lives. I need all the data you can get me on them. And since we're playing with spooks, screw the rules."

"Could you say that again? The screw the rules part. It's such music to my ears."

"You're going to enjoy this one, aren't you?"

"I believe I am." But he didn't look pleased when he said it. He looked dangerous. "Someone has to pay for what's been done to Reva. I'll enjoy being part of that payment."

"There's an advantage to having a friend as scary as you."

"Come sit on my lap and say that."

"Get the data, pal. I need to call in, check with the men on

Reva's house. I don't want anybody sliding in there before we sweep it for devices in the morning."

"If there were bugs, they'd have had an exterminator of their own."

"They had to move fast between the time Reva received the package and the hit, then her arrival." She combed a hand through her hair as she went over the time line. "If they moved right in maybe they swept it out. But somebody was at the Flatiron. Seems to me that an op like this, double murder, would require a small, tight team. Don't want too many in the know."

"It's Homeland," Roarke reminded her. "Orders to sweep out a private residence wouldn't require the exterminators being apprised of the reason."

"Just following orders," she mumbled and envisoned the bloody mess in Felicity Kade's bed. What kind of person gave orders for that kind of brutality? Not assassination, she thought. No way to clean up vicious, bloody murder.

"Yeah, you've got a point. Still, if orders did come down, they could've missed something."

They worked another two hours before he convinced her it was all he could do for the night. He talked her into bed, and when he was certain she slept, he got up, went back. And did more.

It wasn't difficult to access his file as he was already into the main. They had less hard data on him than he'd anticipated. Hardly more, he noted, than was public knowledge—or that he'd adjusted, personally, for public knowledge.

There were a number of *suspecteds, allegeds, probables* running through his somewhat checkered career. Most of them were true enough, but there were a few sins ascribed to him that weren't on his actual plate.

That hardly mattered.

It amused more than annoyed him to find that twice he'd been romantically involved with an operative assigned to him in the hopes of eliciting information.

He lit a cigarette, tipped back in his chair as he remembered the two women with some fondness. He supposed he couldn't complain. He'd enjoyed their company, and was confident enough that though their primary mission had failed, they'd enjoyed his.

They didn't know about his mother, and that was a tremendous relief. Officially, Meg Roarke was listed as his mother, and that was fine by him. What did it matter to the HSO who had birthed him? A young girl foolish enough to love and believe in a man like Patrick Roarke wasn't of any interest.

Especially since she was long dead.

Since they hadn't bothered to go back that far, or dig that deep, they didn't know about Siobhan Brody, or his aunt and the rest of the family he'd discovered in the west of Ireland. His newfound relations wouldn't be watched or approached or have their privacy invaded by the HSO.

But there was a fat file on his father. Patrick Roarke had been of considerable interest to the HSO, as well as Interpol, the Global Intelligence Council, and other covert organizations the HSO had pooled for data. He discovered that they'd considered recruiting him at one point, but had judged him too volatile.

Volatile, Roarke mused with a dark chuckle. Well, he could hardly argue with that.

They'd tied him to Max Ricker, and that was no surprise. Ricker had been a clever man, and his network spread all over the planet, and off, with rich pockets of weapons and illegals running among other business ventures. But he'd been entirely too vain to cover all of his tracks.

Patrick Roarke was considered one of Ricker's occasional tools, and not a particularly deft one. Too fond of the drink and other chemicals. And not discreet enough to warrant a higher position, much less a permanent one on Ricker's payroll.

But seeing the association in black-and-white made the fact that Eve had been the one to lock Ricker in a cage all the more gratifying.

He'd nearly closed the file again when he caught a notation

about travel to Dallas. The time, the place made his blood run cold.

PATRICK ROARKE TRAVELED FROM DUBLIN TO DALLAS, TEXAS, ON CIRCULAR ROUTE AND UNDER THE NAME ROARKE O'HARA. ARRIVED DALLAS 5-12-2036 AT SEVENTEEN-THIRTY. WAS MET AT AIRPORT BY SUBJECT KNOWN AS RICHARD TROY AKA RICHIE WILLIAMS AKA WILLIAM BOUNTY AKA RICK MARCO. SUBJECTS TRAVELED BY CAR TO CASA DIABLO HOTEL WHERE TROY WAS REGISTERED AS RICK MARCO. ROARKE RENTED A ROOM UNDER O'HARA.

AT TWENTY-FIFTEEN, SUBJECTS EXITED HOTEL AND TRAVELED BY FOOT TO THE BLACK SADDLE BAR, WHERE THEY REMAINED UNTIL OH TWO HUNDRED. TRANSCRIPTION OF CONVERSATION ATTACHED.

There was more—standard surveillance reports that covered three days with the two men coming and going, having meetings with others of their kind in bars, in dives.

A great deal of drinking and posturing, and bits and pieces discussed about movement of munitions from a base in Atlanta.

Max Ricker. Roarke didn't need the transcript to tell him both his father and Eve's had been on the fringes, at least, of Ricker's network. They knew the men had met, in Dallas.

Days before, he thought, only days before Eve had been found, battered and broken, in an alley.

They'd known all that, he thought, and so had the HSO.

SUBJECT ROARKE CHECKED OUT OF HOTEL AT TEN THIRTY-FIVE THE FOLLOWING MORNING. HE WAS DRIVEN BY TROY TO THE AIRPORT WHERE HE TOOK A SHUTTLE TO ATLANTA. TROY RETURNED TO HOTEL ROOM SHARED WITH FEMALE MINOR. SURVEILLANCE ON ROARKE PASSED TO OPERATIVE CLARK.

"Female minor," Roarke repeated. "You bastards. You bloody bastards, you had to know."

And with a rage so strong it sickened him, he brought up Richard Troy's HSO file.

It wasn't yet dawn when she stirred, and felt his arms go around her. So gently around her. Half dreaming, she turned to him, turned into him and found the warmth of his body, then the warmth of his lips on her lips.

The kiss was so tender, so fragile somehow, that she could let herself drift into it even as she floated on that twilight sleep.

In the dark, she could always find him in the dark and know he'd be there to soothe her or arouse her. Or to ask those things of her.

She threaded her fingers through his hair, cradling his head as she urged him to deepen the kiss. Deeper, a mating of lips and tongues, and still soft as a dream she was already forgetting.

For now there was only Roarke, the smooth glide of his skin over hers, the lines of him, the scent and taste. She was already filled with him as she murmured his name.

His mouth trailed over her like a benediction. Cheeks, throat, shoulders, then pressed delicately on the slope of her breast to linger where her heart beat.

"I love you." His lips formed the words against her breast. "I'm lost in love with you."

Not lost, she thought, and smiled in the dark even as her pulse thickened. *Found. We're both found.*

He cradled his head there a moment—cheek to heart—and closed his eyes until he could be sure he had his fiercer emotions in check, until he could be sure his hands would be gentle on her.

He had a searing need to be gentle.

She sighed, soft and sleepy, and was content, he knew, to be wakened like this. No matter what had been done to her, her heart was open for him, and that open heart lifted him beyond anything he'd expected to become.

So he was gentle when he touched her, and when he roused her to peak it was lovely and sweet.

When he slipped inside her, they were one shadow moving in the dark.

She held him there, close in the big bed under the sky window where the light was going pearl gray with dawn. She could stay like this for an hour, she thought. Stay quiet and joined and happy before it was time to face the world, the job, the blood.

"Eve." He pressed his lips to her shoulder. "We need to talk."

"Mmm. Don't wanna talk. Sleeping."

"It's important." He drew away, though she groaned a protest. "I'm sorry. Lights on, twenty percent."

"Oh, *man*." She clapped a hand over her eyes. "What is it? Five? Nobody has to have a conversation at five in the morning."

"It's nearly half-five, and you'll have your team here at seven. We need the time for this."

She spread her fingers, squinted through. "For what?"

"I went back last night and accessed more files."

And through those spread fingers, he saw the annoyance. "I thought you said that was all you could do."

"For you, it was. I did this for me. I wanted a look at my own dossier, in case . . . Just in case."

She sat up quickly. "Are you in trouble? Christ, are you in trouble with the fucking HSO?"

"No." He put his hands on her shoulders, ran them up and down her arms. And suffered, knowing she would suffer. "It's not that. While I was at it, I had a look at my father's files."

"Your mother." She reached for his hand, squeezed.

"No. It seems she didn't earn as much as a blip on their radar. They weren't paying much mind to him that long ago, and she didn't matter to them, wasn't useful or interesting, which is all to the good. But Patrick Roarke became of more interest, and they spent time tracking his moves now and again. Mostly, it appears, on the chance he'd give them something to use against Ricker."

"I'd say he didn't, as Ricker stayed in operation until last year."

"He didn't give them enough. It's a long, convoluted file, a great many cross-references, a lot of man-hours that didn't amount to anything that would stick."

"Well, he's away now. Ricker. What does that have to do with this?"

"They had my father under surveillance, believing he was working as a bagman for Ricker, and they tracked him to Dallas, in May. The year you were eight."

She nodded, slowly, but had to swallow. "We knew he'd been in Dallas about that time, helping to set up for the Atlanta job, the sting where Skinner's operation went to hell. It's not important. Look, since I'm up, I'm going to get a shower."

"Eve." He clamped his hands on hers, felt hers jerk as she tried to escape. "He was met at the airport by a man named Richard Troy."

Her eyes were huge now, with fear—the kind he saw when she woke from nightmares. "This has nothing to do with the case. The case is priority. I need to—"

"I've never looked into your past, because I knew you didn't want it." Her hands had gone cold in his, but he held them. He wished he could warm them. "I didn't intend to look now, but only to assure myself that my family wasn't being watched. The connection . . ." He brought her rigid hands to his lips. "Darling Eve, the connection between your father and mine is there. We can't pretend otherwise. I don't want to hurt you. I can't stand to hurt you."

"You have to let me go."

"I can't. I'm sorry. I tried to talk myself out of telling you. 'She doesn't need to know, doesn't want to know.' But I can't hold this back from you. It would hurt you more, wouldn't it, and insult you on top of that if I treated you like you couldn't take it."

"That's tricky." Her voice was scratchy and her eyes burned. "That's pretty fucking tricky."

"Maybe, but no less true for all that. I have to tell you what I've found, and you'll decide how much of it you want to hear."

"I need to *think!*" She yanked her hands free from his. "I

need to think. Just leave me alone and let me think." She sprang off the bed, rushed into the bathroom. Slammed the door.

He nearly went after her, but when he asked himself if doing so would be for her sake or his own, he wasn't at all sure. So instead, he waited for her.

She took a shower, blistering hot. Halfway through her heart rate was nearly normal again. She stayed in the drying tube too long, and felt a little light-headed afterward. She just needed coffee, that was all. Just a few hits of coffee—and she needed to put this *crap* out of her mind.

She had a job to do. It didn't matter, it didn't fucking matter about Patrick Roarke or her father, or Dallas. It didn't apply. She couldn't afford to crowd her head with that kind of *bullshit* when she had work to do.

And she looked at her face in the mirror over the sink, her pale, terrified face. She wanted to smash her fist through it. Nearly did.

But she turned away, yanked on her robe, and walked back into the bedroom.

He'd gotten up, put on a robe of his own. He said nothing as he walked over and handed her a cup of coffee.

"I don't want to know about this. Can you understand? I don't want to know."

"All right, then." He touched her cheek. "We'll put it away."

He wouldn't call her a coward, she realized. He wouldn't even think it. He would just love her.

"I don't want to know about this," she repeated. "But you have to tell me." She walked to the sitting area and lowered to a chair because she was afraid her knees would shake. "His name was Troy?"

He sat across from her, keeping the low table between them because he sensed she wanted the distance. "He had a number of aliases, but that was his legal name, so it seems. Richard Troy. There's a file on him. I didn't read the whole of it, but just the . . . just the business in Dallas. But copied it for you in case you wanted to."

She didn't know what she wanted. "They met in Dallas."

"They did. Yours picked mine up at the airport, brought him to the hotel where you . . . where you were. He registered. They went out later that night and got piss-faced. There's a transcript of their conversation, such as it was, and the same over the three days they were there together. A lot of posturing and bragging, and some speculation on the operation in Atlanta."

"Ricker's gunrunning operation."

"Yes. My father was to go on to Atlanta, which he did the following day. There is speculation that he took payoff money from the cops who were using him as an inside man in Ricker's organization. He took that, and Ricker's money, and—double-crossing both sides—went back to Dublin."

"That confirms what we theorized when we dealt with Skinner. Sloppy job by the spooks if they didn't cop to what your father had in mind, and warn the locals. Puts HSO on the trigger for the thirteen cops who died in that botched raid as much as Ricker, as much as anyone."

"I'd say HSO didn't give a damn about the cops."

"Okay." She could focus on that, pinpoint some of the rage on that. "They'd consider Ricker the prime directive. The Atlanta operation was major, but it wasn't the whole ball. Maybe they were too focused on bringing down Ricker, crushing his network, and doing the victory dance, that they didn't figure a small cog like Patrick Roarke was going to screw all sides. But it's unconscionable they'd let cops die that way."

"They knew about you."

"What?"

"They knew there was a child in that bloody room with him. Female, minor child. The bastards knew."

When her eyes went glassy, he cursed. Shoving the table away, he pushed her head between her knees. "Take it slow, breathe slow. Christ, Christ, I'm sorry."

His voice was a buzz in her ears. His beautiful voice, murmuring in Gaelic now as his control wavered. She could hear it wavering, feel it in the quiver of his hand on the back of her head. He was kneeling beside her, she realized. Suffering as much, if not more, than she was herself.

Wasn't that strange? Wasn't that miraculous?

"I'm okay."

"Just give it a minute more. You're trembling yet. I want them dead. Those who knew you were trapped with him and did nothing. I want their blood in my throat."

She shifted enough to rest her cheek on her knee and look at him. At the moment, he looked every bit like a man who could rip out another's throat. "I'm okay," she said again. "It's not going to matter, Roarke. It's not, because I survived, and he didn't. I need to read the file."

He nodded, then just laid his head on hers.

"If you'd blocked this from me"—her voice was thick but she didn't try to clear it—"it would've set me back. It would've set us back. I know this isn't easy for you either, but telling me . . . Trusting us to get through it, that's going to make it better. I need to look at some of this data."

"I'll get it for you."

"No, I'll go with you. We'll look at it together."

They went back in his private room, and read what he brought up on screen together.

She didn't sit. She wasn't going to let her legs go weak on her again. Not even when she read the field operative's report.

> SEXUAL AND PHYSICAL ABUSE INVOLVING MINOR FEMALE PURPORTED TO BE SUBJECT'S DAUGHTER. NO RECORDED DATA ON MINOR, NO BIRTH MOTHER OR SURROGATE REGISTERED. INTERVENTION IS NOT RECOMMENDED AT THIS TIME. IF SUBJECT BECOMES AWARE HE IS BEING OBSERVED, OR IF ANY SOCIAL OR LAW ENFORCEMENT AGENCY IS INFORMED OF THE SITUATION WITH MINOR FEMALE, SUBJECT'S VALUE WOULD BE COMPROMISED.
> RECOMMEND NONACTION RE MINOR FEMALE.

"They let it go." Roarke spoke softly, too softly. "I hate fucking cops. Saving your presence," he added after a moment.

"They're not cops. They don't give a rat's ass about the law, much less about justice. They sure as hell don't give a damn about an individual. It's all big picture to them, always was, from the moment they formed at the dawn of the Urban Wars, it was big picture and fuck the people in it."

She packed away her rage, her horror, and continued to read. It wasn't until she came to the end that she had to reach out, lay her hand on the console for balance.

"They knew what happened. They knew I killed him. My God, they knew, and they cleaned up after me."

"For security, my ass. To cover their own culpability."

"It says . . . it says the listening devices planted were defective and shut down that night. What are the chances?" she drew a deep breath and read the section again.

SURVEILLANCE RETURNED AT SEVEN HUNDRED AND SIXTEEN HOURS. NO SOUND OR MOVEMENT RECORDED ON PREMISES FOR SIX HOURS. ASSUMPTION THAT SUBJECT HAD MOVED ON DURING DARK PERIOD CAUSED FIELD AGENT TO RISK A PERSONAL CHECK OF ROOM. UPON ENTERING, AGENT OBSERVED SUBJECT DOS. CAUSE OF DEATH DETERMINED TO BE MULTIPLE STAB WOUNDS INFLICTED WITH SMALL KITCHEN KNIFE. FEMALE MINOR CHILD COULD NOT BE LOCATED ON PREMISES.

NO DATA ON PREMISES PERTAINING TO RICKER OR ROARKE. ON ORDERS FROM HOME, AREA WAS CLEANED. BODY DISPOSAL TEAM NOTIFIED.

MINOR CHILD, FEMALE, BELIEVED TO BE SUBJECT'S DAUGHTER, LOCATED UNDER MEDICAL OBSERVATION. SEVERE PHYSICAL AND EMOTIONAL TRAUMA. LOCAL AUTHORITIES INVESTIGATING. MINOR HAS NO IDENTIFICATION AND WILL BE ASSIGNED A SOCIAL CASEWORKER.

SUBSEQUENTLY LOCAL AUTHORITIES UNABLE TO IDENTIFY MINOR CHILD, FEMALE. MINOR SUBJECT UNABLE TO REMEMBER AND/OR RELATE NAME OR CIRCUMSTANCES. NO CONNECTION TO TROY OR THIS AGENCY CAN BE MADE. MINOR SUBJECT HAS BEEN ABSORBED BY THE NATIONAL AGENCY FOR MINORS AND HAS BEEN GIVEN THE NAME DALLAS, EVE.

CASE FILE TROY IS CLOSED.

"Is there a file on me?"

"Yes."

"Did they make the connection?"

"I didn't read it."

"Aren't you just full of willpower?" When he didn't speak, she turned away from the screen, and took a step toward him.

He took one back. "Someone will pay for this. Nothing will stop me. I can't kill him, though God, I've dreamed of it. But someone will pay for standing by, standing back, and letting this happen to you."

"It won't change anything."

"Aye, by God it will." Some part of the fury he'd held inside him since reading the reports lashed out. "There are balances, Eve. You know it. Checks and balances, that's what makes your precious justice. I'll have my own on this."

She was cold, already so cold, but his words, the look of him now all but numbed her. "It's not going to help me to think about you going off and hunting up some spook assigned to this over twenty years ago."

"You don't have to think about it."

A little bubble of panic rose in her throat. "I need you focused on the work—do what you promised to do."

He stepped around the console, up to her. His eyes were blue ice as he took her chin in his hand. "Do you think I can or will let this go?"

"No. Do you think I can stand back and let you hunt someone down and mete out your personal sense of justice?"

"No. So we have a problem. In the meantime, I'll give you whatever you need from me on this case. I won't fight with you over this, Eve," he said before she could speak. "And I won't ask or expect you to change your moral ground. I only ask you do the same when it comes to me."

"I want you to remember something." Her voice wanted to shake. Her soul wanted to tremble. "I want you to think about this before you do something you can't take back."

"I'll do what I have to do," he said flatly. "And so will you."

"Roarke." She gripped his arms, and was afraid she could already feel him slipping away from her. "Whatever happened to me back in Dallas, I came out of it. I'm standing here because of it. Maybe I have everything that matters to me, including you, because of it. If that's true, I'd go through it all again. I'd go through every minute of the hell to have you, to have my badge, to have this life. That's enough balance for me. I need you to think about that."

"Then I will."

"I need to get ready for the morning briefing." To think about something else—anything else. "So do you. This has to be put away for now. If you can't put it away, you're no good for me, or your friend."

"Eve." He said it gently, as he'd loved her gently, and he brushed the tear she hadn't been aware of shedding from her cheek.

She broke when his arms came around her. And because they did, she burrowed into him and let herself weep.

Chapter 8

She was back in form by the time her team arrived for the briefing. Thoughts of what she'd survived in Dallas were locked away to be taken out later when she was alone, when she could stand them. When she could, she would figure out what could and couldn't be done.

He'd kill them. She had no illusions. Left to himself, Roarke would hunt down those responsible for the *nonaction* directive in Dallas and . . . eliminate them.

Checks and balances.

He would do this unless she found the key to his rage, his sense of justice, his need to punish. His need to stand for her and to spill blood for blood for the sake of a desperate and brutalized child.

So she had to find that key, somehow. And while she was looking for it, she was going up against one of the most powerful and self-contained organizations on or off planet.

Her prior plans of expanding the team, of including a strong showing of hand-selected EDD men, had to be put on hold. She had an intricate little bomb on her hands. Too much shifting and passing and it would blow up in her face.

She would keep her team as small and tight as possible.

Feeney. She couldn't do without Feeney. He was currently chowing down on one of his favored danishes while he argued with McNab about some Arena Ball player named Snooks.

EDD ace Ian McNab didn't look like somebody who'd get riled up about Arena Ball. Then again, he didn't look like a cop either. He was wearing purple leather-look pants, pegged tight as tourniquets at the ankles to show off his low-rider purple gel-sneaks. His shirt was purple stripes and snug enough to show off his narrow torso and bony shoulders. He'd pulled his blond hair back in a relatively simple braid that hung between his angel-wing shoulder blades, but had made up for the simplicity with a jungle of silver hoops that curved along his left ear.

Though he had a pretty face, narrow and smooth and set off by clever green eyes, he didn't look like the type the sturdy and steady Peabody would go for. But she did, and in a big way.

You could see what was between them in the casual way his hand brushed Peabody's knee, the way she jabbed him with her elbow when he tried to take her pastry.

And the proof that love was in bloom when Peabody broke the pastry in half and gave it to him.

She needed them, the three of them, and the man—her man—who sipped his coffee and waited for her to start the show.

And once she did, she put them all at risk.

"If everyone's finished their little coffee break, there's a little matter of a double homicide to discuss."

"Got your EDD report there." Feeney nodded toward the disc packet he'd put on her desk. "Every one of the units—house, gallery, studio—was fried. Total corruption. I got some ideas on how to regenerate and access data, but it's not going to be easy, and it's not going to be quick. Easier and quicker with the use of some of the equipment our civilian consultant has at his disposal."

"Then it's at yours," Roarke said, and had Feeney beaming in anticipation.

"I can have a retrieval team here in an hour, with the units. We'll set up a network and—"

"That's not going to be possible," Eve interrupted. "I need to ask you to personally transport a sampling of the units here. Those that remain at Central will require top-level security. They have to be moved from the pen, Feeney. ASAP."

"Dallas, electronics isn't your area, but even you should be able to figure out how long it's going to take me to work this magic on more'n a dozen units. I can't be hauling them over here a couple at a time, and without a retrieval team, six-man minimum, we're looking at days, if not weeks before we pull out anything readable."

"It can't be helped. The nature of the investigation has changed. Information has come into my hands that confirms involvement and possible participation in these murders by the Homeland Security Organization."

There was a moment of absolute silence, then McNab's excited response. "Spooks? Oh baby, ultimately iced."

"This isn't a vid, Detective, or some comp game where you play secret agent. Two people are dead."

"With all respect, Lieutenant, they're dead anyway."

Since she couldn't think of an argument for that, she ignored it. "I can't reveal how this information came to me." But she saw Feeney's glance at Roarke, the speculation and the pride in it. "If it comes down to a court order demanding my source—as it very well may—I'll lie. You need to know that up front. I'll perjure myself without hesitation, not only to protect the source but to maintain the integrity of this investigation, and to protect Reva Ewing, who I'm convinced is innocent."

"I like the anonymous tip myself," Feeney said easily. "Untraceable transmission of data. There's a couple of ways to set that up on your unit right here so it'll look like you got one. Should hold up against most tests."

"That's illegal," Eve pointed out, and he smiled.

"Just talking out loud."

"When each of you took this case, it was on the belief it

was a standard homicide investigation. It's not. You have a choice of stepping out of the investigation before I reveal the data in my possession. Once I relay it, you're stuck. And it could get pretty fucking sticky. We can't bring anyone else into this. It can't be discussed outside of secured locations. Each of us will have to be swept daily for possible bugs and that includes home, workplace, vehicles, and person. You'll be at risk, and certainly under observation."

"Lieutenant." Peabody waited until Eve's gaze shifted to her. "If you don't know we're in, you should."

"This isn't business as usual."

"No, because it's ultimately iced." Peabody grinned when she said it and earned a snicker from McNab.

Shaking her head, Eve sat on the corner of her desk. She'd known they were in, but she had to give them the out. "Blair Bissel was a level-two operative for the HSO, recruited and trained by Felicity Kade."

"It was an HSO hit?"

She glanced at McNab. "I haven't quite tied it all up in a bow for you, Detective. No notes," she said when he got out his book. "Nothing logged or recorded except on cleared units. Here's what I know. Bissel was in Homeland for nine years. At level two he functioned primarily as a liaison. Passing data from point to point, accessing data or accumulating intel, which he passed along to a contact. Kade generally, but not exclusively. Three years ago, Kade was assigned to Reva Ewing for the purposes of developing a relationship, a friendship."

"Why Ewing?" Peabody asked. "Particularly."

"They've had her under observation for a number of years, including her time with the Secret Service. This observation was beefed up after her injury, line of duty, and subsequent retirement. She was approached by a recruiter for the HSO during her recuperation, and—according to the file—was less than gracious in her refusal. As she was offered a substantial incentive package, her refusal and her subsequent employment were suspect.

"Roarke . . . Industries," Eve continued, "is a hot button for the HSO. They've spent considerable time and manpower trying to tie it to espionage, without success. Reva Ewing was considered a strong candidate for information due to her personal and professional relationship with the industry's head, and her mother's position as Roarke's admin. The hope was Reva would chat about her work, her boss, her projects, and so on, and the HSO would be one up."

"But she didn't," Feeney prompted.

"She didn't give them what they were after, but they had a lot invested. And Felicity was committed. She brought in Bissel and set up for the long haul."

"He married her for intel?" Peabody queried. "Sucks wide."

"For intel," Eve agreed. "And for a stronger cover, for the additional contacts that came from her. She's still friendly with some of her associates from the Secret Service, and she has former President Foster's ear, among others. Neither Foster nor the current administration has maintained very friendly relations with the HSO, or vice versa. There's a lot of resentment, one-upmanship, a lot of secrets and backbiting."

"I'm following all this well enough, kid," Feeney put in. "But it doesn't explain why Bissel and Kade were hit, and Ewing set up."

"It sure as hell doesn't. So let's find out."

She glanced at Roarke, silently passing him the ball. "The Code Red must factor into it," he began. "The units were taken out with the Doomsday worm, or a close clone of it. It's possible, though it pains me, that they've infiltrated my security at Securecomp, using Reva as their conduit. The contract came through the Global Intelligence Council, and was heatedly protested by the HSO, and a few other acronyms."

"HSO would've wanted the contract themselves," McNab speculated. "Privatization of this kind of work put the squeeze on the budget of some of these agencies."

"There's that," Roarke agreed.

"Add that if they had the contract and the fee," Peabody continued, "they'd also have all pertinent intel on the Code Red in-house. They don't have to wait to be fed through channels."

Eve nodded. "Using Reva was a way to feed."

"Add that since Roarke Industries is considered suspect by some factions . . ." Roarke let that hang in the air a moment, almost as if amused. "The HSO found it expedient to focus on infiltrating and gathering data and intel—whatever came to hand—in order to attempt to build a case against the corporation. For espionage, double-dipping, tax evasion. Some such thing."

He shrugged it off. He was—since Eve, in any case—a completely legitimate businessman. And if he wasn't, he had no doubt he'd have gotten around Homeland, just as he'd always done.

"I'll be looking into security and plugging any potential holes, but at this point it's a bit like bricking up the hole after the rat's slipped in to nibble the cheese."

"You can always lay out more cheese," Feeney commented.

Roarke smiled a little. "We're of a mind there."

"What about the worm itself?" Peabody asked. "If this was an HSO hit, and the units were corrupted, that means the HSO has the worm, or a clone. Wouldn't they be working on an extermination program and shield themselves instead of . . . Oh."

"Global espionage isn't so very different from the corporate sort." Roarke picked up the pot and topped off his coffee. "If they're working on spec, or have another organization working on the protection programs, it would pay them to know what we're up to."

"And to kill for it. Just another kind of organized crime." Peabody flushed a little. "Sorry, Free-Ager roots showing. Realistically, I know governments need covert organization to gather intelligence, to help predict terrorist attacks, to help dismantle terrorists and politically fanatic groups. But it's the fact that they don't always have to play by the rules that can corrupt the individuals that make up the whole. And that sounded just like my father."

"It's okay, She-Body." McNab gave her knee a squeeze. "I think Free-Agers are hot."

"If the HSO ordered the hit on Kade and Bissel," Eve continued, "they may not pay for it in the public courts. But, if they set up Reva Ewing and left her twisting in the wind, they'll pay for that. She's a citizen of New York, and that makes her ours. I'm going to speak with the commander, then I'm going to Reva Ewing and make full disclosure, unless ordered otherwise. I believe with her contacts I can work a meet with reps from the HSO. And we'll play some ball."

When she'd completed the briefing, she started to walk out with Peabody, then stopped as if just remembering something. "Oh, Feeney, I need just another minute with you. Peabody, go on down. Put in a request with the commander's office for some time, priority one."

"I don't expect to be more than two or three hours at Securecomp," Roarke told Feeney. "You know where everything is here. Set up however it suits you best. Summerset will be able to answer any questions you may have. I'll be back to roll up my sleeves as soon as I can. Lieutenant."

He knew she would wince when he leaned down to kiss her. Which was only one of the reasons he couldn't resist doing so. He let her close the door behind him, and after giving it one speculative look, walked away.

Inside, Eve rubbed her hands over her face. "I've got to ask you for a personal."

"Okay."

"This is . . . a little tricky for me."

"I'm seeing that. We need a sit-down?"

"No. I mean you can. I . . . can't. Shit." She paced away, stared hard out of the window. "I don't know how much you know about when I was a kid, and I don't want to talk about it."

He knew a great deal, enough that having her bring it up tightened his belly. But his voice stayed even. "All right."

"There was an HSO field operative in Dallas when . . . during a period when . . . Goddamn it."

"They had eyes on your father?"

"Yes. Eyes and ears. They . . . it's complicated, Feeney, and I don't have it in me to go through it all. But the fact is there's a file. Roarke's read it and—"

"Hold up. They had eyes and ears, they knew there was a kid, and they didn't intervene?"

"That's not the point."

"Fuck the point."

"Feeney." She turned back and was assaulted by the same rage shooting off him as it had with Roarke. "I shouldn't be telling you any of this. If anything . . . You could, depending on the outcome, be considered an accessory before the fact. But maybe, by telling you, we can change the outcome. He'll look for payback, and he can't. It could ruin him. You know that. I'm asking you to help me stop him."

"Stop him? What makes you think I won't give him a hand with it?"

"Because you're a cop," she snapped. "Because you know you can't take it down to the personal that way. You know what can happen when you do. I need you to keep him busy, too busy for him to spend any time moving on this other thing. I need you to find a way to try to talk him down from this. I think he'd listen to you."

"Why?"

"I don't know." She dragged her hands through her hair. "I just do. Please God, Feeney, don't make me go to Summerset with this. It's hard enough asking you. I just need to buy some time so I can think it clear."

"Keeping him busy's not a problem seeing as there's only three of us working on fourteen units. Talking to him . . ." Feeney's hands retreated to his pockets as he shrugged. "I'll see if I can find an opening for it. Can't promise I will."

"I appreciate it. I appreciate it, Feeney. Thanks."

"Let me ask you something, Dallas. Just between you and me, here and now. We don't have to bring it up again, but I want a straight answer from you. You don't want payback?"

She looked down at the floor, then made herself lift her gaze and meet his eyes. "I want it so bad I can taste it. I want it so bad, so fucking bad, it scares me. I want it, Feeney, so bad that I know I have to put it away. I have to, or I'll do something I'm not sure I can live with."

He nodded, and that was enough for both of them. "Let's go do the job, then."

Commander Whitney was a big man who sat behind a big desk. Eve knew his day was filled with paperwork and politics, with diplomacy and directives. But it didn't make him less of a cop.

He had skin the tone of glossy oak, and the eyes that beamed out of his wide face were dark and intelligent. There was more gray in his hair than there'd been the year before, and Eve imagined his wife nagged him to deal with it.

Personally, Eve liked it. It added one more aspect of authority.

He listened, and she found his silence during her report both heavy and comforting.

She remained standing when she was finished, and though she didn't glance over at Peabody, she knew her partner was holding her breath.

"Your source on this information is reliable?"

"Sir, as this information came to me through unknown sources, I am unable to vouch for the reliability of same, but I'm convinced the data itself is reliable."

He raised his eyebrows and nodded. "Carefully said. It may stand if and when you're pushed on it. How do you intend to proceed?"

"I intend to disclose this information to Reva Ewing."

"That should make her lawyers stand up and dance."

"Sir, she didn't kill Bissel and Kade. I can't in good conscience withhold this information from someone who is, essentially, another victim."

"No. I just hate seeing lawyers dance."

There was the faintest snort from Peabody, hastily transformed into a cough.

"The PA's not going to be happy," Whitney added.

"He may be happy enough to dance himself if we tie the HSO into a double murder, and the deliberate framing of a civilian. That eventuality would make this case very hot," Eve added when she saw the speculative look in Whitney's eyes. "Hot enough to generate considerable media. Global media, with the prosecuting attorney in the forefront."

"That's interesting, and political thinking, Dallas. You surprise me."

"I can push my mind in a political direction when pressed, and assume you'd be able to expand on that area when briefing the PA."

"You can be sure of it."

"Ewing may also prove useful in providing contacts to assist me in pursuing this HSO aspect of my investigation."

"The HSO, once made aware of this aspect of your investigation, will try, very hard, to end said investigation."

Nonaction, she thought. That would be the term, and what they'd want from her.

She'd be damned if they'd get it.

"They have no authority over the NYPSD on a homicide investigation. An innocent woman was implicated, deliberately, in a double homicide."

An innocent child, she thought, couldn't stop the thought, *was deliberately ignored and left to be beaten, to be raped. Left to kill to survive.*

"That isn't national or global security, Commander, it's just dirty." Her throat was starting to burn, but she ignored it and ordered herself to stay with the facts. To stay with the now.

"A legitimate corporation, for which Ewing works, has a viable government Code Red contract to develop an extermination program to block the alleged plans of a techno-terrorist organization. If the HSO has attempted to hamper the research and development currently underway at Securecomp, that isn't a matter of national or global security either. It's dangerous and self-aggrandizing corporate espionage."

"I can promise you, they'll have a different spin."

"They can spin it until they create a new plane of gravity, it won't alter the fact that two people were brutally murdered, and an innocent civilian deliberately framed for it. The media's already smearing Reva Ewing's name all over the screen. She doesn't deserve it. She nearly died standing as shield for President Foster, because that was her job. No more, no less. She's done her job, no more, no less, for Securecomp, and in doing so will be partly responsible for developing another shield against a threat that could, potentially, shut down the Pentagon, the NSC, the GSC, Parliament, and the damn HSO."

He held up a hand. "She'd do better with you than the lawyers. I'm not arguing with you," he added as the insult flickered over Eve's face. "I read her file. You understand you have the option of simply dropping the charges and allowing Ewing to do her own spin. The NYPSD, and you, might look overbearing or foolish initially, but that would wear off before long."

"Two people would still be dead."

"Two operatives, Dallas. By-product of the job." He held up his hand again before Eve could speak. "Do you have an opinion on that, Detective Peabody?"

"Yes, sir. If I went down, line of duty, that'd be a by-product of the job. But I'd expect Dallas and my fellow officers to do everything they could to get me justice. We don't just let murder go because it's a professional hazard."

"You stand up well for yourself, Detective. Now that I see we're all on the same side of the line. Talk to Ewing. I'll take this to Chief Tibble. Only Chief Tibble," he added, "on a need-to-know."

"Thank you, sir. The EDD team will work primarily out of my residence. It has more levels of security than we have at Central."

"That doesn't surprise me. Document everything, Dallas, but for now your reports to me will remain verbal only. I want to be informed the minute you have any kind of contact with any agent or representative of the HSO. Keep your ass covered, because if it takes a hit, so does this department."

"That went well," Peabody commented as they headed down to the garage.

"Well enough."

"When he asked me if I had an opinion, I almost clutched."

"He wouldn't have asked if he didn't want to hear it."

"Maybe not, but brass usually wants to hear what they want to hear. There was this other thing I was thinking." She ran a hand, very casually, down her jacket to smooth the line. "Due to the nature of this investigation and certain sensitivities, it might be more secure, all in all, if members of the team remained at your residence."

"Might it be?" Eve replied.

"Well, yeah, seeing . . ." She trailed off, studied their pea-green city vehicle. "Unit swept and shielded?"

"Maintenance said so, but they're lying sacks of shit. It should be safe enough for you to make your pitch in general terms."

Peabody climbed in. "First, you have those extra layers of security in place, so we don't have to watch what we say or do. Part of investigating is talking through data and information. Also EDD could take shifts, if necessary. And since McNab and I are getting ready to move to our new apartment, my place is a wreck." She smiled prettily. "So how about it?"

"It's not a party."

"Absolutely not." Peabody stifled the smile and looked stern. "I'm proposing this for the good of the team, and the investigation."

"And because there's always ice cream stocked in the freezer."

"Well, yes. Do I look stupid?"

It wasn't unusual for Roarke to call for a spot-check on security in any department at any time. But it was less usual for him to run scanners personally—and to run tests on his own equipment.

The level-ten lab at Securecomp could only be accessed by employees with the highest clearance. Still, none of them grumbled at the body scans, or the delay while the scanner was run through a series of checks, then the scans rerun.

No one mumbled when a team of exterminators in their white skin-suits and black helmets were called in to sweep for bugs. Glances were exchanged, and a few shrugs, but no one questioned the man.

The lab itself was pristine. Filters and purifiers kept the air absolutely clean. Floors, walls, ceilings were all unrelieved white. There were no windows, and the walls were a full six inches thick. Minicams were positioned to record every area, all personnel, every movement, every sound.

Each workstation was a clear-sided cube or series of clear counters, and each held compact and powerful equipment. There were no 'links other than interoffice ones.

Authorized personnel wore encoded badges, and passed through three staging areas each time they entered or exited the lab. Access required voice, retinal, and palmprint verification.

The scanners, alarm, and preventatives made it impossible—so Roarke had believed—to remove any data from the lab without his knowledge and authorization. Planting a bug inside would require sorcery.

He'd have bet his reputation on it. And, essentially, had.

He signaled to the acting lab chief, Tokimoto, and walked into what the techs called "the vault."

It was an office—spartan, almost military—with a single streamlined desk, two chairs, and a wall of sealed drawers. The desk held a muscular data and communications system with a 'link that could only send or receive outside the lab with Roarke's personal voiceprint and passcode.

"Close the door," he ordered Tokimoto. "Have a seat."

Tokimoto did both, then folded his long, neat hands in his lap. "If you've brought me in here to ask me about Ewing, you're wasting our time. And we both value our time. She didn't kill anyone, however much he deserved it."

Roarke sat, adjusted his thinking and approach as he studied Tokimoto.

The man was forty, trim, and long-limbed. He wore his black hair short and close to the scalp. His skin was very white, his eyes tawny beneath long, straight brows. His nose was narrow, his mouth pressed now into a thin line of annoyance.

It was, Roarke estimated, one of the very few times he'd seen Tokimoto annoyed in the six years of their association.

"This is interesting," Roarke commented.

"I'm pleased my opinion is of interest," Tokimoto responded in his clipped, precise voice.

"I didn't realize you were in love with Reva. Obviously, I haven't been paying attention."

Tokimoto remained still, face and body. "Ewing is—was—a married woman. I respect the institution. We are associates and colleagues, nothing more."

"So you haven't told her, or moved on her. Well, that's your business. Your personal business, and none of mine unless it pertains to what goes on inside this lab. But I will say that, at the moment, she could use a friend."

"I don't want to intrude."

"Again, your business." Roarke took a disc out of his pocket, inserted it in his computer. "Have a look at this. I'd like your opinion."

Tokimoto rose, walked lightly around the desk to study the screen. He pursed his lips over the grid, the complex lines and boxes. He scratched his chin.

"Will you enhance? This area." Tokimoto gestured to a section of the grid.

Without speaking, Roarke keystroked to enlarge and enhance the requested area. "There's a shadow, just here in Quadrant B, section five through ten. A bug was there, but is not there now. I think . . . wait. Does it move?"

The question, Roarke knew, wasn't directed at him. But to answer he magnified again and let the disc play forward.

"Yes, yes, it moves. Barely a shadow when it moves. More detectable when it rests."

"And your conclusion?"

"The device is planted on a movable object. A person or droid. It's highly sophisticated. Minute and very well shielded. Ours?"

"I don't think so, but we'll work on that. This is a security print of the lab, Tokimoto. And this . . ." He tapped a finger on the screen where the shadow was darkest. "This is Reva's station."

"There is a mistake."

"It's not a mistake."

"She would never betray you or her associates. She's honorable."

"No, I don't think she'd betray me, or you. I'm going to ask you this once. Have you been approached by any outside party regarding the Code Red?"

"I have not." It was said simply, with no hints of insult, annoyance, or fear. "Had I been, I would have reported to you."

"Yes, I believe that. Because you're honorable, Tokimoto. I'm showing you this because you are. Because in this very delicate matter, I'm trusting you."

"You have my loyalty, but I won't believe this of Reva."

"Neither will I. How, in your opinion, could this bug have infected the lab?"

"On a person, as I said."

"On her person."

Tokimoto's brow creased as he studied the screen again. "This is contradictory to me. She would know if she carried a device, and she would not enter the lab. Therefore, she could not have carried a device. In addition, lab security is meticulous and multilayered and would have detected a device. Therefore, a device could not have penetrated the lab. Yet it did."

"That's very logical, Tokimoto, but expand your thinking. How might Reva have brought a device into the lab, unknowingly, that penetrated lab security?"

"She's an expert, and your scanners are the most powerful available. It's impossible that a device was planted on her person and escaped her detection, and the scanners. It is . . ."

He stopped, straightened, and Roarke watched the idea bloom on his face.

"Internally," Roarke supplied.

"Such things are possible, in theory. Some have been tested. Those in development, including those worked on here, haven't proven effective."

"The device can be injected, under the skin."

"In theory."

"All right, thank you." Roarke rose.

"Is she . . . Is Ewing in some sort of danger?"

"She's protected. It would do her good to hear from a friend who sympathized and believed in her. Meanwhile, I want work on the Code Red to move around the clock. Four shifts. If she's up to it, Reva will be back tomorrow."

"It will be good to have her. She should know of this, but I won't speak of it if that's your wish."

"I'm on my way to tell her myself. If you discuss it with her, do it in the vault." He started for the door, stopped. "Yoshi, life is never as long as we want it to be, and wasted time can never be recovered."

A ghost of a smile curved Tokimoto's lips. "A proverb."

"No. It's my way of telling you to make a goddamn move."

Chapter 9

Eve didn't see how she could be concerned about total security at this point, but she took the cryptic transmission from Roarke on the odd little 'link he'd presented to her that morning.

It strapped on the wrist, but she didn't care for the weight of it, or the absurdity of talking to her sleeve. So she'd stuck it in her jacket pocket, and when it vibrated against her hip, she jolted as if she'd been struck with a laser blast.

"Jesus. Technology is a pain in the—haha—ass." She yanked it out. "What?"

"That's hardly a professional greeting, Lieutenant."

"I'm stalled in traffic. Why don't these people have jobs? Why don't they have homes?"

"And some nerve they have being out and about on your streets. I'm on them myself, and about to pick up a package. I need to take it home. I very much want you to see it, so you'll want to meet me there."

"What? Why? Goddamn asshole maxibus! I'm driving here. I'm heading to the East Side, if I don't indulge in a major vehicular accident just to clear the goddamn *roads!*"

"I'm running that errand for you myself. Come home, Eve."

"But I—" She snarled at the 'link when the transmission ended, then in disgust tossed it at Peabody. "It's gone wonky."

"No, sir. He cut you off. He wants you to go back to the residence, where he's bringing Reva Ewing."

"How do you get that?"

"I watch a lot of spy vids. He must have found something, and he wants to discuss it with you in the most secure location. This is really chilled, you've got to admit."

"Yeah, so chilled. I've yet to talk to Morris, or have another look at the bodies. I haven't booted Dickhead around the lab to see if there's any forensics that might be useful. And, much as I hate it, I haven't talked to the media liaison about a spin when we drop charges on Ewing."

"Those usual routines don't apply as much when you're Bonding."

"Bonding? How am I bonding? I'm not interested in bonding, in fact I dislike bonding intensely."

"No, no, *Bonding*. Like Bond, James Bond. You know, ult spy guy."

"God." Eve shot down a cross-street, and made it a block before she stalled again. "Why me?"

"I really dig the spy vids, even the old ones. Gadgets and sex and sophisticated quips. You know, Dallas, if Roarke was an actor he could completely play Bond on vid. He's a total Bond."

Eve plowed through the light, cast her eyes to heaven. "God, I repeat. Why me?"

She slammed into the house, bared her teeth at Summerset.

"Your associates have arrived. Suitable quarters have been prepared for them. Going by previous experience, I am about to have food supplies completely restocked, with an emphasis on items without any nutritional value whatsoever."

"And you're telling me this because, somehow, I look like I give a shit?"

"You are mistress of this house, and responsible for the comfort of your guests."

"They're not guests. They're cops."

Peabody loitered as Eve charged upstairs. "Is it okay if McNab and I have the room we took last time?"

Summerset's stony countenance softened with a smile. "Of course, Detective. I've arranged it."

"Mag. Thanks."

"Peabody!" Eve's aggrieved voice shot down the stairs. "With me, goddamn it."

"Bad traffic," Peabody grumbled. "Terrible mood."

She had to bolt up the stairs, then streak down the hall to catch up with Eve.

"If you're going to brown-nose the resident cadaver, do it on your own time."

"I wasn't brown-nosing." But the comment had Peabody's nose twitching. "I was merely inquiring about my quarters during this operation. Besides, I don't have to brown-nose Summerset. He likes me."

"That ascribes to him the capacity for human emotions." She swung into Roarke's office, and frowned when she saw him serving coffee to both Reva and Caro. "You might've told me you were bringing them here," she complained, "before I fought my way to the Upper East Side."

"Sorry for the inconvenience, but here is where we need to be."

"This is my case, my investigation, my op. I decide where we need to be."

"This isn't about authority, Lieutenant. And when your knowledge of electronics meets or exceeds mine, we'll reevaluate." His tone was entirely too pleasant. "In the meantime . . . coffee?"

"I don't have time for coffee."

"Help yourself, Peabody," he invited, then took Eve's arm. "If I could have a moment, Lieutenant."

She let him lead her into her office. She didn't like it, but she allowed it. Then she blasted him when he'd closed the door. "We need to set some parameters. You're working in conjunction with EDD. You do not have the authority to transport my suspect, and her mother, whenever and wherever you choose. Your personal feelings for them take a backseat, and if they can't, you're out."

"It was necessary. You're irritable and annoyed," he snapped as she started to steam. "Well, so am I. So we can stand here and piss on each other for the next ten minutes, or get on with it."

She had to take a breath, then two, before she managed to control her temper. He looked ready to brawl. Not that she minded that so much, but she was more interested in why.

"Okay, you *are* irritable and annoyed. What set you off?"

"If you'd give me a few minutes without crawling up my ass, I'll show you."

"I don't like what I see, ace, I'm crawling right back."

He stepped back to the door, then turned to her again. "I realize that I have, on occasion, acted in a way that failed to show the proper respect for your authority and your position. That was wrong. Not that it might not happen again, but it was wrong. This isn't one of those times."

"It feels like it."

"That can't be helped. On the other side, those two women are my employees. Spanking me in front of them demeans my authority and position, Eve."

"That can't be helped either. They know you've got balls." She offered a razor-thin smile. "Now they know I've got them, too."

"This isn't about—" He cut himself off, offered a prayer for patience. "Christ, there's no point to this. We'll have a go at each other later."

"Count on it." She reached around him and opened the door herself.

Thinking of authority and position, she made sure that she strode through the door first. "You've got five minutes," she told him.

"It shouldn't take longer. Computer, lock down this room only, for silent running."

ACKNOWLEDGED. COMMENCING SILENT RUNNING.

"What the hell is—" Eve whirled, hand on her weapon, as titanium shields lowered on the windows behind her. Others slid into place over the doors. The lights took on a red cast, and every machine in the room sent out a series of beeps and hums.

"Totally Bond," Peabody murmured with a big, dazzled grin on her face.

LOCKDOWN COMPLETE. SILENT RUNNING FULLY ENGAGED.

"In your home office." Reva got to her feet, walked over to examine the window shields. "A little paranoid, but excellent. Have you equipped the whole house with SR capability? I'd really like to see the—"

"You kids can play with the toys later," Eve interrupted. "Now I'd like to know why we need them."

"I ran some tests at Securecomp. Very detailed and exacting tests. They showed traces of a mobile bug."

"Mobile?" Reva shook her head. "Someone got through security, all the scanners, with a device on their person? That shouldn't be possible. In fact, it isn't possible."

"So I believed, but the device is also very sophisticated. It wasn't on someone's person, Reva, but in yours."

"In? Internal? That's out of the question. Completely bogus."

"Then you won't object to a body scan?"

Her face went hard, her stance combative. "I submit to one every time I go in or out of the damn lab, Roarke."

"I've something a little more sensitive, a little more specific."

"Go ahead." Reva threw out her arms. "I've got nothing to hide."

"Computer, open Panel A."

ACKNOWLEDGED.

A section of the wall opened. Inside was a small room, hardly bigger than a closet. It held what looked like a high-end drying tube, with clear, rounded sides and a door with no apparent lock. There were no visible controls.

"Something I've been working on, on my own," Roarke said when Reva lifted her eyebrows. "An individual security scanner, higher intensity than what's on the market currently. It'll also read vital signs, which will come in handy for evaluating a subject's state of mind during scan."

"Is it safe?" Caro had risen, walked over quietly. "I'm sorry, but if it hasn't been approved, there may be some risk."

"I've used it myself," he assured her. "It's quite safe. It'll feel warm on the skin as it scans," he told Reva. "Not uncomfortably so, but you'll notice the change in temperature as it moves from area to area."

"Let's just get it done. I've got the Truth Testing scheduled today. I'd like a little time between scans and probes if it's all the same to you."

"Computer, open scanner."

ACKNOWLEDGED.

A door opened on the tube with a little puff of air. At Roarke's gesture, Reva stepped inside, turned to face the room.

"Begin process on Ewing, Reva, full body, full power on my command. It needs to read and record your height," he said. "Your weight, your body mass, and so on."

"Fine."

"When the door closes, the process should only take a few moments. There'll be an audio and video readout, if you don't object."

"Just do it."

"Computer, begin."

The door of the tube closed. The lights inside it turned to a cool blue. Eve listened as Reva's body statistics were noted. A horizontal red beam rose up from the floor of the tube, slowly traveling up the body, down again. Her various injuries were listed, and the evaluation of healing.

"Excellent." Reva's voice sounded hollow through the tube, but she was beginning to grin. Eve could see that most of the temper had drowned in professional fascination. "And thorough. You're going to need to get this on the market."

"A few more tweaks," Roarke said.

Then came a series of red and blue beams, crisscrossing her body, pulsing as they scanned her, section by section from feet to head.

ELECTRONIC DEVICE LOCATED, SUBDERMAL, SECTION TWO.

"What the hell is it talking about?" Her tone a quick jerk of panic, Reva pressed her hands against the tube. "Where's section two? This is bullshit."

Roarke noted the increase in her pulse rate, her blood pressure.

"Let it finish out, Reva."

"Hurry up. Just hurry up. I want to get out of here."

"It's all right, Reva." Caro spoke softly. "Only a little more, and it'll be done. Everything's going to be all right."

"Nothing's all right. Nothing's going to be all right again."

NO SECONDARY DEVICE DETECTED. SINGLE ELECTRONIC DEVICE, OPERABLE, SUBDERMAL, SECTION TWO. REQUEST COMMAND TO MARK LOCATION.

"Do so," Roarke ordered.

There was a quick hum, a flash. Reva slapped a hand at the back of her neck, as though she'd been stung by a bee.

EVAL AND SCAN COMPLETE.

"Save and display all data. Release seal, end program."

The lights in the tube winked off, and the door opened.

"Inside me? Under my skin." She held her hand cupped over the back of her neck. "How could I not know? I swear to God, I swear I didn't know."

"I never thought you did. Sit down now."

"An internal. It would require a procedure. I haven't had a procedure. It can't *be* there."

"It is there." Roarke drew her to a chair, stepped back when Caro sat beside her, took her hand. "Planted there without your knowledge, without your acquiescence."

"I'd have had to have been unconscious. I haven't *been* unconscious."

"You've been asleep, haven't you?" Eve broke in. "Somebody's asleep, it's not hard to give them a little bump with a pressure syringe and take them under. Or to slip something into food or drink so they'd sleep through an implant."

"I sleep at home, in my own damn bed. The only person who'd be able to pull off something like that would've been . . . Blair," she finished on a shaky breath. "But that's crazy. He didn't know anything about internals or subdermal devices."

She saw the look Roarke and Eve exchanged. "What is this? What the hell is this?"

"I didn't tell her, Lieutenant." Roarke inclined his head. "It wasn't my place to."

Eve stepped up to Reva. "You're going to have to toughen up, because this is going to be a punch in the face."

She told Reva the way she'd want to be told. Straight, clean, without emotion. She watched her sag, lose color, saw the tears swim into her eyes. But they didn't fall, and the color came back.

"He . . . they marked me, as a source for information." Her voice was hoarse. "To spy, through me, on Securecomp, and possibly other areas of Roarke Industries through my mother. Also . . ." She paused, cleared her throat and spoke in stronger tones. "It makes sense to assume they were using my connection with the Secret Service, President Foster, and members of her staff I remain friendly with. They would, through this implant, have recorded any and all conversations, professional and personal."

She took the glass of water Peabody brought over without glancing up. "I have, in my supervisory position at Securecomp, numerous discussions every day with techs, giving directives, receiving status reports. It's my habit to log my own reports verbally. It helps me to see the progress, or any necessity for a new direction. They'd know everything about my projects, and any I assisted on, since they put this thing in me. They were sucking me dry, the two of them. Every day. Every day."

She looked up at Roarke. "I betrayed you after all."

"You did not." Caro's tone was harsh and impatient. "You were betrayed, and that's a difficult thing. But feeling sorry for yourself isn't productive. No one's blaming you, and blaming yourself at this point is an indulgence you can't afford."

"I'm entitled to a little brooding time when I've been technologically raped, for God's sake."

"Brood later. How do we remove it?" Caro asked Roarke, then shifted her gaze to Eve. "Or do we?"

"I thought about leaving it in. It's an option, but I'd rather have it out. I'd rather, if anyone's still listening, that they know we're on to them. It could bring them to the surface faster."

"They killed Blair and Felicity, and set me up. Why?"

"The setup? I'd say because you were convenient. As to the hit, I don't know yet. Maybe it was HSO, maybe it was the other side. Either way, they knew how to get in, how to corrupt data, and how to get you where they wanted you to take the fall. All that took some time and some planning. Either Bissel or Kade, maybe both of them, were marked for termination. When I find out why, I can work from there."

"We can have the device removed here. I have someone in-house with medical training," Roarke explained.

"Get it out." Reva rubbed a hand at the nape of her neck. "I want a look at it."

"Set it up," Eve told Roarke. "Reva, you can't discuss any of this on the outside. Not even with your lawyers. Not yet. But I want you to contact someone in the SS, or on Foster's staff, whoever you think best. I want them to set up a meet for me with someone in the HSO with enough grease to know about Bissel and Kade. I don't have time to waste on some office drone. I want someone with juice."

"I'll reach out."

"Good. I'm going to leave the electronics to the people who know what the hell to do about them." She said this, looking at Roarke. "And I'm going to go do some cop work, if you'll open this place up again."

"Computer, end lockdown. Resume normal operations."

ACKNOWLEDGED.

"I'll be a few moments," Roarke told Reva and Caro, then left them alone to walk out with Eve.

"Peabody, go see how the EDD boys are doing. I'll catch up with you."

"Sure."

Eve turned into her own office ahead of Roarke, slipped her hands in her pockets. "I thought you'd told her about the HSO angle, about the conclusions on Bissel and Kade."

"I'm aware of that, and aware that you'd have reason to assume it."

"The assumption factored in to the speed with which I crawled up your ass."

"Understood."

"I'm still irritable and annoyed."

"Well, so am I, so you've company."

"I might still want to have a go at you later."

"I'll pencil you in."

She stepped up to him, and keeping her hands in her pockets, planted a hard kiss on his mouth. "See you," she said, and strolled out.

Since she didn't understand what EDD was doing in Roarke's home lab, she dragged Peabody away and gave her the task of locating and contacting Carter Bissel while she begged a brief consult with Dr. Mira.

"Your assistant's starting to hate me," Eve commented.

"No, she's just very inflexible about schedules." Mira programmed her habitual tea and gestured toward her blue scoop chairs.

She'd gone for red today. Not really red, Eve thought. There was probably a name for the color that looked like faded autumn leaves. She wore a trio of necklaces that were little gold balls strung together like pearls, and matched them with minute gold earrings.

The shoes, some sort of textured heels, were the exact color of the dress. Eve could never figure out how women managed that sort of synchronicity—or really, why they bothered.

But it looked good on Mira. Everything did. Her sable hair with its sunny highlights was drawn back today into some sort of twisty knot at the nape. She was letting it grow again.

However Mira dressed or groomed herself, Eve decided she'd always look perfect, and nothing like the standard image of a top profiler and police psychiatrist.

"I assume this has something to do with Reva Ewing's Truth Test this afternoon, as you requested I handle the test personally."

"It does. This conversation, any conversation with Ewing, and the results of the test are highest classification. My eyes, yours, and Commander Whitney's only."

Mira sipped her tea, pursed her lips. "And what warrants that classification?"

"Global espionage," Eve said, and told her the rest.

"You believe her." Mira rose for another cup of tea. "That she was duped, and is innocent of any involvement—deliberate involvement—in the murders and in the background that may have led to them."

"I do. I expect you to confirm that."

"And if the results contradict her, and your beliefs?"

"Then she'll go back into a cage until I figure out why."

Mira nodded. "She's agreed to level three. That's a very difficult process, as you know from personal experience."

"I got through it, so will she."

Mira nodded, her gaze on Eve's face. "You like her."

"Yeah, probably. But it won't get in the way. Either way."

"The murders were very violent, very brutal. One assumes that a government—even covert government—organization would be less so."

"I don't assume anything about spooks."

Mira smiled a little. "You *don't* like them."

"No. The HSO has a file on my father."

Mira's smile faded. "I suppose that's to be expected."

"They had a field operative monitoring him, and the rooms where we were in Dallas."

Mira set the cup aside. "They were aware of you? Of what was being done to you, and didn't intervene?"

"They were aware, it's in the file. Just like they were aware of what I did to get away. They cleaned up after me, and they let it ride. So no, I'm no fan of the HSO."

"Whoever gave the order not to intervene when a child's welfare—her very life—is at stake, should be locked away—like any abuser. This shocks me. After all I've seen, heard, all I know, this shocks me."

"If they could do what they did in Dallas, they could do what was done to Reva Ewing. But this time, they're not going to get away with it."

"You're going public with Ewing."

"Damn right."

Eve went back to Homicide, taking the glides rather than the elevator to give herself more time to think about her next steps. It still gave her a quick jolt to walk into the bull pen and see Peabody at a desk instead of a cube.

Since her partner was on the 'link, Eve went straight into her own office. She locked the door, then climbed onto her desk to reach the ceiling panel, behind which she was currently secreting her personal stash of candy.

She needed a hit. Genuine chocolate, real coffee. All would be right with the world during the ten minutes she took for this personal, and well-deserved, indulgence.

But instead of her cache of candy, there was a single, empty wrapper.

Son of a *bitch!*" She nearly snatched the wrapper down with the intention of tearing it into bits. But stopped herself. "We'll just see about this, you vicious candy thief."

She hopped down and got her spare field kit. Sealing up,

she climbed back on the desk to remove the wrapper with tongs, then set it on a protective surface on her desk.

"You want to play. We'll play."

Moments later, the knock on her door earned a snarl.

"Dallas? Lieutenant? Your door's locked."

"I know the damn door's locked. I locked it."

"Oh. I have information on Carter Bissel."

Eve rose, kicked the desk, unlocked the door. "Relock it," she ordered, then sat back at her desk with her tools.

"Sure." With a shrug, Peabody secured the door. "I contacted—what are you doing?"

"What the hell does it look like I'm doing?"

"Well, it looks as if you're doing a fingerprint scan on a candy wrapper."

"Then that's probably what I'm doing. You contacted Carter Bissel?"

"No, I . . . Dallas, has a chocolate bar been entered into evidence on this investigation?"

"This is a personal matter. Sealed up," she muttered. "Bastard sealed up. But that's not the end of this. I've got other ways."

"Sir, you also appear to have run a fingerprint scan on a ceiling tile."

"Do you think I'm unaware of what I'm running, Detective? Do I look like I'm in a fugue state?"

"No, you look supremely pissed."

"Again, your powers of observation are keen and accurate. Congratulations. Fuck it." She balled the wrapper up, tossed it. "I'll deal with this later. And I *will* deal. Carter Bissel. And where's my coffee?"

"Uh, as you have declined the services of an aide—"

"Oh, bite me." She shoved away from the desk, stomped to the AutoChef.

"I just wanted the opportunity to say that. But, you know, I don't mind getting you coffee. You could even get it for me sometimes. Like now, for instance, since you're right there."

Eve heaved a huge sigh, and got a second cup.

"Thanks. Okay, Bissel, Carter. I tried the residence, but got no answer. Left a message on his 'link. Then I tried the bar he's listed as owning, and tagged his partner, Diesel Moore. Moore went into a rant and jive the minute I asked about Bissel. Says he wants to find him, too, and called him several uncomplimentary names. He claims Bissel left him high and dry nearly a month ago, and skimmed out of the till. Moore claims to be in dire financial straits. He waited, assuring himself Bissel would come back with an explanation, but that hasn't happened. He filed charges yesterday."

"You verify?"

"Yep. Local authorities are looking for Bissel, and have no record of him leaving the island. Could've taken a boat or a seaplane, island-hopped. They're looking into it, but not very hard. He only skimmed a couple thousand, and part of that would be his due. Also, he has a history of taking off for short periods of time without warning or explanation."

"They check his place?"

"Affirmative. It appears some of his clothes may be missing, and a few personal items, but there's no sign of struggle, foul play, or, for that matter, evidence that he was planning a long trip."

"A month ago, Felicity Kade made a trip to Jamaica. Just what did she and Carter Bissel have to talk about, I wonder?"

"Maybe she was looking to recruit him, too."

"Or maybe she was looking for another goat. I think we should take another look at the crime scene."

Her desk 'link beeped, and she tossed the ceiling tile aside. "Dallas."

DISPATCH, DALLAS, LIEUTENANT EVE. SEE THE OFFICER AT 24 WEST EIGHTEENTH STREET. UNATTENDED DEATH. SINGLE VICTIM, FEMALE. IDENTIFICATION VERIFIED AS MCCOY, CHLOE.

"Acknowledged. Responding. Dallas, out."

Chapter 10

She'd gone with pills, and had dressed in a frothy pink nightgown, done her face and hair carefully, then draped herself on the bed among a mountain of pretty pillows and a stuffed purple bear.

She smelled of something very young, very floral, and might have been mistaken for sleeping if her eyes hadn't been wide and staring, and already clouded with death.

The note lay on the bed beside her, just at her fingertips, with a single line written in dramatic, loopy script on cheap, reconstituted pink paper.

There is no light, there is no life without him.

The empty pill bottle sat on the nightstand, beside a glass of tepid water and a single pink rosebud, shed of all thorns.

Eve studied the room and decided the rose fit with the frilly pink-and-white curtains, the framed posters of fantasy landscapes and meadows. The room was tidy, if overly female, but for a scatter of used tissues lying like snow over the floor by the bed, the remains of a melted pint of Sinful Chocolate frozen dessert, and a half bottle of white wine.

"What does it look like?" Eve asked Peabody.

"It looks like she had herself a major pity party. Wine and ice cream for comfort, lots of tears. Probably used the wine to help herself gear up for the pills. She was young, stupid, and theatrical. The combo led her to self-termination over a sleazeball."

"Yeah, that's what it looks like. Where'd she get the pills?"

With a sealed hand, Peabody picked up the bottle to examine the unmarked green plastic. "It's not a prescription bottle. Black market."

"She strike you as the type who'd have black market connections?"

"No." And the question had Peabody frowning, studying scene and body more closely. "No, but you get fringe dealers working colleges and art circles. She moved in both."

"True enough, true enough. Could be. She'd have had to move fast, but from our brief meeting earlier, I'd peg her as the impulsive type. Still . . ."

Eve walked around the room, into the little bath, out into the stingy living area with its mini kitchen. There were lots of knickknacks, more art reproductions, romantic themes, on the walls. There were no dishes in the little bowl of the sink, no articles of clothing tossed around. No tissues scattered anywhere but the bedroom.

And, she noted, running a sealed finger over a table, not a speck of dust.

"Place is really clean. Funny that somebody so mired in grief they'd self-terminate would tidy up like this."

"Could've always been tidy."

"Could've been," Eve agreed.

"Or she might've buffed the place up, just the way she buffed herself up before she did it. One of my great-aunts is obsessed about making the bed as soon as she's out of it every morning, because if she keels over and dies, she doesn't want anybody thinking she's a careless housekeeper. Some people are weird that way."

"Okay, so she gets the pills, buys herself a pink rosebud.

Then she comes home, cleans the house, spruces herself up. Sits on the bed crying, eating ice cream, drinking wine. Writes the note, then pops the pills, lies down and dies. Could've gone down just that way."

Peabody puffed air into her cheeks. "But you don't think so, and I feel like I'm missing something really obvious."

"The only thing obvious is a twenty-one-year-old girl's dead. And from first look, it appears to be a straight, grief-induced self-termination."

"Just like Bissel and Kade appeared to be a straight, passion-motivated double homicide."

"Well now, Peabody." Eve hooked her thumbs in her front pockets. "You don't say?"

"Okay, I'm picking up the trail, but if this, like the double homicide, is an HSO or terrorist hit, what's the motive?"

"She knew Bissel. She was his lover."

"Yeah, but she was a kid, a toss-away. If she knew anything relevant to Bissel's work, or the Code Red, anything hot, I'll eat my shiny new detective's badge."

"I tend to agree, but maybe someone else didn't. Or maybe it was just housecleaning. The fact is that there's a connection between her and Bissel, and because there is we're not treating this like a straight self-termination. We'll start with the body, then I want this place picked apart. What's the name of the woman who found her?"

"Deena Hornbock, across-the-hall neighbor."

"Do a run. I want to know everything about her before I interview her. Have the uniforms keep her in her apartment and under control."

"Check."

"Contact Crime Scene, and Morris. I want Morris personally on her. And I want CSU to sweep this place down to the last molecule."

Peabody paused at the door. "You really don't think she killed herself."

"If she did, I'll eat my no longer shiny lieutenant's badge. Let's get to work."

* * *

There were no signs of struggle, no evidence of insult or injury to the body that would indicate force. Eve hadn't expected any. She'd died shortly after three A.M. Painlessly, quietly. Uselessly, Eve thought.

Her 'links were in working order, though they'd been shut down shortly after midnight. Reactivating, Eve found her last transmission was an incoming from Deena across the hall at twenty-one hundred and involved a great deal of weeping and sympathy.

I'm coming over, Deena had said. *You shouldn't be alone at a time like this.*

Much tearful gratitude, then the transmission ended.

But the data unit wouldn't boot. Infected, she'd bet the bank on it. What would a silly art student have on a data unit that could worry the HSO, or techno-terrorists?

When she'd done all she could with the body and the bedroom, she moved into the living area where Peabody worked with the sweepers. "They're bagging her for transport. Suspicious death. Give me Deena Hornbock."

"Student, single, twenty-one. A theater major, with an eye toward set design. She's got considerable work on her résumé. Lived at this location for a year. Prior to that did the dorm thing at Soho Theatrical Studies. Prior to that, lived with mother and stepfather in St. Paul. One younger sib, brother. No criminal except a suspended for recreational Zoner when she was eighteen. Pays the rent on time. I contacted the landlord."

"Good."

"McCoy's also up to date on rent, though she tended to pay just before the late fee would kick in. She paid up yesterday, an e-transfer at sixteen thirty-three."

"Yeah? Really tidy to pay the month's rent when you're planning to kill yourself. Let's see what her pal has to say."

Deena Hornbock was shaken but composed as she sat in a plush red chair and sipped continuously from a bottle of water. She was a thin, striking black woman with a small tattoo of a pair of red wings at her left temple.

"Ms. Hornbock, I'm Lieutenant Dallas, and this is Detective Peabody. We need to ask you some questions."

"I know. I'm really going to try to help. I didn't know what to do. I just didn't know, so I ran out and started yelling for somebody to call the police. Somebody did, I guess. I just sat down, right out in the hall until Officer Nalley came."

"How did you get into Chloe's apartment?"

"Oh, I have a key. She's got one for mine, too. We were always in and out of each other's places. Should I give it to you? The key?"

"I'd appreciate that. We'll get it before we leave. Why don't you tell me what happened?"

"Okay." She drew breath in and out, scrubbed a hand over her face. "Okay. I got back from class, and I thought I'd see how she was doing. She was so upset about Blair's death. Just flattened, you know?" Deena let out a long sigh. "I just went right in. When I left her last night I promised to come by this afternoon after class, so I didn't bother to knock or anything. I just went in and called out that I was there."

"The door was locked?"

"Yeah. When she didn't answer, I went back to the bedroom. I was going to try to talk her into going out, or at least over to my place. Cheer her up. God. It's hard to say it," she managed. "It makes me see it again."

"I know."

"I went in. I saw her on the bed. I didn't get it at first, just didn't think . . . I said something like: 'Oh, come on, Chlo.' I said something like that . . ." Her voice started to break. "Jesus, 'Come on, Chlo,' a little impatient, I guess, because it was all so . . . stagey and dramatic. I was a little irritated with her as I walked over to the bed. And then . . ."

"Take your time," Eve instructed, as Deena took a long, long sip from the bottle of water.

"Her eyes were open. Staring and open, and I still didn't get it. For just an instant, I couldn't get it. It was like part of my brain shut down. I've seen someone dead before. My great-grandmother." Deena knuckled a tear away. "She lived with us for a while, and she died in her sleep one night. I found her in the morning, so I've seen somebody dead before. But it's not the same when they're young, when you're not expecting it."

It's never the same, Eve thought. "Did you touch her, or anything else?"

"I think I touched her shoulder, or her arm. I think I reached down to touch her because I didn't see how she could be dead. But she was cold. God, her skin was cold, and I knew. That's when I ran out and started yelling."

"You sat down in the hall, and stayed there until Officer Nalley came."

"Yeah, that's right."

"Did you or anyone else go into the apartment before the officer responded?"

"No. I just sat in front of her door, crying. Some people came out of their apartments, and asked me what was going on. I said, 'She's dead.' I said, 'Chloe's dead,' that she killed herself."

"Okay. You talked to her last night."

"I called when I got home. I'd been out working on a set for a play on the West Side. I knew she was having a rough time. We talked awhile, then I went over. Kept her company for a little while. I stayed till about eleven. I had an early class, and she said she was going to bed. Escape into sleep, that's what she said. She said things like that, but I didn't think she meant . . ." Deena reached out to grip Eve's arm.

"Officer Dallas. I'd never have left her alone if I'd understood what she meant. I'd never have let her do it."

"This isn't your fault. You were a good friend." And because she could see how the guilt was pricking, she didn't correct Deena on her rank. "How was the apartment?"

"I'm sorry?"

"I wondered what sort of state the rooms were in last night when you were there."

"Oh. It was pretty neat, I guess. Chloe liked to keep things neat. Well, there were tissues everywhere. She was crying a lot at first, and tossing them around."

"Did you have anything to eat or drink?"

"We had some wine. I brought over a bottle, and we went through about half of it, maybe."

"Ice cream?"

"Ice cream? No, I didn't think of it. That would've been good, though."

"Did you clean up the wineglasses?"

"The glasses? Ah, no. I didn't think about it. I was tired, and she'd about cried herself out. We just left everything in the living room."

"Not the bedroom?"

"No, we sat on the floor in the living room, just a couple hours. Maybe if I'd stayed over with her . . ."

"I want to ask you to look at this note." Eve took out the pink paper in an evidence bag. "Do you know if this is Chloe's handwriting?"

"Yeah. Big and splashy, that's Chloe. But she was *wrong*. There was life without him. There's always more life. And for Christ's sake, it wasn't going to go anywhere. It was all just a fantasy."

"Did you ever meet Blair Bissel?"

"No." She took a balled-up tissue, blew her nose. "She kept him really close. I didn't even know about him. I mean, I knew there was *somebody*, and I knew the somebody was married, but she wouldn't tell me his name, or anything. Made a vow, she said. A solemn vow. It's so like her to say that: 'I made a solemn vow.' That, and the fact she knew I didn't see him as the love of her life the way she did, meant she didn't tell me a lot of specifics about him. I didn't know his name, or that it was the guy she worked for part-time in the gallery until after it happened. After his wife killed him, I mean, and she told me about it last night."

"So he never came here."

"Yeah, he did. At least I think he did. We had this signal, Chloe and I. If either of us had something going on and didn't want other company—if you get me—we'd hang this pink ribbon on the doorknob. That was her idea. As far as I know, and I'm pretty sure I'd know, she wasn't seeing anybody but the artist for the last few months. And there'd be a pink ribbon on the door about once a week."

"Did she usually turn off her 'links when she was entertaining?"

"Oh yeah. That was Chloe. She didn't want anything from the outside world to disturb the ambiance."

"When you left her last night, did you hear or see anything?"

"I went right to bed. I'd had a couple glasses of wine, and the whole emotional scene. I was wiped. I didn't hear anything until the alarm kicked me out of bed this morning at six-thirty."

"What time did you leave for class?"

"About quarter after seven. Give or take."

"See anything then?"

"No, nothing. I thought about running in and checking on Chloe, but figured she'd be . . ." Her voice wavered again. "I thought she'd be asleep—and I was cutting it close anyway, so I just went straight out, and to class."

"I know this is a tough time for you, and appreciate you answering all the questions." She started to rise, then sat again, as if just remembering something. "Oh, I noticed—when I reviewed the 'link transmissions—that she was wearing a necklace when she talked to you. A heart on a chain, I think. Pretty. She kept playing with it while she talked."

"The locket? I think the artist gave it to her a couple months ago. She never took it off. She was really sentimental."

"She wasn't wearing a locket," Peabody said as they stepped back into Chloe's apartment.

"Nope."

"No locket found on premises."

"Negative."

"So, potentially, whoever killed her or induced her to kill herself took the locket."

"It sure as hell's missing. People put things in lockets, don't they?"

"Sure, pictures, locks of hair, DNA samples."

"If Bissel gave it to her, could be there was something more than romantic inside it—or about it."

"Am I going to have to eat my shiny new badge?"

Eve shook her head. "Doesn't mean she knew what she had. But I'm betting she died because of it, and whatever she might have had on her data unit."

Peabody adjusted her thinking and looked around the living room. "She tidied up, or someone did. I can't see why anyone who came in would wash the neighbor's wineglass or pick up the place. If she did it, she had a reason. Expecting someone? That means she'd have gotten a call, but there's no record of one on any 'link."

"None that show. The data unit's down. Could be somebody sent her an e-mail."

"So we have the EDD whizzes look closer on data and on communication."

"There you go."

"The building's got minimal security, but they should take a look at the run for last night through the 911 call."

"I'll arrange a pickup."

"We can make all those contacts while fueling our bodies with nutrition. After all, you missed your candy fix."

"Don't remind me." She didn't have to look over to know there would be the beginnings of a pout on Peabody's face. "Okay, we'll eat. I want to juggle some things in my head anyway."

Eve couldn't have said why she picked the Blue Squirrel for anything resembling food, and a passing resemblance was as close as anything on the menu came to food. Maybe she needed to touch base with something from her old life—to indulge in a few memories of sitting at one of the sticky tables, half lit on a Zombie while Mavis bounced on stage and screeched out songs for the crowd.

Or maybe, she thought as she studied the soy burger on her plate, she had a death wish.

"I know better than to eat this," she muttered, and took a

bite anyway. "Nothing in this comes from the natural universe."

"You've gotten spoiled." Peabody plowed through a chicken wrap and side of veggie chips with apparent pleasure. "Meat from actual cows, real coffee, genuine chicken eggs, and all that."

Eve scowled and bit into the burger again. Now she could say why she'd opted for the Squirrel. She'd wanted to prove to herself she wasn't spoiled.

"Somebody helps themselves to the coffee from my office AutoChef whenever she damn well pleases."

"Sure, it's the first degree of separation rule." Peabody wagged a veggie chip that was, remotely, carrot-colored. "I get spoiled by association. Or maybe it's second degree, because the coffee comes from Roarke to you. So you're first degree. But since you're married—"

"Shut up and eat."

Obviously, Eve thought, since she was eating the mysterious substance purporting to be meat substitute that was slapped between two bricks of some sort of bread matter, she wasn't spoiled.

A person got used to what they were used to, that's all. And since Roarke insisted on having cow meat and other natural food products around the house, she was accustomed to them. She didn't even notice the difference now. The food was just there, like a chair, or a picture on the wall that she didn't really look at . . .

Because it was day to day.

She yanked out her communicator.

"Feeney." His face filled her screen. "And this better be good."

Eve noted that his hair, however he'd shortened it, was sticking up in mad tufts. Whatever he was working on, she concluded, wasn't going well.

"I need you to take the civilian and his magic fingers over to Queens. Take those sculptures apart."

"You want us to take sculptures apart."

"You didn't find eyes and ears in the house yet, right?"

"I got a couple of boys doing another sweep."

"Move them out, and you and Roarke move in. The sculptures, Feeney. She wouldn't have thought twice about the sculptures. Reva wouldn't have checked them because he brought them in. She wouldn't have thought twice about them, and they're every-fucking-where inside and out. Take them apart."

"Fine, fine. I could use a change of scene."

"Have Roarke talk to her, see if there was anywhere in particular where she might've done some work at home in addition to her office. Or had conversations with him or anyone regarding Securecomp. When you nail those locations, concentrate on the artwork—such as it is—in that sector."

"I got it. I'll leave McNab on this detail here. Boy's young enough a little frustration won't kill him."

Eve stuck the communicator away. "Finish that off," she said with a nod at Peabody's plate. "We're going back to the Flatiron, and tearing down Bissel's works-in-progress."

"You got all that because I said you were spoiled?"

"You never know what's going to kick it off, do you? Another thing I'm thinking: Chloe didn't have any of Bissel's work in her place. Wouldn't you think she'd have wheedled something? Some small piece of her lover's work? She's in love with him, or so she believes. She's an art major, she works in his gallery, but she doesn't have a sample of his genius."

"You're thinking that's gone the way of her locket."

"We'll contact Deena on the way, and see."

Eve stood in the studio, hands on hips, as she studied the complicated twists and marriages of metals that formed the sculptures.

"Okay, I miscalculated this. Taking these apart's going to require specific tools. We've got them around here, but using them's another matter."

"I actually know how to use some of them."

"Why doesn't that surprise me?" Eve circled the tallest of the works. "Thing is, if we cut or melt or just fucking blast, we'd damage or eradicate the device. If there is indeed a device. And we need EDD or one of those handy scanners to verify that."

"The sweepers went over them."

"I'm betting it wouldn't register on a standard sweep. Even on a deeper one. A spook sweep, now that might be different. This guy sold these pieces of crap all over the world. Corporations, private residences, even government facilities."

"And if they're bugged, it's a pretty slick way of getting intel."

"Mmm." Eve kept circling, studying. "I can't see them wasting his talent. This makes sense to me. It's logical. I bet they'd have loved to have had one of these inside one of Roarke's companies. Trouble was, he didn't like the work, and even with Reva's influence he didn't pony up. Didn't matter so much, since they bugged her."

"It's going to sound paranoid, but do you think somebody's watching us now?"

"Maybe." In case, Eve offered a wide grin. Screw security and lockdowns and silent runnings. She hoped they *were* watching. It was time to go hand to hand.

"If they are, they'd better come out and play real soon. Unless they're sniveling cowards on top of murdering bastards and perverted peepers. I'm having these dissected. We're shutting down this floor until I do. So they'd better take a good look while they still have the chance."

She called for the elevator, stepped in. "Peabody, I don't like Carter Bissel in the wind. I want him found."

"I'll give the locals a goose."

"Do that. In person."

"Huh?"

"Go down, talk to the local PSD, interview the partner and everyone who knew him. Get us a line on the brother. There's a reason Felicity went to see him. I want the reason."

"To Jamaica?" Peabody's voice rose three registers. "I'm going to Jamaica?"

"One of us has to stay here, work this from here. You can

get this done in forty-eight, max. I don't want you skipping naked through the surf."

"Can I skip through the surf with appropriate swimwear for maybe one hour?"

It took considerable effort for Eve to keep her lips from twitching. "I don't want to hear about it. Especially since I'm sending McNab with you."

"Oh my God. I'm having the best dream."

Okay, maybe she couldn't quite stop it from twitching. "You can leave as soon as Feeney clears him. This isn't an island holiday."

"Absolutely not. But I could probably have one drink out of a coconut shell—in the line, Lieutenant, since I'll be interviewing the owner of a tiki bar."

"They'll watch you." Peabody's grin faded as Eve spoke. "Whoever's responsible for this will know when you get on the transport, when you get off. They'll know your hotel, what you have for dinner, what you have in that coconut shell. Believe that, and stay ready."

"You're sending McNab with me so he can watch my back."

"So you can watch each other's backs. I don't anticipate anyone will move on you, but I didn't anticipate anyone would move on Chloe McCoy either."

"No one could have, Dallas."

"You can always anticipate," Eve stated as she stepped off into the lobby, and turned to seal off the elevator. "If I had, she wouldn't be dead."

She sent Peabody off to pack and went solo to the morgue. Morris was just suiting up in his protective gear when she walked in.

He had a nice golden tan, and a trio of colorful balls dangling from a temple braid. It reminded her that he'd just returned from vacation.

"Good to see you back in the trenches," she said.

"My return would hardly be complete without a visit from

my favorite murder cop. You've sent me three bodies in as many days. That's a haul, even for you."

"Let's talk about the new one."

"Haven't gotten to her yet. Even I have human limitations. You've sent her in priority one. Since it's you, I assume this poor young thing actually is priority one. Suspicious death." He looked down at Chloe. "Then, I'm always suspicious of death. Called in as a probable ST?"

"Yeah, but I'm not buying."

"No sign of force." He fixed on his goggles, bent low. Eve waited until he'd run his eyes and his gauge over the body, studied readouts and images on his screen. "No punctures, no insults. The note written in her hand?"

"It was, to the best of my knowledge."

"And she was alone, in her apartment. In her bed?"

"On the bed. The security discs show no one other than residents entering the building. There's no security floor to floor."

"Well, I'll open her up and we'll see what we see. Do you want to tell me what you're looking for?"

"I want to know what she took, or was given. The amount, the potency, the time. And I want to know fast."

"That I can do."

"How about the tox on the other two bodies—Bissel and Kade?"

"A moment." He walked over to his data center, called up the files. "Just in. It appears they'd both indulged in several ounces of champagne—French, excellent vintage. Last meal, three hours prior to death . . . very classy. Caviar, smoked salmon, brie, strawberries. No illegals or other chemical enhancements in the female. Small traces of Exotica in the male."

"They have sex?"

"They certainly did. At least they should have died in a jovial and satisfied frame of mind."

"Verified the murder weapon?"

"Yes. Kitchen knife, jagged-edge style. The one recovered from the scene matches the wounds inflicted."

"Zapped, stabbed."

"In that order," he agreed. "No defensive wounds. Some skin under the female's nails that matches the other vic. Conclusion: a bit of passionate scratching, very minor, during the throes. They'd had sex, and from the positioning of the stunner marks, were likely having an encore when they were disabled. Someone was very annoyed with them."

"You'd think." She glanced back at Chloe, lying white and naked and cold on the slab. "Some people would think she got off easy."

"But we know better. I'll take care of her."

"You can reach me at home as soon as you have the results. Morris, repasscode the files on all three of these, will you? And don't let anyone else work on them."

His eyes gleamed with interest behind his goggles. "More and more interesting."

"Yeah. In fact, I'll come back and pick up the data when you're done. Don't send it."

"Now I'm fascinated. Why don't I bring it to you? That way you can offer me some of Roarke's wonderful wine while you explain."

"Works for me."

He'd bought time and space. That was the important thing. Nothing was going exactly as he'd planned, but he could think on his feet. He could, would, keep his head and think on his feet.

He'd thought on his feet with Chloe McCoy, hadn't he? He'd tied that right up.

The police weren't buying it, weren't buying any of it. And that made *no* sense. No damn sense.

He couldn't have handed them a sweeter package if he'd tied a damn ribbon around it.

Sweat wormed down his back as he prowled the well-appointed rooms that were, for now, his prison and his sanctuary. They couldn't tie him to the murders, and that was what counted. That was priority one.

The rest, he'd fix. He just needed more time.

So it was all right, for now it was all right. He was safe. And he'd figure a way out.

He had some money—not enough, not enough even now and a far cry from what he'd been *promised*—but it gave him some breathing room.

And no matter how maddening it was, parts of it were very exciting. He was the star of his own vid, and he was writing it as he went along. He wasn't the patsy people had taken him for, oh no, he wasn't.

He toked a little Zeus, a small reward, and felt like the king of the world.

He'd do what he had to do, and he'd be smart about it. Careful and smart.

Nobody knew where he was, or that he was.

He was going to keep it that way.

Chapter 11

Roarke and Feeney stood contemplating a mixed-metal figure in the garden of the house in Queens.

"What do you think it is?" Feeney asked at length.

"I think it's female. It may be partially reptilian. It may be partially arachnid. It seems to have been built out of copper and brass and steel. Bits of iron and perhaps tin."

"Why?"

"Well, that's a question, isn't it? I imagine it's symbolic of how woman can be as sly as a snake, as cruel as a spider or some such bullshit. I believe it's unflattering to the female sex, and know it's ugly."

"I got that part, the ugly part." Feeney scratched his chin, then took out his bag of candied almonds. After dipping a hand in, he held it out for Roarke.

So they munched nuts and studied the sculpture.

"And people pay large bucks for this shit?" Feeney asked.

"They do. Indeed they do."

"I don't get *that.* Of course I don't know nothing about art."

"Hmm." Roarke circled the piece. "Sometimes it speaks to them on an emotional level, or an intellectual one. Whatever.

That's when the piece has found the appropriate home. Other times, more often than not, the money's spent simply because the buyer feels it *should* speak to him, and is too idiotic or proud or afraid to admit the thing he's just paid for speaks to no one because it's, essentially, an insulting piece of crap."

Feeney pursed his lips, nodded. "I like pictures, the kind that look like what they're supposed to be. A building, a tree, a bowl of fucking fruit. Looks to me like my grandson could've put this together."

"Strangely enough, I believe it takes considerable skill and talent and vision, however odd, to create something like this."

"You say so." Feeney shrugged, but was far from convinced.

"Canny way to conceal observation devices, if that's what it's about."

"Dallas thinks so."

"And she generally knows what she's about." Roarke opened the remote scanner he and Feeney had configured. "You want to run this, or shall I?"

"Your tool." Feeney cleared his throat. "Yeah, she knows what she's about, like you said. A little nervy right now."

"Is she?"

"Hit the jammer on that thing for a minute."

Roarke lifted a brow, but complied. "Are we about to have a private conversation?"

"Yeah." And Feeney didn't relish it. "I said Dallas was a little nervy right now. About what you might do."

Roarke continued to set the gauges on the scanner. "About what?"

"About the file on her father, about what the HSO pus buckets let happen to her back in Dallas."

Roarke looked over now and saw Feeney's face was tight. Rage, he thought, and embarrassment. "She spoke to you?"

"She circled around it some. She doesn't know how much I know about it. Doesn't want to. It's not something I want to talk to her about either, if it comes to that. Since she feels the same, I didn't have to say that you'd told me."

"The two of you amaze me," Roarke replied. "You're

aware of what happened to her, and with her instincts she'd know you are. But the two of you can't say the words to each other. You can't say them, though you're her father, more than that son of Satan ever was."

Feeney hunched his shoulders and stared at the mixed media ugliness of a squat toadlike creature several feet away. "Maybe that's why, and it's not the point. If she's worried enough about you going after some asshole spook, then she's plenty worried. You're not fixing anything if you twist her up."

Roarke set the scanner to analyze the dimensions, weight, and chemical contents of the sculpture. "I don't hear you saying I'm wrong to go after him. That he, or his superiors, don't deserve to pay for standing back while a child was raped, beaten, and brutalized."

"No, I'm not going to say it." Feeney folded his mouth firm, then met Roarke's eyes. "First, it'd be a fucking lie, the sort that'd burn my tongue clean off because there's part of me that'd like to give you a hand with it."

Feeney stuffed the bag back in his sagging pocket, then kicked the base of the sculpture. The gesture was so like Eve, Roarke felt a smile tug at his mouth.

"And second?"

"Second, you wouldn't give a good goddamn about the right or wrong of it. But you give one about Dallas. You give one about how she feels, about what she needs from you." His color came up as he spoke, staining his cheeks with embarrassment. "I don't want to get into that whole thing. Makes me feel like an asshole. But I'm saying you should think, you should think long and hard about what it'd do to her before you do anything."

"I am. And I will."

"Okay. Then let's just move on."

Though he was both touched and amused, Roarke nodded. "Moving on, then." He disengaged the jammer, then studied the readout from the scan. "I'm getting the expected metals, solvents, finishes, and sealants. That's using the strongest setting corporations and facilities would use in high-risk or sensitive areas."

"Bump it up. Let's see what it'll do with the bells and whistles we added."

"Best move aside," Roarke warned. "The beam may not be friendly to cloth and flesh."

Feeney stepped back from the sculpture, then decided the best place was behind the scanner.

The red beam shot out with an insectile hum. As it struck the metal, the entire sculpture seemed to shimmer.

"Shit. Shit! If we set it too high it might melt that crap down to a puddle."

"It's not too high," Roarke responded. "It may soften a few joints, but other than that . . ." Still he pushed it, upping the speed so the beam scanned the piece faster than he'd planned. Even from behind the unit, he could feel the heat and smell the electric buzz in the air.

When he shut down, Feeney gave a whistling breath. "That is some son of a bitch! Some son of a bitch. I'm doing the next one."

"Might be wise to wear goggles next run." Roarke blinked. "I've dots in front of my eyes." But he was grinning, as Feeney was. "Nice rush, wasn't it?"

"You got that right. And look here." Feeney slapped Roarke on the back as he leaned over to scan the readout. "I'm seeing chips, and I'm seeing fiber optics, and some goddamn silicon."

"Bugs."

Feeney straightened, flexed his fingers. "Bugs. Give the girl the brass ring."

When Eve walked back into her office, she wasn't particularly surprised to see on-air reporter Nadine Furst sitting in her visitor's chair and carefully redoing her lip dye.

She fluttered her long, silky lashes and turned that freshly tinted mouth up into a smile. "Cookies," Nadine said with a gesture toward the little bag on Eve's desk. "I culled six for you before bribing your men."

Eve poked into the box, and came out with chocolate chip.

"There's an oatmeal cookie in there. I see no reason for the existence of oatmeal, particularly in cookies."

"So noted. Why don't you give it back to me, then it won't offend your sensibilities?"

Eve pulled out the fat round cookie, handed it over before closing her door. The closed door had Nadine lifting her perfectly arched brows before nibbling on the cookie.

"Is that so you can yell at me for being in your office, or is it so we can exchange juicy girl secrets."

"I don't have any juicy girl secrets."

"You're married to Roarke. You'd have the juiciest on or off planet."

Eve sat, rested her boots on the desk. "Have I ever told you what he can do to the female body with a single fingertip?"

Nadine leaned forward. "No."

"Good. Just wanted to be sure."

"Bitch," Nadine said with a laugh. "Now about this double homicide, and Reva Ewing."

"The charges about Ewing are about to be dropped."

"Dropped." Nadine all but jumped out of the chair. "Let me get my camera, set up an on-the-spot. Take me less than—"

"Sit down, Nadine."

"Dallas, Ewing's huge. The former American hero gone bad and now about to be exonerated? Add in the handsome artist and gorgeous socialite, the sex, the passion."

"It's bigger than Ewing, and it's not about sex and passion."

Nadine sat again. "What could be bigger than that?"

"I'm going to tell you what you can go on-air with, and what you can't."

Nadine's expression went sharp as a blade. "Wait just a minute."

"Or I'm going to tell you nothing."

"You know, Dallas, one of these days you're going to trust me to know what can go on-air and what can't."

"If I didn't trust you, you and your cookies wouldn't be here." She rose as she spoke, and took the scanner EDD had provided her—one Roarke and Feeney had upgraded—to check the office space for any new electronics.

"What are you doing with that?"

"Just being anal. But as I was saying," she continued, when she was satisfied the room was clean, "the fact is, if you hadn't been sitting here playing with your pretty face when I walked in, I was going to contact you. I've got reasons for wanting some of this to go public, Nadine, and they're not all professional."

"I'm listening."

Eve shook her head. "I have to clear every word of the story, and any follow-ups, before you go out with them. I need your word on it. I trust your word, but I have to have it. You have to say it."

Nadine's fingers itched for her recorder, but she curled them into her palm. "This must be big. You've got my word, on all of it."

"Bissel and Kade were HSO."

"You are *shitting* me."

"This information comes from an unnamed source, and it's gold. Bissel's marriage to Ewing was part of an op, and it was without her knowledge or consent. She was used and was framed for the murder of Bissel and Kade to cover up the op, and potentially more."

"Something this hot from an unnamed—gold or not—I need hard facts."

"I'm going to give them to you. No recorder," she said and dug into her desk drawers until she unearthed a stingy pad of recycled paper and an ancient pencil. "Write it down, and keep it and any transcribed discs from your notes in a secure location until you're cleared to air."

Nadine made a few testing squiggles with the pencil. "Let's see how much of that shorthand my mother made me learn is still in my head. Go."

It took an hour, then Nadine flew out of the office to lock herself in at Channel 75 to write the story.

It would explode, Eve knew, even when the initial pieces she cleared hit the airwaves. It deserved to explode. Innocent lives taken or ruined in the name of what? Global security? The sexiness of espionage?

It didn't matter, not when those lives, those innocent lives, looked to her.

Eve finished up most of the grunt work she'd once dumped on Peabody. She had to admit, having an aide the last year or so had come in handy.

Not that she'd gotten spoiled, she assured herself.

She could, of course, pull rank, and continue to dump most of the grunt work on Peabody. And really, it was a learning experience. In the long run, she'd be doing Peabody a favor.

She checked the time and decided to close up shop for the day. She could get considerably more work done at home. With the remaining cookies safe in her jacket pocket, she headed out.

She squeezed into an overburdened elevator, which reminded her why she rarely left at change of shifts. Before the door closed, a hand shot through, yanking it open again to a chorus of groans and nasty curses from the occupants.

"Always room for one more." Detective Baxter elbowed his way on. "You never call, you never write," he said to Eve.

"If you can leave on the dot of COS, you must not have enough paperwork."

"I got a trainee." He flashed his grin. "Trueheart likes paperwork, and it's good for him."

Since she'd had the same thoughts about Peabody, it was hard to argue.

"We got a manual strangulation, Upper East Side," he told her. "Corpse had enough money to choke a herd of wild horses."

"Do horses come in herds or packs?"

"I don't know, but I think herds. Anyway, she had a miserable disposition, a mile-wide mean streak, and a dozen heirs who are all glad to see her dead. I'm letting Trueheart act as primary."

"He ready for it?"

"It's a good time to find out. I'm staying close. I told him I thought the butler did it, and he just nodded, all serious, and said he'd do a probability. Christ, he's a sweet kid."

Cops popped out like corks on every level. There was almost breathable air by the time the elevator reached the garage.

"Heard you had to spring the prime suspect on the double homicide. That's gotta sting."

"It only stings if she did it." She paused by Baxter's shiny sports car. "How do you afford this ride?"

"It's not about afford, it's about the deft juggling of numbers." He looked over to where her pitiful police issue sat dolefully in its slot. "Me, I wouldn't be caught driving that heap if I was wearing a toe tag. You've got rank enough to pull better."

"Maintenance and Requisitions both hate me. Besides, it gets me where I'm going."

"But not in style." He slid into his car, gunned the engine so it roared like a mad bull, then, with another wide grin, zoomed off.

"What is it about guys and cars?" she wondered. "I just don't get how their dicks are attached to cars."

With a shake of her head, she started across the garage.

"Lieutenant Dallas."

Instinctively, her hand slipped inside her jacket and onto the butt of her weapon. She held it there as she pivoted, and studied the man who stepped out from between parked cars.

"This garage facility is NYPSD property, for authorized personnel only."

"Quinn Sparrow, Assistant Director, Data Resources, HSO." He held up his right hand. "I'm going to reach, with my off hand, for my identification."

"Reach slow, AD Sparrow."

He did, drawing out the flip case with two fingers. He held it up, waiting for her to approach. Eve studied the ID, then his face.

He looked young for any real juice in the HSO, but then she had no idea how early they recruited. He might've been forty, she supposed, but calculated he was missing a few years from that date. But he wasn't green. His calm demeanor told her he'd had some seasoning.

His body had the compact, ready look under its black, government employee suit that made her think boxer or ballplayer. His voice had no discernible accent, and he waited, without movement or word, until she'd finished summing him up.

"What do you want, Sparrow?"

"I'm told you want a conversation. Why don't we have one. My car's beside yours."

She glanced over at the black sedan. "I don't think so. Let's take a walk instead."

"No problem." He started to dip a hand in his right pocket. She had her weapon out and at his throat. She heard him suck in air, let it out. She saw the quick flicker of surprise and alarm on his face before it settled into passive lines again.

"Keep your hands where I can see them."

"That's no problem either." He held them out, and up. "You're jumpy, Lieutenant."

"I've got reason, Assistant Director. Let's walk." Rather than holstering her weapon, she slid it inside her jacket as they walked toward the garage exit. "What makes you think I want a conversation?"

"Reva Ewing spoke with a mutual contact in the Secret Service. Given the current situation, I was assigned to come over from the New York base and speak with you."

"What's your function?"

"Data cruncher, primarily. Administrative area."

"You knew Bissel?"

"Not personally, no."

She turned, moved briskly down the sidewalk. "I assume this conversation is being recorded."

He gave her a very easy, very pleasant smile. "Is there something you don't want on record?"

"I bet there's a lot you don't." She swung into a bar and grill, largely patronized by cops. Because it was change of shift, it was packed with them. Eve moved to a high-top where two detectives from her division were sharing beer and shoptalk.

"I got a meet here." She dug out credits, laid them down. "Do me a favor and let me have the table. Beer's on me."

There was some grumbling, but the credits were scooped up, and the detectives moved off. Eve chose a stool that kept her back to the wall.

"Felicity Kade recruited Blair Bissel for the HSO," Eve began.

"How did you come by that information?"

"Subsequently," she went on, "he functioned as a data liaison—data's your territory, right?—transporting same to and from sources, and using his profession as a cover. Was he ordered to marry Reva Ewing, or was that his own suggestion?"

Sparrow's face had gone to stone. "I'm not authorized to discuss—"

"Then just listen. He and Kade targeted Ewing due to her contacts with government officials, and her position in the private sector at Securecomp. She was, without her knowledge, injected with an internal observation device—"

"You're going to wait a minute." He laid a hand on the table. "You're going to wait a damn minute. Your data's incorrect, and if you put this sort of skewed information in your reports, it's going to cause trouble for you. I want your source."

"You're not getting my source, and my data is on the mark. The device was removed from Ewing today. You're finished using her. You shouldn't have set her up on my watch, Sparrow. You want to take out a couple of your own, that's your business, but you don't set up civilians to take the fall for murder."

"We didn't set her up."

"Is that the company line?"

"There was no hit ordered or sanctioned by the HSO."

"You lied when you said you didn't know Blair Bissel. You're the AD, you damn well knew him."

Sparrow's gaze never flickered, and Eve decided she'd been right about the seasoning. "I said I didn't know him personally. I didn't say I didn't know him professionally."

"Being slippery, Sparrow, isn't making me like you any better."

"Look, Lieutenant, I'm doing my job here. The incident involving him and Kade is being investigated, internally. It's believed that the hit was carried out by a cell of the Doomsday Group."

"And why would a group of techno-terrorists bother to build a frame around Ewing?"

"It's being investigated. This is a global security matter, Lieutenant." His voice was very low now, and very cold. "The termination of two operatives is an HSO matter. You're required to step back."

"I'm required to do my job. Another of Bissel's side dishes is dead. This one was a twenty-one-year-old girl, still wet enough behind the ears to believe in true love."

His jaw clenched, visibly. "We're aware of the disposal. We—"

"Disposal? Fuck you, Sparrow."

"It didn't come from us."

"You know everything that goes on inside your organization?"

He opened his mouth, then seemed to check whatever he was going to say. "I've been thoroughly briefed on these matters. This conversation is a courtesy, due to Ewing's exemplary service to her country, and the desire of HSO to cooperate, as much as possible, with local authorities. However, it's only a courtesy. There are details of these matters you are not cleared to know. The charges against Ewing have been dropped."

"And that smooths it all out? You think you can look and listen and sit back, playing with people, nudging them around like pawns in a chess game?"

She recognized the pressure on her chest, knew she'd need to gulp for air if she let it take over. If she let herself think about that room in Dallas.

So she blocked it out, slammed it down, and thought of a young woman in a frilly bedroom with a purple stuffed bear and a pink rosebud.

"A few get broken along the way, well, that's a shame. Chloe McCoy is dead. You got a way to smooth that out?"

His tone never changed. "It's being investigated, Lieutenant. It will be resolved. Responsible parties will be dealt with as appropriate. You need to back off."

"The way you people backed off in Dallas?" It was out before she could stop it. "The way you sat on your asses gathering intel no matter what the cost to the innocent."

"I don't know what you're talking about. Dallas isn't a factor in this matter."

"You look like a smart guy, Assistant Director Sparrow. Look it up, put it together." She slid off the stool. "And hear this: I don't back off. Ewing's not only going to be sprung, she's going to be publically exonerated, with or without your cooperation. And whoever killed Chloe McCoy will be dealt with, as the *law* deems appropriate, not your gang of spooks."

She didn't shout, but neither did she trouble to keep her voice low. A few heads turned—and, she knew, more than a few cops' ears tuned in.

"This time there's going to be payment. You and your listening posts put that into your data banks and analyze it. You approach me again, be ready to deal. Or we have nothing to say."

She strode out of the bar. Her breath was starting to come too fast, and her head was going light. She had to bear down. She wasn't going to think about what had been done to her, but about what she was going to do.

There would be payment, she promised herself. She couldn't get it for the battered, terrified child in Dallas, she would do everything in her power to ensure Roarke didn't, but she would, she damn well would get it for Reva Ewing and Chloe McCoy.

She ignored the tension at the base of her skull as she drove out of the garage. She resigned herself to the iron grip of it as she battled traffic.

Ad blimps blasted out their evening siren song of SALES, SALES, SALES. Fall blowout in EVERY store at The Sky Mall. One hundred lucky customers would receive an In-Touch palm 'link ABSOLUTELY FREE. While supplies lasted.

The noise of it rolled down over her, punctuated by the whispering clack of traffic copter blades, horns blasting against the pollution codes.

The tension began to sneak its way up, squeeze around her temples. When the headache kicked in full, she knew it would be a bitch.

All through the noise of New York, the throb of its violent heart, she heard the cool, composed voice of Sparrow speaking of disposal.

We are not disposable, she told herself when her hands gripped the wheel like iron. No matter how many bodies she'd stood over, no matter how many she'd ordered bagged, none of them, none of them, *none* of them were disposable.

She punched through the open gates of home, and prayed for ten minutes of silence, for ten minutes without the noise screaming in her head.

She rushed into the house, hoping to circumvent her nightly confrontation with Summerset, and was halfway up the stairs when she heard her name called.

She looked around and saw Mavis at the bottom of the stairs.

"Hey. Didn't know you were here." Absently, she rubbed at the ache in her temple. "I was bolting, hoping to miss my nightly treat of Ugly Guy."

"I told Summerset I wanted a few minutes. You look like you're pretty busy, and tired. It's probably a bad time."

"No, that's okay." A dose of Mavis was a better cure than any blocker.

Just one more reminder of who she was, Eve thought. Of who she was now.

She assumed Mavis was in a conservative mood, as she was wearing nothing that glowed. The fact was, she didn't know the last time she'd seen Mavis in something as ordinary as jeans and a T-shirt. Even if the T-shirt stopped a couple inches above the waist and was covered with red and yellow fringe, it was pretty tame on the Mavis Freestone scale of fashion.

Her hair was quietly brown, with only one red and yellow tuft poofed at the crown to liven it up.

She looked a little pale, Eve noticed as she started down, then realized Mavis was wearing no lip dye or eye enhancements.

"You been to church or something?" Eve asked.

"No."

With a frown, Eve took another survey. "Wow, you're sort of starting to poke out. I haven't seen you in a couple of weeks, and—"

She broke off in horror when Mavis burst into tears.

"Oh shit. Oh damn. What did I say? Am I not supposed to say you're poking out?" Frantic, she patted Mavis's shoulder. "I thought you wanted to poke out with the baby and all. Oh boy."

"I don't know what's wrong with me. I don't know what to do."

"Is something wrong with the . . . thing? The baby?"

"No. Nothing's wrong. Everything's wrong," she wailed. "Nothing. Everything. Dallas." On a pathetic sob, she threw herself into Eve's arms. "I'm so scared."

"We should call a doctor." She looked desperately around the foyer as if a medic would magically appear. In her panic, she actually wished, fiercely, for Summerset. "Or something."

"No, no, no, no, no." Mavis wept on Eve's shoulder in great, gulping sobs. "I don't need a doctor."

"Sitting down's good. You should sit down." Lie down? Eve wondered. Be sedated? Oh, help me. "Maybe I should see if Roarke's back yet."

"I don't want Roarke. I don't want a man. I want you."

"Okay, okay." She eased Mavis onto a couch, tried not to be freaked when her friend all but crawled into her lap. "You've got me. Um . . . I was thinking about you today."

"You were?"

"I had lunch at the Blue Squirrel, and . . . Oh, Mother of God," she muttered when Mavis's sobs increased. "Give me a hint, give me a clue. I don't know what to do if I don't know what's going on."

"I'm so scared."

"I got that part. Why? Of what? Is somebody bothering you? You got a crazed fan or something?"

"No, the fans are great." Her shoulders shook as she burrowed into Eve.

"Ah . . . you and Leonardo have a fight?"

Now her head shook. "No. He's the most wonderful man in the world. The most perfect human being in the universe. I don't deserve him."

"Oh, that's just crap."

"It's not crap. I don't." Mavis jerked back, turned her tear-ravaged face up to Eve's. "I'm stupid."

"No, you're not. It's stupid to say you're stupid."

"I never even finished school. I ran away when I was fourteen, and I wasn't even worth looking for."

"If your parents were stupid, Mavis, it doesn't mean you are."

If mine were monsters, it doesn't mean I am.

"What was I when you busted me? On the grift. That's all I knew, cons—short cons, long cons, lifting wallets, or playing the beard for some other grifter."

"Look at you now. You've got the most perfect human being in the universe crazy about you, you've got a mag career, and this baby thing going. Oh God, oh God, please don't cry like that anymore," she begged when Mavis dissolved again.

"I don't know anything."

"Yeah, you do. You know . . . stuff. Music stuff." Such as it was. "Fashion stuff. And you know about people. Maybe you learned it on the grift, Mavis, but you know about people. How to make them feel good about themselves."

"Dallas." Mavis swiped her hands over her face. "I don't know anything about babies."

"Oh. Ah . . . but you're listening to all those discs, right? And didn't you say you were going to go to some class about it? Something?"

Not my area, she thought frantically. *Definitely out of my orbit*. Why the hell had she sent Peabody to Jamaica?

"What good's any of that?" Exhausted from the crying jag, Mavis flopped back, resting her head on the pillows on the end of the couch. "All that's just how to feed a baby, or change one, or pick them up so you don't break them. Like that. How to *do* things. They can't tell you how to *know*, how to *feel*. They can't tell you how to be a mom, Dallas. I don't know how to do it."

"Maybe it just comes to you. You know, when you finally push it out, it just happens. And you know."

"I'm scared I'm going to mess it up. That I'm not going to be able to do it right. Leonardo's so happy and excited. He wants this so much."

"Mavis, if you don't—"

"I do. I want it more than anything in the world and beyond. That's what's so scary. Dallas, I don't think I could stand it if I messed this up. If I have this baby and I don't feel what I'm supposed to, don't know what it needs—the real needs, not the food and the diapers. How will I know how to love it when nobody ever loved me?"

"I love you, Mavis."

Mavis's eyes filled again. "I know you do. And Leonardo. But it's not the same. This . . ." She laid a hand on her belly. "It's supposed to be different. I know it is, but I just don't know *how*. I guess I panicked," she said on a long sigh. "I couldn't talk about it to Leonardo. I just needed you."

She reached for Eve's hand. "Some stuff you can only tell your best pal. I'm better now. Probably just hormones weirding me out."

"You're the first real friend I ever had," Eve said slowly. "You had it stuck in your head to get close to me, and I just couldn't shake you off. Before I knew it, there we were. We've seen each other through some rough spots."

"Yeah." Mavis sniffed, and the first hint of a watery smile touched her lips. "We have."

"And because you're my first real friend, I'd tell you if you were stupid. I'd tell you if I thought you'd make a crappy mother. I'd tell you if I thought you were making a mistake having the baby."

"You would? Really?" Mavis clutched Eve's hand, stared hard at her face. "Swear to God?"

"Swear to God."

"That makes me feel better. It really does." She let out a long, shaky breath. "Oh boy, it really does. Could I hang for a while? Maybe call Leonardo and tell him to— Oh God. Oh my God."

Eve popped up as Mavis's teary eyes went wide, as she sat straight up, pressing a hand to her belly. "What? Are you going to get sick or something?"

"It moved. I felt it move."

"What moved?"

"The baby." She looked up at Eve, and now her face glowed, as if someone had flicked a switch under her skin. "My baby moved. Like . . . like little wings fluttering."

Eve felt her own color drain, right down to the bone. "Is it supposed to do that?"

"Uh-huh. My baby moved, Dallas. Inside me. It's really real."

"Maybe it's trying to tell you not to worry so much."

"Yeah." Mavis wiped away fresh tears and smiled beautifully through them. "We're going to be fine. Better than best. I'm glad you were here when it happened. When I felt it. I'm glad it was just you and me and the baby, this one time. I'm not going to screw it up."

"No, you're not."

"And I'll know what to do."

"Mavis." Eve sat beside her again. "Looks to me like you already do."

Chapter 12

Roarke walked into the house and saw Eve sitting on the steps, head in hands. Alarm twisted through his belly as he hurried to her.

"What's wrong? What's happened?"

She blew out a huge breath that hitched on the end. "Mavis."

"Ah, God. Is it the baby?"

"It's all about the baby. At least I think. What do I know? She wasn't even wearing lip dye. What was I supposed to do?"

"I think we'd better start over. I'll go first. Is everything all right with Mavis and the baby?"

"It must be. It moved."

"Where?" He caught himself, cast his gaze to heaven. "Now you've got me turned around. She felt the baby move, then? Isn't that a good thing?"

"She thought so, so it must be."

She sat back, looked at him. He was holding her hand still, studying her face. Waiting.

All so normal, unless you felt, as she felt, that subtle change of rhythm. Things weren't normal between them right now, and maybe they'd never be again. But they were both willing to pretend otherwise.

The pretense that there was nothing hanging over them was oddly terrifying.

But if it was all she had, she was as willing to hide behind it as he was.

"She was all down and teary when I got back," Eve continued. "Figured she'd mess up with the kid because she was messed up as a kid, or something. Afraid she wouldn't know what to do or how to feel. Had herself a serious weep."

"I've heard that's fairly normal for pregnant women. The weeping. I imagine she's a bit scared. It must be considerably scary if you think about the whole process."

"Well, I don't want to think about it, that's for sure."

He'd let go of her hand, and he'd shifted, just the slightest bit away from her. So she knew he felt it, too.

She called herself a coward, but she pushed it out of her mind.

"Anyway, she calmed down mostly, then the baby did whatever it did in there and she got all happy again. She was practically doing handsprings when she left to go tell Leonardo."

"Well, then, why are you sitting here looking miserable?"

"She's coming back."

"That's good. I'd like to see her."

"She's bringing Trina." Eve's voice rose nearly an octave as she gripped Roarke's shirt. "And their instruments of torture."

"I see."

"You *don't*. They don't gang up on you and come at you with strange, sharp implements or goop unknown substances all over your face and body. I don't know what they're going to do to me, and whatever it is, I don't want it."

"It's hardly as bad as all that, but you could actually have used work as an excuse and put all this off for a while."

"I couldn't fight her." She dropped her head back in her hands. "She had me with that naked face, how often do you see Mavis with a naked face?"

He touched her hair, the lightest stroke. "Never."

"Exactly. And her eyes are all puffy and red—and shiny. And her belly's poking out. This little white lump sticking out. What was I supposed to do?"

"Exactly what you did." He shifted to kiss the top of her head. "You're a good friend."

"I'd rather be a bitch. It's easier, and more satisfying emotionally, to be a bitch."

"And you're so good at it. Well, this should be a fine time for me to fire up that barbecue grill again."

"I can't believe you'd kick me when I'm down."

"I've a handle on it now. I've been practicing on the side. We'll have burgers. They're the simplest."

She could've told him she'd had a burger for lunch, but that would have put too glossy a shine on what she'd swallowed at the Blue Squirrel.

"I just want to work," she complained. But it was for form. It might do them, do everything some good, to have people around. Making noise, taking up energy.

Keeping the illusion all was normal, in place.

"I just want to spend a regular evening working through the insidious and murderous plots of the HSO and foreign technoterrorists. Is that too much to ask?"

"Of course not, but life will intrude. Would you like me to tell you how Feeney and I did in Queens?"

"Shit. *Shit!*" She threw out her hands and nearly caught Roarke on the chin with a fist. "See? This has got me so messed up I didn't even remember what's going on with my own case. Where's Feeney?"

"He stayed back in Queens to supervise the removal of some of the sculptures. They're being impounded. You were dead-on about the bugs."

Look how you watch me, he thought. *Trying to see inside my head, to read what's there. So we won't have to talk about it again.*

What are we going to do about this? he wondered.

"We found six sculptures—three out and three in—that were bugged." He smiled. He couldn't make it reach his eyes, but he smiled. "Very sexy technology, too, from the looks of it. It'll be fun to take one of the devices apart for analysis once we hack it out of the metal."

"Eyes or ears?"

"Both. From preliminary study, using a satellite bounce. No question whoever was watching and listening knows we've found them."

"Good." She pushed to her feet. "If Bissel was spying on his own wife for the HSO, they already know we're making moves. I had a meet with an assistant director today."

"Did you?" He said it very softly, very coolly, and sent a chill up her spine.

"Yeah. And if Bissel turned and was working with the other side, though I don't see a hell of a lot of differences between sides here, they'll be scrambling. I'm going to handle it," she said, and let the pretense drop, for a moment. "I'm going to handle it."

"No doubt. I don't intend to tell you how to handle it," he added, very carefully. "Can you say the same?"

"It isn't the same. It—" She pulled back, like a woman who felt herself sliding over a cliff. "Let's just table that. Concentrate on what is."

"Happy to. What is?"

"The investigation. We should take this upstairs, fill each other in."

"All right." He touched her face, then leaned in, brushed his lips over hers. "We'll do what's most normal for us, for now. Go up and talk about murder, then have a meal with friends. That suit you?"

"Yeah, it does." She made the effort, kissed him back. Then got to her feet. She rolled her shoulders. "This is better. Briefing and a burger. Keeps my mind off Trina and her scary bag of tricks."

Because he wanted her to smile, needed her to, he walked his fingers up her arm as they started upstairs. "What flavor skin cream do you suppose Trina will put on you?"

"Shut up. Just shut up."

* * *

"This," McNab said as he took in a gulp of tropical air, "is living."

"We're not living. We're investigating. There'll be no living until we've completed the investigative purpose of this trip."

He cocked his head, studied her from behind his fuchsia-tinted sunshades. "You sounded just like Dallas. I find that strangely arousing."

She elbow-jabbed him, but didn't put much behind it. "We're going straight to Waves and interview Diesel Moore regarding Carter Bissel. We'll go by Bissel's residence, speak to any neighbors or associates."

"Now you sound bossy." He gave her butt, currently covered in thin summer pants, a friendly pat. "I like that, too."

"You've got a grade on me, but I'm Homicide." And boy, did she *love* saying that. "So I'm in charge of this hunting party. And I say first we do the job, then we . . . live."

"I hear that. Still, we gotta rent transpo."

He slid his gaze to a line of scooters chained outside a hut beside their hotel. They were as colorful and bright as a circus parade, and screamed tourist.

Peabody grinned. "And I hear that."

Waves was a hole-in-the-wall joint screwed into a clapboard building on one of Kingston's less welcoming streets. They'd gotten lost twice—or had pretended to get lost as they'd scooted along narrow streets with the island breeze fluttering over their urban cheeks. After some heated debate, they'd agreed that he'd drive to, and she'd drive from. Peabody found it just as much fun to ride pinion with her arms clutched around his waist as it would've been to man the controls.

But as they made their way into the poorer and less hospitable section of the city, she was glad she had her weapon strapped under her summer-weight jacket.

She saw three illegal transactions in a two-block radius, and spotted a pair of funky-junkies jittering together on a stoop. When a flash all-terrain sportster cruised by, and the driver aimed his dark, dangerous eyes at her, she almost wished she was wearing her uniform.

Instead, she aimed hers right back, and deliberately, visibly, laid her hand on her weapon.

"Nasty vibes," she said into McNab's ear as the car gunned and slid off down a side street.

"Oh yeah. Penalties for illegals are stiff as a teenager's dick down here, but nobody seems to care in this sector."

There were sex shops and clubs, and the street LCs who sold the same commodity. But none of them looked particularly alluring. She could hear music pumping out of a few doorways, but the exotic charm of it was lost in the bored and repetitive come-ons of the hookers and the front men.

Tourists might wander in here, she thought, but unless they were looking for sex, illegals, or a blade in the back, they'd hurry out again quick.

They parked the scooter in front of the mean little bar, and while McNab used the chain the rental agent had provided to lock it to a lamppost, Peabody looked around.

"I'm going to try something," she said. "You might have to back me up."

She selected the two young men, one black, one white, sitting on a stoop and smoking Christ knew what out of a black pipe they passed between them. Gearing herself up, she put on her coldest cop face and swaggered up to them. And ignored McNab's hiss of warning from behind her.

"See that scooter?"

The black man smirked, took a long slow drag on the pipe. "Got eyes, bitch."

"Yeah, looks like you've got a pair each." She shifted her weight, used her elbow to ease the jacket back so her badge and weapon peeked out. "If you want to keep them in your skulls, you'll keep them on that scooter. Because if I come back out and it isn't where I left it, in the same condition I left it, my associate and I are going to hunt you down like sick dogs. While he's shoving that pipe up your ass," she said, showing her teeth to the white guy, "I'm going to pop your fellow asshole's eyes out. With my thumbs."

The white guy bared his own teeth. "Hey, fuck you."

Her stomach jittered, a little, but she kept the fierce and

toothy expression in place. "Now, if you talk like that you're not going to earn the nice prize I have for you at the end of our contest. The scooter's there, untouched, when I come back out, I don't haul your ugly asses into a cage for possession and use, and I give you a nice shiny ten credits."

"Five now, five later."

She shifted her gaze to the black. "None now, and none later unless I'm happy with you. Hey, McNab, what happens when I'm not happy?"

"I can't talk about it. Gives me nightmares."

"Do yourselves a favor," Peabody suggested. "Earn the ten."

She turned, sauntered toward the bar. "I've got sweat running down my spine," she said out of the corner of her mouth.

"Doesn't show. You even scared me."

"Dallas would've gotten in their faces more, but I thought that was pretty good."

"Frigid, babe." He yanked open the door, and they were hit by a blast of cold air that smelled of smoke, liquor, and humans who didn't have a working arrangement with soap and water.

It wasn't yet sundown and business was sluggish. Still there were pockets of patrons, such as they were, huddled at tables or slumped at the bar. On a narrow platform that stood as a stage, a malfunctioning holographic band played bad reggae. The image of the steel drummer kept winking out, and the looping was just a hair off so that the singer's lips moved out of synch, reminding McNab of the really poorly dubbed vids his cousin Sheila got such a charge out of.

His toeless airsneaks made little sucking sounds as he crossed the sticky floor.

Moore was manning the bar. He looked a little thinner and a lot more harassed than he had in the ID photo they'd studied. He wore his hair in dreadlocks, a kind of explosion of horsey black tails McNab admired. They suited the mahogany cast of his face, the diamond point of his chin.

There was a necklace of what looked like bird bones

around his neck, and his skin was glossy with sweat despite the chilly pump of air.

His eyes, an angry black, skimmed over Peabody and McNab as if they were one unit. He shoved a muddy-looking brown brew into the waiting hands of a customer, then used a dingy bar rag to wipe at his shiny chest exposed by a snug electric-blue tank.

He stepped down the bar, and curled his tattooed lip. "I'm paid up for the month, so if you've come in here to shake me down for another *deposit* go fuck yourselves."

Peabody opened her mouth, but McNab set his foot over hers to keep her quiet. "We're not local badges. The locals got a Survivor's Fund going here, we're not in that mix. Fact is, we'll be happy to make a contribution to your personal fund if you have information that merits it."

Peabody had never heard that cool and faintly bored tone out of McNab before.

"Cop offers to give me money, he usually finds a way to skin me for it."

McNab took a twenty out of his pocket, palmed it on the bar while keeping his attention on Moore. "In good faith."

The money was exchanged, slick as a magic trick. "What're you paying for?"

"Information," McNab repeated. "Carter Bissel."

"Asshole son of a bitch." Somebody hammered a fist on the far end of the bar and called for some goddamn service. "Shut the fuck up," Moore shouted back. "You find that goddamn Carter, I want a shot at him. He owes me two large, not to mention the ass pain I've had running this place solo since he decided to go on fucking holiday."

"How long did you run the place together?" Peabody asked him.

"Long enough. Look, we had some previous business, you could call it shipping. Decided we'd go into this little enterprise here, and each anted up the rent. Carter, he's got a good head for business in that asshole brain of his. We did okay. Maybe he'd go on a bender time to time. Guy likes his rum and his Zoner, and you run a place like this you can get 'em. Couple days off and on maybe he'd be no-show. I'm not his fucking mother, so what? He takes off, next time I take off. Works out."

"But this time," Peabody prompted.

"This time he's just gone." Moore pulled a bottle from under the counter, poured something brown and thick into a short glass, then downed it. "Took two thousand from the operating expenses, which damn near wiped them for the month."

"No warning?"

"Shit. He talks about a big score. Big score and living high, maybe getting us a class place. Carter, he's full of that crap. Always going to score big, and ain't never gonna 'cause he's small-time. Enough rum, he'd really get rolling on it, and how his brother got all the luck."

"You ever meet his brother?" Peabody asked.

"Nope. Figured he was making it up till I saw this scrapbook deal Carter kept at his place. Full of media reports and some shit on his brother, the artist."

"He kept a scrapbook on his brother."

"Yeah, loaded with shit. Don't know why 'cause the way he talked, Carter hated the son of a bitch just for being."

"Did he ever talk about going to New York to see him?"

"Shit. Carter, he talked about going everywhere to see everybody. Just talk."

"Did you ever hear him mention Felicity Kade?"

"Mmm. Slick blonde." Moore licked his lips. "She's some number. She came around a couple of times."

"No offense," Peabody said pleasantly, "but this doesn't look like the sort of place a woman like that would spend much time."

"You never know what's going on with a fancy piece like that. Why I steer clear of them. Come in one night and made a play for Carter. Didn't have to play very hard. Didn't get the nitty-gritty out of him. Usually, he'll brag on the women he bags. Likes to think he's king in the sack. But with this one, he buttoned up. Slylike." Moore shrugged. "No big to me. I get my own action."

"She spend much time with Carter?"

"How the hell do I know? She come in a couple of times. They went out together. Sometimes he'd take a couple of days. If you're thinking he went off with that piece of work, your aim's off. No way she'd take him for more than the quick ride."

"Did he have any other business, any other women, something along those lines that he might've gone off with?"

"Been through all this with the locals. He banged women when he could get them. Didn't shack with any for long. If he had any side jobs, he didn't let me in. In or not, likely I'd've heard. It's a small island."

"Small island," Peabody agreed after they'd finished with Moore. "Not many places to hide."

"Not many ways to get off either. You got air, you got water."

She stepped out, saw with pleasure the scooter was in place, and apparently untouched. "Pay those guys off."

"Why do I have to pay them?"

"I lined them up."

McNab grumbled, but he flipped them a ten before unchaining the scooter.

"You handled that business about the shakedown really smooth." She wanted to pinch his butt in appreciation, but decided it wouldn't look professional. So it would wait. Instead, she climbed on the scooter. "Just as glad we're getting out of this sector before dark."

"You and me both, She-Body." Apparently he wasn't as concerned with professional image as she was 'cause he pinched her butt as he slid on behind her. "Let's ride."

Carter Bissel lived in a two-room shack that was hardly more than a tent pitched on a mix of sand and crushed shells. It had what Peabody considered a very slight appeal due to its proximity to the beach, but that same proximity made it a handy target for tropical storms.

She could see where patches had been slapped on, just as she could see from the sagging rope hammock that Carter had preferred to spend his free time swinging rather than worrying overmuch about household maintenance.

Scraggly tufts of beach grass poked up through the shells. An ancient and thoroughly rusted scooter was chained to a dead palm.

"A long way from Queens," McNab commented as he kicked a broken bottle aside. "He might have beat his brother out on the view, but the rest of the living conditions put him way back on the sib rivalry chart."

"When you look at this, you can see that he might just walk away." Peabody took out the key they'd picked up from the local PD. "Everything we're seeing spells out loser."

"It doesn't spell out what Felicity Kade wanted down here."

"I've been thinking about that. Maybe they wanted to use him for a setup. It's not the kind of place you'd expect an HSO branch office or a terrorist cell. And that could've been just the point."

She unlocked the door, creaked it open. Inside, the air was stale and hot. She saw an enormous bug scurry into the shadows and had to bite back a squeal. She was no particular fan of anything that skittered or slithered.

She tried the lights, found them inoperable. Both she and McNab drew out penlights.

"I've got a better idea. Hold on a minute."

She struggled not to cringe when he left her alone. She could almost hear the spiders spinning. She shined her light over the living area.

There was a single couch. One cushion had exploded and left a kind of gray mushroom of filler growing up from the torn fabric. There were no rugs, no art, a lone unshaded lamp on a crate that served as a table. But the entertainment screen was new, top of the line, and, she noted after a quick scan, bolted to the floor.

Not the most trusting of men, she decided. In addition to being a slob and a loser.

The kitchen was along one wall of the living quarters. A counter cluttered with take-out boxes and a blender, a cheap AutoChef and a grimy minifridgie. She'd just opened the fridgie to peruse the contents of homebrew, a withered fuzzy tube that might have once been a pickle, and a golfball-sized lime when McNab puttered in on the scooter.

The headlight beamed brightly.

"Good thinking," she decided. "Strange but good." She opened the lone cupboard and found three glasses, two plates, and an opened bag of soy chips.

"You know, his financials weren't stellar, but he had enough to live better than this." She turned around as McNab poked under the cushions of the couch. "And you can bet not all his money was reported."

"Probably couldn't hold on to it. Slippery fingers. Spent it on women and illegals." He held up a small bag of white powder he'd pulled out of the damaged cushion.

"How'd the locals miss that?"

"Didn't care enough to look. My question is why'd he leave it behind?"

"Because he left in a hurry and planned to come back . . . or he didn't leave voluntarily." She started toward the bedroom. "Bring the scooter."

The bed was unmade. But the sheets, Peabody noted, were prime quality. They matched the entertainment unit more than the rest of the house. The skinny closet held three shirts, two pair of trousers, and one bunged-up pair of gel-sandals. The dresser held four pair of boxers, a dozen T-shirts or tanks, five pair of shorts.

There was a 'link, but it had been turned off. The data unit sat on the floor and looked as if it had been through several wars. She left McNab to fiddle with it while she searched the tiny bathroom.

"No toothbrush, but there's a half tube of toothpaste," she called out. "No hairbrush or comb, but there's shampoo. There's another set of sheets—whoa, baby, very smelly sheets—stuffed in the hamper in here, along with a moldy towel."

She stepped back out. "Looks to me like he packed up a few essentials, and before he did, he had company. Female company who earned the fresh, fancy sheets."

"What're you doing?" McNab asked absently.

"We're taking the sheets in for testing. He put them on, but the bed's not made. That tells me they got used. That says sex, so maybe there's some DNA."

He grunted and continued to work with the computer.

"I'll tell you what else isn't here, besides his toothbrush and comb. There's no scrapbook on his brother. That's interesting."

"So's this." He scooted around until he faced her, with the headlight from the scooter shining on his face. "It's really interesting that this unit is fried. That it appears to have been infected with the same worm as the ones in New York."

In New York, Eve paced Roarke's locked-down office with her secured 'link on privacy mode as she listened to Peabody's report. It was, she supposed, still possible for someone to copy the transmission even through the lockdown, even through the layers of security, but it would take time and effort.

"I'm going to pull strings, and pull them hard with the locals," she told Peabody. "And get you cleared to transport any and all items from that location that you deem applicable to this investigation. It may take a few hours, but I'm going to see to it that you and those items are on a transport in the morning. Sit tight. I'll be back to you."

She broke transmission, then paced a moment longer as she calculated how best to start the wheels turning.

"If I may suggest," Roarke put in. "I could have a private shuttle bring them back, circumventing any of the red tape with the local police."

She frowned, but considered it. "No. I don't want to circumvent. It'll take a little more time this way, but we'll keep it clean. When this comes out, and I'm going to make damn sure it does, I want our end to sparkle. I'll start by playing diplomat with the local chief, and if that doesn't work, I'll toss him to

Whitney. But it should work. What do they care if we haul off a busted data center and some sheets?"

"Then I'll leave you to it and go back to our company. Some grilled meat should set you up for the ordeal yet to come."

"Don't remind me. I don't like the way Trina was eyeballing me."

He lifted the lockdown and left her alone. Once she'd reestablished it, she sat down at his workstation. She could stay here all night, she mused. Locked in, nice and safe, away from hair products. There was access to food, to drink, to communications. It would be so . . . soothing to hunker down and work alone again.

Then she thought of Mavis, who'd bounced in twenty minutes before with a beaming Leonardo.

At times like this, Eve decided, alone was nothing but a fond and distant memory.

She engaged the 'link and prepared to grease the wheels.

Chapter 13

Eve considered it strength of character not to keep the room sealed, with her inside. But she braced herself, went downstairs, then wound her way through the house to the back patio.

And stared at the scene.

She knew her scenes. Normally, there would've been a corpse somewhere in the vicinity, but she still knew how to read a scene where death wasn't part of the landscape.

There was a bird singing a two-note repetitive chirp that was both cheery and insistent. Butterflies with wings of bold orange and black massed like a fanciful army on the purple spires of a bush that fountained just beyond the west corner of the stone patio.

Roarke's newest toy, an enormous silver monstrosity on wheels, was smoking away, with the man himself at the helm with a long-handled spatula. The smoke smelled like meat—real meat from real cows. Several individuals were currently chowing down on it in the form of thick burgers on buns.

They were seated at tables or standing around chatting, in full party mode.

The city's medical examiner was swigging beer from the

bottle and having what appeared to be an amusing conversation with Mavis. Mira—and where the hell had *she* come from—was seated at a table scattered with food and flickering candles while she held some sort of confab with Leonardo and the terrifying Trina.

The captain of EDD stood munching a burger one-handed and giving Roarke advice on the mysteries and mystiques of outdoor cooking.

Everyone seemed pretty damn jolly and well-fed, and to Eve's mind out of place. Hadn't she just left a sealed room where she'd spent considerable time picking her way through red tape and the land mines of diplomacy and palm greasing? Wasn't she in the messy middle of a murder investigation involving covert organizations and state secrets?

Now it was burgers and beer in the twilight with birds and butterflies.

Her life, she decided, was just plain strange.

Leonardo spotted her first, and with a wide grin splitting his big caramel-colored face, glided over to her in what Eve supposed was his casual cookout-wear of shimmery white pants and a bright yellow shirt that crossed over his impressive chest in a skin-tight X. He bent down, his soft, curling hair brushing her cheek just before his lips.

"Mavis told me she'd been upset, and came to you. I wanted to thank you for being there for her, for giving her this time tonight to feel normal and steady again."

"She just needed to spew."

"I know." Then he wrapped his big arms around Eve, pressing her hard against the rock wall of his chest. This time when he spoke, his voice was thick and shaky. "The baby moved."

"Yeah." She wasn't quite sure what response was called for, and gingerly patted him somewhere on the miles of exposed skin of his back. "She said. So, ah, everything's good now."

"Everything's perfect." He heaved a sigh. "Perfect." He drew back, and his gold eyes were gleaming. "Good friends, the woman I love with our child inside her. Life is so precious. I realize that now more than ever before. I know Dr. Mira needs to speak with you, but I just wanted to have a moment first."

Drawing her close to his side he all but carried her to the table where Mira sat.

"Now don't start." He wagged a finger at Trina. "Dallas needs to speak with Dr. Mira, and to have a moment to relax."

"I can bide my time." Trina grinned, a wide magenta smile that sent a chill up Eve's spine. "I have plans. Lots of plans." She scooped up her plate and wandered off on six-inch platform sandals.

"Oh my God."

With a look caught between sympathy and amusement, Mira patted the chair beside her. "Sit. What a gorgeous evening. I'm stealing an hour of it to be here, on what was supposed to be a quick professional call. Now I'm having this lovely glass of wine and this rather magnificent hamburger."

"Did he actually cook it?" Eve glanced back at Roarke. "On that thing?"

"He did. I'm probably telling tales out of school, but he talked to my Dennis at some length about how to use the grill." Mira took another bite. "He seems to have figured it out."

"Nothing much gets over on Roarke. A professional call?" she prompted.

"Yes. I could've waited until tomorrow, but I thought you'd like to know as soon as possible that Reva Ewing passed her level three."

"Thanks. How's she doing?"

"A little shaky and tired. Her mother took her straight home. I think she's in good hands there."

"Yeah, Caro's another who always seems to know what she's doing."

"She's afraid for her daughter, Eve. However efficient and steady she is on the surface, under it, she's desperately worried. I could speak with her, or Roarke could. I'm sure he will.

But the fact is you're the one in authority. And you're the one whose thoughts and opinions she'd respect most in this."

"Did you come by to tell me about the level three, or to tell me I should talk to Caro?"

"Both." Mira patted her hand. "Also, I looked over the results of her blood tests taken just after she was taken into custody."

"There was nothing. No chemicals, illegal or otherwise. And the medicals found no trauma to indicate she'd been physically knocked out."

"No." Mira picked up her wine. "But we both know there are some anesthetics that can debilitate quickly, and dissipate without a discernible trace within two or three hours."

"The sort of thing Homeland would have in its pantry."

"I imagine so. When I had Reva under, I took her back through the steps and stages of that night. She recalled a movement to her left as she was facing the bed. She doesn't remember this, not clearly, except under hypnosis. A movement," Mira went on, "then a scent, something strong, bitter, and the taste of it in the back of her throat."

"Probably sprayed her." Eve looked over the gardens, but she wasn't seeing the busy butterflies now, or hearing the insistent bird. She saw the candlelit bedroom, the bodies curled close together on bloody sheets. "Waited for her to come up, came in on her on her off-side, hit her with the spray. Set the rest of it up while she was out."

"If so, it was organized thinking. Cold and organized. And still . . . much of what was done was overly dramatic—beyond the violence that shows the capability for brutality, there were added steps, complications that were unnecessary for the result we're assuming was desired."

"Because he was having fun with it."

"Yes." Pleased, Mira enjoyed her hamburger. "He was. Several misjudgments and flourishes—when simplicity would have served his purposes better—indicate to me that he gets caught up in the role he's playing. Enjoying it, and perhaps wanting to prolong it."

"Adding touches to a pretty tight and simple plan that unbalance the whole. What do they call it? Ad-libbing."

"Very well put. You have organized thinking but impulsiveness as well. I doubt he was working alone. I also doubt that the one who conceived the core of the plan was the one to carry it out. Now I'm going to pass you to Morris so you can get the business over with and enjoy some of your evening."

"It's a little tough to enjoy anything when I know Trina has *plans*." But Eve rose, walked over to Morris. "Got something for me?"

"Dallas!" Mavis popped up. "Did you know Morris played the sax?"

"The what?"

"Saxophone," Morris said. "Tenor. It's a musical instrument, Lieutenant."

"I know what a saxophone is," she muttered.

"He used to play with a band in college," Mavis went on. "And sometimes they still get together for private gigs. They're The Cadavers."

"Of course they are."

"We're going to jam sometime, right?" Mavis asked Morris.

"Name the time, name the place."

"Too mag to lag!" she danced off and into Leonardo's arms.

"That's a very happy young woman."

"You wouldn't've thought so if you'd seen her two hours ago."

"Gestating ladies tend to swing. They're entitled. Want a beer?"

"What the hell." She snagged one from the cooler. "What've you got for me?"

"Nothing as wonderful as this cow patty. Chloe McCoy. No evidence of recent sexual activity. But . . . it would appear she'd expected some as she'd inserted protection. An over-the-counter product called Freedom. This coats the vaginal area with both spermicide and a lubricant, which protect against STDs and conception."

"Yeah, I know what it is. You can use it up to twenty-four hours before you rock. When did she use it?"

"My best guess? An hour, possibly two premortem. And she'd also ingested fifty milligrams of Sober-Up at approximately the same time."

"Well now, isn't that interesting?"

To show their unity on that point, he tapped his bottle of beer against hers. "At least one hour before she ingested the termination pills. And if those were purchased on the black market, someone has a very valuable source. They weren't generic or clones or homemade. And, the kicker: They were dissolved in the wine before they were ingested."

"So she protects herself against pregnancy or STD, sobers herself up, cleans her apartment, gets herself a sexy outfit, and does her face and hair. Then drops a couple of fatals in her wine and offs herself." Eve took a long pull on the beer. "And you said you didn't bring me anything as interesting as that burger."

"You haven't tasted the burger yet."

"I'll get to it. What's the ruling on this matter by the Chief Medical Examiner of New York City?"

"Homicide, staged to look like self-termination. That girl didn't knowingly eat those pills."

"No, she didn't." And that made Chloe McCoy hers. "Termination pills require a prescription—after considerable testing and counseling. If she didn't get them that way, and she didn't, and they weren't black market, would you say that a strong possible source for meds of that type and potency would be a covert government organization?"

"I wouldn't say no."

"Neither would I." She pondered for a few minutes. "There's something I'd like you to check out."

When she was finished with Morris, Eve headed over to the grill. "I've got some new juice," she said to Feeney, then found a plate shoved into her hand.

"Take a minute. There's always time for meat."

The scent of the burger had saliva pooling in her mouth. "A

lot of new juice, Feeney. ME's ruling homicide on McCoy, and I've got the gears oiled in Jamaica so Peabody and McNab can haul the evidence back here. Mira says—"

"Go ahead." Roarke lifted the burger off her plate and to her mouth. "Take a bite. You know you want to."

"This isn't the time for a family picnic."

"Think of it as a combination family and company event."

"You gotta eat, Dallas," Feeney told her. "That's primo cow. You don't wanna waste it."

"Fine. *Fine.*" She bit in. "Mira says—okay, this is really good, and I see absolutely no reason I can't sit down and eat this while I brief you."

"Just let me set this on auto, and you can brief both of us."

She moved to a table, and sitting, gripped the burger in both hands. Even as she took another bite, Roarke was dumping some sort of grilled vegetables on her plate.

"To balance it out," he told her.

"Whatever." If he wanted to play as if everything was dandy between them, she could get on board. There was enough inside her head without marriage weirdness. "Okay, here's how I think it went down, and I need EDD to dig into McCoy's links and verify. Whoever took her out contacted her. She's happy and excited enough to take some Sober-Up to counteract the wine she's been guzzling with her neighbor. She uses birth control. She fixes up the place, and herself."

"Sounds like someone expecting a hot date, not a girl getting ready to pop termination pills." Feeney shook his head. "She's been rolling with Blair Bissel, and Bissel's dead. You figure she had another guy dangling?"

"Possible. More possible that whoever contacted her made her think one of several options. That he had news on Bissel—the whole thing was a mistake, a cover-up, maybe an operation. He's going to bring Bissel to her place, for hiding out until it's safe. Or he made her think he was Bissel."

"That'd be a trick."

"Not if you're the man's brother. You got a strong resemblance, and you could augment that. You've been jealous of the bastard all your life, and here's your chance to get some young stuff on his back."

Feeney contemplated the beer he'd brought to the table. "That's a good one. Damn good one. Had to contact her, though, if she had time to prep herself. We'll go deep on the 'links, and put her unit in the mix. If he used e-mail, it's going to be a bitch to find."

"That's your deal. I'm looking at Carter Bissel. He knows what big bro's been up to. He's had a side deal going with his trainer. Blair's working with Kade, and sleeping with her. She knows about McCoy, and about whatever Bissel gave her that was secreted in the locket. There's a reason that was taken from the scene. McCoy's a loose thread, and she has to be snipped."

"I said it's good, but why not just go in and snip?" Feeney questioned. "Why the big show?"

"Same deal as Ewing. Lots of bells and whistles, lots of show and smoke. He likes to improvise. He's having fun with this. And maybe because the need for cover seemed to warrant it, maybe for the drama. Maybe both."

"Follows." Feeney nodded at Roarke. "I did a good job with her."

"You did, yes. She's cop to the bone."

"Let's try to stick with the point." But Eve took a healthy and satisfying bite of burger. "Either way, it's the same MO under the surface. Kill, and go to considerable lengths to make it seem like what it's not. Hang the murder on somebody else. Ewing in the first case, McCoy herself in the second."

"Plays well," Roarke agreed. "When her killer arrived, however, wouldn't she question or object if Bissel wasn't along?"

"He gets inside. Tells her they have to be careful. They need her help. The more theatrical the story, the quicker she'd buy it and go along. All he has to do is talk her into starting a note. Hell, she might've written it herself beforehand, just a dramatic sort of touch. He slips the meds into her wine. After she drinks it, all he has to do is lay her out, then walk away.

"Or"—Eve ate a grilled pepper without thinking about it—"the HSO could've staged the whole thing. Gotten in, disabled her. But that doesn't explain the BC, or the Sober-Up. Whoever killed her didn't know she'd used either. He's not as smart as he thinks he is."

Roarke remembered the young woman clinging tearfully to Eve's shins in the gallery. It fit. It was just sad enough to fit. "You're heading back to Bissel's brother."

"Yeah, I'm liking the looks of him. He's been MIA for almost a month. Plenty of time to have a little face work done, make himself look more like his brother." She polished off her burger, took another drink of beer. "But there's one more possibility, a little out there, but interesting."

"Blair Bissel killed her," Roarke put in.

"You're pretty quick for a guy who grills burgers in his spare time."

"Smoke's gotten to you two," Feeney said. "Bissel's in a cold drawer at the morgue."

"It looks that way. It probably is that way," Eve agreed. "But let's take this into spy vid territory for a minute—which Reva said was one of his hobbies—and which we know was his profession. What if Bissel was playing both sides? Or he was doing a double agent thing with, or without, HSO sanction. They find out Kade's turned, or he's just pissed she's playing with his brother. He sets them up, knocks them down, and handily frames his wife, who he's done with. He snips McCoy and gets back whatever she was holding for him in the locket."

"You don't think somebody as sharp as Morris would see the body didn't match the ID photo? Even with the couple of bashes in the face, there's dental. There's fingerprints. There's fricking DNA. All of it matches Blair Bissel's."

"Yeah, and he's probably on ice. I said it was out there, and Carter Bissel heads my list. Morris is going to run a scan and see if he had any recent facial surgery. And because, if this is true, it would be another thread, I need you to hit IRCCA, find me a recently deceased face fixer. I'm betting Carter Bissel had work done—either to play Cain or to be tricked into playing Abel. One of the Bissel brothers is alive. We just need to figure out which."

Eve told herself not to think about what was being done to her. Otherwise, she might scream like a girl. Her hair was plastered to her head with a thick pink goop. A new product according to Trina, guaranteed to add luster, body, and bring out the natural highlights.

None of which, to Eve's mind, mattered.

Her face and throat were slathered with something green, and sealed with some sort of spray. Before that, her skin had been buffed and scrubbed, examined and critiqued. And not just the skin on her face and throat, Eve thought, still inwardly shuddering, but every inch that covered her body. From the throat down she'd been painted yellow, then sealed with the same spray before having her mortified body wrapped in a heat sheet.

At least she was covered. Small blessings.

She'd quietly turned off the VR goggles Trina had programmed when Trina had given the delighted Mavis her full attention. Eve didn't want the mindless nature sounds or the soft, swimming colors of the relaxation program.

She might have been naked on a padded table and covered from head to feet in goo. But she was still a cop, and she wanted to think like one.

Back to the victims. It was always back to the victims.

Bissel, Kade, McCoy, with Bissel as the focal point. Who or what stood to gain from their deaths?

The HSO. During the early days of the Urban Wars, the government had formed the arm as a way to protect the country, to police the streets and gather intel covertly from radical factions.

It had done the job. It had been necessary. And over the years since, some said it had morphed into something closer to a legalized terrorist group than a protection and intel operation.

She happened to agree.

So, the murders could have been a cleanup operation. If

Bissel and Kade had turned, and McCoy unwittingly knew too much, all three might have been terminated to protect some global security project. The Code Red was the obvious linchpin. The data units had been corrupted. What data needed to be eliminated? Or was the use of the worm simply a ploy to point toward the techno-terrorists?

The Doomsday Group. Assassinations, terminations, large- and small-scale destruction and loss of life through technological sabotage were their reasons for being. Kade and Bissel could have been playing both ends, or on assignment to infiltrate. They could have been targeted by the terrorists, taken out, and McCoy treated as collateral damage.

But then why weren't they taking credit? Media play with a lot of bloody fist-pumping and skewed messages were a big part of the program for any terrorist group. There'd been enough time for an acknowledgment to have been leaked to the mainstream press.

In either case, why the frame on Ewing? Why—if either organization for reasons of its own wanted to keep the lid on the terminations—go to so much time and trouble to implicate Reva Ewing?

To slow, hamper, or eliminate her work on the extermination program, and utilize whatever data Bissel had gathered from his devices to create one first, in the HSO's case, or to reformulate the worm to override the extermination, in Doomsday's case.

Possible, and she wouldn't close those doors. She'd run probabilities and give them a push.

But with either of those scenarios she still had Carter Bissel floating around like a goddamn dust mote. Had Kade recruited him with or without HSO sanction? With or without Blair Bissel's knowledge?

And where the hell was he?

She tried to bring a picture of him into her mind, but it was blurry and kept dissolving in all the melting colors that swirled lazily in her brain.

She'd stopped hearing Mavis's and Trina's birdlike chatter at the edge of her focus, so there was only the gentle *whoosh,* like a heartbeat inside a womb.

Even as she realized the relaxation program had been reactivated, she sank under it.

In Roarke's home computer lab, Feeney sat back at his station and pressed the heels of his hands hard against his aching eyes.

"You ought to take something for that eye-strain headache," Roarke commented. "Before it blows on you."

"Yeah, yeah." Feeney puffed air into his cheeks, let it out. "Don't do as much geek work as I used to." He studied the unit currently laid out in sections and small bits over his counter. "Got spoiled handing this sort of detail over to one of my young guns."

He glanced over at Roarke's station and was somewhat mollified to see the civilian's progress was as slow and exacting as his own. "You got an estimate on when we might have one of these up and running again—working like this, just the two of us?"

"I figure sometime in the next decade if we're lucky, into the fourth millennium if we're not. This bitch is toasted." Roarke shoved back, scowled at the burned-out guts of his current project. "We can replace, repair, reconfigure, and beat it with a hammer. We'll retrieve data. I'm annoyed enough at the moment to make it my bloody life's work. But Christ knows we could do it all faster and easier with a few more hands and brain cells. McNab's good. He's got the hands and the geek quotient to keep him at something like this for hours on end, but he won't be enough."

They sat in brooding silence for a moment, then eyed each other.

"You talk to her," Roarke said.

"Oh no, I'm not married to her."

"I'm not a cop."

"It's your setup here."

"It's an NYPSD investigation."

"Like that means a damn to you. Okay, okay." Feeney waved a hand before Roarke could speak again. "Let's settle this like men."

"Want to arm wrestle?"

Feeney let out a snort, then dug into his pocket. "We'll flip a coin. You call it."

Eve heard what sounded like flutes. For a moment she saw herself running naked through a flower-strewn meadow where small, winged creatures played long, reedlike instruments. Birds sang, the sun shone, and the sky was a perfect bowl of cerulean blue.

She woke with a start and said: "Gak."

"Wow, Dallas, you were really out."

Blinking, Eve focused on the figure spread out on the table beside her. She thought it was Mavis. It sounded like Mavis, but it was tough to make a positive ID when the form was covered with hot pink from shoulders to toes, the face coated with electric blue, and the hair plastered down with a mix of green, red, and purple.

She'd have said *gak* again, but it seemed redundant.

"You didn't drool or anything," Mavis assured her. "In case you were worried."

"Let out a couple of sex moans." Trina's voice came from somewhere near her feet, and Eve froze.

"What are you doing?"

"My job. You're all rinsed off. Blissed right through that part. Got your derma revitalizer rubbed in. Your man's going to like this one. Going to finish up with your hair and face after I do your feet."

"Do what to my feet?" Gingerly, Eve boosted herself on her elbows and looked down. "Oh my God! God almighty! You painted my toes."

"Just a delux ped. It's not a satanic ritual."

"My toes are *pink*."

"Yeah, I went conservative with you. Sun-kissed Coral. Nice with your skin tone. Your feet were a disgrace," Trina added as she sprayed on sealer. "Good thing you were under VR while I was working on them."

"How come she's not under?" Eve demanded, pointing at Mavis.

"I get more out of it if I'm aware of the treatments. I like getting souped and rubbed and scrubbed down and painted. It's the ult of ults for me. You hate it."

"Mavis. If you know I hate it, why do you make me *do* this?"

Mavis smiled an electric-blue smile. " 'Cause it's fun."

Eve lifted a hand to rub her face, then gaped in shock as she saw her nails. "You painted my fingers. People will see them."

"Neutral French job." Trina walked back up, slid a finger over one of Eve's eyebrows. "Need trimming. You oughta chill, Dallas."

"Do you understand that I'm a cop? Do you understand that should I have to restrain a suspect and he gets a load of my shiny yet neutral French job, he's going to break his neck laughing? Then I'll be under IAB investigation for the death of a suspect at my hands."

"I know you're a cop." Trina showed her teeth in a smile. The left eyetooth was decorated with a tiny green stud. "That's why I threw in the little boob-tat gratis."

"Boob? Tattoo?" Eve sat up as if she'd been propelled out of a catapult. *"Tattoo?"*

"Just a temp. Came out really good."

She was almost too horrified to look. To counter the fear, she took a handful of Trina's glossy black hair, yanked her tormentor's head down. If necessary, she would beat that head against the padded table until unconsciousness ensued. Ignoring Trina's yelps and struggles, and Mavis's giggling calls for peace, Eve tipped down her chin and looked at her breast.

There on the curve of the left was a painted replica of her badge, minutely detailed though it was no bigger than her own thumbnail. Her grip loosened a bit as she tilted her own head to read her name. And Trina escaped.

"Jesus, are you whacked? I said it was a temp."

"Did you give me any hallucinogenic substance while I was under VR?"

"What?" Obviously steamed, Trina shook back her abused hair, folded her arms, and glowered at Mavis. "What is *wrong* with her? No, I didn't give you anything. I'm a certified personal body and style consultant. I don't have illegals on my menu. You ask me something like that, and—"

"I asked something like that because I'm looking at what you painted on a personal area of my body, and I kind of like it, so I want to make sure I'm not under some illusionary drug haze."

Trina sniffed, but there was a light that was both pleasure and humor in her eyes. "You like it, I can make it permanent."

"No." In defense, Eve slapped a hand on her breast. "No, no, no. No."

"Got it. Just the temp. Mavis has to cook awhile more, so we'll finish you up." Trina pressed a mechanism on the table and a section lifted up like the back of a chair.

"How come you've got all those colors in the gunk on your hair?"

"I'm getting multied," Mavis explained. "I'm going to have some red curls, and purple spikes, and—"

"There wasn't any of that in mine." Fear clutched at her throat. "Was there?"

"Relax." To get back some of her own, Trina yanked Eve's head back by the hair. "The pink streaks'll wash out."

"She's just kidding," Mavis said as Eve went pale. "Honest."

By the time it was over, Eve was limp as a noodle. The minute she was alone, she dashed into the nearest bathroom, shut the door, and braced herself for a look in the mirror.

Her knees went weak with relief when she saw there were no streaks of pink, or anything else, in her hair. Nor were her eyebrows the carnival of colors Mavis's had been when Trina finished with them.

She wasn't vain, Eve assured herself. She just wanted to look like she looked. There wasn't anything wrong with that. And since she did, the ball of tension between her shoulder blades dissolved.

Okay, maybe she looked a little better than usual. Trina did something to her eyebrows whenever she got her hands on them that made the arch more defined and framed out her eyes. And her skin had a nice glow to it.

She shook her head, pleased when her hair fell into place without any fuss.

Then her eyes widened in shock. She *was* vain, or edging perilously close to it. And it had to stop. Deliberately, she turned away from the mirror. She needed to get out of this stupid robe and into clothes. As soon as she did, she'd check on the lab.

Work, she assured herself, was the only thing worth being vain about.

Chapter 14

She'd barely nipped into the bedroom when Roarke stepped in from the elevator.

"I just need to change, then I was coming by the lab."

"Well, I need a minute to speak with you, and saw that Mavis and Trina had gone."

"What about?" She started rummaging through her dresser for old, comfortable sweats. It gave her something to do with her hands as she prayed it had nothing to do with a field operation in Dallas. "Did you guys have a breakthrough?"

"No. It's painstaking and exacting work. Slow and tedious. Feeney's taking an hour restorative. It's hell on the eyes."

"Okay." She could hardly complain about the break when she'd spent a good chunk of the evening flat on her back and covered with goo. "I'm not much help in the comp-jock area, but I've got some probabilities to run, some theories I want to play with. Mind's clear. I hate that."

"You hate that your mind's clear?"

"No." Her shoulders relaxed again. She was tuned to every nuance in his voice, and everything was all right. For now. "I hate that the stuff Trina does actually works—on the brain. I'm pumped," she said, hauling out a ragged and ancient short-sleeved sweatshirt she'd buried under a stack of silk and cashmere tees. "And I'm thinking . . . what're you looking at?"

"You. Darling Eve, you look—"

"Don't start." She waved the shirt at him and backed up two steps. Even that was a fake, she thought. It was such a tremendous relief to know he could look at her that way. To know, when he did, her blood warmed, her body tightened. "Don't even start."

"You've had a pedicure."

Instinctively, her toes curled in embarrassment. "She did it while I was under VR, and she won't tell me how to get it off."

"I like it. Sexy."

"What's sexy about pink toes? What could possibly be sexy about that? Wait, I forgot who I was talking to. If she'd painted my teeth pink, you'd think it was sexy."

"A fool in love," he murmured and stepped close enough to brush a thumb over her cheek. "Soft."

"Stop it." She slapped his hand away.

"And you smell . . . exotic," he said after easing closer for a testing sniff. "A bit tropical. Like a lemon grove in spring, with just a hint of . . . jasmine, I think. Night-blooming jasmine."

"Roarke. Down."

"Too late." He laughed and gripped her hips. "A man needs his restorative, you know. Why don't you be mine?"

She was his, but still she gave him a shove as his lips came down on hers. "I've already had my break."

"You're about to extend it. You taste incredible." His lips skimmed over her jaw, then under it, and his busy hands had already unbelted her robe, slipped beneath it. "Let's just see"—he tugged on her bottom lip—"what else Trina's been up to."

He eased the robe off her shoulders, skimmed his teeth over bare skin.

The little ball of lust that had curled in her belly expanded. She tipped her head to the side to give him better access. "I'm giving you twenty minutes, thirty tops, to get yourself under control."

"Thirty should give me just enough time to . . ." He trailed off as his gaze lowered to her breast. "Well now." His voice came out in a purr as he rubbed his thumb lightly over the replica of her badge. "What have we here?"

"One of Trina's little brainstorms. It's just a temp, and actually I got kind of a kick out of it after I got over the shock."

He said nothing, only continued to stroke and circle the image with his thumb.

"Roarke?"

"I'm amazed to find myself ridiculously aroused by this. How odd."

"You're kidding."

His gaze lifted to hers, and that hot blue slammed through her. "Okay." Nerves danced under her skin. Over it. "Not kidding."

"Lieutenant." He gripped her hips again, and hitched her up in one clean jerk until her legs wrapped his waist. "You'd best brace yourself."

There was no bracing against that kind of assault on the senses, that sort of brutal invasion of the system. Since the bed was too far away, he simply spilled them both onto the sofa and took her over with lips and hands.

She clamped around him. It seemed if she didn't hold on, hold tight, she might shoot out of her own body. Sensations crowded inside her, careening through blood and muscle and nerve until she was quivering, until she was coming in a screaming rush.

Staggered, she fought for air, then met, finally met, those hungry lips with her own. Partly in lust, partly in desperate relief that they were together, at least here, they were together, she tugged at his shirt. He wasn't the only one who wanted the taste and texture of flesh. His was hot, as if he burned from the inside out for her.

Her miracle.

"Let me." She fought with his belt. "Let me."

And they rolled off the sofa, hit the floor with a solid thud.

Her breathless laugh shimmered through him. God, he'd needed to hear her laugh.

He'd needed to hold her, and be held.

Her scent, her shape, her flavor all burned through the lines on his already straining control. He wanted to lap her like cream, to devour her like a feast after famine. He wanted to bury himself in her until the world ended.

If it was possible to love, to want, to need too much, he'd already passed the boundary with her. There was no going back. She shuddered under him, moved under him. Her hand reached out and closed over him, and took the hard length of him into the wet, wild heat of her.

Pleasure swamped him, drenched him, a saturation of mind and body as her hips plunged up, and he drove down.

He could watch her dark amber eyes that were blurry with arousal, and he could see her lips tremble an instant before her head arched back and the throaty moan escaped her.

Undone, he pressed his lips to the symbol of what she was, and felt the heart that thundered for him beneath it. His cop. His Eve. His miracle.

He gave himself over to it, surrendered himself to her.

Her pulse was nearly back to normal when he rolled so she was sprawled over his chest instead of pinned under his weight. From that vantage point, she folded her arms and propped her chin on them to study his face.

He certainly looked relaxed at the moment, she thought, all loose and satisfied, like a guy about to take a nice little nap.

"Pink toenails and boob tats. What is it with men?"

His lips curved, though he didn't yet open his eyes. "We're so easily played. Really, we're at the mercy of the female, with all her mysterious wiles."

"You're at the mercy of your glands."

"That as well." He sighed happily. "Praise God."

"So you really go for all that stuff? The potions and lotions and paints and all that?"

"Eve. Darling Eve." He opened his eyes now and stroked a hand over her hair. "I go for you. That should be obvious."

"But you get off on all the jazz."

"With or without the jazz." He scooted her up until he could brush his lips to hers. "You're my own."

Her lips twitched. "Your own what?"

"Everything."

"Slick talker," she murmured, and gave in to nuzzle him. "You're some slick talker. Just so you know, I'm not keeping the tattoo, even if it turns you into my sex slave. Just a few days, and that's it."

"Your body, your choices. But I can't say I'd want you to make it permanent. Something about the surprise of it certainly flicked a switch in me. A bit baffling, really."

"Maybe I'll surprise you every now and again."

"You always do."

She liked knowing that, and gave him a quick pat on the cheek before she rolled away. "Restorative period's over."

"There's no surprise in that."

"Get some clothes on, civilian, and report."

"I'm not entirely sure I used up my full thirty minutes. Someone was in a bit of a hurry."

She picked up his pants, threw them into his face. "Cover up that pretty ass of yours, pal. You said you needed to speak to me before you were overcome by my pink toenails. What about?"

"Before I get to that, I'd like to express the hope that you remain barefoot as much as possible the next several days. And moving on," he said with a laugh when she sent him a steely stare. "Feeney and I both agree we need more jocks in the lab. With just the two of us this restoration may take weeks at best."

"McNab will be back tomorrow."

"So that's three of us, except when at least one of us is pulled off for something else. If you want answers, Eve, you have to give us the tools to get them."

"Why isn't Feeney, as head of EDD, requesting this?"

"Because I lost the bloody flip, which wouldn't have happened if I'd gotten my hands on the coin long enough to switch it for one of my own. But he said—I believe this is a direct quote—'you don't get bit by the same dog twice.' Which is his colorful way of saying he's aware I've rigged a coin toss on him before."

"He's no easy mark."

"He's not, no. And neither of us is green when it comes to electronics, nor are we slackers. As much as it pains both of us to admit it, we need help. I've some in mind who—"

"If you're thinking Jamie Lingstrom, forget it. I'm not dragging a kid into an unstable situation like this."

"I wasn't. Jamie's in classes, and I'm set on his remaining there. I want Reva. She's already aware of the situation," he continued before Eve could speak. "She's one of the best, her clearance is top level, and she already knows what's going on."

"Because she's one of the elements. It's a tricky business to bring in one of the prime elements. To bring in another civilian."

"She won't have to be brought up to speed, which saves us all time. She has a personal investment so she'll work harder than anyone. She's not a suspect, Eve, but another kind of victim." He paused, and his tone was cooler when he continued. "Shouldn't a victim have a right to stand for herself, as much as to have someone stand for her, if the opportunity's there?"

"Maybe." They were veering toward it, toward that gulf with the jagged edges. She wanted to step back from it, and worse, pretend it wasn't there. But the gap was building even as she stood with her body still warm from him.

"Did you run this by Feeney?"

"I did. And circled the same ground you and I are dancing on now. Then I showed him her qualifications. He's anxious to work with her."

"You seduced him."

That made him smile, just a little. "That's a bit of an uncomfortable image for me. I prefer that I convinced him. Regarding Reva, and Tokimoto."

"Another of yours. Another civilian?"

"Yes, and there are several reasons for the choice. First, civilians with as high a security rating as these two are less likely to leak something to the media. Don't blow," he said, mildly, when she showed her teeth. "These choices would be less likely to leak than any others. Reva for obvious reasons, and Tokimoto because he's in love with her."

"Well, fucking A."

"She doesn't know it," Roarke continued without missing a beat. "And he may never move in that direction, but the facts are the facts. Due to his feelings for her, and his natural interest in the work, he'll put more energy and effort into it than most. Love does that sort of thing to you."

When she didn't respond to that, he turned to open a panel, and the minifridgie behind it. He took out a bottle of water. Opened it, sipped.

It wet his throat, but didn't cool the anger that was starting to build. "Aside from that, if you bring in cops, you have to do the paperwork, deal with the budget, clear them for this level of operation, and so on. I have a bigger budget than the NYPSD."

"You have a bigger budget than Greenland."

"Perhaps, but the point is I have a vested interest in solving this problem, and protecting my Code Red contract. I've quite a bit to lose if we don't find the answers with some expediency. Because of that, because of what was done to a friend of mine, because I know what the bloody hell I'm about in this area, I'm recommending we bring in the best people for the job."

"You don't have to get pissy about it."

"I feel pissy about it. About the whole shagging thing. I don't sit easy when people I care about are in this kind of turmoil, and it's fucking frustrating to be picking my way through the holy mess of those units working toward retrieval, and to be doing that, spending my time there instead of spending it finding out exactly who was responsible for what happened in Dallas."

A small, hard ball of ice dropped in her belly. And there it was, the big, glowing elephant in the room she'd hoped to ignore, and it was trumpeting. "That's what's under it, isn't it? All of it."

"Aye, that's under it and over it, it's around it and through it."

"I want you to put it away." Her voice stayed calm even as her belly clenched. "I want you to put it aside before you cross a line I can't ignore."

"I have my own lines, Lieutenant."

"That's right, that's right. Lieutenant." She picked up her badge that lay on the dresser, and slapped it down again. "Dallas, Lieutenant Eve, NYPSD. You can't stand there and talk about doing murder to a murder cop and expect me to ignore it and pretend it's nothing."

"I'm talking to my wife." He slammed the bottle down so water sloshed out and onto the glossy surface of the table. "A woman I vowed to cherish. There's no cherishing, there's no living with myself if I stand back and do bloody nothing. If I fold my hands while those responsible for what happened to you go on with their lives as if *that* was nothing."

"Their lives don't matter to me. Their deaths, at your hands, do."

"Goddamn it, Eve." He spun away from her and dragged on his shirt. "Don't ask me to be what I'm not. Don't ask it of me. I never ask it of you."

"No." She steadied herself. "No, you don't. You don't," she repeated, very quietly as that one point struck her as truth, inarguable truth. "So I can't talk about this. I can't think about it or fight about something we'll never come close to agreeing on. But you'd better think about it. And when you're thinking, you should remember I'm not a child like Marlena. And I'm not your mother."

He turned slowly, and his face was cold, and set. "I never mistake who you are, or who you're not."

"I don't need your kind of justice because I survived what happened to me, and made my own."

"And you cry in your sleep, and shake from the nightmares."

She was close to shaking now, but she wouldn't cry. Tears wouldn't help either of them. "What you're thinking about won't change that. Bring in whoever Feeney agrees to. I have to work."

"Wait." He walked to his own dresser, opened a drawer. He was angry, as she was, and wished he knew how they'd so seamlessly turned from intimacy to temper. He took out the small, framed photograph he'd placed there, then walked over to hand it to Eve.

She saw a pretty young woman with red hair and green eyes, healing bruises on her face, and a splint on the finger of a hand she held against the boy.

The gorgeous little boy with the Celtic blue eyes who had his cheek pressed against the woman's. Against his mother's.

Roarke and his mother.

"There was nothing I could do for her. If I'd known . . . I didn't, so that's that. She was dead before I was old enough to fix her face in my memory. I couldn't even give her that much."

"I know it hurts you."

"It isn't about that. They knew about him. The HSO, Interpol, all the global intel organizations. They knew about Patrick Roarke long before he traveled to Dallas to meet with Richard Troy. But she, the woman who birthed me, the woman he murdered and tossed away, didn't even merit a footnote in their files. She was nothing to them, as a small, helpless child in Dallas was nothing to them."

She hurt for him, for herself, and for a woman she'd never met. "You couldn't save her, and I'm sorry. You couldn't save me, and I'm not. I'm good at saving myself. I'm not going to argue with you about this because it doesn't fix anything. We've both got a lot of work to do."

She set the photo on his dresser. "You should leave this out. She was beautiful."

But when Eve left the room, he put the photo away. It was still too painful to look at those images for long.

They gave each other a wide berth, working in their separate areas late into the night. Sleeping, for once, with a sea of bed between them and neither attempting to bridge it. In the morning, they circled around the distance that had spread between them, carefully avoiding each other's territory, and cautious of their moves when that territory overlapped.

She knew Reva Ewing and Tokimoto were in the house, and was leaving them to Feeney while she bunkered in her office, waiting for Peabody and McNab to get in.

She could focus on the work at hand for long periods, running her probabilities, then sifting through data to create other scenarios. She could study her murder board and reconstruct the crimes, the motives, the methods from what evidence she had and begin to see a picture.

But she only had to shift that evidence to one side and a different picture formed.

And if her concentration wavered, even for an instant, there was yet another image. One of herself and Roarke on opposing sides of a bottomless chasm.

She hated that her personal life interfered with work. Hated more that she couldn't stop it from creeping into her thoughts when she needed to train them on the job.

And what was she upset about, really? she asked herself as she stalked back into the kitchen yet again for coffee. That Roarke wanted to hunt up and bloody some HSO agent she didn't even know? She was fighting with him, and just because they weren't yelling and slamming around didn't mean they weren't fighting still.

She'd figured out that much of the marriage game.

They were fighting because he had a rage like a trapped tiger about what had been done to her as a child. Layered over it, sharpening the claws and teeth of the trapped tiger was the rage over what had happened to his mother.

Brutality, violence, neglect. Christ knew they'd both lived with it and survived. Why couldn't they live with it still?

She shoved through the kitchen door to stand on the little terrace beyond, and just breathe.

And how did she live with it? The work—and, yes, sometimes she used the work until it dragged her down to exhaustion, even misery, but she needed what it gave her, through the process, through the results. Standing not just over the victim but for the victim, and working to find whatever balance the system allowed. Even hating the system from time to time when that balance didn't meet her own standards.

But you could respect something, even when you hated it.

The nightmares? Weren't they some sort of coping mechanism, an unconscious outlet for the fear, the pain, even the humiliation? Mira could probably give her a whole cargoload of fancy terms and psychiatric buzz on the subject. But at the base they were just triggers, for events she could stand to remember. Maybe a few she wasn't sure she could stand. But she coped.

God knew she coped better with Roarke there to pull her out of the sticky grip of them, to hold on to her, to remind her she was beyond them now.

But she didn't deal with what had been done to her by meeting brutality with more of the same. How could she wear her badge if she didn't believe, at the core, in the heart and soul of the law?

And he didn't.

She scooped a hand through her hair as she stared out over the riotous late-summer gardens: the full green trees, the sheen and sparkle of the world he'd built, his way. She'd known when she met him, when she'd fallen in love with him, when she married him, that he didn't, and never would, have the same in-the-bone beliefs as she had.

They were, on some elemental plane, opposite.

Two lost souls, he'd once said. So they were. But as much as they had in common, they would never meet smoothly on this one point.

Maybe it was that opposition, the pull and tug of it, that made what was between them so intense. That gave that terrible and terrifying love such power.

She could reach his heart—it was so open to her, so miraculously open. She could reach his grief, give a kind of comfort to him she hadn't known herself capable of. But she couldn't, and never would, fully reach his rage. That hard knot inside him he covered so skillfully with elegance and style.

Maybe she wasn't meant to. Maybe if she could reach in, take hold of that knot and loosen it, he wouldn't be the same man she loved.

But God, my God, what would she do if he killed a man over her? How could she survive that?

How could they?

Could she continue to hunt killers knowing she lived with

one? Because she was afraid of the answer, she didn't look too deeply. Instead she stepped back inside, filled her cup again.

She walked back into her office, stood in front of her board, and pushed her mind back into work. Her answer was an absent and faintly irritated "What?" when someone knocked on her door.

"Lieutenant. I'm sorry to disturb you."

"Oh. Caro." It threw her off to see Roarke's admin in her sharp black suit at her office door. "No problem. I didn't know you were here."

"I came in with Reva. I'm going into the midtown office, to work. I needed some details from Roarke on a project. Well, that doesn't matter." She lifted her hands in a rare flustered move, then dropped them again. "I wanted to speak to you before I left, if you have a moment."

"Sure. Okay. You want coffee or something?"

"No. Nothing, thank you. I . . . I'd like to close the door."

"Go ahead." She saw Caro's gaze go to the board, the stills of the murder scenes, the garish ones of the bodies. Deliberately, Eve moved to her desk and gestured to a chair that would put the images out of Caro's line of vision. "Have a seat."

"You look at this sort of thing all the time, I imagine." Caro made herself take a long look before she ordered her legs to move, and took the chair. "Do you get used to it?"

"Yes. And no. You look a little wobbly yet. Maybe you shouldn't be going back to work so soon."

"I need to work." Caro straightened her shoulders. "You'd understand."

"Yeah, I get that."

"As does Reva. I know getting back to what she does will help her state of mind. She's not herself. Neither am I. We're not sleeping well, but we pretend we are, for each other's sake. And this isn't at all what I came here to say. Rambling isn't like me either."

"Guess not. You always struck me as being hyperefficient. Have to be to handle Roarke's stuff. But if something like this didn't throw you off stride, I'd have to figure you for a droid."

"Just the right note." Caro nodded. "You know what note to take with victims and survivors, witnesses or suspects. You were brisk, even brusque with Reva. That's the sort of tone she responds best to when she's stressed. You're very intuitive, Lieutenant. You'd have to be . . . to handle Roarke."

"You'd think." Eve tried not to let the words that had passed between them the night before replay in her head. "What do you need, Caro?"

"Sorry. I know I'm taking up your time. I wanted to thank you for everything you've done, and are doing. I realize you look at variations of what's on that board every day. That you deal with victims and survivors, listen to statements and questions, and work toward finding the answers. It's what you do. But this is personal for me, so I wanted to tell you, to thank you, in a personal way."

"Then you're welcome in a personal way. I like you, Caro. I like your daughter. But if I didn't, I'd be doing the same thing I'm doing now."

"Yes, I know. But that fact doesn't change my gratitude. When Reva's father left us, I was devastated. My heart was broken, and my energies scattered. I was only a bit older than you," she added, "and it seemed the end of the world. I thought, 'What will I do? How will I get through this? How will I get my baby through it?' "

She stopped, shook her head. "And this isn't of any possible interest to you."

"No." Eve gestured Caro back down when she started to rise. "Finish it out. I am interested."

Caro sat again, sighed. "I will, then, as all this keeps running through my mind. I had, at that time, very few personal resources—some secretarial skills I'd let rust as I'd wanted to be a professional mother. There were debts, and though he'd incurred most of them, he was smarter and, well, meaner than I was."

"Must've been pretty smart, then."

"Thank you. I wasn't as . . . seasoned then as I am now. And he had better lawyers," she added with a ghost of a smile. "So I was in a pit, financially, emotionally, even physically as

I let myself become ill with the stress and grief. I was very, very frightened. But it was nothing—no more than a bump that leaves you momentarily off-balance—compared to this. Reva might've been killed."

Caro pressed a hand to her lips, visibly fought for control. "No one's said that, but it's there, the possibility of what might have been. Whoever did this thing might have killed her instead of using her to cover the tracks."

"She wasn't. Might-have-beens shouldn't scare you."

"You don't have children," Caro said with another, stronger smile, but her eyes were beginning to shine with the tears she was fighting off. "Might-have-beens are the monster in the closet for parents. She might have been killed, or she might be in prison waiting for trial if you weren't so very good at what you do. If you and Roarke hadn't been willing to help. I owe him a great deal. Now I owe him, and you, a great deal more."

"You figure he wants payback for pitching in for you and Reva?"

"No. He never does." She opened her purse, took out a tissue and dabbed at her cheeks. Every movement was economical. "It annoys him. And you, I imagine. You're so well-suited."

Eve felt her throat close, and only managed a shrug.

"I wondered if you would be. When you first came to the office, so fierce and tough. And cold. At least that's how I saw you. Then I saw him, after you'd gone. He was baffled and dazzled and frustrated. A rarity for Roarke."

"Really? Well, that made two of us."

"It's been an education watching the two of you find each other." She replaced the tissue, closed her neat black handbag. "He's an important part of my life. It's good to see him happy."

She didn't know what to say to that, so asked a question that was circling in her brain. "How did you come to work for him?"

"I took a secretarial position, entry level, and did drone work at an advertising agency here in New York. My skills weren't as rusty as I'd thought, and I'd scraped together the money for some classes to reacquaint myself with them. For the most part I was a gofer in one of the legal departments for a time. Then I was a revolving clerk, moving from department to department, filling in where and how I was needed."

"Getting a little bit of everything."

"Yes. It pleased me, and I thought of it as training. It was good work, and paid well. At a point, I suppose it's been about a dozen years ago now, Roarke took over the company where I worked, and the company—along with several others—moved into the midtown building."

Her voice was stronger now as she took herself back. Took some distance from the present.

"Shortly after, I was promoted to an assistant to an assistant in one of the project development arms of the company. A year or so into that, I was asked to sit in on a meeting—just to keep notes, fetch coffee, and look presentable as Roarke himself would be attending. The New York branch was quite young then. There was such energy, and most of it came from him."

"He's got more than his share," Eve added.

"He certainly does. During the meeting, one of the execs snapped at me when I didn't move fast enough to suit him, and I responded with something about his manners being as unattractive as his suit, or some such thing."

"So Reva gets her temper from you."

Caro let out a half-laugh. "I suppose she does. Roarke ignored the little altercation—or so I thought—and continued with the meeting. At some point he asked me to run the holo of the building he was designing, and later to bring up the data on something else. He had me hopping around, doing tasks that weren't in any particular domain, but those years of revolving had paid off. Still, once my annoyance with the exec was cleared, I was terrified I was going to be fired. The meeting lasted more than two hours, and it seemed like years. When it was over, all I wanted to do was find a corner and collapse. But he gestured to me. 'It's Caro, isn't it,' he said in that wonderful voice of his. 'Bring those files and come with me, would you?'

"Now I *knew* I was going to be fired, and I was frantic thinking of how I'd find another job, keep Reva in college, make the payments on the condo I'd bought three years before. He took me in his private elevator, and I was shaking inside, but I wasn't going to let him see it. I'd had enough humiliation from my ex-husband to last me a lifetime, so I wasn't going to let this young turk see how frightened I was."

"He knew," Eve commented, picturing it.

"Of course. He always knows. But at the time I was proud of my composure, and assumed it was about all I had left. He asked me what I thought of . . ." Her forehead creased. "I've forgotten his name. The exec who'd snapped at me in the meeting. I answered back, very crisply as I thought I was already heading out the door, did he mean personally or professionally, and he grinned at me."

She paused a moment, angled her head. "I hope you won't take offense if I add something here."

"Go ahead. I don't offend all that easy."

"I was old enough to be his mother, and when he looked down at me and grinned, I felt it in the pit of my belly. The power of his sexuality, in a situation that wasn't, in any way, sexual. I'm surprised I could form a coherent thought or word after the exposure."

"I get that, too."

"Undoubtedly you do. When he grinned at me and said he was interested in both my personal and professional opinion of this exec, I was just mortified and stunned enough by my own completely inappropriate reaction to tell him I thought the man was competent enough in his job, but on a personal level he was an ass.

"The next thing I know I'm in his office, and he's offering me coffee, and asking me to wait just a moment. He went to his desk and went to work while I sat there in complete confusion. I didn't know then that he'd pulled up my file, was checking my work evals, my security ratings."

"And very likely what you'd had for breakfast that morning."

"It wouldn't surprise me," Caro agreed. "Then he said, pleasantly, that he was looking for an administrative assistant who could think on her feet, who had good judgment of situations and people, and who wouldn't serve him a plate of bullshit when he wanted the truth. She'd have to be efficient, tireless, and loyal, as she'd answer only to him and there would be times he'd ask the . . . unusual. He continued on, outlining the job description, but I'm not sure I was hearing it all clearly. And he named a salary that made me very grateful I was sitting down. Then he asked me if I was interested in the position."

"Guess you were."

"I said, with heroic calm, that, yes, sir, I would be very interested in applying for the position. That I'd be happy to sit for an interview and any tests required. He said we'd just had the interview and I'd already passed the tests, so I might as well start now."

"He'd had his eye on you before."

"Apparently so. And because of it, I was able to finish raising my daughter in comfort, in security. And to discover myself. So I owe him a great deal. You've settled me down," Caro said with a sigh. "Just by taking me through all that. You've reminded me that you get through a crisis by doing what needs to be done next. So I'll leave you to do what you have to do next." She rose. "Thank you for taking the time."

"I figure Reva's got some of your spine. So she'll get through this and out the other side."

"I'm counting on that." Caro walked to the door, then turned. "This is a small thing, but I think it might please you, that it might be just a little something I can give back. A lot of busy people have their assistants or admins select gifts for their spouses. Birthdays, anniversaries, tokens to make up for an argument. He never does. Whatever he gives you comes from him. Perhaps that's not such a small thing after all."

Chapter 15

Peabody hustled in on lime-green high-tops. She no longer clopped, Eve noted, but sort of . . . *boinged.* It was just something else to get used to. She also had a big, toothy grin and a line of colorful little beads worked into her hair from crown to chin.

"Hey, Dallas. I gotta say, Jamaica rocks."

"You have beads in your hair."

"Yeah, I got this little braid." She tugged on it. "I can do that now. I'm not in uniform."

"But why would you? Never mind. Where are the units?"

"Detective McNab and I transported the units, personally, through customs and security and accompanied them directly here to the off-site lab for analysis and study. They were never out of our control. McNab is with the EDD team at this location now. I left him there to come report to you. Sir."

"No point in getting sulky because I ragged on your beads."

"Maybe I just won't give you your present."

"Why would you get me a present?"

"To commemorate my first out-of-town as detective." She dragged it out of her bag. "But you don't deserve it."

Eve stared at the little plastic palm tree with the little plastic naked man lounging under it. He held a tiny bowl-shaped glass filled with shimmering green liquid. Alcoholic in nature, no doubt, Eve concluded, from the goofy grin on his face.

"You're right. I don't deserve this."

"It's kitschy." Miffed, Peabody set it on Eve's desk. "And amusing. So there."

"Uh-huh. I'm going to bring you and the rest of the team up to speed momentarily. We'll have a short briefing that includes the civilians, then . . . Hold on," she said when her 'link beeped. "Dallas."

"We've got trouble."

From the tone of Morris's voice, and the grim look on his face, Eve knew the trouble was serious. "You at the morgue?"

"I'm at the morgue," he confirmed. "Bissel isn't."

"You lost the body?"

"Bodies aren't lost," he snapped, though he'd spent the last thirty-five minutes doing both a computerized and a personal search and scan. "And our guests rarely get up and take a walk to the corner deli for a bagel and schmear. Which means someone came in here and helped themselves to him."

"Okay." He sounded more insulted than angry. She was about to change that. "Lock the place down."

"Excuse me?"

"Lock it down, Morris. Nobody in, nobody out—living or dead—until I get there. And it's going to take me close to an hour."

"An hour to—"

"Seal off the room where the body was stored. Retrieve all security discs for the last twenty-four, and have any and all records of your work on Bissel copied for me. And I want to know everyone who had work or business in the dead zone since the last time you, personally, saw the body. Kade still there?"

"Yes, Kade's still here, damn it, Dallas."

"I'll be there as soon as I can." She cut him off. "Get the rest of the team," she told Peabody, then let out a curse of her own when her 'link beeped again. "Move." She snapped out the order and had Peabody hot-footing it to the door. "Dallas."

"Lieutenant." Whitney's face filled the screen and looked no cheerier than Morris's. "Report to the Tower for a meeting with the chief and Assistant Director Sparrow of the HSO. Nine hundred."

"It'll have to wait."

He blinked once, and his voice went to ice. "Lieutenant?"

"Sir, I'm about to brief my team. I'll keep it to the bones, but it has to be done. My presence is then required at the morgue. I've just spoken to Chief Medical Examiner Morris. Bissel's body is missing."

"Misplaced or gone?"

"I assume gone, sir. I've ordered a lockdown, seal, and retrieval. Detective Peabody and I will meet with Morris and evaluate within the hour. I believe this takes precedence over the Tower meeting. Homeland and Sparrow will just have to wait their turn to dance with me."

"I want the details, every last one of them, ASAP. The meeting will be rescheduled for eleven hundred. Be there, Lieutenant."

She didn't bother to respond as he'd cut her off as neatly as she'd cut off Morris. So she just scowled at the 'link and said, "Fuck."

Then she rose, turned the murder board face to the wall.

She got her first look at Tokimoto when he walked in beside Reva, and had to remind herself to trust Feeney and Roarke to pick their own people, even when she didn't know who the hell they were. She decided Reva looked sturdy enough, if a bit gaunt in the face, and that Roarke was off on the love vibes as Tokimoto didn't touch her, or so much as glance at her as they took seats.

"Captain Feeney will have briefed you on the electronics area," she began, "so I'm not going there except to say that I need data, any data, and I need it fast. Retrieval is first priority. The Code Red is now secondary."

"Lieutenant." Tokimoto spoke in his modulated voice, with

his interesting face carefully bland. "May I say that by its very nature a Code Red cannot be secondary. In order to retrieve the data, we have to know how it was corrupted. Learning how it was corrupted will lead us to prevention. It is all of a piece, you see."

"No, I don't, which is why I'm not EDD. You were brought in to assist in a homicide investigation. Since the units were corrupted, there was data on said units that concerned person or persons unknown who have killed at least three people. When I see the data, I'll know why this was of concern, therefore the data is my priority. Understood?"

"Yes. Of course."

"Good. The units that Detectives McNab and Peabody transported from Carter Bissel's residence are now in-house. Carter Bissel is missing. It must be assumed he is or was part of this. The extent of his involvement is yet to be determined."

"Blair rarely mentioned him, but if he did he talked about him as a screwup. I don't know if that helps at all," Reva said to Eve. "But he gave me the impression that Carter was an embarrassment to him more than anything else."

"As far as you know, when was the last time they communicated with each other?"

"I think about a year ago Carter might've contacted Blair and asked for money. I walked in while he was setting up an e-transfer and he said something about pissing away money on the monkey on his back named Carter. He was upset, and didn't want to talk about it, so I let it go. Looking back, I can see I let a lot of things go."

"Is that the term he used? Monkey on his back?"

"Yeah. He was upset, and pissed off. I remember being surprised he'd lend Carter money, and said so. He shut down the machine and yelled at me that it was his money, his business, and slammed out. Since it was, and I didn't see the point in having a fight about some jerk I'd never met, I let it pass."

"Interesting. Roarke, squeeze out some time and find me whatever private and secret accounts Blair Bissel may have had. I'd like to see how often he fed the monkey." She paused, scanned the room. "It will have been explained to the civilian members of this team that any and all information learned or imparted during this investigation is not to be discussed with anyone on the outside. Friends, neighbors, lovers, media, or the family pets. I'm going to reiterate that and add that if any information is passed, it will be considered an obstruction of justice. If there's a leak, the leak will be plugged, prosecuted, and will spend some quality time in a cage. I don't have time to play nice," she added, reading Roarke's mind. "These may be your people, but they're not mine."

"I don't believe anyone in this room could mistake your stand on that," he said. "Lieutenant."

"If anyone's offended by that," she said evenly, "that's the breaks. I don't think Chloe McCoy's too concerned about sensibilities and tender feelings just now. On another level, Bissel, working on his own or in conjunction with the HSO, inserted spy devices into his artwork. We know these devices were in place in various locations in the home he shared with Reva Ewing, and must assume the purpose was to gather intel on projects she was involved in for Securecomp."

She watched Reva as she spoke, saw her jaw tremble, then firm.

"We'll need the records of sales so we can track the locations of his other sculptures. They'll have to be scanned. When that happens, this is going to blow out of the water. You're going to get wet, Reva, by association."

"I can handle it."

"Surely as someone who was victimized, and so intimately, by this very plot, Ewing can't be blamed for the actions of a man who used and deceived her."

Reva offered the irate Tokimoto a weak smile. "Sure I can. It's the way of the world."

"Some of that backlash may come sooner than later," Eve continued. "Bissel's body is missing."

She watched, watched carefully. Reva's face went blank as if she'd just heard a phrase in an unknown language. Beside her, Tokimoto jerked in his chair, then reached out without looking and closed his hand directly over Reva's.

So, Eve surmised, Roarke was right again. She should never bet against the house.

"I don't understand what you mean." Reva spoke carefully. "I don't think I understand."

"I've spoken with the ME, who informed me that Bissel's body is no longer in the morgue. We'll proceed on the assumption that it was removed."

"But . . . why would anyone take . . ." Reva's hand came up, rubbed at her throat as if pushing the words out of a clog. "I just can't follow this."

"It's my job to follow it. Can you verify your whereabouts last night?"

"You're cruel," Tokimoto said softly.

"I'm thorough. Reva?"

"Yes. Yes. Um. We had dinner in. My mother and I. We watched screen. Her idea, all comedies. We ate popcorn, drank wine. I had a lot of wine." She sighed. "We sat up until about one. I fell asleep on the couch. I woke up about four. She'd covered me up. I just rolled over and went back to sleep. Best sleep I've had in days."

"All right. I need the civilians to go back to the lab." She looked directly at Roarke. "I'd like a complete progress report by fourteen hundred."

"Yes, I'm sure you would." He walked to Reva, offered her a hand to bring her to her feet. "Would you like some air first, or a moment to yourself?"

"No. No, I'm fine. Let's get to work. Let's just get to work."

Eve waited until Roarke shut the door, after one last cool look at her.

"Wow." McNab gave a mock shudder. "Chilled down in here."

"Button it, moron," Peabody said under her breath. "Sorry, Lieutenant, the five hundred tiny little braids have cut off the circulation to his brain."

"Hey."

"Let's move on. I've run numerous probabilities, none of which has been satisfactory or particularly enlightening. It all depends on how I input the data. But what it comes down to is we don't yet know what we're dealing with. Covert operations, a rogue agent, family violence. What we do know is we have three murders, one missing body, a connection in Jamaica.

"Chloe McCoy was killed for what she knew or had in her possession. The autopsy confirmed that she had inserted birth control. She was expecting a lover. The only lover who has come to light is Blair Bissel."

"Who's dead, and among the missing," Feeney put in.

"There's little doubt she *believed* she was expecting Blair Bissel. This was a naive, theatrical, and gullible young woman. Play it right and she would've believed her lover had risen from the dead and was coming over to play—to tell her all, to seek her help, to ride off into the sunset with her. The killer had only to gain access to her apartment, keep her calm, induce her to drink the drugged wine. I'm Blair's friend, associate, brother. He asked me to explain everything to you. He'll be here as soon as it's safe."

"She'd have let him in," Peabody agreed. "She'd have loved the excitement of it."

"She certainly would have let him in if it was Blair Bissel."

McNab stifled a snort. "Risen from the dead."

"He wouldn't have to, if he'd never died at all. If he'd set it up."

"The body was identified, Dallas," Peabody said. "Prints, DNA, the whole shot."

"He was HSO, so I'm not ruling out falsified identification. But McCoy throws it off for me. If she had something, knew something, why not take care of it before you perform the main act? Then there's motive. Why die—taking your lover, setting up your wife? There's nothing in his files to indicate he was in any trouble with Homeland. From all appearances, he had it locked. Sexy secret job, loving wife who unknowingly feeds you regular intel, a couple of lovers to add variety, a successful career, financial security. Life's pretty damn good, so why die?"

She sat on the side of her desk. "We could move to the brother. Jealousy, resentment. We know Kade went to see him in Jamaica, and have reason to believe she took him as a lover. Was this HSO sanctioned? Or was she working on her own, or in league with Blair Bissel? And why? Maybe it was a setup that went wrong. Maybe it was a Cain and Abel, and Carter upped the stakes, took out his brother—too bad about the woman—and set Reva up. It's a nice nest egg, the estate. If Reva's tried and convicted of the murders, she won't inherit. He'd get a chunk of it."

"Maybe he was blackmailing Blair," Peabody suggested. "The monkey on his back."

"Good, that's what Roarke's going to help us find out. Carter has something on Blair—the HSO connection, the extramarital, something else—and taps him regularly. Blair's had about enough of that and decides to shake off the monkey. But killing three people seems a little over the top. Why not just slip down to the islands, do the brother, and go back to your life? Some of these answers have to be on those units. Feeney, I need some answers."

"Got one for you. Top-drawer face sculptor out of Sweden was killed in what appears to be a botched burglary at his office. Two weeks ago. His patient records have not been retrieved as his data unit was damaged."

"Damaged?"

"According to the report. Jorgannsen, that was his name, had his throat cut. His drug supply was taken, and his data unit damaged. I'm figuring infected, but there's no way to verify without seeing the unit."

"See if you can play nice with your counterpart in Sweden, maybe they'll transport it to us."

"Give it a shot."

"Shoot fast." She pushed to her feet. "I've been called to the Tower at the request of the fucking HSO. I'm taking steps to cover all of our asses because this isn't going to be neat and pretty. The shit's going to hit the fan, and if it blows the way I'm hoping, the spooks are going to be up to their knees in it. But there's bound to be some backdraft. For the duration of this area of investigation, we bunker down here."

"God." McNab grinned like an idiot. "How will we stand it?"

"And work twenty-four/seven," Eve added and watched the grin turn to a wince. "In shifts. Let's get started. Peabody."

"Yes, sir. I'm with you."

"Communication by secured lines only," she added as she walked out the door and nearly into Roarke.

"Lieutenant, a moment of your time."

"Walk and talk. I don't have any moments to spare."

"I'm just going to ah . . ." *Be somewhere else,* Peabody thought, and hurried past them.

"If you've got a beef about the way I handled your people, you'll have to save it. I'm in a hurry."

"It would take more than a moment to discuss the areas of your sensitivity and people skills. I realize you're not looking at Reva and were, in your way, establishing her alibi."

"So?"

"I won't work in the dark, Eve. If you want my help you can't give me tasks to perform one moment, then close me out the next. I expect you to trust me with the details."

"You know all you need to know. When you need to know more, I'll tell you more."

He grabbed her arm, spun her around. "Is this your way of slapping at me because I refuse to stand on the same elevated moral ground as you?"

"If I slap at you, pal, believe me, you'll feel it. This, and that, are two separate issues."

"Bollocks."

"Oh, *fuck* you and the big-ass dick you rode in on." She jerked away from him and lost control long enough to shove him back.

She saw his eyes fire, but he didn't shove back, didn't touch her. She hated herself for resenting that he could keep that violence in line when she couldn't.

"This is my work, goddamn it, and I don't have the time or the luxury to think about anything else right now. You don't like the way I'm running this investigation and this team, then step out. Step the hell out. You don't know what I'm dealing with."

"You've just made my point. I've some concerns, reasonable concerns, about having my wife go up against the HSO. This isn't just a murderer, or even organized crime. It isn't some wild-eyed group of terrorists. This is one of the most powerful organizations in the world. If they're involved in this, as it seems they must be in some aspect, it logically follows that they'd have little compunction about harming a New York City cop who got in their way. Personally or professionally harming that cop. My cop."

"Deal with it. That's part of the package you took on. You want to keep my ass out of the sling on this, get me the information. That's what you can do. That's all you can do."

"It's part of the package I took on," he agreed in a tone that was dangerously soft. "You'd do well to remember the whole of the one you took on. The whole of it, Eve. You have to live with that, or without it."

She stood, shocked to the bone, when he turned and walked away from her. Her skin went cold with it, and her stomach cramped and twisted as she rushed down the stairs out of the house. Something of it must have shown on her face as Peabody turned to her when she climbed into the car.

"Dallas? You okay?"

She shook her head. She wasn't sure she could get out words. Her throat was burning. Punching the accelerator, she sent the car speeding down the drive, which was flanked by lovely trees and bushes beginning to fire with the first hints of autumn.

"Men are tough nuts," Peabody said. "The more I'm around them, the tougher they get. It seems to me that one like Roarke would be tougher than most."

"He's pissed, that's all. Really pissed." She had to press a hand to her troubled stomach. "So am I, goddamn it, so am I. But he got under my guard. He's really good at getting under your guard. The son of a bitch." Her breath wanted to hitch so she sucked it in, sucked it in hard. "He knows just where to jab."

"The more somebody loves you, the better their aim."

"Christ, he must really love me. I can't do this now. He knows I can't do this now."

"Never a convenient time for relationship upheaval."

"Who the hell's side are you on?"

"Well, since I'm sitting beside you, and you punch really hard, I'm on yours. You bet."

"Gotta put it away." But she was afraid the sickness in her belly was going to plague her throughout the day. Still, she engaged the dash 'link and took the next step.

"Nadine Furst."

"I can't make lunch. We'll have to reschedule. As soon as possible."

"All right." Nadine didn't bat a carefully groomed lash. "I'll clear some time and let you know."

"Looking forward to it." Eve signed off.

"What the hell was that?" Peabody demanded.

"Spooks aren't the only ones who can be covert. That was me telling Nadine to break the story that Blair Bissel was HSO, with a few selected details to confirm and expand upon. We're going to see whose ass is red by the end of the day."

"Roarke's not going to be the only one who's really pissed."

"Thanks." Eve managed a weak smile. "That makes me feel considerably better."

Morris had done exactly as instructed. Because it took ten full minutes to clear her and Peabody into the morgue, she decided he was more than a little annoyed. He admitted them personally, then led the way through the chilly white tunnel toward the autopsy and viewing rooms.

"What time did you get here this morning?" Eve asked his rigid back.

"Around seven. Early, as I was doing a cop a favor, or had intended to do one by coming in ahead of schedule and running tests on Bissel to see if he'd had any recent facial enhancements or sculpting. I got coffee and reviewed my previous notes on the case, then came down here, about seven-fifteen."

He used his pass and a voice command to open the secured doors on one of the storage/viewing areas.

"Was this door locked?"

"It was."

"I'll have Crime Scene check it for tampering," Peabody said.

"Bissel's slot was empty," Morris continued, and approached the wall of stainless steel refrigerator drawers. He opened one and it let out a whoosh of air and chilly white vapor. "Initially I was annoyed, assuming he'd been moved or misfiled, so I checked the last log-in, which verified he'd been stored properly. I called the AME, Marlie Drew, who was on the night shift. She was still here as she wouldn't end shift until eight. She had no record of anyone entering this area, adding or removing anything."

"I'll need to speak with her."

"She's in her office, waiting. We ran a thorough search. His data is still here, his body is not."

"How many bodies do you have in at this time?"

"Twenty-six. Four came in last night. There was a vehicular accident logged in at two-twenty."

"You've checked all storage areas?"

Insult flashed over his face. "Dallas, this isn't my first day on the job. When I tell you a body isn't here, it isn't here."

"Okay. So you only had twenty-two before the new ones checked in at two-twenty?"

"No, we had twenty-three. Two were scheduled for disposal—city expense. Two sidewalk sleepers, unclaimed."

"Disposal."

Now, fresh irritation layered over the insult and made his voice an icy slash. "You know the damn drill. Unclaimed, indigent, the city cremates after forty-eight hours. We deal with them during the night shift, send them out to a crematorium."

"Who goes with them?"

"Driver and orderly." Because he saw where she was heading, he set his teeth. "They wouldn't have taken Bissel by mistake, if that's what you're thinking. We don't run a damn comedy hour around here. It's serious and sensitive work to care for the dead."

"I'm perfectly aware of that, Morris." Her own temper was

beginning to fray as she stepped up to and into his face. "But Bissel's not here, so let's go through the steps."

"Fine. There's a staging area. Bodies slated for transfer and disposal would be logged out from storage—and the records checked—by the AME on duty, and those records would be cross-checked to avoid any mistakes. The transfer team would take them to the staging area, log them out through another series of checks. This isn't a matter of someone mistakenly slating Bissel for disposal and leaving one of the city jobs behind. I've got a damn body missing. The count's wrong."

"I'm not thinking it was a mistake. Contact the crematorium first. See how many they did for you last night. And I want the names of the ones who transported the bodies. Are they still on site?"

"Different shifts." Looking more worried than angry now, Morris led the way out, resecured the door. "They'd have been off by six." He walked quickly toward his office. He called up the previous night's schedule even as he engaged his 'link.

"Powell and Sibresky. I know both these men. They're big on jokes but they're efficient. They're careful. This is Chief Medical Examiner Morris," he said into the 'link. "I need to verify a delivery for disposal, city contract, made early this morning."

"One moment please, Dr. Morris, I'll connect you with Receiving."

"Does anybody but me think this is kind of sick?" Peabody wondered. "I mean, Receiving. Yuck."

"Shut up, Peabody. Do a quick run on this Powell and Sibresky, get me pictures."

"I gave you pictures," Morris objected. "People around here don't just fry up any loose body. There's a very exacting system in place to . . . Yes, this is Morris," he said when Receiving got on the line. "We delivered a John and a Jane Doe early this morning for disposal. Order numbers NYC-JD500251 and 252. Will you verify?"

"Of course, Dr. Morris. Just let me pull those up. I have

those deliveries, and disposal was completed. Do you need the verification numbers?"

"No, thank you. That's enough."

"Do you need to verify the third delivery?"

Eve didn't need to see his stomach to know it sank. It showed by the way he slowly lowered his body into his desk chair. "A third?"

"NYC-JD500253. All three were delivered and signed for by the Receiving supervisor, Clemment, at one-oh-six A.M."

"Disposal is completed?"

"Oh yes, Doctor. Disposal was completed at . . . three-thirty-eight A.M. Is there something else I can help you with?"

"No. No. Thank you." He broke transmission. "I don't know how this could happen. It makes no sense. The order is here, right here." He tapped his screen. "For two, not three. There's no third disposal order, no third body cleared from Staging."

"I need to talk to Powell and Sibresky."

"I'm going with you. I need to follow this through, Dallas," he said before she could object. "This is my house. The guests may be dead, but they're still mine."

"All right. Get Crime Scene in here, Peabody. And let's get Feeney to pick us a hotshot from EDD to look at Morris's unit. I want to know if any of the data's been altered in the last twenty-four."

They got a very irritated Sibresky out of bed. Though he mellowed a bit when he saw Morris, he still scratched his butt and bitched.

"What the hell? Me and the old lady work nights. You gotta sleep some time. You day people think everything runs on your clock."

"Real sorry to disturb your sleep, Sibresky," Eve began, "and I'm real sorry you didn't use a mouthwash before this little conversation."

"Hey."

"But the fact is I'm conducting one of those pesky daytime

investigations. You took a delivery to the crematorium early this morning."

"Yeah, so what? That's my fricking job, lady. Hey, Morris, what the fuck?"

"Sib, this is important. Did you—"

"Morris," Eve interrupted, more gently than she might have with anyone else. "How many did you take in?"

"Just the one run from the city morgue. We do 'em in groups if it's under five. Five or more, you gotta take it in two trips. More of that in the winter when the sleepers kick off from exposure and shit. Good weather like this, it's pretty slow."

"How many in the run?"

"Shit." He poked out his bottom lip in an expression Eve gauged as concentration. "Three. Yeah, three. Two Johns, one Jane. Jesus, we went through the routine, the logs, the paperwork, the sign off, sign in, and shit. Not my fault if somebody decided to claim one of the bodies after the forty-eight."

"Who authorized the transport for you and Powell?"

"Sal, I guess. You know, Morris, Sally Riser. She logs 'em out usually from Staging. It was already done when I clocked in, but it wasn't Powell."

"What wasn't Powell?"

"Powell called in sick, so the new guy was working. Real hotdogger," Sibresky said with a grimace. "Had all the paperwork done when I clocked on. Don't matter a shit to me. I just drive 'em."

"What was the new guy's name?" Eve demanded.

"Shit, I gotta remember everything at ten in the fricking morning? Angelo, I think his name was. What the hell do I care, he was just filling in for Powell. Wanted to do all the paperwork himself, and that's fine with me. Like I said, he was a real hotdogger."

"I bet he was. Peabody."

Understanding, Peabody pulled photos of Blair and Carter Bissel out of her file bag. "Mr. Sibresky, are either of these the man you know as Angelo?"

"Nah. Hotdogger had a big, stupid mustache, lots of eyebrows, hair all slicked back and hanging to his butt like some kinda fag-ass vid star. Scar on his face, too." He tapped a finger on his left cheek. "Nasty one, went from the corner of his eye nearly to his mouth. Teeth bucked out, too. Guy was pretty damn ugly."

"Sibresky, I'm going to ruin your day," Eve told him. "You'll need to get dressed and come down to Central. I need you to look at pictures and work with a police artist."

"Ah, come *on*, lady."

"That's Lieutenant Lady. Go get your pants on."

Chapter 16

She wasn't surprised to find herself standing over Joseph Powell's body, but she was furious. She had to control the fury, coat it thickly before it clouded judgment.

He'd lived alone, and that had been one of the many breaks for his killer. He'd been scrawny, with little meat on his bird bones and a crop of hair cut short around the ears and trained, somehow or other, to stand up straight from his head in a six-inch crown dyed lightning blue.

From the looks of his place, he'd liked music and cheese-flavored soy chips. He was still wearing his headphones, and an open bag of the chips was in bed with him.

There were no privacy screens on the single bedroom window, but a shade, blue as his hair, had been drawn. It blocked out the sun well enough, turned the room to gloom, and let all the traffic sounds—air and street—rumble against the glass like a storm rolling in.

He'd toked a little Zoner along with his chips. She could see the remnants of paper and ash in the dish shaped like a stupendously endowed naked woman on the table beside the bed.

Another break for the killer. He'd been zoned out, music pounding in his head, and couldn't have weighed more than one-thirty. It was unlikely he'd even felt the jolt from the laser pressed to his carotid artery.

Small blessings.

Across from the bed, tacked up for the view she was sure, was a life-sized poster of Mavis Freestone, exploding into a midair leap, arms extended, grin wide and full of fun. She wore little more than the grin and strategically placed glitter.

MAVIS!
TOTALLY JUICED!

The sight of it, hanging on the dingy beige wall, laughing down at the dead, made Eve incredibly sad and sick.

Because Morris was there, and she knew he needed to take some control, she stayed back and let him handle the initial exam.

"One jolt," he said. "Full contact. Burn marks from the weapon are clearly evident. No other visible trauma. No signs of struggle or defensive wounds. His neurological system would have been immediately compromised. Death instantaneous."

"I need positive ID, Morris. If you want I can—"

He whipped around. "I know the drill. I know what the fuck has to be done here, and don't need you . . ." He lifted both hands. His breath shuddered in, then out. "And that was so uncalled for. I'm sorry."

"It's all right. I know this is rough on you."

"Close to home. This hits very, very close to home. Someone came into this room and killed this . . . boy as carelessly as you might swat a fly. He did that without knowing him, without having any feelings about him. Did this only to remove a small barrier so he could walk into my house. This really meant nothing more to him than putting on his shoes so he wouldn't stub his toe.

"Victim is positively identified as Powell, Joseph. I'm going to take just a minute, Dallas, to pull myself together so I can do him, and you, some good."

She waited until he left the room. "Peabody, I need you to

work this. Do the on-scene, call the sweepers, start the knock-on-doors. I have to get to the Tower."

"I need to be there."

"They ordered me, not you."

Peabody's jaw tightened. "I'm your partner, and if your ass is getting fitted for a sling, mine is, too."

"I appreciate the sentiment, however strange the visual, but I need my partner to pull the weight here. He needs you," she said, looking down at Powell. "You have to start the process for him, and you need to help Morris. And if they're fitting my ass for a sling, Peabody, I need you to keep pushing this investigation through, to keep the team solid. I'm not protecting you. I'm counting on you."

"Okay. I'll handle it." She stepped up, stood with Eve over Joseph Powell. "I'll take care of him."

She nodded. "Do you see what happened here? Tell me."

"He let himself in the door. He knows how to bypass security, and there's not much here to bypass. No cams, no doorman. He picked Powell instead of Sibresky because Powell lived alone, and as orderly, probably handled more of the paperwork. It was business here, and he went straight for it. Powell's in bed, zoned or asleep, probably both. He just leaned down, pressed the weapon to his throat, zapped him. Um . . ."

She took a quick scan of the room. "There's no pass or ID sitting around. He might've taken it, altered it for his own use. We'll check on that. Then he just walked out again. We'll get time of death, but it was probably middle of the day yesterday."

"Start with that. I'll head back to the house as soon as I can. Morris may want to notify next of kin himself. If not—"

"I'll take care of it. Don't worry about this end, Dallas."

"Then I won't."

She started out, paused in front of the poster of Mavis. "Don't ever tell her," she said, and left the scene.

Inside the lab, Reva worked side by side with Tokimoto. They rarely spoke, and when they did it was in an abbreviated computerese only the true data jock could translate. But for the most part, there were no words between them. One thought, the other anticipated.

But Reva couldn't anticipate how badly he wanted to speak, how the part of his mind not focused on the work formed and re-formed the words and phrases.

She was in trouble, he reminded himself. She was just widowed, and widowed by a man she'd learned was using her. She was vulnerable, and emotionally fragile. It was . . . ghoulish—wasn't it?—to even consider approaching her on any personal level at such a time.

But when she leaned back on a quiet sound of exhaustion, the words simply popped out.

"You're pushing too hard. You need to take a break. Twenty minutes. A walk in the fresh air."

"We're close. I know it."

"Then twenty minutes will make little difference. Your eyes are bloodshot."

She worked up a twisted smile. "Thanks for pointing that out."

"You have lovely eyes. You're abusing them."

"Yeah, yeah, yeah." She shut them on a sigh. "You don't even know what color they are other than red."

"They're gray. Like smoke. Or fog on a moonless night."

She opened one eye, peered at him. "Where'd that come from?"

"I have no idea." Though he was flustered, he decided to push on. "Perhaps my brain is as bloodshot as your eyes. I think we should take a walk."

"Why not?" She studied him as she got to her feet. "Sure. Why not?"

Across the room, Roarke watched them step out. "About damn time," he muttered.

"You got something?" Feeney asked, and nearly pounced on him.

"No. Sorry. I was thinking of something else."

"You're a little off today, aren't you, boy?"

"I'm on right enough." He reached for his coffee mug,

found it empty, and had to struggle against the urge to just heave it against the glass wall.

"Why don't I fill that up for you." Feeney nipped it handily out of Roarke's hand. "I was about to do my own."

"Appreciate it."

When he'd done so, Feeney came back, swiveled his chair beside Roarke's. "She can handle herself. You know that."

"Who would know it better?" Roarke took a tool as thin as a dentist's probe and scraped delicately at corrosion. Then because Feeney merely sat and sipped, he set the tool aside once more.

"I gave her a difficult time before she left. She deserved it, by God, didn't she deserve it. But I regret the timing of it."

"I'm not getting between a man and his wife. Those who do usually come out looking like they've been set on by wild dogs. I will say when the wife's in a mood to cook my brains for breakfast, I can usually save myself with flowers. Pick 'em up from a street vendor, take them home to her—with a big sappy look on my face." He sat, he sipped. "Flowers wouldn't work on Dallas."

"Not in a million years," Roarke confirmed. "A sack of diamonds from the Blue Mines on Taurus I wouldn't work on her, unless you knocked her in that block of wood she calls a head with them. Christ Jesus, that woman's a frustration to me. Beginning, end, and all the middle."

Feeney said nothing for five humming seconds. "See, you want me to agree with you. To say something like, 'Oh yeah, that Dallas sure is a blockhead.' If I did, you'd end up kicking my ass. So I'm just going to drink my coffee."

"That's a big help to me."

"You're a smart boy. You know what you have to do."

"And what would that be?"

He patted Roarke on the shoulder. "Grovel," he said, and scooted his chair out of harm's way.

It wasn't over. No, by God, it wasn't over, and he was in the pilot's seat now.

He paced and prowled his rooms—rooms he was so proud

of, rooms he'd celebrated having completely to himself. No one knew about them.

Well, no one living.

They were a perfect place to strategize his moves. And to congratulate himself on yet another job well done.

The blue-haired freak had been child's play. Absolute child's play. He took a minute hit of Zeus to keep his energies up, keep his mind alert, as he had business, very personal business, to conduct shortly.

He was protecting himself, step by stage by layer. And that, self-preservation, was paramount. The quick thrill of the kill, of outwitting those who would have *erased* him, was a nice benefit, but it wasn't the point.

The point was to cover his ass, which he had done—and beautifully, if he did say so himself. The cops were up the creek now, without a body to work with.

The next was funding. And he couldn't quite figure out, yet, how to get his hands on the money due him.

He paused to study his reflection in a mirror. He was going to have to change that face, and it pained him. He liked the face that looked back at him. Still, sacrifices would have to be made for the good of the whole.

Once he finished his work, tied up some more loose ends, he'd find a surgeon who wouldn't ask too many questions. He had enough to pay for that, sure he did. And he'd find a way to get the rest, all the rest, when he could just *think* without all these complications springing up on him.

So that was level one and two. But the third level was payback, and he knew exactly how to collect that debt.

He wasn't going to be used and betrayed, and played for a fool. What he was going to do was take care of business.

Eve blanked everything out of her mind but the moment. She kept her sights on the goal, striding briskly toward the waiting area outside the vaulted office of Chief Tibble. And had to check that stride when Don Webster cut across her path.

"Move it. I've got business."

"So do I. Same place, same business."

Her heart tripped. Webster was Internal Affairs. "I wasn't informed IAB was part of this. That's a serious breach, Webster. I'm entitled to a departmental rep."

"You don't need one."

"Don't tell me what I need," she hissed. "Somebody sics the rat squad on me, I get a rep."

"The rat squad's on your side." He took her arm, then released it quickly when her eyes went to hot slits. "I'm not hitting on you, for God's sake, Dallas. Give me a minute. One minute." He gestured her around the corner.

"Make it fast."

"First, let me say this isn't personal. Or let me say this isn't intimate. I don't want Roarke trying to beat my brains into veggie hash again."

"I don't need him to do that."

"Acknowledged. I'm here to help you."

"Help me what?"

"Kick a little Homeboy ass."

They had a history, Eve reminded herself as she studied his face. That history included a single night between the sheets, years before. For some reason she never quite understood, that night had gotten under Webster's skin. He had a . . . thing for her, which she was fairly sure Roarke had tromped out of him before she could do so herself.

She supposed they were, in some strange way, friends by this point. He was a good cop—wasted, in her opinion, in IAB, but a good cop. And an honest one.

"Why?"

"Because, Lieutenant, IAB doesn't like outside organizations trying to mess with what's ours."

"No, you like to mess with us yourselves."

"Ease back, would you? We're informed the HSO is looking at one of our cops, we're obliged to take a look at that cop. That cops comes up whistle clean—and you do—we take exception to the waste of our time and resources. Somebody outside tries to target a good cop, IAB offers a shield. Consider me your knight in shining fucking armor."

"Get out." She turned away.

"Don't ditch a shield, Dallas. IAB's required to be in on this meet. I just want you to know going in where I'm standing."

"Okay, okay." It wasn't easy, but she buried her temper and her resentment. She was probably going to need all the help she could get. "It's appreciated."

She kept her head up as she approached Tibble's office. "Dallas, Lieutenant Eve," she said to the uniformed admin stationed outside. "Reporting as requested."

"Lieutenant Webster, IAB, as directed."

"One moment."

It didn't take long. Eve stepped into Tibble's office just ahead of Webster.

Tibble was at the window, hands loosely held at the back of his waist, watching the city below. He was a good cop, in Eve's opinion. Smart, strong, and steady. It had helped put him in the Tower, but it was his political dexterity, she knew, that kept him there.

He spoke without turning, and his voice carried authority. "You're late, Lieutenant Dallas."

"Yes, sir. I apologize. It was unavoidable."

"You know Agent Sparrow."

She glanced at Sparrow, who was already seated. "We've met."

"Have a seat. And you, Lieutenant Webster. Webster is here representing Internal Affairs. Commander Whitney is present per my request." He turned, swooped his hawk's gaze over the room, then moved to his desk.

"Lieutenant Dallas, it seems the HSO has some concerns about the nature of your current investigation, the direction thereof, and your techniques. They have requested, through me, that you halt the investigation and turn over all notes, data, and evidence to AD Sparrow, thereby passing this case into HSO aegis."

"I am unable to comply with this request, Chief Tibble."

"This is a matter of global security," Sparrow began.

"It's a matter of murder," Eve interrupted. "Four civilians have been killed, in New York City."

"Four?" Tibble asked.

"Yes, sir. I was detained due to the discovery of a fourth victim. Joseph Powell, a city employee assigned to transportation and disposal at the morgue. My partner and ME Morris are on scene."

"How is this connected?"

"Dr. Morris contacted me this morning to inform me that the body identified as Blair Bissel had been removed from storage."

Sparrow lunged out of his chair. "You lost the body? You lost a key factor in the investigation and you sit there and refuse to hand it over to us?"

"The body was not lost," Eve said evenly, "but removed. Covertly. That sort of thing falls under your aegis, doesn't it, Assistant Director?"

"If you're accusing the HSO of stealing a corpse—"

"I've made no such accusation, but merely commented about the covert nature of your work." She reached into her pocket and drew out a microtracker. "This is the sort of thing you play with, right?" She held it up, turning it between her thumb and forefinger. "Funny. I found this on my vehicle—my official police unit—which was parked outside the morgue. Does the HSO consider it a matter of global security to track and spy on a NYPSD officer while she is carrying out her sworn duty?"

"This is a sensitive matter, beyond your—"

"Electronic surveillance of a police officer, who has not been charged or is not suspected of a crime or an infraction of law," Webster put in, "violates federal and state privacy codes as well as departmental regs. If Lieutenant Dallas is suspected of a crime or an infraction by the HSO that requires said surveillance, Internal Affairs would like to see the paperwork, the order, the charge, the evidence that led to the surveillance."

"I am unaware of any such surveillance by my agency."

"Is that what you call plausible deniability, Sparrow?" Eve asked. "Or just a big, fat lie?"

"Lieutenant," Tibble said, quietly, authoritatively.

"Yes, sir. I apologize."

"Chief, Commander, Lieutenants." Sparrow paused, let his gaze scan the faces. "The HSO wishes to cooperate with local law enforcement whenever this cooperation is possible, but global matters take priority. We want Lieutenant Dallas removed from the investigation and all data pertaining thereto given over to me, as representative."

"I am unable to comply with the request," Eve repeated.

"Chief Tibble," Sparrow continued. "I've given you the letter of request and authorization from the director."

"Yes, I've read it. As I've read the reports and the case file provided by Lieutenant Dallas. Of the two, I find hers more compelling."

"I can, if this request is denied, obtain a federal warrant for those reports and case files, and authorization to have the investigation terminated."

"Let's cut the bullshit here, Assistant Director." Tibble folded his hands and leaned forward. "If you could have, you would have, rather than wasting this time. Your agency is hip-deep in the mud on this. Two of yours are dead, and they were, allegedly, exploiting an innocent civilian without her knowledge or consent to gather information from a private concern."

"Securecomp is on the agency's watch list, Chief Tibble."

"I can only imagine what's on your agency's watch list. Regardless of this, or the very legitimate reasons you may have for that list, Reva Ewing was unforgivably—and illegally—used, her reputation impugned, her life turned inside out. She is not one of you. Chloe McCoy is dead. She was not one of you. Joseph Powell is dead. He was not one of you."

"Sir—"

Tibble merely held up a finger. "My count makes it three victims to two, weighed on this side of the fence. I will not compel my lieutenant to step out of an active investigation."

"During the course of her investigation, your lieutenant illegally received or accessed data from the HSO. We can pursue charges on that issue."

Tibble spread his hands. "You are free to do so. It may be

necessary for you to pursue charges against Commander Whitney and myself as well, as we have both received that data from the lieutenant."

Sparrow kept his seat, but Eve watched his hands ball into fists. The way things were going from his side, she couldn't blame him for wanting to punch something.

"We want her source."

"I'm not required to divulge my source."

"You're not required," Sparrow snapped out the words, "but you can be charged, you can be held, and you can very possibly lose your badge."

The more anger and frustration she read from him, the less she felt herself. "I don't think you're going to charge me, because if you do, it's going to look really bad for your team. The media gets their teeth into some of the dirty little games the HSO authorized Bissel to play—and they start speculating that he was taken out, he and his partner brutally murdered by your organization, which then callously staged a frame for Bissel's innocent and exploited wife—why they'll just tear you to bloody pieces."

"Bissel and Kade were not HSO-sanctioned terminations."

"Then you really better hope I find the answers that prove your agency is not responsible."

"You hacked into government files," he tossed at her.

"Prove it," she tossed right back.

He started to speak, or, more likely from his expression, spew, but his 'link beeped. "I'm sorry for the interruption, but that's a priority signal. I have to take it. Privately."

"Through that door," Tibble told him with a gesture. "There's a small office you can use." When Sparrow closed the door at his back, Tibble tapped his fingers on the edge of his desk. "They may charge you, Dallas."

"Yes, sir, they may. But I don't think they will."

He nodded, seemed to drift off into thought. "I don't like their use of private citizens in this maneuver. I don't like them planting devices to spy on my officers, and circumventing the standards of privacy and decency and law to do so. These organizations have their purpose, and require a certain amount of latitude, but there are lines. Those lines were crossed with Reva Ewing, and she's a citizen of New York, of the goddamn United States, and as such has a right to expect her government to treat her fairly. As such, she deserves the full efforts of this police force. I'm backing you on this, but I'm warning you, get it wrapped quickly. They're bound to send bigger guns than Sparrow to knock you out."

"Understood. Thank you, sir, for your support."

Sparrow stormed back in, and his face was a study in barely suppressed fury. "You went to the media."

Nadine worked fast, Eve thought, and kept her face blank. She'd just fall back on a little plausible deniability herself. "I don't know what you're talking about."

"You leaked Bissel's association with the agency to the press. And Kade's. You've involved the HSO in a goddamn media circus to protect your damn hide."

Slowly, very slowly, Eve got to her feet. "I leaked nothing to the media to protect my hide. I can protect my own hide. You make accusations like that, Sparrow, you'd better be able to back them up."

"They didn't pluck it out of thin air." He spun toward Tibble. "With this development, it's more vital than ever that this officer be removed from the investigation and her case files be turned over to the HSO."

"Media attention directed at the HSO doesn't, in any way, alter the circumstances of my lieutenant's position."

"Lieutenant Dallas has a personal vendetta against the agency and is using this investigation to revenge herself for what transpired over twenty years ago in—"

"Hold it." Her stomach shuddered. "Hold it right there. Sir," she said to Tibble, "Assistant Director Sparrow is about to bring up a personal matter. One that has no bearing whatsoever on this investigation, or on my conduct as an officer. I'd like to discuss that matter with him, to resolve it. I request, respectfully, sir, that I be given that opportunity. In private. Commander . . ."

Don't lose it, she ordered herself. *God, don't lose it.*

"Commander Whitney is aware of the matter. I have no objection to him being present."

Tibble said nothing for a moment, then rose. "Lieutenant Webster, let's step out."

"Thank you, sir."

She used the time it took to clear the room to gather herself. And still, she couldn't quite manage it. "You son of a bitch," she said softly. "You son of a bitch, you'd throw that in my face. You'd use what was done to me—by him, by your precious agency—to get your way in this."

"I apologize." He seemed nearly as shaken as she. "I apologize, sincerely, Lieutenant, for allowing my temper to cloud my judgment. The incident has no place here."

"Oh yes, it does. You bet your ass it does. You read the file?"

"I read it."

"And you stomached it."

"Actually, Lieutenant Dallas, I couldn't quite stomach it. I believe in the work we do, and I know that sometimes sacrifices have to be made, that choices are made that seem—that are—cold. However, I could find no rationale, no purpose, no excuse for the lack of intervention in your case. Knowingly leaving a minor in that situation was . . . inhumane. You should have been removed, and the decision to leave status quo was ill-advised."

"The HSO was aware of your situation in Texas?" Whitney asked.

"They were surveilling him, due to his connection with Max Ricker. They knew what he did to me, they listened to it. They listened while he raped me, and while I begged. While I begged."

"Sit down, Dallas."

She could only shake her head. "Can't. Sir."

"Do you know what I'll do with this information, AD Sparrow?"

"Commander," Eve began.

"Stand down, Lieutenant." Whitney pushed to his feet, towered over Sparrow. "Do you, or your superiors, understand what I can and will do with this information if you continue to harass my officer, or in any way attempt to infringe on her duties or smear her reputation? It won't be leaked to the media. It'll be flooded to them. You will be washed away in the tidal wave of the public outcry. Your agency will need generations to recover from the legal tangle and the public relations nightmare. You take that back to whoever holds your leash, and you make sure they know who it came from. Then, if you want to take me on, you come ahead."

"Commander Whitney—"

"You're going to want to walk away now, Sparrow," Whitney warned. "Walk away before you end up taking the punch for something that happened when you were still drooling on your bib."

Sparrow walked over to retrieve his briefcase. "I'll relay this information," he said and went out.

"You need to pull yourself together, Dallas."

"Sir. Yes, sir." But the pressure in her chest was outrageous. In defense, she dropped into a chair, lowered her head between her knees. "Sorry. Can't breathe."

She waited until the worst of the weight eased and air squeezed down her throat, into her lungs.

"Steady it out, Lieutenant, or I'm going to have to call the MTs." She sat up, had him nodding. "Thought that would do it. Need water?"

She could have swallowed a small ocean of it. "No, sir. Thank you. I understand that Chief Tibble may need to be apprised of—"

"If Tibble needs to be apprised of incidents that took place in another state more than two decades ago, he will be so apprised. But in my judgment this is a personal matter. I think you can rest assured it will stay one. You fired the first volley with the media leak. They'll have their hands full trying to spin and swim through that. They won't want to risk a second whirlwind. You'd already calculated all that."

"Yes, sir."

"Then you'd better get back to work and close this up. And if you have to fry a few spooks along the way, that's just a nice bonus." He showed his teeth in a grin. "A real nice bonus."

Chapter 17

Eve walked out on the garage level at Central, and laid her hand on her weapon as Quinn Sparrow stepped out from behind a column.

"You take chances, Sparrow."

"You don't know the half of it. I shouldn't be speaking to you outside of authorized parameters, Lieutenant. But between us, we've got a hell of a mess on our hands. You won't back off so we have to find some level ground, some area of compromise."

"I've got four bodies. Well, had four." She eased her hand away from her weapon and moved toward her vehicle. "I don't compromise."

"Two of those bodies are ours. You may not think much of our organization, of me, of our directives, but it matters when we lose people."

"Let's get this straight. What I think or don't about your organization isn't relevant, but the fact is I'm not naive enough to think it doesn't serve a purpose. Covert operations helped end the Urban Wars, prevented numerous terrorist attacks on U.S. soil, and globally. I might find some of your methods questionable, at best, but that's beside the point."

"Then what is the point?"

"You wired, Sparrow?"

"You paranoid, Dallas?"

"Oh yeah."

"I'm not wired," he snapped. "I shouldn't even be talking to you."

"Your choice. Here's the point. Four people are dead, and your organization is part of it."

"The HSO does not murder its own operatives, then frame a civilian."

"No?" She lifted her eyebrows as she slid a scanner out of her pocket. "They just sit back and watch while a child is brutalized, raped, and tortured, then tidy up after her when she takes a life desperately defending her own. When she's traumatized and broken. And they leave her alone, to wander the streets."

"I don't know what happened." He looked away from her. "I don't know why. You've read the file, so you know data was deleted. Covered up. I'm not denying it, or the poor judgment of—"

"Poor *judgment?*"

"There's nothing I can say to you. Nothing that can balance the scales after what was done. No excuses I can make, so I won't make them. But I will say, as you have to me, that's not the point."

"Score one for you." She moved away from him to run a program on the scanner, checking her car for devices. "I'm pissed, Sparrow, and I'm tired, and it's very, very difficult for me to accept that strangers know my private business. Because of that, I've got no reason to trust you, or the people you work for."

"I'd like to try to give you one, and to find some area of compromise that will satisfy us both. But I've got to ask you, where the hell did you get that thing?"

She found herself amused, and she hadn't expected to be, by the look of fascination and avarice on his face. "I have my connections."

"I've never seen one quite like it. Very compact. Will it

multitask? Sorry." He laughed a little. "I'm big on gadgets. One of the reasons I got into this line of work. Look, if you're satisfied your car's clear, maybe we could take a ride. I'll give you some data that may convince you to find that compromise."

"Open the briefcase."

"No problem." He set it on the trunk of her vehicle, manually entered a code on the lock. When he opened it, Eve blinked.

"Jesus, Sparrow, got enough hardware?"

She saw a stunner, a miniblaster, a complex little palm 'link, a recharger, and the smallest data system she'd ever come across. There was also a number of the same sort of tracking devices she'd taken off her vehicle earlier in the day.

She took one out, held it up, and looked him dead in the eye.

He gave her a winning smile. "I didn't say the tracker you removed from your vehicle wasn't HSO, I just said I was unaware of any directive to place said tracker on your vehicle."

"Smooth." She tossed the tracker back in the briefcase, and watched as Sparrow meticulously fit it back in its slot.

It occurred to her that under other circumstances he and Roarke would have bonded like brothers.

"I like gadgets," he repeated. "I didn't bug your vehicle. That's not to say I—or someone else from the organization—won't do so if ordered, but I didn't lay the tracker today. Nothing in here's activated. Your scanner will verify."

When it did, she looked him up and down. "What about you?"

"I've got a lot on me." He held his arms out to the side for the scanner. "All deactivated. You see, we're not having this conversation. We will have had it if the outcome's satisfactory. Otherwise, we left things up in Tibble's office."

Eve shook her head. "Get in. I'm heading uptown. I don't like what you have to say, I'll dump you in the most inconvenient spot I can manage. And I know all the inconvenient spots in this city."

He got in the passenger seat. "You really mucked up the works with that media leak."

She sent him her version of a winning smile. "I don't believe I confirmed playing any part in any media leak." She set the scanner on the seat beside her, activated. "Just in case you decide to flip something on," she said when Sparrow frowned at it.

"With that level of cynicism and paranoia, you ought to be one of us."

"I'll keep that in mind. Start talking."

"Bissel and Kade were not in-house terminations. We believe, though we have no confirmed intel, that Doomsday broke Bissel's cover, and took them out."

"Why?" She backed out of her slot. "If they knew about him, and his connection to Ewing and hers to the Code Red, it would make more sense to watch him, or haul him off and pull data out of his toenails."

"He was working a double. We worked over a year to set him up with a Doomsday operative. Look at his profile, and what do you see? An opportunist, a man who cheats on his wife—and his mistress, who likes the good life, spends lavishly. That's how we wanted him to look, and that part was easy, as what you see with Bissel was what you got. It's how and why we used him to pass carefully arranged data to Doomsday. He took their money. There was no way they'd believe he was behind their philosophies. Just in it for the shine."

"You set him up to get close to Ewing to spy on Securecomp, and you set him up to get close to Doomsday to screw with them. You guys are something."

"It was working. The worm they're developing, have developed," he corrected, "could undermine governments, give the terrorists an open door. If our data banks and surveillance apparatus are severely compromised, we can't track, we can't know how and when they might hit. That doesn't touch on internal crises: banks, military, transport. We needed to slow them down, and to gather intel, to have our defenses fully in place."

"And to steal the technology from them to create your own version of the worm."

"I can't confirm that supposition."

"You don't have to. Where does Carter Bissel come in?"

"Loose cannon. He has serious issues with his brother, and took the time and trouble to learn about the extramaritals. Blackmailed him. That actually worked for us. Solidified Bissel's cover, gave him another reason for needing quick money. We don't know where he is, or if he's alive or dead. Maybe they took him out, maybe they just took him. Maybe he ran or is on a fucking bender." Frustration eked through. "But we'll find him."

"This just doesn't jibe for me, Sparrow. Not all the way." She paused at the exit of the garage. "Terminating Bissel and Kade in that manner was sloppy. And Doomsday hasn't taken credit. They like credit."

"Yeah, but they don't like being conned. He conned them for months. We've gathered significant intel on the worm through Bissel. Enough bits and pieces that we should be able to develop the shield before . . ."

"Before Securecomp? God, you're a piece of work."

"Look." He shifted in his seat. "Personally, I don't give a flying fuck where the shield comes from, as long as we have it in place. But there are some who don't like the idea of a man with Roarke's . . . questionable connections having his fingers in a pie this sensitive."

"So you undermine Securecomp, get busy like bees to beat Roarke to the punch, so you can beat your red, white, and blue chests and add the big fee to your budget."

"Everything about the NYPSD is sunshine and roses, Dallas? You got a perfect system here?"

"No, but I don't screw somebody just so I can take the collar." She eased out into traffic. "I'm seriously thinking about ditching you in front of this nice little cafe where Zeus addicts hang."

"Come on, Dallas, give a little, get a little. We need a look at the units you confiscated, and have locked down. The ones you took from the various crime scenes. Or at least the scan and analysis reports. Doomsday has the worm. Even Roarke can't put together the brain trust we can to complete the shield and complete it now. Without it, we could be facing a crisis of goddamn biblical proportions."

At those words, the wrath of God hit. She felt the intense blast of heat, and saw the blinding flash of light. Glass imploded, and the dust of it spewed into her face.

Instinctively, she wrenched the wheel sideways, slammed the brakes, but her tires were no longer in contact with the road. Dimly she realized they were airborne.

She choked out a warning for Sparrow to hang on, and through the haze of smoke saw the world revolve. They hit, and the impact snapped her safety harness. She tumbled, stomach pitching, head ringing, and thudded hard on the safety bags that deployed with an explosive snap. The last thing she remembered was the taste of her own blood in her mouth.

She wasn't out long; the stink of the smoke, the quality of the screams told her she hadn't lost consciousness more than a minute or two. That, and the fact that the pain hadn't had time to fully process in her brain. Her vehicle—what was left of it—was on its top, like a turtle laying on its shell.

She spat out blood and shifted enough to reach Sparrow, to check for a pulse in his throat. She found a weak one, though her hand came away slick with blood that was still running down his face.

She heard the sirens now, and the rush of feet, the shouted orders that said *cops*. Dimly she thought, *If you are going to take a sudden, unexpected air trip while still in road mode, it is good to do so within a block of Cop Central.*

"I'm on the job," she called out and began to try to wriggle her way back, out of the smashed driver door and window. "Dallas, Lieutenant. There's a civilian pinned in here—bleeding bad."

"Take it easy, Lieutenant. MTs are on the way. You probably don't want to move until—"

"Get me the hell out of here." She tried to dig into the roadbed with the toes of her boots, searching for traction. She made it two inches before hands gripped her legs, her hips, and eased her out of the wreckage.

"How bad you hurt?"

She managed to focus on the face, recognized Detective Baxter. "I can still see you, so I'm in considerable pain. But I think I'm just banged up. Passenger's bad."

"They're getting to him."

She winced as Baxter ran his hands over her, checking for breaks. "You better not be using this to cop a feel."

"Just one of those little bonuses life hands you. Got some lacerations, probably going to have contusions all over that nifty bod of yours."

"Shoulder burns."

"You gonna punch me if I take a look?"

"Not this time."

She rolled her head back, closed her eyes as he unbuttoned her ruined shirt. "Friction burns from the harness, looks like," he told her.

"I want to stand up."

"Just take it easy until the medicals look at you."

"Give me a damn hand up, Baxter. I want to see the damage."

He helped her up, and when her vision didn't waver, she figured she'd gotten off lucky.

The same couldn't be said of Sparrow. The passenger side had taken the brunt when it rammed a maxibus on one of its revolutions. Trueheart was working with another uniform to sheer away the metal trapping Sparrow inside.

"He's pinned between the door and the dash," Trueheart called out. "Looks like his leg's broken, maybe his arm, too. But he's breathing."

She stepped back as the MTs hustled up. One wriggled into the driver's side where she'd wriggled out. The calls turned to medical jargon and orders. She heard talk about spinal and neck injuries, and cursed.

Then she looked at the car.

"Holy Jesus Christ."

The front end was all but disintegrated. Metal was blackened, melted, fused to metal. Window glass had gone to powder and continued to smoke.

"It looks like . . ."

"Like it was hit with a short-range missile," Baxter finished. "You'd be toast if it'd broadsided you instead of skimming the front end. I was heading in to Central, and saw this flash, this streak. Big boom, and a vehicle, yours, flew right over mine. Flew up, came down, flipped three times then spun around like a top. Smashed a couple of civilian vehicles, laid waste to a glide-cart, skipped the curb, skipped back, then plowed into a maxi like a torpedo."

"Civilian casualties?"

"I don't know."

She could see some of the injured, and hear weeping, some screaming. Soy dogs, soft drink tubes, candy sticks were scattered over the street and sidewalk like some nasty buffet.

"Harness held, until the last minute." She wiped absently at a trickle of blood on her temple. "It held, or God knows . . . Reinforcements in the roof kept us from being crushed like a couple of recycled milk cartons. Major damage on the passenger side from the crash. He got the worst of it."

Baxter watched the MTs fix the unconscious man to a back-and-neck board. "Friend of yours?"

"No."

"You piss somebody off enough to fire missiles at you or did he?"

"Good question."

"You need to have the MTs look you over."

"Probably." The pain was seeping through now, making mincemeat of the adrenaline and shock. "I hate that. Really do. And you know what else? The guys in requisitions are going to slap me around for this. They're going to slap me around, then give me some piece of shit transpo to punish me."

She hobbled over to the curb, sat among the confusion and noise. Then sneered in warning at the MT who headed, with his kit, in her direction. "You even think about using a pressure syringe on me," Eve told him, "and I'm taking you down."

"You want the pain, you keep the pain." The MT shrugged and opened his kit. "But let's have a look."

It took her another two hours to get home, and then she had to catch a ride with Baxter as she'd been ordered not to drive. Since she didn't have anything *to* drive, it wasn't hard to follow orders.

"I guess I'm supposed to ask you in for a drink now or some happy shit."

"That's right, but I'll take a raincheck. I got a date. Scorching date, and I'm running behind."

"Appreciate the ride."

"That's your best comeback? You're in bad shape. Take a pill, Dallas," he suggested as she eased her aching body out. "Flake out awhile."

"I'm okay. Go bang the bimbo of the week."

"Now that's more like it." He gave a cheery chuckle and drove away.

She limped into the house, but couldn't quite limp past Summerset.

He looked down his nose, sniffed. "I see you've managed to destroy several more articles of clothing."

"Yeah, I thought I'd rip and burn them while wearing them, just to see what happened."

"I assume your vehicle suffered similarly as it's not in evidence."

"It's trash. But then, it always was." She headed for the stairs, but he blocked her path, then scooped up the cat who was trying to climb up her legs.

"For God's sake, Lieutenant, take the elevator. And you may as well take something voluntarily for the pain before you have to be humiliated into it."

"I'm walking it off so I don't stiffen up and start to look like you." She knew it was stubborn, she knew it was stupid, but she took the stairs. The worst was, if he hadn't been there at the door, lurking, she'd have taken the damn elevator in the first place.

She was dripping with sweat by the time she made it to the bedroom, so she simply stripped off her ruined clothes, tossed her weapon and her communicator on the bed, and whimpered her way into the shower.

"Jets on half power," she ordered. "One hundred degrees."

The soft spray of hot water stung, then soothed. She braced her hands against the tile wall, dipped her head, and let it flow over her.

Who had they been after? she wondered. Her or Sparrow? She was betting on herself. Sparrow, and the civilians in the line of fire, were just what they'd call collateral damage. So why try to take her out, and why hadn't they done a better job of it?

Sloppy, sloppy, she thought. It's all been sloppy.

"Jets off," she grunted, and feeling a bit steadier, stepped out of the shower.

She knew her heart shouldn't have jolted when she saw Roarke. Summerset—the big, fat tattletale—would have told him.

"The MTs cleared me," she said quickly. "I'm just banged up, that's all."

"I can see that. You don't want the drying tube. The hot air won't do you any good. Here." He picked up a bathsheet, walked to her, and wrapped it gently around her. "Do I have to force a blocker on you?"

"No."

"Well, that's something." He feathered his fingers over the abrasions on her face. "We may be angry with each other, Eve, but you should have contacted me. I shouldn't have heard you'd been in an accident from a damn media bulletin."

"They didn't release names," she began, then trailed off.

"They didn't have to."

"I didn't think. I'm sorry, I really didn't think about it. It's not because I'm—whatever I am with you right now. I didn't think about the media, or that you'd hear anything about it until I got back and could tell you myself."

"All right. You need to lie down."

"I'll take the blocker, but I'm not going down. AD Sparrow's bad. He was with me. His spine's messed up, and there's severe head trauma. The passenger side was—shit. Shit. I don't know how he lived through it. It was a short-range missile."

She scooped her hair back and went into the bedroom to sit. "You said missile."

"Yeah. Probably one of those nifty one-man jobs. Handheld launcher. He must've fired from the roof across from Central. Had me staked out. Maybe Sparrow, but I'm thinking me. To mess up the investigation? To mess you up? Both?" She shook her head. "Maybe to put the HSO on the hot seat, taking out a cop when they couldn't get her to pass the investigation over to them. Maybe to throw the suspicion onto the terrorists."

He handed her a small blue pill and a glass of water. "Your word you'll swallow it or I'll check under your tongue."

"I'm not quite feeling up to sex games. Leave my tongue alone. I'm swallowing it."

Some of the warmth came back in his eyes as he sat beside her. "Why isn't it the HSO or Doomsday?"

"Not very covert to launch a missile at a cop car in New York traffic in the middle of the day. If they wanted me out, they'd find a more subtle way and without losing one of the assistant directors in the process."

"Agreed."

"So, this is like a quiz?"

"The MTs may have cleared you, but you look as if you've been run over by a truck. I'd like to see if you're thinking clearly at least. Why not Doomsday, then? Subtle isn't their style."

"First, technos don't send a man out to shoot missiles. That's why they're technos. And if they did break pattern, they wouldn't have missed. And it was a miss. Couple of feet down, hit the car broadside, and we're gone. They send somebody to take out a cop and/or an operative, they're not going to be so half-assed about it. Plus, I think they'd have gone bigger. If they could get a man into position, why not use a bigger toy, and take out a chunk of Central? Hit Cop Central and you've got the kind of media foray they love. Take out a car, and it's a little bulletin. Not big. This has the earmark of desperation or temper, not organization. How'm I doing?"

"Your brain doesn't appear to have been unduly scrambled." He rose, wandered to the window. "Why didn't you tell me you'd been called to the Tower?"

"We're straddling a line here," she said after a moment. "I don't like it, I don't like feeling . . . apart from you. But that's the reality of it."

"So it seems."

"Someone tried to kill me today. Will you hunt them down?"

He didn't turn. "It's entirely different, Eve. I've had to . . . adjust myself when it comes to your work, what you do, what may be done to you. I love you, and loving you I have to accept that you are what you are, and do what you do. It costs me."

He turned now, looked at her with those wild blue eyes. "Considerably."

"It was your choice. It was always your choice."

"As if I had one, from the minute I saw you. What you face now, I can accept, and admire you for facing it. What you faced then, what was forced on you when you had no defense, I can't accept."

"It won't change anything."

"That's a matter of perspective. Does it change anything to put a killer in a cage after his victim's in the ground? You believe it does, and so do I. And debating this now is only going to push us both further over on our own sides of that line. We both have work."

"Yeah, we both have work." She got to her feet. She would stand, she thought. Had to. Even if she couldn't stand with him.

"Before we were so rudely interrupted, Sparrow told me that Bissel was a double agent. The HSO was using him to get intel from Doomsday. Giving them structured intel in return for payment. It was a long con. They wrapped Ewing up in it due to her position at Securecomp. They wanted a handle on your technology and projects, and most particularly in recent months, whatever they could get on your Code Red. They want, and apparently seriously want, to scoop you on the shield."

"I suppose the idea of the private sector having that kind of technology irritates them. Using Bissel was sensible. He plays all ends—using Reva to gain data on Securecomp, posing as the greedy turncoat to gain knowledge of Doomsday."

"His brother was blackmailing him over the extramaritals. But that suited their purposes. Sparrow claims they don't know where Carter Bissel is. He might be telling the truth, but I'm not buying little brother as your standard blackmailer. No reason to corrupt his personal units, no reason for him to disappear or be disappeared. Doesn't jibe."

"He who can play turncoat can actually be one."

She smiled. "There you go."

She hated to admit it but the blocker helped. Even so the thin cotton pants and loose T-shirt felt heavy on her abused body. When Peabody took one look at her and winced, Eve decided she probably looked worse than she felt.

"You don't look like you can hit me at the moment," Peabody began, "so I'm going to ask. Don't you think you should be in the hospital?"

"Don't let appearances deceive you. No, I shouldn't be in the hospital, and yes, I can still hit you. Bring me up on Powell."

"Single full-contact, full-power shot with hand laser, as evaled on scene. Time of death, ten-fifteen yesterday morning. No forced entry. CSU believes a master was used. Powell's ID, his vehicle code, his employee pass were all missing from the premises. He'd made no transmissions from his home 'link since the previous afternoon when he ordered pizza from a local place. But he did receive one at just after eight A.M. on the morning of his death. The caller cut transmission after Powell answered, groggily. We traced it to a public 'link at a subway station three blocks away from the scene. Conclusion: The killer verified Powell was home, and in bed. Gave him enough time to fall back to sleep, then entered the premises and killed him."

"Sweepers?"

"Only the prelim, but they haven't identified any prints other than the victim's, no DNA, no trace. But I do have a neighbor, Mrs. Lance, who was coming back home from the deli. She saw a man coming out of the building at about ten-thirty. Description matches the one Sibresky gave us of this Angelo."

"How about the artist's rendering? We got that?"

"Working on it. When I checked I was told Sibresky isn't being particularly cooperative or open-minded. I promised the artist a backstage pass to the next Mavis Freestone concert in the city if he got us something this afternoon."

"Good bribe. I'm so proud."

"I had an excellent trainer."

"Suck up later. Have you been in to see McNab?"

Peabody pokered up. "I only stopped by the lab to check on the progress of their work."

"Yeah, and to give his bony ass a pat."

"Unfortunately, he was sitting on said bony ass at the time of my visit, so I was unable to complete that part of my mission."

"Because, despite all my efforts, the image of that bony ass is starting to form in my fevered mind, tell me about the rest of the mission. How's it going in there?"

Peabody wanted to ask why Eve hadn't been in to see for herself, but from the snags of tension around her and Roarke, she thought she knew.

"Well, there's a lot of techno-talk, some pretty creative cursing. I like how Roarke says 'bugger.' Tokimoto stays iced, and Reva's like a woman on a religious quest. McNab's in heaven, hacking away. But what tipped me was Feeney. There's this gleam in his eyes. I think they're getting close."

"While they're making the world safe for democracy, let's see if we can solve a few murders."

"Excuse me, Lieutenant," she said when her communicator signaled. "I'll get on that little task as soon as I take this. Detective Peabody," she announced. "Hey, Lamar, you got something for us?"

"You got my backstage pass?"

"My word's my bond."

"Then I got your face. How do you want me to send it?"

"Laser fax," Eve ordered from her desk. "And a file to my unit here. I want a hard copy, and I want one on my computer."

Peabody relayed, then walked over to retrieve the fax herself. "Lamar's good. Could probably make a better living doing portraits than detailing bad guys. Not the prettiest petal on the flower," she added, passing the printout to Eve. "But not as ugly as Sibresky said. The scar just messes up the face."

"Yeah, it draws the eye, too, doesn't it? You're going to think scar when you see this face. Big, nasty scar, so maybe you don't look too close, because, gee, that's rude."

"Sibresky doesn't seem to have had that problem."

"I get the feeling Sibresky's not too big on sensitivity and etiquette. Let's play a game, Peabody."

"Really? Okay."

"We'll start by you going in the kitchen, getting a pot of coffee and . . . something. There's gotta be something to eat."

"You want food?"

"No, my stomach's still shaky. You get food."

"Hey, so far I like this game."

"Don't come back in until I tell you."

"No problem."

Eve turned to her computer, rubbed her hands together. "Okay, let's play."

It didn't take long because the process and the possibility had been brewing in her brain for some time. She used the imaging program, shooting the visuals on the wall screens as she worked the details.

"Okay, Peabody, you're up, and bring me coffee."

"You should have some of this apple-cranberry cobbler." She came in with a bowl of it, and a mug for Eve. "It's really mag."

"What do you see?"

Peabody eased a hip onto the edge of the desk, spooned up

cobbler. "The artist's rendering of the suspect known only as Angelo."

"Okay. Computer split screen, keep current image and display image CB-1."

WORKING . . . IMAGE DISPLAYED.

"Now what do you see?"

"Carter Bissel, split screen with Angelo." She frowned, and though she understood immediately what direction Eve was taking, she shook her head. "I'll go with the Angelo person being a disguise. I don't see Carter Bissel in there. There's no data on him being an expert on disguise. Buy a wig, slap on a mustache, sure. Even maybe manage the scar. But the line of the jaw's off—an implant for the bucked teeth would change the shape of the mouth, but not the jaw. He'd need more for that, and even if Kade was working him, or with him for a few months, how'd he get so skilled in disguise?"

She scooped up more cobbler and continued to study and compare the two images. "And Carter Bissel's ears are bigger. That's the tip. Ears are a good giveaway. He could make them bigger for Angelo, but not smaller."

"You've got a good eye, Peabody. But watch and learn."

Chapter 18

Peabody ate cobbler and watched as Eve and the computer added the hair from image one onto the head of image two.

"You know, you can do it all with one command if you—"

"I know I can do it all with one command," Eve said irritably. "It doesn't make the same damn point that way. Who's running this game?"

"You know, getting shot at with a short-range missile makes you really testy."

"Keep it up, and the next short-range missile's going straight up your ass."

"Dallas, you know how I love that sweet talk." Shifting to a more comfortable position, Peabody licked her spoon, then waved it at the screen. "Okay, you add the bad hair, but it doesn't change jaw structure or ear size and shape. Also, the witness makes Angelo slimmer, considerably slimmer than Carter Bissel. Fifteen pounds, easy. Bissel carried some extra weight according to his ID stats. The witness said Angelo was trim, in good physical shape. Again, you can add weight in a disguise, but you can't shave off fifteen pounds overnight. If you could, I'd be signed up for the program."

"If you don't want to play, take your cobbler and scram. Computer, replicate facial scar from image one onto image two."

"The entry into Powell's apartment, as in the Bissel home, was slick." Peabody scraped at the bowl, looking for any escaping cobbler as the computer complied with the command. "Has to be someone with experience or training. And all the murders in this case have been particularly cold, even the first ones, which were staged to look hot-blooded. It's the very staging that makes them cold."

"Nobody's arguing that. Give me motive. Computer, assume front top teeth of image one is an implant. Calculate and replicate same on image two."

"Covert organization screwup—either one. Or, I've been thinking about this—a kind of gang war. The worm is complete so Doomsday must want to utilize. They know a shield's being created. HSO and its associates create havoc to slow technos down or circumvent, or destroy the worm. Doomsday creates havoc to scatter resources, create havoc, which is what terrorists do anyway, and circumvent the creation of the shield until they get some use out of all the time, trouble, and expense they've gone to. One side murders a couple of operatives, the other snips off a potential loose thread—McCoy. One side grabs operative's brother. The other steals dead operative's body, and does the overkill attack on the primary investigator. Escalated espionage," Peabody said with a shrug. "Not as iced as Bond, but plenty convoluted. It seems to me spies convolute everything."

"Look at the images, Peabody."

Peabody complied, and tapped the spoon gently on her teeth. "I see a resemblance, largely superficial, between the two images. Dallas, you put my image up there and do computer composites, you could make me look like Angelo. But don't, okay, 'cause I just ate."

"Still hung up on the variation of jawline and the ears?"

"If you tried to take this into court, they'd throw you out."

"Guess you're right. Computer, remove image two and replace with image three."

Peabody's brows knit when the split screen showed two images of Angelo. "I don't get it."

"Don't get what?"

"Why are you projecting two images of the same guy?"

"Am I? You sure they're the same guy? Maybe getting tossed around earlier's messed up my vision."

"You got Angelo up there side by side." Concerned, Peabody shifted to study Eve's face. "Look, if you don't want to go to the hospital, maybe you could call Louise. She'd make a house call for you."

"I don't want to bother the busy Dr. Dimatto. Let's just see what I . . . oh yeah, that's right. Here's what I meant to do. Computer, remove all replications from image three and display original."

Eve sat back with a very satisfied grin as Peabody dropped the spoon. "That's Bissel. That's *Blair* Bissel."

"It sure is, isn't it? You know, I'm thinking reports of his death have been largely exaggerated."

"I know you ran that theory, but I never thought you put real weight on it. The DNA, the prints, were Blair Bissel's. His own wife ID'd him."

"HSO training, several years on the job, even at a lower operative level, should give a guy the skills to doctor records, change his to his brother's. Add overkill, the blood, the gore, the fact that Ewing was shocked, and the fact that in all probability Carter Bissel had undergone some recent surgery to enhance his fairly strong family resemblance to his brother. Body weight was high for Blair's records, but not more than a lot of people lie about on official documents anyway. Nobody pays any attention to an extra ten or fifteen pounds."

"I skim ten off mine. I don't know why. It's a compulsion."

"We expect to see Blair Bissel, so we see him. Why should we question the identity of the victim?"

"But why would he go along with it? Carter? There wasn't any sign of force, no ligatures. How do you induce somebody to undergo surgery, change appearance?"

"Could've paid him. Money, sex—probably both. Let's

screw with big brother and screw his girlfriend while we're at it. No love lost between the brothers."

"There's a wide gulf between no love lost and deliberately, coldly murdering your brother and your lover. If Kade was helping to set Carter up—"

"Then Blair planned to do her all along. Yeah, that's what I think. You want to fake your own death, do it in a big way. A vicious way that tosses the blood in your wife's face, at least initially, and gets rid of the monkey on your back and one of the people who knew you intimately enough to muck the deal. They'll say you were a cheat, a liar, a bastard. What do you care, you're dead."

"I have to think about this." Peabody pushed away from the desk to pace. "With this theory, Blair and Kade did a number on Carter outside the HSO directive."

"Maybe they started inside, probably did, but I figure they started coloring outside the lines at some point."

"As a solution for the blackmail."

"Partially. It's money, it's adventure, it's risk. All those fit their profiles. But they had bigger goals. Keep going."

"Crap. Blair was a liaison, doubling under HSO directive as a liaison for Doomsday. Feeding them selected data for payment, and establishing himself as a source, a traitor, a free agent. Part of this cloak was his marriage to Reva Ewing, blueprinted by the HSO."

"Corporate espionage on one hand—a lucrative game, and with so much privatization of intel- and data-gathering sources over the last couple of decades, the HSO has to compete with civilian companies for revenue."

"Like Securecomp."

"Like that, and the dozens of others on and off planet they arranged for Blair to plant his listening posts. And think about this, Peabody. You always have to have a backup plan. You require plausible deniability. What contingency plan do you suppose the architects of this blueprint drew up in the event one of the sculptures was detected?"

Peabody stopped in front of the screens, studied the faces. "Blair Bissel, fall guy."

"You bet, and by association, Reva would fall with him and Securecomp is compromised. It could—and I think would—have been said that they'd worked together. After all, they were husband and wife."

"So they were building a frame after all."

"Contingencies. Blair'd been in the organization long enough for this to occur to him. And if not him, it occurred to Kade."

"So he took steps to protect himself?" Peabody shook her head. "Really big steps."

"Not only protection. Factor in the satisfaction of getting back at his blackmailing brother, Homeland—the people, the government who'd use and discard him if things went wrong. Then add a big shit-pile of money."

"From the technos? He makes a deal with them. Unauthorized information. Something big."

"He's the bridge between points A and B, and he knows more about both points, in this aspect, than either point knows of each other. Because he's the one passing the data. He's in control of that. Heady stuff for a guy with his personality profile. Why not take more? More control, more power, more money, and get out? Only one way out. Go rogue, and they'll hunt you down. Both sides."

"But they won't hunt if they think you're dead."

"There you go. Add to that the HSO busy trying to cover up the mess you left behind, the cops busy investigating a prime suspect handed to them on a platter, and the death of the only person who had knowledge of your plans, and you're in the cozy part of fat city."

"What went wrong? Why isn't he sitting in the surf on some island paradise, slurping rum punch and counting his money?"

"Maybe the payment wasn't made. You don't want to go putting all your eggs in a terrorist's basket. They often end up scrambled. But he'd been trained well enough to have a contingency plan of his own. He gave McCoy something. He had to go back for it. She had to die for it."

"And meanwhile, the primary isn't buying his served-on-a-platter prime suspect. With the cops taking a closer look, so's everyone else."

"Yeah, things got screwed for him, almost from the start. Roarke's into this Yeats guy who's an old, dead Irish writer. He said something about things falling apart. The center doesn't hold. The center hasn't been holding for Blair Bissel."

"And it's been falling apart since you walked into the first crime scene."

"He's desperate, and he's pissed, and he overthinks. He's so worried about covering his ass, he keeps exposing it. He needs to stay dead, needs to collect his fee. Hard to do both. Killing Powell and destroying the body identified as his own was stupid. It prevents positive ID, but it also turns the trail around and heads it right back at him. He's the only one who'd want that evidence destroyed."

"Then he tries to take you out."

"Like I said, he's pissed. And he's desperate. And you know what he is, under all this espionage, artsy, woman-sniffing bullshit, Peabody? He's a screwup. The kind that keeps making bigger, splashier mistakes to cover up the last one. He thinks he's a stone-cold killer, but he's a selfish, spoiled little boy playing—what's that guy's name—James Bond—then having a tantrum when he doesn't quite pull it off."

"He may not be stone-cold, but he's killed four people, knocked you around pretty good, and put an assistant director of the HSO in the hospital."

"I didn't say he wasn't dangerous. Kids having temper tantrums are pretty damn dangerous. Scare the hell out of me."

"So, according to your theory, we have a cranky, immature, HSO-trained killer."

"Pretty much."

Peabody blew out a breath that fluttered her ruler-straight bangs. "That is pretty scary. How do we catch him?"

"Working on that." Eve started to prop her feet on the desk, had the twinge of revolting muscles shoot straight through her body. "Shit."

"You'd better work on those bruises."

"I don't have bruises on my brain. I can still think. Let's get the rest of the team in here, civilians included, and kick this ball around."

"You want Ewing in on this?"

"She was married to him for two years. It might have been a convenience to him, but she still would've learned something about him. Habits, fantasies, hangouts. If Sparrow lives, regains consciousness, and opts to share information on Bissel, that may help, but right now, Reva Ewing's our best source."

"You're going to tell her that the husband she was accused of murdering is not only alive, in your opinion, but is the one who set her up?"

"If she can't deal with it, she's no help and we're no worse off. Let's see if she inherited any of her mother's spine."

Feeney came in muttering figures and command codes into a PPC. His chin was stubbled with ginger and gray and the bags under his eyes could've held a week's marketing for a family of three—but there was a gleam in them.

"Bad time to interrupt, kid," he said to Eve. "We're on the verge."

"There's another prong to this investigation, and that may be on the verge, too. Where are the others?"

"Roarke and Tokimoto are finishing up running a series. Don't want to walk away in the middle of that, not after what it's taken to get there. We got one of Kade's units as clean as it's going to get. McNab and Ewing are just about done reinstalling some . . ."

He stopped, pursed his lips as he finally lifted his head and took a good look at her. "Said you got slammed around. They meant it. Ought to put some ice on that eye."

"Is it going black? Damn it." She pressed her fingers gingerly along the top edge of her cheekbone, and felt the bolt of pain right down to her toes. "I took a blocker. Isn't that enough?"

Peabody came out of the kitchen with an ice bandage. "If you let me put this on it, it'll sting a minute, and look stupid.

But it'll decrease the bruising and swelling. You may not end up with a full shiner."

"Just do it, don't talk about it."

Eve set her teeth while Peabody fixed the bandage. The sting drowned out the throbbing, which wasn't that much of an improvement.

"Ouch," McNab commented with a sympathetic wince as he strolled in. "Heard you lost your ride, too."

"Wasn't much of a loss. Where's Ewing?"

"Right behind me. Just had to make a pit stop. Okay if I pump some fuel? I'm empty."

"There's cobbler," Peabody called out as he was already heading to the kitchen. "Apple-cranberry."

"Cobbler?" Feeney repeated.

"Jeez. Go ahead." Eve threw up her hands. "Eat, drink, be merry. Every multiple homicide investigation should have cobbler."

"I'm going to get you something cold to drink," Peabody decided. "You should probably be pushing fluids."

With that Eve found herself alone in her office, wondering how she'd so easily lost the reins of her team.

Marital discord, she decided, was like some sort of low-grade fever that threw the whole system just slightly out of whack so you couldn't manage to function at full capacity.

She wasn't at the top of her game, that was for sure, and had no idea how to get back there again.

"You want food," she snapped out the minute Reva came in, "get food. You want drink, get drink. But make it fast. This isn't a damn twenty-four/seven."

Reva merely angled her head. "I'm fine, thanks. But I'm betting you feel as bad as you look. Roarke and Tokimoto are going to be a few more minutes. They're at a flash point."

"They aren't the only ones. We're not going to wait for them. Or for anybody else!" she called out. "You're going to want to sit down for this."

"Because this is going to be a really long lecture or because you're going to, metaphorically, give me a punch?"

"I'm hoping you can take a punch."

Reva nodded and took the closest chair. "Don't pull it. Whatever it is, I'd rather you go for the knockout instead of a lot of testing jabs. I'm tired. And with every hour that passes, I feel more of an idiot for not seeing what was in front of my face, day after day, for over two years."

"What was in front of your face was a guy who behaved and portrayed himself as someone who loved you, and was brought into your life by someone else you trusted."

"Goes a long way to measuring how well I judge people."

"They were pros at what they did, and they worked hard to set you up, right along. Were you supposed to look at this guy and think: Hey, secret agent?"

"No." Reva's lips curved. "But you'd think I'd get some vibes about liar and cheat."

"They screened you and they studied you. They knew everything there was to know about you before you met either of them. They knew what was public and private. You were laid up for months for shielding a president, for doing your job. Maybe they hoped you'd have some resentment about that, or that your work for the government would make you open to working with them."

"Fat fucking chance."

"And when they got that, they moved on you personally. He knew what you liked to eat, what flowers you preferred, your hobbies, your finances, who you slept with or cared about. You were nothing to them but a tool, and they knew how to use you."

"The first night, at the art showing, he asked me if I'd have a drink with him. Great-looking guy, funny, sweet, hey, why not. We sat for hours, talking. I felt like I'd known him all my life. Like I'd been waiting for him all my life."

She looked down at her hands. "I'd been involved before, pretty serious involvement before I was injured, then that fell apart. But nothing came close to what I felt for Blair. And it was all fabrication. It wasn't perfect. He'd get sulky or irritated at the least slight or criticism, but I figured that was part of the deal, you know? Part of being married and figuring each other out, making each other happy. I wanted to make him happy. I wanted to make it work."

"It's never perfect," Eve said half to herself. "Whenever you think it is, something sneaks up and bites you on the ass."

"I'll say. Anyway, I'm tired. Tired of feeling stupid, of feeling sorry for myself. So tell me why I'm sitting down. One punch."

"Okay. It's my belief that Blair Bissel orchestrated and committed the homicides at Felicity Kade's apartment, killing her and his brother in order to fake his own death and implicate you."

"That's just crazy." The words wheezed out as if the punch had landed hard on her throat. "He's dead. Blair's dead. I *saw* him."

"You saw what you were meant to see, just as you saw what you were meant to see when he approached you two and a half years ago. And this time, you were in shock and almost immediately incapacitated."

"But . . . it was verified."

"I think he switched his identification records with his brother's, in preparation. I believe he set an elaborate stage so that you, the police, and the clandestine organizations he'd been playing against each other would believe him dead. Nobody looks for the dead, Reva."

"It's insane. I'm telling you it's *insane*, Dallas." Reva got to her feet as the others came in from the kitchen. "Blair was a liar and a cheat. He used me. I'm doing everything I can to accept all that. I'll live with that. But he wasn't a killer, he wasn't someone who could . . . could hack two people to death."

"Who stood to gain from his death?"

"I—you mean financially?"

"In any way."

"I did, I guess. There's money, decent money. You know all that."

"Decent money," Eve repeated. "You've got decent money of your own. He'll have hidden accounts, and once we find them—"

"Located, listed, and filed on your computer," Roarke said as he walked in. "As requested, Lieutenant."

"How much?"

"In excess of four million spread over five accounts."

"Not enough."

Roarke inclined his head. "Perhaps not, but it's all there is. He was neither particularly frugal nor skilled in investment areas. All the accounts have slow, steady leaks over the six years they've been opened. He spends, and he speculates, and most usually loses his capital."

"That plays." She began to reevaluate. "Okay, that plays. He goes through money, he needs more money. A big score."

"So he kills Felicity and his brother to get it, implicates me? You're painting a monster. I wasn't married to a monster."

"You were married to an illusion."

Reva's head jerked back as if the blow had landed. "You're grabbing at air because you don't have anything else. And because you don't want to leave me with nothing. I *loved* him, whether or not he was an illusion. Do you understand the concept?"

"I'm familiar with it."

"You want me to believe I loved someone capable of murder. Cold-blooded, cold-minded murder."

It took all her will to keep her gaze from flicking, even for an instant, toward Roarke. And to keep her heart and mind from asking herself that same question.

"What you believe is your own business. How you handle this is up to you. If you can't deal with the direction of my investigation, you're no use to me."

"You're the cold-blooded one. The cold-minded one. And I've been used just about enough."

When she strode out, Tokimoto eased away from the door and followed her.

"Gee, she took that well." Now Eve allowed herself a slow scan of faces. "Would anyone like to complete this briefing, or should we break for comments about my need for sensitivity training?"

"It's a hard knock, Dallas," Feeney said. "No way for you to pretty it up for her. She'll be back when she shakes it off."

"We'll work without her. Bissel has accounts in various locations, odds are he's got a bolt-hole—a lavish one, maybe more than one. He's still in the city, cleaning up after himself, so he must have one here. We find it."

"I found two properties," Roarke put in. "One in the Canary Islands, the other in Singapore. Neither were very well cloaked, meaning if I found them so easily, others would."

"So they're probably blinds. He's not completely stupid. Let's look in his brother's name, or Kade's, Ewing's. He might have set himself up, using them as cover, then if . . . No, no. Shit! McCoy. Chloe McCoy. He had to have more use for her than the occasional bang. Check it out. See if he tucked away funds and/or property in her name somehow. He killed her for a reason, and my take is this guy kills for money and self-preservation."

"I'll take that," McNab volunteered. "Working on a cobbler rush."

"Get started. I'm going to check on Sparrow, see if he's coherent and I can dig anything out of him. Feeney, I'm leaving you and Roarke on the machines. If Reva's backed out and Tokimoto's busy patting her head, you're going to be shorthanded."

"Another tanker of coffee ought to keep us in the game."

"You may want an update before you rush off, Lieutenant. We're retrieving data from Kade's unit. It's encrypted, but we'll get through that."

"Great, good. Let me know when—"

"I'm not finished. Each of Kade's units was corrupted, but not through a networking worm. They were burned individually."

"So what? Look, this is EDD territory. All I need is the bottom line. I need the data."

"You don't give electronics enough respect," Feeney stated.

"And neither, I'd venture, does Bissel." As Eve hadn't

touched the glass of chilled juice Peabody had brought her, Roarke picked it up and helped himself. "The potential worm's import is its theoretic ability to corrupt an entire networking system, however small or large, however simple or complex, with one stroke, to corrupt and shut down, irretrievably. That's not what we're dealing with. It's a shade of that, an early version perhaps, but not nearly as powerful as we've been led to believe. It's been relatively easy to clean and retrieve from the units we've got."

"Relatively." Feeney rolled his aching eyes. "It's nasty business, but it's not global security shit. What it is, is smoke."

"Which means he doesn't have what he thought he had—what he was going to parlay into a nice retirement fund. But maybe someone else does, or maybe . . . Son of a bitch. He wasn't trying to take me out." She tapped her fingers absently over her bruised eye. "He hit his target. Aim was a little off, but he hit."

Roarke inclined his head as his thoughts marched with hers. "Sparrow."

"It'd help to have somebody on the inside, somebody with some juice who could adjust or create data in-house. And provide protection. Sparrow. He's the organized thinker. The planner. Look at Bissel. He's not brave, he's not very smart, he hasn't been able to work himself up in the organization. Just a delivery boy. And here's a big opportunity, handed to him from one of the brass. The big score. Little scores all along. The corporate espionage. Could be, just could be, some of that was outside Homeland, a little personal partnership. Bissel though, he can't capitalize. Just a screwup with money. I bet his partner's done better. A hell of a lot better."

"Why not just kill Bissel then?" Peabody asked.

"Because you need a contingency. You need a fall guy. He set the putz up. Still the delivery boy. Bissel goes to deliver the worm disc to the high bidder, and it's not the deal. He gets the shaft. Now he's a dead man, a desperate one. He's running, he's hiding, and at all costs he has to stay dead. Our friend from the HSO wants him to stay dead, too, and he's ready with the company line about global security when the investigation doesn't turn the way he anticipated."

"I imagine he planned to make an honest man out of Bissel by turning him into a dead man," Roarke said. "Quietly, at some point."

"Should've moved on that sooner rather than later, and he wouldn't be in the hospital. I think he forgot to factor one vital element into the equation. When somebody like Bissel starts killing, it gets easier every time."

She pulled out her communicator. "I want a block on Sparrow. I don't want anybody, not even the medicals, talking to him until I get my shot. Start reeling in that data."

"Hook up that tanker of coffee," Feeney reminded her, then headed out.

"I need a moment, Lieutenant." Roarke glanced at Peabody. "A private one."

"I'll wait outside." Peabody slipped out, shut the door.

"I don't have time to go into personal business," Eve began.

"Sparrow has access to your data, to what happened in Dallas. If you're right about all of this, he might very well use it against you. Make it public, even altering it in some way that twists the truth."

"I can't worry about that."

"I can make it disappear. If you want that . . . element removed, I can remove it. You're entitled to your privacy, Eve. You're entitled to be secure that your own victimization won't be used to draw speculation, gossip—and the pity you'd hate more than either."

"You want me to give you the nod to tamper with government files?"

"No, I want you to tell me if you'd prefer those files didn't exist. Hypothetically."

"Which would let me off the hook. Legally. I wouldn't be an accessory if I just made a little wish, and poof. This is a hell of a day. This is a hell of a funny day."

Because emotion was flooding her throat again, she turned away. "You and me, we haven't been this far apart from each other since the beginning. I can't reach you, and I can't let you reach me."

"You don't see me, Eve. When you look at me, you don't see the whole of me. Maybe I've preferred that."

She thought of Reva, of illusions, and a mockery of a marriage. Nothing could be further from what they were dealing with. Roarke had never lied, nor pretended to be something other than what he was. And she had seen him, right from the first moment.

"You're wrong, and you're stupid." There was more weariness than temper in the words, and as such struck him more forcefully. "I don't know how to get through this. I can't talk to you about it, because it just circles. I can't talk to anyone else, because if I tell them what's ripping at us, it makes them an accessory. You think I don't see you?"

She turned back, looked straight into his eyes. "I'm looking at you, and I see you. I know you're capable of killing, and feeling justified, feeling right. I know that, and I'm still here. I don't know what the hell to do, but I'm still here."

"If I wasn't capable, I wouldn't be who I am, what I am, where I am. Neither of us would be here, wrestling with this."

"Maybe not, but I'm too tired to wrestle. I have to go. I need to go." She walked quickly to the door, wrenched it open. Then she shut her eyes. "Make it disappear. Fuck hypothetical. I take responsibility for what I say, what I do. Make it gone."

"Consider it done."

When she left him, he sat down at her desk in the quiet, and wished, with everything inside him, that he could make the rest of it vanish as easily.

Reva waylaid her on the way outside. "I don't have time," Eve said curtly and kept moving.

"It'll only take a minute. I want to apologize. I asked you to give it to me straight, and when you did, I didn't handle it. I'm sorry, and I'm pissed off at myself for reacting the way I did."

"Forget it. Are you going to handle it now?"

"Yeah, I'm going to handle it now. What do you need?"

"I need you to think. Where he might go, what his next steps would be in a crisis. What's he doing now besides trying to find a way out? Think it through, lay it out. Have it ready for me when I get back."

"You'll have it. He'd have to work," she called out as Eve streamed out the door. "His art wasn't just a cover, it couldn't have been. It's his passion, his escape, his ego. He'd have to have a place to work."

"Good. Keep it up. I'll be back."

"That was well done." Tokimoto stepped out of the parlor, into the foyer.

"I hope so. I'm not doing so well otherwise."

"You need time to adjust, to grieve, to be angry. I hope you'll feel able to talk to me when you need someone."

"I've been talking you black-and-blue so far." She sighed. "Tokimoto, can I ask you something?"

"Of course."

"Are you hitting on me?"

He stiffened like a rod. "That would be inappropriate under the circumstances."

"Because I might still be married or because you're not interested?"

"Your marriage would hardly be a factor, considering. But you're not in a state of mind where . . . An advance of a personal nature is clearly inappropriate while your emotions and your situation are in flux."

She found herself smiling, just a little. And found something opening inside her again, just a little. "You didn't say you weren't interested, so I'll just say I don't think I'd mind. If you worked up to hitting on me."

To test it out, she rose on her toes and touched her lips lightly to his. "No," she said after a moment, "I don't think I'd mind. Why don't you think about it?"

She was still smiling, just a little, as she started back upstairs.

Chapter 19

Quinn Sparrow would live. He might, with several months of intensive therapy and treatments, walk again—if he had the same level of will and guts Reva Ewing had called upon to recover from her injuries.

It was, to Eve's mind, a solid kind of justice.

He had broken bones, a fractured spine, and a concussion among other insults. He would require reconstructive surgery on his face.

But he would live.

Eve was glad to hear it.

He was and would remain in Intensive Care for at least forty-eight hours. He was sedated, but Eve's badge and some bullying got her through.

She left Peabody posted at the door.

He was either sleeping or zoned when she walked in. She was banking on the zoned and shut off his IV drip of blockers without a twinge of remorse.

It only took a few moments for him to surface, moaning.

He looked considerably worse for wear, brutally bruised around his bandages, with a skin cast on his right arm, another along with a stability cage—that looked a little like one of Bissel's sculptures—around his right leg.

The wedge of collar prevented any movement of his head or neck.

"You in there, Sparrow?"

"Dallas." White at the lips, he shifted his eyes, tried to focus on her. "What the fuck?"

She moved closer, making it easier for him to keep her in his line of vision, and laid a hand in what she considered a "survivors of the battle" gesture on his shoulder. "You're in the hospital. You're strapped in to restrict movement."

"I don't remember. How . . . how bad?"

It was, she thought, a nice touch to look away for a moment as if she was struggling to speak. "It's . . . it's pretty bad. He hit us, hard. You took the worst. Vehicle went up like a rocket, crashed like a bomb. Slammed into a maxi on your side. You're messed up bad, Sparrow."

She felt his shoulder tremble as he tried to move. "Christ, Christ, the pain."

"I know. It's gotta be rugged. But we got him." She closed a hand over his now, squeezed. "We got the bastard."

"What? Who?"

"We got Bissel, wrapped and locked. Still had the shoulder launcher he used on us. Blair Bissel, Sparrow, alive and well, and singing like a canary."

"That's crazy." He groaned. "I need the doctor. I need something for the pain."

"I want you to listen, to dig down and pay attention. I don't know how much time you've got."

"Time?" His fingers jerked under hers. "Time?"

"I want to give you a chance to clear your conscience, Sparrow. To set the record straight. You deserve that much. He's dumping the whole ball on you. Listen to me. Listen." She tightened her fingers on his. "I've got to give it to you, and you've got to prepare yourself. You're not going to make it."

His skin went sickly gray. "What are you talking about?"

She leaned in close so he could see only her face. "They

did everything they could. Worked on you for hours. There's too much damage."

"I'm *dying?*" His voice, already a weak tremble, cracked. "No. No. I want a doctor."

"They'll be back in a minute. They'll give you . . . they'll give you a humane dose. You'll go out easy."

"I'm not going to die." Tears swam, and spilled over. "I don't want to die."

She pressed her lips together, as if overcome. "I thought you'd want to hear it from me, from . . . a colleague. His aim had been better, we'd both be on our way out. But he just sheered the front end, and we flipped. They saved your leg," she continued, and paused to clear her throat. "They hoped that . . . Christ. The impact messed up your insides, messed them up bad. The son of a bitch killed you, Sparrow, and tried for me."

"I can't see. I can't move."

"You've gotta stay quiet, still. It'll buy you time. You've been out of it, Sparrow, and he's using that. He tried to wipe us both, and because of that I'm trying to give you a chance to go out with some dignity. I'm going to read you your rights." She paused again, shook her head. "Jesus, this sucks."

He began to tremble as she recited the revised Miranda. "You understand your rights and obligations, Assistant Director Sparrow?"

"What the hell is this about?"

"It's about setting the record straight, and getting some of your own back here. A good lawyer's going to get Bissel off with a few slaps if you don't tell me how it went down. He's counting on you just dying. Dying and taking the hard rap. He says you killed Carter Bissel and Felicity Kade."

"That's bullshit."

"I know it, but he might convince the PA. Jesus, Sparrow, you're dying! Tell me the truth, let me shut this down, put him away. He killed you." She leaned in close, lowered her voice. "Make him pay."

"Stupid fuckup. Who knew he had it in him? How'd it all end up like this?"

"Tell me, and I'll see to it he goes down. You've got my word on it."

"He killed Carter Bissel and Felicity Kade."

"Who?"

"Blair! Blair Bissel killed Carter Bissel and Felicity Kade. He sniffed a little Zeus to give himself some backbone and sliced them up."

"Why? Give me some juice so I can drown him in it."

"He was going to disappear, with a big chunk of change. Set up the wife so the cops closed the book. Open, shut. Shoulda been open, shut."

"You sent Reva the photographs of Blair and Kade?"

"Yeah. I took them, dropped them on her when the rest was in place. I can't feel my legs. I can't feel my legs."

"Hold on. Just hold on. I'm recording this, Sparrow. You're going on record. You're going to put him away for doing this to you. Why'd he kill Kade?"

"Needed her to tie the bow on the package. And she knew too much about both of us. Couldn't risk it."

"You were the brains in this. You can't tell me that jerkoff thought this up on his own."

"I had it all worked out. Should've been a walk. Couple more weeks, I'd be on a beach sipping fucking mai tais, but he just kept screwing things up."

"Kade was in on it? She pulled the brother in."

"Know a hell of a lot, don't you?" He stared at Eve with dead eyes.

"I'm putting it together. I've got to be straight with you. You deserve that. A deathbed confession . . ." She trailed off, watching his face blanch and crumble. "Well, you know the weight of that. You'll be the one to lock the cage on him. I want to give you that last act. Professional courtesy. Felicity Kade drew Carter Bissel into the mix."

"Pulled him in." Sparrow's breath wheezed in, wheezed out, and Eve had the sudden thought that the bastard might die on her just through the power of suggestion. "Had the stupid son of a bitch convinced he was working for the HSO. Going to take over his brother's position. He bought it. Change his face, make a few deliveries. Get to sleep with his trainer. He was a dunk."

"I bet. Who took out the guy who did the face and body work? Kade?"

"No. No, she wouldn't get her hands dirty. She had Bissel do it—Carter. She was good at getting men to do what she wanted."

"But you were the architect, right? Not Kade, certainly not Blair Bissel. You're not stupid enough to go around killing people right and left, but you knew how to pull the strings. He thought he had the comp worm. He thought he could sell it. Live off the proceeds the rest of his life. But he never had it."

"Can't have what doesn't exist. I made it up." His smile turned to a grimace. "I can't take this pain, Dallas. I can't take it."

His whine set her teeth on edge, but she gave his hand another bolstering squeeze. "It won't be much longer. There's no worm?"

"Yeah, there's a worm. It's just not as advertised. I invented it, hyped it, documented the skewed data and intel. Doomsday's been trying to create one, a fricking decade. Works in theory, but in practice it just self-cannibalizes or mutates when it hits the shields. You insert at port, it'll mess up a unit, fry its ass, but it won't network, and won't infect by remote. But if it did"—his pale, battered face shone for a moment with pleasure—"it'd be worth billions."

"So it was all just a con—on HSO and the global agencies, on Doomsday. You created the intel that supported the myth that the worm was real, that it was a threat. Then you planted your man with the project head of the company who nabs the Code Red. Feed the HSO data, sell same to interested parties. You're raking it in on both ends, and all over something that doesn't yet exist, and may never exist. But Securecomp's working on it, and they might just create the worm for you. Yeah, you're smart."

"They were getting close. Roarke's got some brain trust at Securecomp. I get what they've got together with what I've got, what I'm pulling from Doomsday, maybe I can put it together and get myself a nice bonus. You know what you make annually as an AD? You make shit. Just like a cop."

"And being as we're so underpaid, you didn't figure the cops would dig too deep into the Bissel/Kade murders."

"Served it up so neat and pretty. But things went wrong."

"You could stall, though, pressure to have the locals turn over the investigation. And you had your goat with Bissel. He tries to sell the disc, and it's worthless."

"Figured the buyer would execute him, bury the body, once they figured out the worm wasn't what he claimed. That would take some time, put some distance between him and me. He wiggled out of that, though. He talks a pretty good game."

"But he can't access his money without sending up a flag, to you. And even if he got desperate enough to try, we started finding and freezing his accounts. So he stages McCoy's suicide. What did she have that he wanted?"

"I don't know. I don't know where she fits. He should've slipped off, counted his losses, but the stupid son of a bitch panics, kills her, kills that stupid orderly, steals the body. What's he think the cops're going to do? Might as well have taken out a fricking ad on an airblimp."

"How long have you two been doing the corporate espionage on the side?"

"What the hell does it matter?"

He was pouting now, she thought. Wimp was pouting because his big plans had blown up in his face and killed him.

"The more you give me, the deeper I can bury him."

"Six, seven years. I've got a nice retirement fund, got a place on Maui, and another I've got my eye on in Tuscany. I'd've been set, living large, before I was forty. Had to start covering my tracks."

"Eliminate your partners," Eve agreed. "Better, smarter, have them eliminate each other. And move to a one-man, more profitable organization. All those listening posts planted in Bissel's sculptures all over the world—and off—all yours alone now. You can gather your intel, invest, anticipate. Yeah, you'd've been sipping mai tais, and *still* raking it in. I gotta say, Sparrow, it's brilliant."

His damp eyes shone for a moment in pleasure. "It's what I do. Crunch data, think up scenarios, blueprint dirty tricks to compromise or dispose of targets. You have to know how and when to use people."

"And you knew how to use Bissel. Both of them. And Kade. And Ewing."

"Wasn't supposed to be so complicated. Bissel hits Kade, goes under. Was supposed to go under for a few weeks, then make the sale. But he went right after it. Didn't give it time to settle, for me to see if it worked and cooled off."

"Cooled off so you could make certain you didn't need him, so he could be eliminated."

"You don't throw away tools until you're sure they've outlived their usefulness. Terminations are part of the game. You know that. Death's necessary. I've never killed anybody, and I wouldn't have had to do him. Leak some intel, point the right person in the right direction. He'd be taken out. I'm not a murderer, Dallas. I just engaged a tool. Blair Bissel did the killing. Every one of them. I was at the Flatiron, corrupting his data units, when he did the hit on his brother and Kade."

"Why go there?"

"I needed to upload any data he might've kept on the operation there, and to crash his units so he couldn't use them. Just covering tracks. I wasn't anywhere near Kade's place when it went down, and I've got alibis for the hits on McCoy and Powell. Blair Bissel did the terminations. I'm going to die, but I'll be damned if he's going to hang me with murder."

"I think we can make that conspiracy to murder, accessory to murder, before and after the fact. Multiple counts. We can probably throw in all sorts of nice pluses like obstruction of justice, tampering with government files, espionage, and that big mama, treason. I think you can say bye-bye to Maui, Sparrow, and those pretty hills in Tuscany."

"I'm fucking dying. Give me a break."

"Right." She pulled her hand free of his and smiled. "I've got some good news and some bad news. Good news, from your point of view, is you're not dying. I exaggerated your medical condition a bit."

"What?" He struggled to sit up and only went sheet-white with the pain. "I'm going to be all right?"

"You'll live. You might not walk again, and you're going to have some serious pain with the physical therapy and treatments over the next few months. But you'll live. Bad news? Doctors say you're pretty strong and healthy otherwise, so you should last decades in a cage."

"You said I was dead. You said—"

"Yeah." She hooked her thumbs in her front pockets. "Cops're such liars. I don't know why you assholes believe us."

"Bitch. Goddamn bitch." He fought to raise himself, going white, then red as he strained against the stabilizers. "I want a lawyer. I want a doctor."

"You can have both. Excuse me, Sparrow, I've got to go arrange for a meeting between your superiors and mine. I bet they're going to have a high old time with this recording."

"You walk out of here with that . . ." He gasped against the pain, and the fear. Eve read them both in his eyes. "You walk out of here with that recording, and I'll have your records all over the media within the hour. Everything that happened in Dallas. Everything in that file, including the speculation that you committed patricide. You're finished as a cop when I get finished spinning those records out to the media."

Eve tilted her head, and smiled. "What records?"

She let her smile widen as she pushed open the door. "Nailed, to the wall," she said to Peabody.

And she could hear Sparrow screaming for a doctor as she strode away.

"I need you to take the recording, copy it, write the report. I want him charged fast. Go through Whitney, push the grease."

"What are the charges?"

"It's all on the record. He's not going anywhere," Eve added as they started down in the overcrowded elevator. "And I don't think Bissel will try for him again, but I want a man on the door."

"Okay. Are you going somewhere?"

"I want to play some of this off of Mira, see if any of this new data gives her an idea how and where Bissel might move next. He's seriously screwed with Sparrow alive and wrapped, and that might make him more dangerous. Nobody's left for him to go for."

"There's you."

"Yeah. That'd be a nice plus."

"You sure have a twisted sense of optimism."

"Yeah, I'm Polly-freaking-anna. Take the ride. I'll track Mira down and grab public transpo."

"I get to drive the mag civilian vehicle. Again?" Peabody did a quick tap and shuffle. "Man, I love being a detective."

"Get Sparrow secured, write the report, get Whitney to push through the arrest warrant, then get back over here and serve it. Then see how much you love it."

She pulled out her pocket 'link. "Oh, and requisition us a new ride."

"You're the superior officer," Peabody reminded her. "The request should come from you."

"And my name is kick-her-ass in Requisitions. I put in, they'll dig up some piece of shit heap with an attitude. They save them for me."

"That's a factor. You know, we could bog down the request, and keep using one of Roarke's. I mean, he's got plenty of vehicles."

"We're cops. We use a cop car."

"Spoilsport," Peabody grumbled when Eve hiked away.

She took a cab to Mira's residence because her body was one massive ache, and the idea of the subway with its crowds and smells seemed like more punishment than she deserved.

Mira answered the door herself, and had already changed out of her work gear into rust-colored pants and a roomy white shirt.

"Thanks for making the time."

"It's absolutely no problem. Look at you," Mira said with concern as she lifted a hand to Eve's face. "The incident's all over the news. With speculation it was a botched terrorist attack on Central."

"It goes back to Bissel, and it's a lot more personal. I'll explain."

"You should sit down, and we'll . . ." She turned, beamed as her husband came toward her with a loaded tray. "Dennis, you remembered."

"Eve likes coffee." He winked at Eve with his dreamy eyes. He was wearing a baggy cardigan with a hole in the sleeve and worn brown trousers. He smelled, Eve thought, a little like cherries.

His expression sobered as he scanned the bruises. "Was there an accident?"

"It was pretty much deliberate. It's nice to see you, Mr. Mira."

"Charlie, you should take care of this girl."

"Yes, I will. Why don't we go upstairs, and I'll take a look at you?"

"Thanks, but I really don't have time—"

Dennis was already starting up with the tray. "We can discuss the case while I treat you," Mira said, and took a firm hold of Eve's arm. "Otherwise, I'll be distracted."

"It looks worse than it is," Eve began.

"Yes, so they always say."

There was a lot of color. It was one of the things Eve always noted about Mira's home. All the color and pretty little whatnots sitting around. Flowers and photographs.

Mira took her into a cozy sitting room done in quiet blues and misty greens. Over a small fireplace was a family portrait of the Miras, their children and spouses, their grandchildren. It wasn't a formal pose, but a casual kind of grouping, as if a conversation was taking place.

"Nice," Eve said.

"Yes, isn't it? My daughter had it done from a photograph and gave it to me last Christmas. The children have already grown so much since. Well. I just need to get a few things. Dennis, entertain Eve for a moment."

"Hmm?" He'd set down the tray and looked around absently.

"Keep Eve company."

"Your husband's not coming?" Dennis poured the coffee. "Nice boy."

"No, he's . . . this is really a professional visit. I'm sorry to interrupt your evening."

"Pretty girl's never an interruption." He patted his pockets, looked around blankly. "I seem to have misplaced the sugar."

There was something about him—the mop of hair, the baggy sweater, the bemused expression—that stirred a little glow of affection inside her. "I don't use any."

"Good thing. Don't know where the hell I left it. Remembered the cookies, though." He picked one up, handed it to her. "Look like you could use one, sweetie."

"Yeah." She stared at it and wondered why it, the gesture, the room, the scent of the flowers on the mantel combined to make her eyes sting. "Thanks."

"It's rarely as bad as we think it is." He patted her shoulder and had her throat going hot. "Unless it's worse. Charlie'll fix you up. I'm going to take my coffee out on the patio," he said when Mira came back. "Let you girls gab."

Eve bit into the cookie, swallowed hard. "I've got a crush on him," she said when she and Mira were alone.

"So do I. You'll need to take off your clothes."

"Why?"

"I can tell by the way you move you've got injuries, and pain. Let's deal with it."

"I don't want—"

"And you can take your mind off what I'm doing by telling me about Bissel."

Accepting that an argument would only drag things out, Eve stripped off the shirt, then the trousers. Mira's quick wince of sympathy had Eve hunching in defense.

"Mostly from the safeties. You know, the harness, impact bags."

"And would have been considerably worse without them, yes. You were treated on scene?"

"Yeah." Eve felt her insides draw up as Mira opened a medical bag. "Look, they did all the stuff. And I took a blocker, so—"

"When?"

"When what?"

"When did you take something for pain?"

"Before . . . awhile ago. A few hours," she mumbled when leveled by Mira's patient gaze. "I don't like meds."

"All right, let's see what we can do without them. I'm going to put the chair back. Relax. Close your eyes. Trust me."

"That's what they all say."

"Tell me what you've learned about Bissel."

It wasn't so bad, Eve thought. Whatever Mira was doing didn't add to the pain, or layer on any stings or twinges. Best, it didn't make her feel light-headed and stupid.

She ran through the progress of the case, and didn't pause when Mira began to work on her face.

"So he's alone now," Mira said. "Angry, displaced, and probably feeling very, very sorry for himself. A dangerous mix with a man of his emotional content. His ego has been severely attacked. He should be patting himself on the back now, lavishly. Instead things continue to go wrong—through no fault, in his mind, of his own. He has a very vaulted opinion of himself, so someone else must be to blame. He sacrificed his wife, his brother, both his lovers without a qualm. He has no capability for real emotion, real attachments."

"Sociopathic?"

"Of a kind, yes. But it's not simply that he has no conscience. It's that he sees himself as above the behaviors, needs, attachments, rules of general society. An artist on one hand, a spy on the other. He's wallowed in the thrill of these parts of himself, preened on the pleasure of his own cleverness. He's spoiled, and wants more. More money, more women, more adulation. He would have enjoyed the risk of killing. The planning stages, the idea of playing both ends for his own means."

"Sparrow did the planning."

"Yes, our organized thinker, but Bissel wouldn't see it that way. He was the field operative, thinking on his feet and getting the job done. Adding his flourishes. In his capacity for the HSO, he was, basically, a delivery boy. This has given him the opportunity to show them, show everyone, how much more he is."

"But if it had worked, no one would know."

"He would know. He'd have fooled everyone, and he would know. Eventually, he'd have been compelled to share this with someone, to brag. He'd had Kade, his associates within the HSO, he'd had Sparrow. He could show his true face to these people. With them gone, he'd have to seek other outlets. Self-satisfaction wouldn't hold him long."

Gently, she brushed Eve's hair back and treated the laceration on her temple. "Sparrow's mistake was in not factoring in how much Bissel would enjoy the limelight, the thrill of killing and being a critical part of the plan."

"Now that it's all gone to hell?"

"Bissel will only have more to prove. He may go to ground, but he won't stay there. In the past, his art fed that part of his ego that needed public acknowledgment, praise, admiration. That spotlight's been taken, too. He needs a show. A platform."

"If I make it public that he's still alive, that he's . . . the star, that would give him the show. He'd need to come out, wouldn't he? Take a bow."

"I believe he would. But with his violent tendencies, with his rapid descent into them, he'll be dangerous. His killing pattern has escalated. The first, though the most brutal, was specific, and personal, and part of a blueprint already drawn for him. McCoy was more cruel, more cold, and orchestrated completely on his own. Powell took it beyond. This was a stranger. And the last—while his target was certainly the man he felt had ruined everything—injured a number of bystanders. They meant nothing to him. No one does but himself."

She closed her bag. "I'm going to bring the chair back up now. You can get dressed. And have another cookie."

Eve opened her eyes, looked down at herself. Cuts and bruises were covered with something pale gold that didn't, in her opinion, look any better than the injuries themselves. But the aches had largely subsided.

"Feels better."

"I imagine. I used topicals. An internal blocker would help, but we won't push it."

"Appreciate it." She rose, began to dress. "I've got the technos on my team working on finding any bolt-holes, and I can continue to tie up his funds, making it tough for him to access anything. The only people I can figure he might go for, out of spite, are his wife and his mother-in-law, and they're both tucked up. I'm going to let the media have his name as suspect, and enough of the circumstances to light a fire under him. I'm going to smoke him out."

"It'll be your fault then. He'll panic first, but then he'll try to find a way to punish you for upending the rest of his plans."

"He's stupid." Eve buttoned her shirt. "He's gotten this far largely on dumb luck. His luck's about to change. I've got to get back, work a release through the media liaison. I want this one real official."

"Could you sit down another moment?" To ensure she did, Mira sat herself. "Will you tell me what else is hurting you?"

"I think you hit all the hot spots."

"I'm not talking about physical injuries. I know your face so well now. I know when you've exhausted yourself with work, and when there's something more, something other that's pushing you to the edge. You've worn yourself out. You're hurt and you're unhappy."

"I can't talk about it. Can't," she said before Mira could speak. "There's a problem, and there's no point in me telling you there isn't. I don't know if it can be fixed."

"Everything can, one way or the other. Eve, whatever you tell me here stays here. In confidence. If I can help—"

"You can't." Despair worked its way to the surface and made her tone sharp. "You can't help, you can't fix it, and there's no point in you saying things you think I want to hear to draw me out, or to put a damn topical on it. I've got work."

"Wait." Mira got to her feet as Eve did. "What does that mean—that I would say what I think you want to hear?"

"Nothing." Eve dragged her hands through her hair. "Nothing. I'm in a pisser of a mood, that's all."

"I don't think that's all. We've had what I feel is a good, an important, personal rapport. If there's something that's interfering with that, I'd like to know."

"Look, Dr. Mira, it's your job to dig under, and to use whatever tools it takes. I appreciate the help you've given me, the personal help as well as on the job. Let's let it go at that."

"I certainly won't. Do you think I've been dishonest with you?"

She didn't have the time, and less of an inclination, to get into personal matters. But noting the set expression on Mira's face, Eve calculated it was best to approach this as she had the treatment for her injuries: Strip down and get it over with.

"I think you . . . Okay, it's a method, right, for the therapist to find or create a mutual ground with a patient? A kind of connection."

"It can be, yes. And I did this with you by . . ."

"You told me, a long while back, you told me you'd been raped by your stepfather."

"Yes. I gave you that personal information because you didn't believe I could understand what you'd been through as a child. How you felt remembering being raped by your father."

"It opened me up, and that was your job. Mission accomplished."

Obviously baffled, Mira lifted her hands. "Eve?"

"Earlier this summer, you sat on the patio of the house, drinking wine, relaxing. Just a nice little moment. It was after I told you Mavis was pregnant. And you told me about your parents. Your mother, your father, how they had this nice, long-term marriage, how you had all these pretty memories."

"Ah." Mira let out a little laugh, and sat again. "And this has been troubling you ever since? Yet you said nothing."

"I couldn't quite figure out how to call you a liar . . . and what would be the point? You were just doing your job."

"It wasn't just the job, and I didn't lie. Either time. But I certainly see why you'd believe I did and how it would make you feel. I'd like you to listen to me. Please."

Eve fought the urge to check the time on her wrist unit. "All right."

"When I was a girl, my parents' marriage disintegrated. I don't know why, except that there was some elemental problem, something they couldn't, or wouldn't, resolve. They pulled away from each other, ripped the fabric of their relationship. They divorced."

"You said—"

"Yes, I know. It was a difficult time for me. I was angry and hurt, confused. And like most children, self-absorbed. So, of course, I believed I was at fault. Believing that, I was only more angry, with both of them. My mother was, is, a very vital, attractive woman. She was financially well-off, had an important career. And she was miserably unhappy. Her way of coping was to surround herself with people, to keep busy. Mothers and daughters sometimes fall into a pattern of bickering, especially when they're a great deal alike. We were, and we did.

"During this difficult and hostile time, she met a man." Mira's voice changed, subtly, went just a bit tight at the edges. "Charming, personable, attentive, handsome. He swept her off her feet. Flowers, gifts, time. She married him impulsively, less than four months after she and my father divorced."

She rose, went to the coffeepot. "I shouldn't have a second cup of this. I'll be buzzing around driving Dennis to distraction half the night. But . . ."

"You don't have to tell me this. I get the picture. I'm sorry."

"No, I'll finish it. Though I'll shorten a long story for both our sakes." She set the coffeepot down again, and spent a moment just tracing her fingers over the purple pansies that decorated it.

"The first time he touched me, I was shocked. Outraged. He warned me that she'd never believe me, that she'd send me away. I'd been in a little bit of trouble. Acting out, you might say." She smiled, sat again. "Won't go into that. But my mother and I were at odds, very much at odds. He was convincing, and frightened me. I was young, and felt powerless. You understand."

"Yeah."

"She traveled quite a bit. I think—well, it came out later, that she'd realized she'd made a mistake, marrying him. But she'd already had one marriage fail, and she wasn't going to give up so quickly. She focused on her career for a time, and he had many opportunities to molest me. He used drugs to keep me . . . quiet. It went on for a very long time. I told no one. In my mind, my father had deserted me, my mother loved this man more than she loved me. And neither of them cared if I lived or died. I attempted suicide."

"It's hard," Eve managed, "really hard to feel like you're alone in all that."

"You were alone. But yes, it's equally hard to feel alone, and helpless, and guilty. Fortunately, I bungled the suicide. My parents, both of them, were in my hospital room, at their wits' end. It came spewing out of me, all of it. The rage, the fear, the hate. It all came out, two and a half years of rape and abuse."

"How'd they handle it?" Eve asked when Mira fell into silence.

"In a most unexpected way. They believed me. He was arrested. Imagine my surprise," she murmured. "That it could be stopped, just by speaking of it. That saying it out loud could make it stop."

"That's why you became a doctor. So you could make it stop for other people."

"Yes. I didn't think of it then. I was still angry, still hurt, but yes. I had therapy—individual, group, family. And sometime during that healing period, my parents found each other again. They mended what was ripped. We don't often talk of that time. I don't often think of it. When I think of my parents, I think of them as they were before things began to unravel, and as they've been since they repaired the damage. I don't think of the bitter years."

"You forgave them."

"Yes, and myself. They forgave each other, and me. We were stronger for it," Mira added. "And I think I was drawn to Dennis because of his bottomless well of kindness, and decency. I'd learned the value of those things because I'd seen their opposite."

"How do you find the way back? How do you find the way when a marriage crumbles under you, and you turn away from each other? When it's bad, so bad you can't talk about it, or think about it?"

Mira reached out, laid her hands over Eve's. "You can't tell me what's hurting you, and Roarke?"

"I can't."

"Then I'll tell you the simple and most complex answer is love. It's where you start, and where, if you work hard enough, want hard enough, you end."

Chapter 20

She didn't want to go home. It was, Eve knew, evasion at its worst, but she didn't want to go home to a houseful of people. She didn't want to go home to Roarke.

The answer couldn't be love—simple or complex—she didn't see how that could be it. She couldn't find her way through this thing that was strangling her marriage. And if she loved the man any more than she did, she'd burn up from it.

She didn't see how the answer could be evasion either, though it helped at the moment. Walking in the city on a balmy evening, the familiar ground, the familiar sounds of irritable traffic, the smell of overdone soy dogs, the occasional *whoosh* through the vents of a train zooming by underground.

Clutches of people, ignoring each other—ignoring her—as they went about their own business and thought their own thoughts.

So she walked, and it occurred to her she never did this anymore. Never simply walked around the city when she didn't have a specific destination, a specific purpose. She'd never been the meandering sort. And she sure as hell wasn't interested in browsing from window to window to study whatever was being sold.

She could've rousted a couple of the sidewalk grifters hawking knockoff wrist units, PPCs, fake python handbags—all the rage this season—but she didn't feel quite mean enough to bother.

She watched two women shell out seventy dollars each for snake bags complete with fangs for fasteners and wondered what the hell was wrong with people.

More because it was there than because of hunger, she dropped some credits on a glide-cart for a soy dog. The stink of the cart's smoke followed her, and the first bite reminded her how disgusting, and oddly addicting, the fake meat on a stingy bun could be.

She watched a couple of teenagers weave through pedestrian traffic on an airboard. The girl riding pinion had her arms around the boy's waist in what looked like a death grip, and she was squealing in his ear. From the expression on his face, he didn't seem to mind. Probably made him feel like a man, Eve decided, to have some girl holding on to him and pretending she was afraid.

Not bothering to pretend anything was why she'd been so lousy at the mating rituals, she supposed. Then, with Roarke, she hadn't had to pretend.

A messenger droid whizzed by on his zip-bike, risking smashed circuits and vehicular madness as he threaded through the breath of space between two Rapid cabs, then buzzed the bumper on another. The cab driver responded with a vicious blast of horn, which set off several other horns like dogs howling together at the moon.

"I'm driving here!" The driver shouted with his head and upper body popping out his side window. "I'm driving here, you asshole!"

But the red cap and boots of the messenger droid were only a blur as he cut through the light on the yellow, and kept jetting.

She heard snatches of conversations as she walked—bits

and pieces of sexual, shopping, or business escapades—all delivered with the same passion.

A licensed beggar squatted on a rag of blanket and played a mournful tune on a rusty flute. A woman with a python bag and matching boots glided out of a shop trailed by a uniformed droid carting several glossy bags. She slid into a shiny black limo.

Eve doubted she'd heard the flute—she'd bet the beggar wasn't even on her plane of existence. People didn't pay enough attention, she decided, and tossed a couple of credits into the beggar's box as she passed by.

The city was awash with color and sound and energy, with petty meanness and careless kindnesses. *She* didn't pay enough attention. She loved it, but she rarely looked at it.

And if that was some sort of subconscious metaphor for her marriage, it was time to ditch the rest of the soy dog and get back to work.

She saw the bump and snatch. The man in the suit, carrying a briefcase who crossed toward the curb to hail a cab. The boy of about twelve who bumped against him, the quick exchange of words.

Watch it, kid.

Sorry, mister.

And the fast hands, very fast, very light, that nipped into the pocket of the suit and palmed the wallet.

Still munching her soy dog, she strode toward them just as the boy turned to melt into the crowd. She caught him by the collar.

"Hold on," she said to the suit.

He sent her a look of irritation as the boy struggled against her hold. "I'm in a hurry."

"You're going to have a hard time paying for that ride without your wallet," Eve told him.

Instinctively he patted his pocket, then whirled. "What the hell is this? Give me back my wallet, you little bastard. I'm calling the cops."

"I am a cop, so just throttle back. Hands off," she snapped when he started to reach for the boy. "Give it over, ace."

"Don't know what you're talking about. Lemme go. My ma's waiting."

"Whoever's waiting missed the pass, so give me this man's wallet and let's call it a day. You're good," she said studying his soft, lightly freckled face. "Not only look harmless, but you've got good hands. Slick and smooth. If I hadn't been right here, you'd have gotten away clean."

"Officer, I want this delinquent arrested."

"Give it a rest." Eve reached into the goodie pouch inside the boy's jacket, pulled out a billfold. Flipped it open and read the ID. "Marcus." She tossed him the wallet. "You've got your property back. No harm, no foul."

"He belongs in jail."

She had a strong hold on the boy now, and felt him tremble. She thought of Roarke running the streets of Dublin, picking pockets and going home with his take to a father who'd likely beat him no matter what the day's work had brought in.

"Fine. Let's all go downtown and spend the next couple of hours filling out forms.

"I don't have time—"

"Then you'd better catch that cab."

"It's hardly a wonder the city is overrun with crime when the police treat law-abiding citizens with such disdain."

"Yeah, that must be the reason," she replied as he climbed into the cab, slammed the door. "And you're welcome, sunshine."

She hauled the kid around, studied his young, angry face. "Name, and don't bother to lie, just give me the first name."

"Billy."

She saw it was a lie, but let it pass. "Okay, Billy, like I said, you're good. But not that good. Next time you're going to get caught by somebody without my mushy compassionate nature and winning personality."

"Shit." But he grinned a little.

"Ever been in juvie?"

"Maybe."

"If you have, you know it sucks. Food's lousy and they lecture you every damn day, which is worse. You got a problem at home, or wherever, need some help, you call this number."

She dragged a card out of her pocket.

"Dufus? What the hell is that?"

"*Duchas*. It's a shelter. Hell of a lot better than juvie," she said when he sneered. "You can tell them Dallas sent you."

"Yeah, sure."

"Put it in your pocket. Don't throw it away until you're out of sight at least. No point in insulting me after I kept your ass out of lockup."

"You hadn't caught me, I'd have the wallet."

Smartass, she thought. God, she had a weakness for a smartass. "Well, you've got me there. Scram."

He bolted, then spun around, grinned at her again. "Hey! You're not a total asshole, for a cop."

And that, she figured, was a better thanks than the suit had managed. Feeling marginally better, she hailed a cab of her own.

She gave the driver Reva Ewing's home address. He turned around, gave her a pained stare.

"You want I should drive you to fricking Queens?"

"Yes. I want you should drive me to fricking Queens."

"Lady, I gotta make a living here. Whyn't you take a bus or the subway or an airtram?"

"Because I'm taking a cab." She yanked out her badge, pressed it to the safety shield that caged in the driver. "And I gotta make a living here, too."

"Oh jeez, lady, now you're gonna want the cop rate. Now I'm going to be driving you to fricking Queens at ten percent off. You know how long that's going to tie me up?"

"I'll give you the standard fare, but get this bucket of shit moving." She shoved her badge away. "And don't call me lady."

She ruined the driver's evening when she told him to wait, then recorded his name and license number to ensure he did. He drooped behind the wheel as she got out to unseal and unlock the gates.

"How long am I supposed to wait?"

"Let's see. Oh yeah. Until I get back."

EDD had removed the statuary, and it was an improvement. Still, she imagined Reva would sell the place. She wouldn't want to live where she'd lived with the man who used and betrayed her.

She unsealed and unlocked the front door and stepped inside.

It had the feel of an empty house, an abandoned one. A home that was finished, she supposed, being a home.

She didn't know what she was looking for, but she wandered the house much as she'd wandered the streets. Just to see what popped out at her.

The sweepers and EDD had both combed the place. The faint, metallic smell of chemicals lingered.

To satisfy herself she browsed through Bissel's closet. Large wardrobe, expensive clothes. She knew how to recognize expensive material and cuts now.

He'd indulged himself in the two-level space with its revolving racks, automatic drawers, computerized menu of contents, and their location.

Jesus, even Roarke didn't computerize his wardrobe. Of course, his brain was a damn computer so he probably knew just where the specific black shirt he wanted would be, when he'd last worn it, for what occasion, and with what pants and jacket. Shoes. Fricking underwear.

She blew out a breath and scowled at the little wall screen.

Bissel hadn't fried his closet unit. Because there was nothing on there worth bothering with, or because there was something on there he wanted to retrieve?

Curious, she engaged it. "List last wardrobe selection, and date."

WORKING . . . LAST SELECTION ON SEPTEMBER 16, AT TWENTY-ONE SIXTEEN, BY BISSEL, BLAIR. CONTENTS REMOVED AS FOLLOWS . . .

She listened to the list, mentally matching it with the contents taken from Bissel's bags and Kade's closet after the murders. They seemed to jibe.

"Okay, let's try this. Last use of this unit by Bissel, Blair, for any purpose."

LAST USAGE SEPTEMBER 23, AT OH SIX HUNDRED TWELVE HOURS.

"This morning, the son of a bitch was here this morning? What was the purpose of usage?"

PURPOSE BLOCKED. PRIVACY ENGAGED.

"Yeah, screw that." She keyed in her police code, her badge number, and spent several annoying minutes trying to override the system. The fourth time the computer spat PRIVACY ENGAGED at her, she kicked the wall.

The sound was hollow in the lavish space. "Well, what's this?" She crouched and began to thump and press on the wall.

She considered, briefly, hunting up a really big knife and just hacking at the wallboard. But cooler heads prevailed. Instead she pulled out her communicator and contacted Feeney.

"I'm in Queens, in Bissel's closet."

"What the hell you doing in a closet in Queens?"

"Just listen, he was here. This morning. There's a comp menu thing in the closet. He used it this morning, but the little bastard won't tell me why. Privacy block. And there's something behind the wall here, a hidey-hole or something. How do I get the computer to let me in?"

"You beat on it yet?"

"No." She perked up a bit. "Can I?"

"Won't do any good. Can you open her up?"

"I don't have any tools."

"You can give me a look at it, and I can try to walk you through, or one of us can come over there and work on it. Probably be faster to deploy one of the team."

"That's an insult, and don't think I don't know it. It's a damn closet menu, Feeney, get me in."

He puffed out his cheeks, made little noises while she

scanned the unit so he could see it on his screen. "Okay, key in this code."

He read it off as she input the numbers manually. "What's this? A privacy override?"

"Just keep going. Snap your fingers and say, 'Open Sesame.' "

She started to obey, then set her teeth. "Feeney."

"Okay, okay, just a little joke. Code's from the data we've been pulling out here. Let's see if he used it on that unit, too."

"Computer, what was removed by Blair Bissel at last usage?"

WORKING . . . CONTENTS LISTED AS EMERGENCY PACKAGE.

"Emergency package. What was in the emergency package?"

THAT DATA IS NOT AVAILABLE.

"Computer, open the compartment from which said emergency package was removed."

ACKNOWLEDGED.

The panel slid open, revealing a small safe. "Bingo. Computer, I said to open the compartment."

ACKNOWLEDGED. COMPARTMENT IS OPEN.

"You have to be specific, Dallas," Feeney told her. "You want the safe open, you tell it you want the safe open. It can't read your mind."

"Open the damn safe."

ACKNOWLEDGED. COMMENCING INTERFACE.

There was a low hum and some blinking red lights on both the safe and the wall unit as they communicated. When it stopped, Eve wrenched open the safe door.

"Empty," she said. "Whatever it was, he got it all."

* * *

She asked herself what Blair Bissel would have secreted away for an emergency. Funds, forged ID, codes or passkeys into bolt-holes. But surely he'd have taken all that with him before he killed Kade and his brother.

What else, she thought, would a man who prepared to run require enough to risk breaking into his own house for?

Weapons seemed the most logical.

He hadn't stored a rocket blaster in that little safe, but he might've stored smaller weapons and passkeys.

Stupid to have left them behind in the first place, she thought as the cab drove through the gates of home. Sooner or later the safe would have been discovered, and whatever he'd left behind found.

Then again, it would all have been a kind of mystery, wouldn't it? His body would have been long since cremated, ensuring he'd stay dead. But people would wonder about the safe, its contents.

He might have left behind something that would have hinted at the HSO, at his association. It would make him important, talked about.

Another kind of immortality for the dead man who didn't die.

Yeah. Yeah. That would be right up his alley.

"You want I should wait? Again?"

Eve broke out of her thoughts, stared at the big house with lights gleaming in some of the windows. "No, last stop. You're sprung."

She pulled out a debit card, swiped it over the scanner.

"You telling me you live here?"

She verified the meter charge and decided to cut him a break and give him a decent tip. "So?"

"So then you ain't no cop."

"Surprises me all the time, too."

She went straight in and straight up to her office. She wanted, very much, to go straight to bed. Still playing the evasion game, she bypassed the lab.

She found her team had been busy in her absence. The full

report on Quinn Sparrow was filed, and copied. He'd been charged. Peabody's attached personal memo told Eve that there was already political wrangling taking place between the HSO and the NYPSD on who owned him.

She couldn't work up the spit to care who won that battle. Sparrow was done, and that was that.

Reva had left her a list of Bissel's habits, routines, favorite haunts and getaways. Most of those haunts and getaways leaned toward the trendy or exotic.

She would, in the morning, contact local authorities in all the out-of-town and foreign locations Reva listed and ask for their assistance.

But he wasn't out of town, he wasn't in some foreign location.

He was, for now, in New York. Maybe not for much longer, but for now.

She read McNab's report. He'd found nothing under Chloe McCoy and was now pursuing variations and codes based on that name.

What had she died for? What use had she been for him that had made her a victim when that use was over?

A locket, a sculpture, and corrupted data on a cheap desk unit.

She made a note to ask Feeney to have the team focus on McCoy's unit.

She worked late, and she worked alone, soothing herself with the quiet, the routine, with the puzzle until her brain began to fuzz.

After shutting down for the night, she used the elevator. The bedroom was empty. It seemed Roarke knew how to play the evasion game, too.

The cat padded in while she undressed. Grateful for his company, she picked him up, nuzzling as he purred. He curled up beside her in the dark, blinking his bicolored eyes at her.

She didn't expect to sleep. Prepared herself to spend most of the night staring at the dark.

And was out in minutes.

* * *

He knew the moment she'd passed through the gates in the cab. He knew she'd worked after most of the team had gone to bed. The fact that she hadn't sought him out was a small ache. It seemed he had so many small aches these last days he'd forgotten what it was like without them.

He stood over her now as she sprawled facedown on the bed in exhaustion. She didn't wake. The cat did, enough to stare so those odd eyes gleamed at him in the dark. Roarke couldn't have said why he was sure the stare was accusatory.

"I'd think you'd understand well enough the primal, the instinctive, and be a bit more on my side in this."

But Galahad only continued to stare until Roarke cursed softly and turned away.

He was too restless to sleep, too unsettled to lie beside her knowing there was a great deal more than a fat lump of feline between them.

The knowledge so infuriated, so terrified, that he strode away from her, left her sleeping. He moved through the house where others slept, and accessed entry to the tightly secured room where he kept his unregistered.

He'd given Eve and Reva all of his time. His work was suffering because of it and he would begin to mend that in the morning. But tonight was for himself. Tonight, he *was* himself, and he would gather the data he wanted on the people, all of them, who'd had a part in Dallas.

In Eve.

"Roarke," he said, his tone was cold as ice. "Open operations."

She stirred in the dark, in the dead quiet just before dawn. The whimper sounded in her throat as she tried to turn herself out of the dream. And sweat pooled at the base of her spine as she fell into it.

The room, always the same. Freezing, dirty, and washed with the erratic red light from the sex club across the street. She was small, and very thin. And very hungry. Hungry enough to risk punishment for a bite of cheese. A little mouse, sneaking toward the trap when the brutal cat was away.

Her stomach clenched and knotted—part fear, part anticipation, as she cut the mold off the cheese with the knife. Maybe he wouldn't notice this time. Maybe. She was so cold. She was so hungry. Maybe he wouldn't notice.

She held on to that even when he came in. Richie Troy. Somewhere in her unconscious brain his name echoed, over and over. She knew him now, she knew his name. Nothing, no monster was ever as terrifying if you could name him.

She had a moment of hope. He would be drunk, drunk enough to leave her alone. Drunk enough not to care that she'd disobeyed and gotten food.

But he came toward her, and she saw in his eyes there hadn't been enough drink that night. Not enough to save her.

What are you doing, little girl?

And his voice turned her bowels to ice.

The first blow stunned her, but she fell limply. A dog who'd been kicked often enough knew to stay down and submit.

But he had to punish her. He had to teach her a lesson. Despite her fear, despite her knowing, she couldn't stop herself from pleading.

Please don't please don't please don't.

Of course he would. He did. Bearing down on her, striking her. Hurting her, hurting her while she begged, while she wept, while she struggled.

Her arm broke with a sound as thin as her shocked scream.

The knife she'd dropped was in her hand again. She had to make him stop. Make him *stop*. The pain, the horrible pain in her arm, between her legs. He had to stop.

Blood gushed warm over her hand. Warm and wet, and she scented it like an animal in the wild. When his body jerked on hers, she plunged the knife into him again, again. Again and again as he tried to crawl away. Again and again and *again* as the blood splashed her arms, her face, her clothes, and the sounds she made were nothing human.

When she crawled away, shivering, panting, to huddle in

the corner, he was sprawled on the floor, drowned in his own blood.

As always.

But this time she wasn't alone with the man she'd killed. She wasn't alone with the dead in the hideous room. There were others, countless others, men and women in dark suits, sitting in row after row of chairs. Like people at a play. Observers with empty faces.

They watched as she wept. Watched as she bled and her broken arm hung limply at her side.

They watched, and said nothing. Did nothing. Even when Richie Troy rose, as he sometimes did. When he rose, pouring blood from all the wounds she'd put into him and began to shuffle toward her, they did nothing.

She awoke bathed in sweat with the scream tearing at her throat. Instinctively she rolled and reached out for Roarke, but he wasn't there. He wasn't there to gather her in, to soothe away those horrible jagged edges.

So she curled into a ball, battling the tears while the cat bumped his head against hers.

"I'm okay, I'm okay, I'm okay." She pressed her damp face against his fur, rocked herself. "God. Oh God. Lights on, twenty-five percent."

The low light helped, so she lay in it until her chest stopped burning. Then, still shivering, she rose to drag herself to the shower, and the heat of the water.

Rose to drag herself into the day.

Chapter 21

It was too early for the team to be up, and she was glad of it. She wasn't quite in the frame of mind for teamwork. She'd close herself up in her office and review everything again. She would walk through it all with Bissel one more time.

She resisted checking the house monitoring system to see where Roarke was. It was more important where he hadn't been, and that was in bed with her. If he'd slept—and there were times she thought he needed less sleep than a damn vampire—he'd slept elsewhere.

She wouldn't bring it up, wouldn't mention it, wouldn't give him the *satisfaction* of that. They'd finish the investigation, they would close this case, and when Bissel was wrapped, they would . . .

She wished to God she knew.

She programmed coffee in the kitchen off her office. Just coffee as even the thought of food made her stomach pitch. But she took pity on the pathetic begging from the cat, and poured him a double shot of kibble.

She turned, and there he was, leaning against the doorjamb watching her. His beautiful face was unshaven—a rarity—and as expressionless and remote as those in her dream had been.

The comparison turned her blood cold.

"You need more sleep," he said at length. "You don't look well."

"I got all I'm getting."

"You worked late, and no one's going to be up and around for at least another hour. Take a soother, for pity's sake, Eve, and lie down."

"Why don't you take your own advice? You don't look so hot yourself, ace."

He opened his mouth. She could almost see the venom. But whatever poisonous thing he'd been about to say, he swallowed. She had to give him points for it.

"We made some progress in the lab. I assume you'll want to brief the team, and be briefed." He moved in to program coffee for himself.

"Yeah."

"Bruises look better," he said as he lifted his cup. "On the face, anyway. How's the rest?"

"Better."

"You're very pale. If you won't lie down, at least sit and have something to eat."

"I'm not hungry." She caught the petulant tone, hated it and herself. "I'm not," she said in a calmer voice. "Coffee's enough."

She braced the mug in both hands when the first one trembled, just a bit. He stepped forward, took her chin in his hand. "You had a nightmare."

She started to jerk her head away, but his fingers tightened. "I'm awake now." She put a hand to his wrist, nudged it away. "I'm fine."

He said nothing as she walked back into her office, but stood staring down into the black pool of coffee in his cup. She'd pushed him away, and that was more than a small ache. It was a vicious tear through the heart.

He'd seen she was exhausted and hurt, and knew how much more susceptible she was in those states to the nightmares. But he'd left her alone, and that was another tear.

He hadn't thought of her. He hadn't thought, so she'd awoke in the dark alone.

He walked to the sink, upended the contents into it, set the cup down very carefully.

She was already at her desk when he walked in. "I want to review, shuffle some of this around. It's easier for me to do that alone, in the quiet. I took a blocker yesterday, and I let Mira treat me when I went by her place. I'm not abusing or neglecting myself. But I have work. I need to do my job."

"You do, yes. You do." There was a space, just under his tattered heart, that felt hollowed out. "I'm up early to catch up on a bit of my own."

She glanced up at him, then away with a small nod.

So she wouldn't ask, he realized, where he'd slept or what he'd been doing. She wouldn't say what was so clearly in her eyes. That he was hurting her.

"You've given a lot of time to this," she said. "I know both Reva and Caro appreciate all you're doing. So do I."

"They're important to me. So are you." And thought: *Aren't we polite? Aren't we just fucking diplomats?* "I know you need to work, as do I, but I need you to come in my office for a moment."

"If it could wait until—"

"I think it best it doesn't, for all involved. Please."

She rose and moved away from the desk without her coffee. A sure sign, he thought, that she was agitated. He led the way through the connecting door, then closed it, and called for a lockdown.

"What is this?"

"Given the circumstances, I prefer absolute privacy. I looked in on you last night. Must've been near to two. Your feline knight was guarding you."

"You didn't come to bed."

"I didn't. I couldn't . . . settle. And I was angry." He searched her face. "We're both so angry, aren't we, Eve?"

"I guess we are." Though anger seemed the wrong term

somehow, and she thought he knew it as well as she did. "I don't know what to do about it."

"You didn't let me know when you got home."

"I didn't want to talk to you."

"Well." He drew a breath as a man did after a quick, surprising blow. "Well. As it happens, I didn't want to talk to you either. So after I saw you were sleeping, I took myself off to the unregistered to do the business I needed to do."

Whatever color had still been in her cheeks drained now. "I see."

"Aye." His eyes never left hers. "You see. You may wish you didn't, but you do." He unlocked a compartment with a quick play of fingers over a panel, and took from it a single disc.

"I have here the names, the whereabouts, the financials, the medicals, the professional evaluations, and all other matter of data on the field operative, his supervisor, the director of the HSO, and any who were attached to the task force involving Richard Troy in Dallas. There's nothing about them that's relevant—and quite a bit that likely isn't—that's not on this disc."

The weight dropped on her chest, pressing against her heart so she could hear the panicked beat of it roaring in her ears. "None of that changes what happened. Nothing you can do changes what happened."

"Of course it doesn't." He turned the disc in his hands, and its surface caught light and shot it out again. Like a weapon. "They've all had very decent careers, some more than decent. They continue to work, or consult, play golf or, in one case, squash, of all things. They eat and they sleep. Some cheat on a spouse, some go to church every bloody Sunday."

His gaze whipped up to hers, a bolt of blue. Another weapon. "And do you think, Eve, do you suppose any flaming one of them gives that child they sacrificed all those years back a single thought? Do they wonder, ever, if she suffers? If she wakes weeping in the dark?"

Her head felt light now, and her knees weak. "What do I care if they think of me? It doesn't *change* anything."

"I could remind them." And his voice was utterly flat, more frightening than the hiss of a snake. "That would change something, wouldn't it? I could remind them, personally, what they did by sitting back and leaving a child to defend herself against a monster. I could remind them how they listened and recorded and sat on their fat government asses while he beat and raped her, and she cried for help. They deserve to pay for that, and you know it. You bloody well do."

"Yes, they deserve to pay!" The words burst out, hot as the tears that burned behind her eyes. "They deserve it. Is that what you need to hear? They should fry in hell for what they did. But it's not up to you, and it's not up to me to send them there. If you do this thing, it's murder. It's murder, Roarke, and their blood on your hands changes nothing that happened to me."

He paused a long, long moment. "I can live with that." He saw her eyes go dark, and dead. "But you can't. So . . ."

He snapped the disc in two, then shoved the pieces into the recycle slot.

She only stared, and in the silence there was only the sound of her own shaky breaths. "You . . . you're letting it go."

He looked down at the slot and knew his rage would never be so easily destroyed. He'd live with it, and the impotence that walked with it, the whole of his life. "If I did anything else it would be for myself, not for you. Hardly a point in that. So yes, I'm letting it go."

Her stomach fluttered, but she managed to nod. "Good. That's good. Best."

"So it seems. End lockdown." His cool order had the shields going up, and the light pouring in the windows. "I'll give you some time later this morning, but I need to see to some matters. If you'll close the door on your way out."

"Sure. Okay." She started out, then pressed a hand on the door to brace herself. "You think I don't know, that I don't understand what that cost you. But you're wrong." She couldn't keep her voice steady, gave up trying. "You're wrong, Roarke. I do know. There's no one else in the world who would want, who would need, to kill for me. No one else in the world who would step back from it because I asked it. Because I needed it."

She turned, and the first tear spilled over. "No one but you."

"Don't. You'll do me in if you cry."

"I never in my life expected anyone would love me, all of me. How would I deserve that? What would I do with it? But you do. Everything we've managed to have together, to be to each other, this is more. I'll never be able to find the words to tell you what you just gave me."

"You undo me, Eve. Who else would make me feel like a hero for doing nothing."

"You did everything. Everything. Are everything." Mira was right, again. Love, that strange and terrifying entity, was the answer after all. "Whatever there is, whatever happened to me, or how it comes back on me, you have to know, you need to know that what you did here gave me more peace than I ever thought I'd find. You have to know that I can face anything knowing you love me."

"Eve." He stepped away from the slot, away from what was gone. And toward her, toward what mattered. "I can't do anything but love you."

Her vision blurred as she ran, wrapped herself around him. "I missed you. I missed you so much."

He pressed his face to her shoulder, breathed her. Felt the world steady again. "I'm sorry."

"No, no, no." She clung, then eased back only to take his face in her hands. "I see you. I *know* you. I love you."

She watched the emotion storm into his eyes before she pressed her lips to his.

"It was like the world was off a step," he murmured. "Nothing quite in time when I couldn't really touch you."

"Touch me now."

He smiled, stroked her hair. "That's not what I meant."

"I know, but touch me. I need to feel close to you again." She turned her lips back to his. "I need you, and I need so bad, so bad to show you."

"In bed then." He circled her toward the elevator. "In our bed."

When the elevator doors closed, she pressed against him, strained.

"Gently now." He ran his hands down her sides, then boosted her into his arms. "You're bruised."

"I don't feel bruised anymore."

"All the same. You look so delicate." When her brow creased, he laughed and dropped a kiss on it. "That wasn't an insult."

"Sounds like one, but I'm going to let it pass."

"You look pale," he continued as he walked off the elevator into the bedroom. "And a bit fragile. There are tears on your lashes yet, and shadows under your eyes. Do you know how I love your eyes, your long golden eyes, Eve. My darling Eve."

"They're brown."

"I like the way they watch me." He laid her on the bed. "There are tears still in them." He kissed them closed. "It kills me when you cry. A strong woman's tears can cut a man to ribbons faster than a knife."

He was soothing her, seducing her, with words and those patient hands. It amazed her that a man of his energy, his needs, could be so patient. Violent and cold, tender and warm. The contradictions of him, the whole of him that meshed, somehow, with the whole of her.

"Roarke." She bowed up, wrapping her arms around him.

"What?"

She opened her eyes, laid her lips on his cheek, and searched for her own tenderness. "My Roarke."

She could soothe, she could seduce. She could show him that whatever the world threw at them, whatever reared up from the past or lurked in the future, they were together.

She unbuttoned his shirt, pressed a kiss to his shoulder. "You're the love of my life. I don't care how corny that sounds. You're the start of it, and the end of it. And you're the best of it."

He took her hands, cupping them in his own and bringing

them to his lips as love washed through him. It cleansed, he thought, this flood of feeling between them. And despite all the odds, what it left behind was pure.

He parted her shirt, then traced his fingers lightly over the bruises.

"It hurts me to see you marked like this, and to know you'll be marked again. At the same time it makes me proud." He brushed his lips lightly over injuries, pressed them softly to the image of her badge. "I married a warrior."

"So did I."

His gaze came back to hers, and held, as their mouths found each other's. Hands stroked, in comfort, in passion. They moved together in the quiet of the morning and words slipped into sighs.

When she rose over him, took him in, their fingers linked. Locked. With the pleasure, with the thrill, was the steady beat of love.

She curled up beside him, realizing they both needed this space of intimacy as much as they'd needed the reassurance and release.

Her world had been rocked. She only understood how violent the shake had been now that it was steady again. Only understood, she thought, that it had been the same for him now that they were reconciled.

Reconciled, she realized, because he'd given her what she needed. He'd submerged or denied his own ego for her. And there was nothing simple or easy about it. His ego was . . . she'd just call it *healthy* since she was feeling so grateful.

He'd given in, given up his own needs, not because he stood on the same moral ground as she at the end of the day, but because he valued her and their marriage more than that ego.

"You could've lied to me."

"No." He watched the light strengthen in the sky through the window over the bed. "I couldn't lie to you."

"I don't mean you, I mean in a general sense." She shifted, skimming his hair away from his face with her fingers, then running those fingers over the stubble he'd neglected to remove that morning. "If you were less of a man you could have lied to me, done what you wanted to do, stoked your ego, satisfied yourself and moved on."

"It's hardly a matter of ego—"

"No, no." She rolled her eyes, but made sure she did so out of his range of vision. "Ego always plays a part, and I don't mean that in an insulting way. I've certainly got an ego."

"Tell me," he muttered.

"Look, look, follow along here." She shifted, scooting up so she could sit and face him.

"Can't we just lie here quietly for a few moments, so I can admire my naked wife?"

"You should like most of this because it involves all sorts of compliments and admiring comments about you."

"Well then, don't let me interrupt your train of thought."

"I really do love you."

"Yes." His lips curved. "I know."

"Sometimes I think it's because of that Plutonian-sized ego, sometimes despite it. Either way, I'm stuck on you, pal. But this isn't about that."

He stroked the back of his fingers along her thigh. "But I'm liking this very much."

"I might be feeling a little sloppy yet, but—" She slapped his hand away. "I'm back on the clock."

"Yes, I'm admiring your badge right now."

The laugh snorted out before she could stop it, but she grabbed her shirt. "What I'm saying is you're an important man, a successful man. Sometimes you make a splash about it, sometimes you don't. Depends on the purpose. You don't *need* to make a big deal about stuff because you are a big deal. That's one part."

"Of what, exactly?"

"Of the whole ego thing. Guys have a different kind of ego than women. I think. Anyway, Mavis claims it's connected to the dick. She's usually right about stuff like that."

"I don't know how I feel about you discussing my dick with Mavis."

"I always say you're hung like a bull and can go all night."

"That's all right, then." But since the direction of the discussion made him feel just a little exposed, he reached for his pants.

"What I'm saying is you've got a . . . powerful ego. You needed it to get where you are, and I must be feeling sloppy because I'm going to say you've earned it. You're confident, confident enough in yourself, in who you are, to back away from a fight because it was important to me. You don't agree with me. What you said before, that you'd be able to live with the consequences, is true. You'd have felt justified. You'd have felt right."

"There was complicity in their neglect. They're guilty because they ignored you. More guilty because they were in a position of authority."

"I'm not arguing that." She tried to put her thoughts into cohesive words as she dressed. "You understood me enough to know if you took action in that direction it would damage me. Us. You put that first, subjugating your own ego. It takes balls to do that."

"I appreciate the sentiment, but I wonder if you could formulate metaphors that didn't include my genitalia. It's beginning to weird me out."

"You're courageous enough to do something that in some part of your heart you see as cowardly." She stepped toward him when he stopped buttoning his shirt, when he looked over at her. "You think I don't know that about you? That I don't understand the nasty little war this waged?"

She tapped a finger to his heart. "And what it cost you to surrender? It makes you the bravest man I know."

"There was nothing courageous about hurting you. And I was hurting you."

"You put me first. That was brave and that was strong. You didn't circumvent the issue by pretending to go along, then going behind my back to do what you wanted. You didn't want a lie between us."

"I don't want anything between us."

"No, because you know how to love. You know how to get the job done. How to be a man. How to take care of the people who matter, even those who don't. You're really smart, and you're capable of very scary behavior, and incredibly kind behavior. You see the big picture, but you never miss the details. You have power, more than most people could dream of, but you don't trample the little guy with it. Do you know what that makes you?"

"Words fail me."

"It makes you the exact opposite of Blair Bissel."

"Ah. So this entire praisefest was just your way of getting back around to your investigation. That certainly crushes my ego."

"You couldn't crush your ego with a hydrovice. That's part of my point. His is fragile, because it's based on smoke. He's not really smart or clever, he's not even talented. His art is just crap, trendy and expensive crap. He doesn't have relationships. He has conquests. He got sucked into this, initially, by a woman who undoubtedly got hooks in his cock, and therefore his ego. 'Aren't I iced? I'm a fricking spy.' "

"And?"

"He should never have been recruited. Look at his profile. He's unstable, immature, reckless. But those are part of the reasons Kade and Sparrow wanted him. He has no genuine ties to anyone. He's attractive, can be charming, has some arty connections, knows how to travel."

"He also has no conscience. It seems to me that would be useful in some areas of covert work."

"That's right, as long as they controlled him. But Sparrow got greedy, and asked for more than Bissel could deliver. He used Bissel to kill, and never figured that Bissel would do more than scamper away with his tail between his legs when he realized he'd been set up just as Reva was. And if he caused any trouble, well, they'd keep it in the HSO, and he'd tag Bissel as rogue, schedule him for termination, or feed enough intel to Doomsday or some other group to have them do it."

"I'm sure you're right, but I also think neither of them figured on you. They, or Sparrow at least, would have had some idea you'd be involved in some way. Using Reva meant using me, which meant you. But, it would seem, neither of them understood how far you'd go, not just for me or Reva, but for the emblem you're currently wearing over your heart."

"So it got sticky. Sparrow does what you'd expect. He uses his position in his organization, tries muscle first, then reason, then cooperation, but always behind the shield of the HSO."

"If Bissel hadn't put him in the hospital, he'd have tried to kill you, or, from what you say, have you killed as he didn't have the stomach for doing the job himself. That would have been his next step."

"I'm sure that was in his pack of contingencies. But a last resort. He should've been smart enough to factor in what it would do to Bissel's twisted ego when Bissel's hands got bloody. He'd killed. He wasn't a stinking level-two now. He'd succeeded in two terminations, and I guarantee he liked the rush."

"But the rush doesn't last."

"No, then you're out in the cold. Isn't that what spies call it? Out in the cold."

She focused, with some surprise, on the plates Roarke set on the table in the sitting area. "Are we eating?"

"Yes."

Thoughtfully, she pressed a hand on her stomach. "I could eat." She sat down to eggs, crisp slices of bacon. "So anyway, he's out in the cold. His direct supervisors are either dead by his own hand or hunting him. He's been betrayed, used, fucked. Cops are looking into the murders in a way he'd been assured they would not, and sooner or later he's going to get squeezed from that side, too. There's nobody to tell him what to do, what to think. He kills twice more to protect himself, to cover his tracks. Both are unnecessary, and mistakes, because the murders only serve to lead the police investigation to the fact that he's still alive. What would you have done?"

"In his place?" He spread jam on toast as he considered. "I'd've gone under, deep. Accessed some of the funds I'd squirreled away, and buried myself until I could plan a way to either kill Sparrow or expose him as a traitor. Wait and watch. A year, two, maybe longer, then hit him. One way or the other."

"But he won't. He can't. He can't suppress his ego that long, or think that clearly. That coldly. He needs to slap back at everything and everyone who had a part in screwing this up for him. At the same time he's scared, like a little boy whose mommy and daddy left him home alone. And he needs to feel safe. He's still in New York, somewhere he feels safe. And he's going to make a move."

She could almost see him, almost see him. "Bigger, more violent, more reckless. Each of his kills was a degree away from the bull's-eye. And each was less carefully thought through, and with more risk of collateral damage than the last. He doesn't care who gets hurt now, as long as he proves himself."

"You think he'll go after Reva."

"Sooner or later. She didn't cooperate. She's not curled up in a cage crying over her dead husband and proclaiming her innocence. But we're not going to give him a chance to go after her."

She took the toast Roarke handed her, bit in. "We're going to lock him down before that, before he starts contacting the targets again. He'll try for Sparrow again sooner. I'm not averse to using that schmuck as bait, but I don't like the idea of taking Bissel at the hospital and risking civilians. We need to track him down, take him in his hole, with minimal risk to civilians. Where would you hide? If you were staying in New York?"

It soothed his soul to sit with her like this, sharing a meal and the work that drove her. It settled, and it comforted, he found, as much as the lovemaking. And when he smiled at her, she smiled back.

"Am I thinking like myself, or like Bissel?"

"Like you."

"A small apartment in a lower middle-class neighborhood where no one pays attention to anyone else. Better, something just outside the city, convenient to public transportation so I could get back and forth easily."

"Why not a house?"

"Too much overhead, too much of a paper trail. I wouldn't

want to waste my capital on the roof over my head, or deal with lawyers and so forth. Just a simple, short-term lease on a modest couple of rooms where I'd be invisible."

"Yeah, that would be smart, and patient."

"Which means you think he's likely in the heart of the city, in something more suited to his taste."

"Yeah, I do. Something big enough where he can work. Someplace with plenty of security where he can lock himself up, stew, rant, plot."

"You probably don't need to be told that there are countless places in the city that fit those requirements."

"You should know, you own most of them. And I . . ." She trailed off with a forkful of eggs halfway to her mouth. "Jesus, would he be that dumb? Or that smart?"

She shoveled in the eggs, snagged her coffee as she rose. "Let's roust the team. I want to check something out."

"You may want to put some shoes on first," Roarke suggested. "You look like you're about to kick some ass, and there's no point in bruising your pretty pink toes."

"Cute." But she winced when she looked down at her feet. She'd forgotten about the pink toenails. Hauling open a drawer, she yanked out some socks and hastily covered all evidence of pedicure.

"Lieutenant?"

She grunted as she pulled on her boots.

"It feels good to know you and I are a team again."

She reached out, took his hand. "Let's go kick some ass together."

Chapter 22

As the techs outnumbered the nontechs on her team, Eve took the briefing to the lab.

She didn't understand the nature of the work, or the purposes of the tools meticulously arranged on work counters and workstations. She couldn't decipher the patterns of the color-coded boards, the gibberish scrolling by on screens, or the constant hum and clack that was the odd communication in the network of machines.

But she knew what she was looking at was a great number of man-hours and a large dose of brain power.

"You'll kill the worm."

"We will, yes. It's already failing." Roarke glanced at the lines of code and commands on one of the screens. "It's a clever bug that can look more dangerous than it is."

"You can say that makes it plenty dangerous."

"You could," he agreed. "Its limitations don't negate the fact that it can and would play hell with most home units. We're tracking it back to Sparrow, and its origin."

"Tokimoto's largely responsible for that," Reva put in.

"I'm hardly working alone. And," Tokimoto added,

"wouldn't have researched or explored that possibility of origin without the data supplied to me."

"Which is what Sparrow counted on. He creates the worm, then assigns Bissel to play double agent. Our side believes Doomsday has the worm, they believe our side has it. Both sides, due to his planted intel, believe the worm is more powerful than it actually is, and shell out a lot of money. Bissel funnels the money, or most of it, back to Sparrow through Kade."

"A good con," Roarke commented. "And might've been a tidy one in the short haul. He'd have been wiser to keep it on a smaller scale, induce a couple of corporations to haggle over it rather than involving the HSO and the like."

"Ambitious guy. And greedy," Eve added. "He supplies the data on the progress Securecomp's making on the worm, and in that way can cover himself anytime the direction the R and D's taking gets too close. Good setup for him."

"But his thinking was narrow." Roarke watched the codes whiz by, noted the progress. "He believed he could control it all, without getting his own hands bloody, and keep Bissel on a leash until he was of no more use."

"Coward." Eve remembered how he'd wept and wailed in the hospital. "Bissel's getting blackmailed and wants more. Kade wants more. And Securecomp's getting close to ending his nice, profitable enterprise."

"He gives Bissel a new assignment that solves all those problems." Peabody shook her head. "It's way over the top, and Bissel's too dim to see the frame going up. Sorry," she said to Reva.

"No problem."

"Not just too dim," Eve added. "Too egocentric. He's living his fantasy. He's got his license to kill."

"Sir!" Peabody beamed. "You've been boning up on Bond."

"I do my homework. But now he's in hip-deep. He can't go to the HSO. He can't go to the other side. He waited too long to run, so his accounts have been located and frozen. He killed to stay dead, but that cover's been blown. He took a hit at Sparrow, but he missed. Instead of being dead, Sparrow's in custody, and he'll use whatever juice he can to cut a deal and bury Bissel. He's lost his fantasy job, and all the glory and polish he garnered from his art."

"If you can call that crap art." Reva grinned when everyone looked at her. "Hey, Blair isn't the only one who can fake it. I never liked his stuff." She rolled her shoulders as if shedding weight. "Feels good to be able to say that. It's starting to feel good all around."

"Don't get too happy yet," Eve warned. "He needs to make a statement, but first he needs to lick his wounds, to reassert himself and find some satisfaction. Reva, you said his art was his genuine passion."

"Yeah. I don't see how that could've been faked. He's worked for years, studied, pursued. He'd sweat days over a piece, hardly sleep or eat when he was in full mode. I might not have liked the shit he turned out, but he put heart and soul into it—his black, withered and rotting heart and soul. I'm going to be bitter for a while," she continued, "and take as many cheap shots at him as humanly possible." She grinned again. "Just FYI."

"I think it's healthy," Tokimoto said. "And human."

"So his art, such as it is, is the real deal to him. They can take away his fantasy job, but he's still an artist." Eve nodded. "He can still create. He has to create. McNab, do a tenant search, look for any connection to Bissel. Target the Flatiron."

"Of course," Roarke murmured. "I can help you with that, Ian," he said to McNab, but he continued to look at Eve. "He'd want to be close to his work, to where he'd felt powerful, and in charge. If he had another place in the building, it's possible Chloe McCoy knew of it."

"Guy like that, he'd want to take her there, to ball her, sure, but also to show her how important he was. Look, I've got this secret place. Nobody knows about it but you."

"And then things went wrong and he needed the place," Peabody finished. "She had to die, just because she knew it was there."

"Lieutenant." Roarke tapped the screen where he worked

with McNab. "LeBiss Consultants. LeBiss is an anagram for Bissel."

"Yeah, he'd want his own name. Another ego thing." She leaned over Roarke's shoulder. "Where is it?"

He gave a command and a diagram of the Flatiron came on screen, revolved, then magnified a highlighted sector. "One floor below his gallery. He'd have enough skill to be able to go between floors with minimal risk should he want to access his studio."

"Fully soundproofed, right?"

"Of course."

"And privacy shades on the windows. Monitors. Add another level of security and he'd be able to know if anyone tried to get on the elevator or through the door. He could muck that up, the way Sparrow did on the night of the first murders. Then clear out before anybody got in.

"Probably work at night," she said half to herself. "Probably work mostly at night when the building's shut down, offices closed, nobody's going to bother him. Cops've already been through, and there's nothing in there that applies to the investigation. Lease is paid up. So until the estate's settled, he can use it without much risk of detection."

"He loved that studio." Reva stepped forward, studying the diagram herself. "I'd bring up the possibility of him building one at home, and he wouldn't consider it. I know it could've been because he wanted the freedom of being away, having accessibility to the women he was sleeping with, but I know, at the core, he just loved that place. Damn it, I'm slipping. I didn't think to put it on the list you wanted of his habits and hangouts."

"Why would you? It was already on my list."

"Yeah, but this was *his* place, and if I'd had my head on straight, I'd have put it together. He always said he needed the stimulation, the energy of the city, of that spot, just as he needed the serenity and privacy of our house. One to charge him up, the other to relax him."

"We need to go in," Eve said.

"Dallas," Reva added. "He wouldn't just work at night, not

if some piece had him. He wouldn't be able to step away from it. I think, unless I've misjudged everything about him, that the risk wouldn't factor into it. Or maybe it would, in some way, fuel the creative drive."

"Good. Good point. We need to assume he's in there, just as we need to assume he's armed and dangerous. The building's full of civilians. We need to move them out."

Feeney, who'd continued to work on McCoy's data unit throughout the briefing, finally glanced up. "You want to clear out a twenty-two-story building?"

"Yeah. Without Bissel knowing it. Which means first we should verify he's in there. Don't want to clear it out while he's around the corner picking up a sandwich at the deli. So let's figure out how to verify, then how to clear out the civilians."

Feeney puffed out a breath. "She don't ask for much. Side note: I've got some data out of this. Reads like a diary. Enough sex stuff with who she calls BB to make a seasoned LC blush." He colored a bit himself when he glanced toward Reva. "Sorry."

"It's not a problem. Not a problem," she repeated in three viciously bitten off words. "He lied to me, screwed around on me, he tried to frame me for murder. Why should knowing some poor little twit romped around naked—"

She paused, breathed deep when the room remained silent but for the machine. "Okay, I'm making it a problem by trying to prove it's not. Let me put it this way." She looked at Tokimoto now. Directly. "Love can die. It can be killed, no matter how alive it was, it's not invulnerable. Mine's dead. It's dead and it's buried. I just want one thing more, and that's the chance to look him in the face and tell him he's nothing. If I can do that one thing, it'll be enough."

"I'll make sure you have the chance," Eve promised. "Now, how do we get him?"

"A bomb scare would clear it, but there'd be injuries," Peabody decided. "People panic, especially when you tell them not to. And even soundproofed, he'd get wind of it."

"Not if you go floor by floor." Eve paced as she thought it

through. "Not a bomb scare. An electrical problem? Something that irritates but doesn't panic."

"A potential leak—hazardous waste, chemicals. And keep it vague," Roarke suggested. "Floor-by-floor evac will take considerable time, and a great many cops."

"I don't want to pull any more into this than necessary. A small, tight unit of the Crisis Team for backup. Move fast, keep it smooth, and we can evac in under an hour. We box him in, that's what we do. We box him in." She stopped, studied the diagram again. "Three exits on the studio?"

"That's correct. Main corridor, elevator to lobby, and the cargo elevator to the roof."

"No glides on the Flatiron, that's a plus."

"And more aesthetically pleasing," Roarke added.

"We block off the elevators. We can bring in a unit from CT on the roof. And we come in from the corridor after he's boxed. If we can get him in this end, the narrow end, he won't have much room to maneuver. We work out the tacticals on this space, and we work out tacticals on the studio. And on the space below. He might be in there. But we need to know where he is when we go in, and we need to blindfold him to the fact we're coming."

"We can do that."

She angled her head, looked down at Roarke. "Can we?"

"Mmm." He took her hand and, watching her horrified expression, brought it smoothly to his lips before she could jerk it free. "The lieutenant doesn't like me to nibble on her when she's coordinating an op. So I can never resist."

"There's just too much sex around here," Feeney grumbled from his station.

"How can we verify his position inside the building and blindfold him?" Eve demanded with what she considered admirable patience.

"Why don't you work out your tacticals and leave those pesky details tails to me. Reva, how much time do you need to shut down the security and undermine the monitors in this sector of the building?"

Brow creased, Reva fisted her hands on her hips. "I'll let you know after I study the specs."

"You'll have them in a minute. I'll need a few things from Securecomp," Roarke said to Tokimoto. "Would you mind getting them?"

"Not at all." His lips curved. "I think I know what you have in mind."

"Let's leave the geeks to it, then." Eve started out, turned back. "I meant the civilian geeks," she said when Feeney and McNab stayed in place.

It took her an hour to work out an approach that minimized risk to civilians and her team, and longer to push through the red tape for clearance to evacuate an entire building.

"We know he's got a short-range launcher. We don't know what other toys he has in there. Boomers, chemical weapons, flash grenades. He won't hesitate to use them to protect himself or to expedite an escape. He's more dangerous because he's not trained in weaponry. Guy who doesn't know what the hell he's doing with a few flash grenades will do more damage than one who does."

"We clear the building, we could pump some gas in the vents, put him to sleep," McNab suggested.

"We can't be sure he doesn't have filters or a mask. He likes the secret-agent toys. Once we verify where he is, we box in that sector. We close off alternate exits, take down the door. We go in fast, and we get him under control. There's nothing in his dossier that indicates any training or skill in hand-to-hand beyond the basics. That doesn't mean he's not dangerous."

"He's going to panic." Feeney pulled on his bottom lip. "First kills were incapacitated when he took them out. He drugs the McCoy girl, does Powell while he's zoned. Tried to hit Sparrow from a distance. This is face-to-face, so if he isn't taken quick, he's going to panic. More dangerous that way."

"Agreed. He's an amateur who thinks he's a pro. His life's screwed. He's pissed off and scared, with no place to go and nothing much to lose. Civilians are our first priority because he won't think twice about taking any out, and we don't know what kind of firepower he's got in there. We remove the civilians, box him in. Take him out. And we want him breathing. He's a key to the case against Sparrow. I don't want to lose him."

"You're going to end up fighting the spooks for him," McNab said. "They're going to want him."

"Exactly. I need Bissel to lock down the case on conspiracy to murder. I want to win this one. Feeney, I need you working with the geeks—with Ewing and Tokimoto," she corrected. "However much Roarke trusts them, I want you at the helm on whatever electronics go into this op. Ewing's tough, and she's pulling her weight, but she might lose it in the crunch."

"She's held up better than most, but I'm with you on that." Feeney dug out his bag of almonds. "This is going to shake her some. I'll stay on top of it."

"The Crisis Team is backup, backup only. I don't want them cowboying this. Four of us go in, two teams of two. McNab and Peabody, I don't want you guys thinking of each other as anything but cops. No personal feelings go through the door. If you can't deal, tell me now."

"It's a little hard for me to think of McNab as a cop when he's wearing a shirt the color of a persimmon." Peabody sent him an arched look. "But otherwise, no problem."

"We'll do the job," McNab assured her. "And this shirt matches my underwear."

"That's something we all needed to know. If we all agree to keep our minds off McNab's underwear, let's get started."

"You said four of us," Peabody pointed out.

"Roarke goes in. McNab can handle any electronics Bissel may have on site, but he's not trained in weaponry. Not the kind we may have to handle. Roarke knows his war toys. And he knows how to go through a door. Any objections to that?"

"Not from me." McNab shrugged. "I've seen his weapon collection. It's beyond."

"Then let's put both ends of this team back together and close this down. Feeney, I just need a word with you."

She waited until they were alone, and shook her head when he held the bag of almonds in her direction. "The . . . data we discussed before, the personal data that had come into my hands. I wanted to let you know it's not going to be a problem. No action will be taken."

"Okay."

"I put you in a bad spot by telling you about the data, and my concerns. I shouldn't have done that."

He folded the top of the bag, put it back in his pocket. "We go back too far for you to say that to me. Because we do, and I know where it's coming from, I'm not going to be pissed at you for saying it."

"Thanks. My head's been pretty screwed up."

"On straight now?"

"Yeah."

"Then let's load up the rockets and get the sucker launched."

"I've got one more thing to do, then I'll be right behind you." She went to her desk when he walked out, turned on her 'link.

"Nadine Furst."

"Dallas. It looks like I'm going to be able to clear my schedule in a couple hours. Three anyway. Since we missed that lunch, why don't we get together today. Just you and me."

"Sounds like fun. Where should I meet you?"

"I've got some business to take care of. Why don't you meet me at Fifth Avenue, between Twenty-second and Twenty-third. Around two. My treat."

"Perfect. Looking forward to seeing you."

Eve disconnected, satisfied Nadine had understood the offer of a one-on-one. And that she'd be giving the top media hound in the city a story that would send the HSO scrambling for cover.

She joined the others in the lab as Roarke demonstrated equipment for Feeney.

She frowned at the screen, and the colors moving on it. "I assume this is not a new vid game."

"Sensor. Configured to body heat. You're looking at Summerset puttering around in the kitchen downstairs. You input the coordinates of the location you want to scan, and the nature of the object you want to track. It'll read through solid objects like walls, doors, glass, and so on. Steel. Flatiron's a steel skeleton. The distance it will work depends on basic interference. Other objects with similar makeup will, of course, interfere. But once you've homed in on your target, you can lock and follow."

"What's this?" She tapped the screen where a red-and-orange blob circled. "Is that—"

"The cat." Roarke grinned at her. "Hoping for a handout, I'd say. Got ears, Tokimoto?"

"Nearly. Another moment."

"We're locked on," Roarke explained. "Interface the audio sensor, and find the right combination of filters, and we should be able to pick up sound."

"Two floors down? Without direct linking or satellite bounce?"

"We're utilizing satellite. With equipment we've got in the lab, we'd be able to see and count Galahad's whiskers. But with this portable 'link, we'll make do with body heat image." Roarke glanced up. "It should be enough for your purposes."

"Yeah. It'll work just fine." She pursed her lips when she heard what might have been violins coming from the equipment, then the unmistakable sound of Galahad's most persuasive meows.

"This," McNab said with an avaricious sigh, "kicks solid ass."

"How about his security and monitors?" Eve asked.

"I can shut them down by remote. We can bypass his building audio so he won't hear the evacuation orders. We can have this equipment set up, on site, in twenty minutes, have him scanned and locked within thirty."

"We start boxing and locking him first, then evacuate. We'll need to clear out a space on the floor below his for base.

Keep that quick and quiet, then set up this equipment there. Feeney?"

"On that."

"Peabody, break out the body armor for the takedown team. Load up. Roarke, with me."

"Always," he said and followed her out.

She said nothing until they were back in her office. She checked her weapon, her clutch piece, then opened a drawer in her workstation and took out a stunner. "You'll need this. I want you to go in with me."

He turned the weapon over in his hand. He had more powerful and certainly more efficient weapons of his own. But it was, he decided, the thought that counted. "You're not going to make me ask."

"No. You've earned it. I want you going through the door with me. More than that, I don't know what he's got in there. When we go in, I need you to focus on the weaponry. Leave him to me. Leave him to me, Roarke."

"Understood, Lieutenant."

"There's something else. I've given Nadine a heads-up. When this is over, if you wanted to say something to the media about how Bissel and Sparrow screwed over an employee and attempted to steal data from Securecomp, to sabotage a Code Red and so on, it wouldn't hurt my feelings."

"You're feeding them to the dogs." His lips twitched as he skimmed a finger down the dent in her chin. "Why, Lieutenant. You excite me."

"I figure they'll be cleaning up the blood and bones for some time. And a lot of the blood and bones are going to be scattered throughout HSO. There's all kinds of payback, Roarke."

"Yes." He slipped the weapon into his pocket so he could take her face in his hands, lay his lips on her brow. "There is. If this satisfies you, it'll do me as well."

"Then let's go kick some righteous ass."

It made it stickier, and just a little nerve-racking, to have Commander Whitney and Chief Tibble step into the operation as observers. She did her best to ignore them as she coordinated her personnel.

"Both protocol and courtesy demand that the HSO be informed if and when we verify the location of Blair Bissel," Tibble commented.

"I'm not immediately concerned with protocol or courtesy, sir, but with the locating, restraining, and capture of a multiple murder suspect. It's entirely possible that other members of the HSO were involved in or privy to the plans and actions that involved three operatives. Informing the organization at this time of this operation may, in fact, compromise same if Bissel has some contact in-house."

"You don't believe he does, not for a minute. But it's good," Tibble said with a nod. "Logical, and you can be sure I'll use that angle when the shit falls. You miss Bissel here, or fail to wrap him up tight, some of that shit will fall on you."

"He'll be wrapped." She turned back to the monitors, marking the time. Waiting.

They were in a suite of offices one floor below LeBiss Consultants. The occupants had been swept out, and she only needed Roarke's confirmation that the security in LeBiss and the penthouse level had been shut down to start the next stage.

"They'll want to take him, Lieutenant," Tibble added. "Move both him and Sparrow into federal territory."

"Bet they will," she started. "As long as they both face the murder and conspiracy to murder charges, I don't care who locks the cage."

"They'll want it quiet. This sort of screwup within their own ranks won't play well with the public."

Yeah, she thought, definitely stickier. "Are you ordering me to sweep this under the rug, Chief Tibble?"

"I'm giving no such order, Lieutenant. But I will point out that public statements regarding certain details of this case would be politically unwise."

"I'll bear that in mind." She looked over as Roarke walked in.

"Done," he said. "Your man's blind and deaf. The elevator to the studio is disabled."

"Acknowledged." She picked up her communicator. "Dallas. I want those stairways blocked and manned. Do not, I repeat, do not move in on either target location. Begin evac."

She gestured to the monitor. "Find him."

"I'd like to scan and locate," Reva said. "I'd like to man the controls on that."

"That's Feeney's call."

Feeney gave Reva a little pat on the shoulder and had to fight off the itch to run the program himself. "Go."

She input the designated coordinates for LeBiss, configured for body heat imaging, then did a slow scan. "Nothing there." Her voice shook a bit, but she cleared her throat and changed the coordinates for the penthouse.

When she saw the mass of red-and-orange light, she simply stared. "Target confirmed," she said as Eve stepped forward. "He's alone. Coordinates put him in the studio sector."

"What's this?" Eve demanded, circling a line of blue.

"Fire. Flame. Intense heat. He's working."

"He's armed," Roarke put in. "See here, this space, the angle and position on the body. "Sidearms, would be my guess."

"Okay. Suit up." She grabbed her own body armor.

"Bringing up audio. He's got music on. Trash rock," Reva said after a moment. "He's excited, buzzed up," she added. "He listens to that when he's revving. He's got a lot of metal in there. Equipment, works-in-progress. It's going to be tricky to tell if any of what I'm getting is weaponry."

"We assume he has it. Keep him locked." Eve fit on her headset. "I want to know where he is and what he's doing at all times. I want to know the instant the building's clear. Let's move into position."

"Go." Feeney spoke into his communicator. "Unit Six, this is base. Friendlies moving into your sector. I repeat, friendlies moving through."

"They'll give us the picture," Eve began as they started toward the stairwell. "Weapons on stun. Dallas on the door," she said into her headset, then opened the door to the stairwell.

The two-man crisis unit stood ready. "All quiet," she was told.

"We stun him. I don't want him drawing a weapon. Nobody gets hurt on this op. We put him down, restrain, and move him out clean."

"I can get behind that," McNab muttered.

A full frontal, she thought, all four through the same door, was too risky if he was armed.

"You and Peabody on the gallery door. Roarke will open the door between the sections by remote on my command. We'll go in the studio door. Take him in a pincer. Move on my signal."

She moved through the stairwell door, signaled McNab and Peabody to position on the other side of the corridor.

She could hear the progress of the evacuation through her headset. It was slow, but it was moving. She rolled her shoulders.

"Jesus, I *hate* these vests. Can they make them any more uncomfortable?"

"In another age, Lieutenant, you'd have been my knight in shining armor. And that protection you'd have hated a great deal more."

"Could've taken him, probably could've taken him without the evac. Could wait, stake him out. He's got to sleep sometimes. But . . ."

"Your instincts told you to move people out of harm's way and take him now."

She removed her headset, gestured at his. "If it'll help you to be the one to take him down, I'll hold back."

He skimmed a fingertip along her jawline. "Soft on me, aren't you?"

"Pretty much."

"Same goes. And no, don't hold back. It doesn't matter who."

"Okay, then." She put her headset back in place. Then rolled on her toes a few minutes later when the all-clear came through.

"Peabody, on the door. Roarke, get them into the gallery."

He keyed in on his remote. "Done."

"Move in. Stay ready." She took her position by the studio door, nodded to Roarke. "Go!"

She broke through the door, went in low with Roarke high beside her. An instant later, the door between sections opened and Peabody and McNab charged through.

Bissel stood by one of his sculptures, wearing a safety helmet and goggles, light body armor. And two hand blasters in a cross-body harness. He held a torch that spurted a thin line of flame.

"Police! Put your hands in the air. Do it now!"

"It's not going to matter. Not going to matter." He swept the torch toward Peabody and McNab, and jerked back as he was stunned.

"Not going to matter." He tossed down the torch and flame bounced along the reflective surface of the floor. "I rigged this. Are you hearing me!" he shouted. "I've got a bomb. If you come at me, I'll blow it. I'll blow up half this building and everyone in it. You put down those weapons and *listen* to me."

"I'm all ears, Blair." She heard the order go out for Bombs and Explosives through her earpiece. "Where's the bomb?"

"Put down your weapons."

"I'm not going to do that." She watched out of the corner of her eye as Roarke shifted, then crouched to retrieve the torch and turn it off. "You want me to listen, I'll listen. Where's the bomb? You could be bullshitting me. You want me to listen, you've got to tell me where it is."

"This. The whole damn thing." He slapped his hand on the twisting column of metal. His face was sheened with sweat. From the work, she imagined, and from excitement. And panic.

"There's enough in here to blow this place, hundreds of people, to hell and back again."

"You'd go with them."

"You listen." He shoved back his helmet and she saw his eyes. Zeus, she thought. He was riding on it. Between that and the body armor, he'd take a few stuns before he went down.

"I said I was listening. What do you have to say?"

"I'm not going to jail. I'm not going in a cage. Sparrow, Quinn Sparrow's the one who set this up, who set me up. I'm not going in a cage. I'm an HSO operative, on assignment. I don't answer to the NYPSD."

"We can talk about that." She kept her voice even, the tone interested. "You can tell me about your assignment, unless you blow yourself up first."

"We're not going to talk. You're going to listen. I want transportation. I want a jet copter, and pilot, on the roof. I want ten million in nontraceable currency. When I'm clear I'll send you the deactivation code. Otherwise . . ."

He held up his left hand and displayed the remote trigger strapped to his palm. "I use this. I'm HSO!" he shouted. "Do you think I won't use this?"

"I don't doubt you'll use it, Agent Bissel. But I have to verify the explosive exists. Unless I can confirm the threat and tell my superiors, they're not going to listen. I need to verify, so you can stay in control."

"It's there. And one twitch—"

"You know procedure and protocol. We're professionals. I've got to answer to my superiors. Let's confirm, then we can move on to your demands and negotiate."

"It's inside, you stupid bitch. I put it inside. You'd stayed out of this, I'd've had it drop-kicked to fucking HSO Base for screwing with me."

"We'll scan it. No point in anybody getting hurt. We've got Sparrow. He's enough for me. He's the one who got you into this mess. I've just got to confirm, so we can start the process."

"Scan it, then. You'll see. I want that jet copter. I want you to pull back, pull the hell back. I want transportation to a location of my choice."

Roarke held up both hands. "Let me just get out my scanner, configure it for reading an explosive device. You know I own part of this building. I don't want it damaged."

Bissel shifted his gaze from Eve's face to Roarke's. Wet his lips. "Make one move, just one I don't like, it goes."

Roarke reached in his pocket, held out the scanner for Bissel's approval.

"You've been dipping in Zeus, Agent Bissel," Eve said to bring his attention back to her. "It's not good for you. It can cloud your thinking."

"You think I don't know what I'm doing?" Sweat was running down his face, pooling at the base of his throat. "You think I don't have the balls?"

"No. You couldn't do what you do, be what you are, if you didn't have balls. Sparrow hadn't screwed you up, you'd be fat city."

"The son of a bitch."

"He thought you were his dog, that he could keep you on a leash." She didn't look at Roarke, but sensed him at her side. "But you showed him what you were made of. I think all you wanted to do was get away after your assignment was complete. To get what was owed to you and get away, and things kept going wrong. You know, I bet Chloe would've gone with you. You didn't have to kill her."

"She was an *idiot!* A decent roll, but she'd irritate the hell out of you out of bed. I used her data unit to store information, to formulate plans. I know how to make my own plans. Contingencies. And what do you think I saw when I peeked in through the listening device I planted in the bedroom? She was trying to get into it, trying to break my passcode. Probably thought I was screwing around on her. Stupid, jealous little bitch."

"What about the locket you gave her?"

He looked blank, then his jittery eyes smiled. "Passkey, drop box. Think I don't know how to cover myself? I had drop boxes all over the damn place. Emergency funds, weapons, whatever I needed. Can't put everything in one spot. Gotta spread out."

"And she knew about this place. She knew, and she had that incriminating data buried on her unit, and one of your passkeys. I guess I was wrong. You did have to kill her."

"Damn straight. It should've worked. It should've. I even

got her to write the note. Just write it down for me, baby. One line, just one to say how you felt when you thought I was dead. And she was stupid enough to do it."

"It was a good plan. So was Powell. It was just bad luck."

"Explosive device confirmed," Roarke said coolly. "My, my, Bissel, you certainly put all your eggs into one very volatile basket. If you discharge that, they wouldn't be able to sweep up the pieces."

"I told you. Didn't I *tell* you? Now get me that copter. Get it now!"

"If you discharged it," Roarke continued. "But you won't, as I've just deactivated the timer. You're clear, Lieutenant."

"Thanks." She aimed for Bissel's unprotected legs. He staggered, roared, and his eyes went wild as he closed his hand into a fist to try to set off the explosive.

She hit him a second time when he reached for the sidearms, and Peabody came in from the side, bowling in mid-body to send them both flying across the now scarred floor.

Pumping on Zeus, he backhanded her, but she held on.

McNab leaped, diving in to catch Bissel in a headlock, and, using his fist instead of his weapon, rammed three short, hard punches to the face.

Her nose was streaming blood, but Peabody grabbed her restraints. Between the two of them, they held him down and cuffed his wrists.

"Get his ankles, too," Eve suggested, and tossed over her own restraints. "He's still pretty hopped. This is Dallas," she said into her headset. "Suspect is secured. Send in Bombs and Explosives to remove device."

When Peabody panted and sat hard on Bissel's still bucking back, McNab offered her a polka-dotted handkerchief. "Here you go, baby. Your nose is bleeding. I mean, Detective Baby," he added with a glance at Eve.

"Doing okay, Peabody?" Eve asked her.

"Yeah. It's not broken." She held the colorful cloth to her nose. "We got him, Lieutenant."

"Yeah, we got him. Arrange to have the prisoner transported to Central. Good job, Detective Baby. You, too, McNab."

"You held back," Roarke said when Eve stepped out of the way to let the bomb squad deal with the sculpture. "So McNab could punch him a few times for Peabody."

"I think Peabody might have handled it on her own, but he deserved a shot. Got a good, solid right for such a skinny guy."

She checked her wrist unit. It looked as if she was going to be right on time for Nadine.

Screw political wisdom.

"I'm going to have to go in, do the paperwork, warm up Bissel in Interview. Going to take some time. Maybe you could fill in Reva and Tokimoto, make sure they know their assistance and cooperation have been noted and appreciated. Let Reva know I'm going to clear it so she gets five private minutes with Bissel. And maybe you could tell Caro she did a good job raising her kid."

"You could tell her that yourself."

"Guess I could. Meanwhile"—she jerked a thumb so he'd step with her into the relative quiet of the gallery—"you've been putting in a lot of time and energy as regards this investigation. Personal interest or not, that's also noted and appreciated."

"Thank you."

"I guess it's going to take you some time to get your own stuff back in order. All that universal magnate and corporate god stuff."

"A few days. A week or so, we'll be on balance again. I'm going to have to be out of town for a bit. Some of it needs to be hands-on."

"Okay. But you figure you'll be back in order in about a week?"

"More or less, why?"

"Because when you're all set, I'm going to take you away for a long weekend. So you can relax."

His eyebrows shot up. "Are you?"

"Yeah. You've been revving on all engines. You need a break. So we'll say . . . a week from Friday. Where do you want to go?"

"Where do I want to go? And you're doing this because I need a break?"

She glanced through the doorway, just to make sure nobody was paying any attention. Then cupped his face in her hands. "You do. Then there's the fact that I intend to make you my sex slave for a couple days. So where do you want to go?"

"We haven't been to the island in a while." He didn't bother to check if anyone was watching, but leaned down and kissed her. "I'll make the arrangements."

"No. I'll make the arrangements. I can do it," she said when he didn't quite hide the wince. "I can. Jesus, I can coordinate a major op, I should be able to coordinate some damn travel. Have a little faith."

"In you I have more than a little."

"Then I'll see you later. I've got to go let the dogs out."

She headed out, then walked back and gave him a hard, short kiss. "Later, Civilian Baby."

She heard him laugh as she walked out, skirted around other cops. And when she was alone, riding down alone, she tapped her finger—the one that wore her wedding ring—against the image of the badge on her heart.

Turn the page for a preview of

Visions in Death

The next exciting novel
featuring Lieutenant Eve Dallas and Roarke

She'd gotten through the entire evening without killing anyone. Lieutenant Eve Dallas, cop to the bone, figured the restraint showed enormous strength of character.

Her day had gone smoothly enough. A morning court appearance that had been as routine as it was tedious, paperwork both extensive and mind-numbing. The single case she'd caught had involved pals and their dispute over who had dibs on the last of the illegals—a party mix of Buzz, Exotica, and Zoom—they'd been toking on while lazing around on the roof of an apartment building on the West Side.

The dispute had been resolved when one of the afternoon partyers had taken a header off the roof, clutching the last of the illegals in his greedy fist.

He probably hadn't felt much, even when he'd splatted onto Tenth Avenue, but it sure as hell had broken the party mood.

Witnesses, including an uninvolved Good Samaritan from a neighboring building who'd called in the nine-one-one, all stated that the individual who'd been scooped off the sidewalk and into a bag had leaped of his own volition onto the roof ledge, danced an energetic keep-away boogie, lost his precarious balance, and had taken flight with a giggling *wee-haw*.

Much to the surprise—and possible entertainment—of the afternoon passengers on an airtram who'd also witnessed the last dance of one Jasper K. McKinney.

One inappropriately delighted tourist had managed to capture the entire incident on his pocket vid.

It all jibed, and the books would close on Jasper as death by misadventure. Unofficially, Eve labeled it death by stupidity, but there wasn't a place on the sheet for that particular observation.

As a result of Jasper and his eight-story dive, she'd clocked out of Cop Central barely an hour past end-of-duty, only to get bogged down in ugly midtown traffic because the temporary vehicle some sadist in Requisitions had tossed at her limped along like a blind, three-legged dog.

She had rank, for God's sake, and was entitled to a decent ride. It wasn't her fault she'd had two units destroyed in two years. Maybe she'd forget strength of character and go maim somebody in Requisitions in the morning.

It sounded like fun.

And after she'd gotten home—okay, almost two hours late—she'd had to transform herself from kick-ass murder cop to fashionable corporate wife.

She was a good cop, she reminded herself, but more than a little shaky in the corporate wife arena.

She supposed she'd been fashionable, since her husband had the entire getup—down to the underwear—set out for her. Roarke knew clothes.

She just knew she was wearing something green with sparkles all over it, and where it wasn't green and sparkly, it showed a lot of skin.

There hadn't been time to argue about it, but only to dive into the outfit and shove her feet into shoes—also green and sparkly. With high enough, needle-thin heels, she'd been nearly eye to eye with her man.

It wasn't a hardship to be eye to eye with Roarke. Not when his were that wild, unearthly blue in a face drawn by artistic angels. But it was tough being social with strangers when you were worried you might tip over and fall on your ass any second.

But she'd gotten through it. Through the quick-change, the quick shuttle trip from New York to Chicago, through the cocktail hour where her brains were nearly bored to suet despite truly excellent wine, and the corporate dinner with Roarke entertaining about a dozen clients, with her playing hostess.

She wasn't quite sure what kind of clients they were since Roarke had his fingers in every pie known to man or beast, so she didn't attempt to keep up. What she did know was that most of them could take the prize for most tedious during the four-hour ordeal.

But there had been no casualties.

Points for her.

What she wanted now was to get home, get out of the sparkly green thing, and fall into bed to sleep for the six hours she'd have before the clock started ticking again.

The summer of 2059 had been long, hot, and bloody. Fall, with its cooler temperatures, was coming. Maybe people wouldn't be as inclined to kill each other.

But she doubted it.

She'd barely settled into her seat on the plush, private shuttle when Roarke lifted her feet into his lap and slipped off her shoes.

"Don't get any ideas, pal. When I finally get out of this dress, I'm not getting back in."

"Darling Eve." His voice was a purr that echoed of Ireland. "That's the sort of statement that gives me ideas. However lovely you look in that dress, you'd look even lovelier out of it."

"Forget it. No way I'm dragging this thing back on, and I'm surely not getting out of this shuttle wearing what you laughingly call underwear. So just . . . Oh, sweet baby Jesus."

Her eyes crossed, then did a slow roll to the back of her head when he pressed his thumbs into her arch.

"I owe you a foot rub, at the very least." He smiled as she let her head fall back and moaned. "For services above and beyond. I know you detest the sort of thing we did tonight.

And I appreciate you not pulling out your weapon and stunning McIntyre over the canapés."

"The guy with the big teeth who laughed like a donkey, right?"

"That would be McIntyre. He's also a very important account." He lifted her left foot, kissed her toes. "So thanks."

"It's okay. Goes with the package."

Hell of a package, she thought, studying him through barely open eyes. All gorgeously wrapped six feet two inches of him. Not just the lean, muscled build or the heart-stopping face framed with the sweep of black silk hair. But the brains, the style, the edge. The whole shot.

And best of all, he not only loved her, but he *got* her. Of all the things they fought about—and it was never hard to find something—they never butted heads over this.

He never expected any more of her in the corporate-wife arena than she could give. A lot of people would, and she got that. Roarke's enterprises included holdings, properties, factories, markets, and God knew, on and off planet. He was absurdly rich with all the power that went with it. A lot of men in his position would expect a spouse to be at their beck, to drop everything and drape themselves over his arm at a moment's notice.

He didn't.

For every business event or social occasion she managed to attend as his wife, there were probably three she missed.

Moreover, there were countless times he arranged his schedule to suit hers, or put in time as consultant on a case.

In fact, when she thought about it, he made a much better cop's husband than she made corporate wife.

"Maybe I owe you a foot rub," she considered. "You're a pretty good deal."

He skimmed a finger down her foot, from toes to heel. "I certainly am."

"But I'm still not getting out of this dress." She scooted down in her seat, closed her eyes. "Wake me up when we land."

She'd only started to drift when the communicator in her

evening bag signaled. "Oh, come *on*." She didn't open her eyes but reached out, clamped a hand on the bag. "What's our ETA?"

"About fifteen."

With a nod, she pulled out the communicator and engaged. "Dallas."

DISPATCH, DALLAS, LIEUTENANT EVE. REPORT TO BELVEDERE CASTLE, CENTRAL PARK. OFFICERS ON SCENE. HOMICIDE, SINGLE VICTIM.

"Contact Peabody, Detective Delia. I'll meet her on scene. My ETA is thirty minutes."

ACKNOWLEDGED. DISPATCH OUT.

"Shit." Eve dragged a hand through her hair. "You can dump me and go on."

"I dislike dumping my wife. I'll go with you and wait."

She scowled down at the fancy dress. "I hate going to scenes in these getups. I hear about it for weeks."

It was worse because she had to put the shoes back on, and then navigate in them over the grass and on to the paths of the city's greatest park.

The castle sat at the highest point of the park, with its skinny tower rising up into the night sky and the rocky ground giving way to the lake at its feet.

It was a pretty enough spot, she supposed, for tourists to take their snaps and vids during the day. Once the sun set, areas like this were the natural habitat of the street sleepers, chemi-heads, unlicensed companions on the troll, and those with nothing better to do than look for trouble.

The current city administration made a lot of noise about keeping the parks and monuments clean. And to their credit they even tossed money at the process with some regularity. There would be volunteers as well as city workers combing the park for litter, blasting off graffiti, sprucing up gardens and such.

Then everyone would get cozy and comfortable and put their efforts into other matters until it all went to hell again.

At the moment it was in decent shape with hardly enough litter to make the predawn clean-up crews work themselves into a lather.

With Roarke beside her, she strode as best she could toward the barricades the cops had already put in place. The castle was lit up like day with crime-scene lights.

"You don't have to wait," she told him. "I can catch a ride."

"I'll wait."

Rather than argue, she shrugged and, pulling out her badge, went through the barricades.

No one made any comments about the dress or shoes. She'd figured her rep for ass-kicking would have kept the uniforms quiet, but it surprised her not to detect a single grin or snicker behind her back.

It surprised her more when her partner stepped toward her without a smart remark on her wardrobe.

"Dallas. It's bad."

"What've we got?"

"Female, caucasian, about thirty. I got the scene recorded. I was about to run her for ID when they told me you'd arrived on scene." They walked together, Peabody in her comfortable airskids, Eve in the arch-killing heels. "Sexual homicide. Raped and strangled. But he didn't stop there."

"Who found her?"

"A couple of kids. Jesus, Dallas." Peabody stopped a moment, stood in her hastily thrown-on clothes, rubbing a hand over her tired face. "Snuck out of the house, thought they'd have a little adventure. Sure as hell got more than that. We've contacted the parents and child services. We've got them in a black-and-white."

"Where is she?"

"Down there." Peabody led the way, then pointed.

She lay on the rocks, just above the dark, still water of the lake. She wore nothing but what looked to be a red ribbon tied around her neck. Her hands were clasped together between her breasts, as if in prayer, or plea.

Her face was smeared with blood. Blood, Eve thought, that had spilled out of her when he'd taken her eyes.

She had to ditch the shoes or risk breaking her neck. Using the can of Seal-It from the field kit Peabody handed her, she coated her hands, her bare feet. Even so, it wasn't an easy climb down in the party dress, and she imagined she looked completely ridiculous, completely uncoplike sparkling her way over rocks toward a body.

She heard something rip, and ignored it.

"Oh man." Peabody winced. "You're going to ruin that dress, and it's totally iced."

"I'd give a month's pay for a goddamn pair of jeans and a normal shirt. A pair of fucking boots." Then she put it out of her mind, set her feet solidly, and turned to the body.

"Didn't rape her down here. There's going to be a secondary scene. Even a lunatic doesn't rape a woman on a heap of rocks when there's all this grass. Raped her somewhere else. Killed or incapacitated her somewhere else. Had to carry her down here. Had to have some muscle and bulk to manage that—unless there was more than one of them. She's what, maybe a hundred and thirty pounds anyway. Deadweight."

More to protect the scene than the dress, Eve hitched the skirt up. "Let's get an ID on her, Peabody. Find out who she is."

While Peabody used the Identi-pad, Eve studied the position of the body. "Posed her. Praying? Begging? Resting in peace? What's your message?"

She crouched to examine the body. "Visual evidence of physical and sexual assault. Facial bruises, torso, forearms—those look defensive. She's got some matter under her nails. Tried to fight, scratched at him. It's not skin. Looks like fibers."

"Her name's Elisa Maplewood," Peabody said. "Central Park West address."

"Not so far from home," Eve stated. "She doesn't look uptown. No pedicure. Hands aren't smooth and pampered. Got calluses."

"Lists employment as a domestic."

"Yeah, that's more like it."

"She's thirty-two. Divorced. Dallas, she's got a four-year-old kid. A daughter."

"Oh, hell." Eve drew it in, then set it aside. "Bruises on her thighs and the vaginal area. Red corded ribbon around her throat."

It was dug into her skin so the bruised flesh puffed around it, then the tails draped down to her breasts.

"Time of death, Peabody?"

"Getting it." Peabody drew back the gauge, studied the readout. "Twenty-two twenty."

"About three hours ago. And the kids found her?"

"Just after midnight. First on scene responded, dealt with the kids, took a visual from above, and called it in at quarter to one."

"Okay." Steeling herself, she took the microgoggles, slipped them on, then bent over the ruined face. "Took his time here. Didn't hack at her. Neat, precise cuts. Almost surgical, like he was doing a fucking transplant. So the eyes were what he was after. They were the prize. The beating, the rape, those were just the prelude."

She eased back and took off the goggles. "Let's turn her, check the back."

There was nothing but the darkened flesh from the settling of blood, and what Eve identified as grass stains on the buttocks and down the thighs.

"Came at her from the front, that's what he did. Didn't matter to him if she saw him. Knocked her down—sidewalk or pavement. No, gravelly path. See the scrapes on her elbows? Smacks her around. She tries to fight him off, tries to scream. Maybe she does scream, but he's hauling her away, somewhere he can have his fun without anyone trying to interfere. Drags her across the grass. Beats her into submission, rapes her. Ties the cord around her neck, kills her. When that part of the job's over, it's time for the real business."

Eve replaced the goggles. "Strip off what's left of her clothes, take her shoes, anything else she was wearing. Jewelry, anything that individualizes her. Carry her down here.

Pose her. Take the eyes—carefully. Check the pose, make any necessary adjustments. Wash off all that blood in the lake if you want. Clean up, take your prize, and be on your way."

"Ritual killing?"

"His ritual anyway. They can bag her," Eve said as she straightened. "Let's see if we can find the kill site."

Roarke watched her slide her feet back into the shoes. She'd have been better off barefoot, he mused, but that wasn't an option the lieutenant would consider.

Despite the heels, the glamorous dress—worse for wear now—the glitter of diamonds, shc was every inch the cop. Tall, lean, steady as the rocks she'd just climbed on to view some new horror. You wouldn't see the horror in her eyes, those long, golden brown eyes. She looked pale in the harsh lights, and the glare of them only accentuated her sharp features. Her hair, nearly the same color as those eyes, was short, choppy, and mussed now from the breeze off the water.

He watched her stop, hold a brief conversation with a uniform. Her voice would be flat, he knew, and brisk, and reveal nothing of what she felt.

He saw her gesture, and saw the stalwart and more comfortably dressed Peabody nod. Then Eve was peeling off from the group of cops, and heading back to him.

"You're going to want to go on home," she told him. "This is going to take some time."

"I suspect it will. Rape, strangulation, mutilation." He lifted a brow when her eyes narrowed. "I keep my ear to the ground when it involves my cop. Can I help?"

"No. I'm keeping civilians—even you—out. He didn't kill her down there, so we need to find where he did. I probably won't make it home tonight."

"Would you like me to bring you, or send you, a change of clothes?"

Since even with his amazing powers, he couldn't just snap his fingers and put her in boots and trousers, she shook her head. "I've got spare stuff in my locker at Central." She glanced down at the dress, sighed at the smears of dirt, the small tears, the stains from body fluid. She'd tried to be careful, but there you go, and God knew what he paid for the damn thing.

"Sorry about the dress."

"It's not important. Get in touch when you can."

"Sure."

She struggled—knew he knew she struggled—not to wince when he skimmed a finger down the dent in her chin, when he leaned down and brushed his lips to hers. "Good luck, Lieutenant."

"Yeah. Thanks."

As he walked back to the limo, he heard her raise her voice. "Okay, boys and girls, fan out. Teams of two. Standard evidence search."

He wouldn't have carried her far, Eve deduced. What would be the point? The added time, trouble, the additional risk of being seen. Still, they were talking Central Park, so it wasn't going to be quick and easy unless they ran into incredible luck.

She did, inside of thirty minutes.

"Here." She held up a hand to stop Peabody, then crouched. "Ground's torn up some. Hand me the goggles. Yeah, yeah," she said after she'd strapped them on. "We got some blood here."

She went down on hands and knees, her nose nearly to the ground, like a hound scenting prey. "I want this area cordoned off. Call the sweepers. I want to see if they can find any trace. Look here."

She got tweezers out of the field kit. "Broken fingernail. Hers," she decided when she held it up to the light. "Didn't make it easy for him, did you, Elisa? You did what you could."

She bagged the nail, then sat back on her heels.

"Dragged her over the grass. You can see where she tried to dig in. Lost a shoe. That's why she's got grass stains and dirt on one foot. But he went back for it. Took her clothes with him."

She pushed to her feet. "We'll check bins in a ten-block radius in case he dumped them. They'll be torn, bloody, dirty. We'll see if we can get a description of what she was wearing, but even without it, we'll look. Kept them though, didn't you?" she murmured. "Kept them as a memento."

"She lives a couple blocks from here," Peabody commented. "Grabbed her close to home, dragged her here, did the job, then carried her over to the dump site."

"We'll canvass. Let's get this coordinated, then take her residence."

Peabody cleared her throat, studied Eve's dress. "You're going like that?"

"Got a better idea?"

It was hard not to feel a little ridiculous, striding in her ruined dress and mile-high shoes toward the night droid on door duty in front of Maplewood's building.

At least she had her badge. It was one of those things she never left home without. "Lieutenant Dallas, Detective Peabody, NYPSD. Regarding Elisa Maplewood. She lives here?"

"I'll need to scan your IDs to verify."

He looked pretty spiffy for so early in the morning, but that was a droid for you. He wore a natty red uniform with silver trim, and was designed to replicate a man in his mid-fifties, just a bit of silver at the temples to match the braid.

"These are in order. Mrs. Maplewood is a live-in domestic, employed by Mr. and Mrs. Luther Vanderlea. What's this about?"

"Did you see Ms. Maplewood tonight?"

"I'm midnight to six. Haven't seen her."

"We'll need to see the Vanderleas."

"Mr. Vanderlea is out of town. You'll need to clear a visit with the desk. Comp's on this time of night."

He unlocked the doors, walked in with them. "Secondary scan for ID," he informed them.

It irritated, but Eve passed her badge through the electronics on the fancy desk in the black-and-white lobby.

YOUR IDENTIFICATION IS VERIFIED, DALLAS, LIEUTENANT EVE. WHAT IS THE NATURE OF YOUR BUSINESS?

"I need to speak with Mrs. Luther Vanderlea, regarding her employee, Elisa Maplewood."

ONE MOMENT WHILE MRS. VANDERLEA IS CONTACTED.

The droid hovered while they waited. Quiet music played. It had switched on when they'd started across the lobby. Set to activate, Eve assumed, when a human entered.

Why people needed music to cross a room, she couldn't say.

The lights were dim, the flowers fresh. A few good pieces of furniture—in case you wanted to sit down and listen to the recorded music—were arranged tastefully. There were two elevators in the south wall, and four security cameras to sweep the lobby.

The Vanderleas had a lot of bucks under the belt.

"Where's Mr. Vanderlea?" she asked the droid.

"Is this an official inquiry?"

"No, I'm just a nosey so-and-so." She waved her badge under his nose. "Yes, this is an official inquiry."

"Mr. Vanderlea is in Madrid on business."

"When did he leave?"

"Two days ago. He's due back tomorrow evening."

"What—" She broke off as the comp signaled.

MRS. VANDERLEA WILL SEE YOU NOW. PLEASE TAKE ELEVATOR A TO THE FIFTY-FIRST FLOOR. YOU WILL FIND MRS. VANDERLEA IN PENTHOUSE B.

"Thanks." Even as they crossed the checkerboard floor, the elevator doors opened. "Why do we thank machines?" Eve wondered out loud. "They couldn't possibly give a shit."

"One of those innate human traits. That's why programmers have them thanking us, too, I guess. You ever been to Madrid?"

"No. Maybe. No," she decided. She'd been a lot of places over the last couple of years. "I don't think. Do you know who designs shoes like the ones I'm wearing, Peabody?"

"The shoe god. Those are magolicious shoes, sir."

"No, not the shoe god. These are the product of a man, a devious flesh-and-blood man who secretly hates all women. By designing shoes like this, he can torture them for profit."

"They make your legs look a hundred feet tall."

"Yeah, that's what I want all right. A pair of hundred-foot legs." Resigned, she stepped off on fifty-one.

The door to Penthouse B was wide as a truck, and opened by a petite woman in her thirties wearing a moss-green dressing gown.

Her hair was long and sleep-tousled, and was a deep, dark red with subtle gold streaks streamed through it.

"Lieutenant Dallas? God, is that a Leonardo?"

Since she was goggling at the dress, it didn't take Eve long to conclude she was talking about it. "Probably." As Leonardo was not only the current darling of the fashionable set, but also the main squeeze of Eve's closest friend. "I was . . . at a thing. My partner, Detective Peabody. Mrs. Vanderlea?"

"Yes, I'm Deann Vanderlea. What's this about?"

"Can we come in, Mrs. Vanderlea?"

"Yes, of course. I'm confused. When they called from downstairs and said the police wanted to see me, my first thought was something happened to Luther. But I'd have gotten a call from Madrid, wouldn't I?" She smiled, uncertainly. "Nothing's happened to Luther, has it?"

"We're not here about your husband. This concerns Elisa Maplewood."

"Elisa? Well, she's in bed at this hour. Elisa can't be in any trouble." She folded her arms. "What's this about?"

"When did you last see Ms. Maplewood?"

"Right before I went to bed. About ten. I went to bed early. I had a headache. What *is* this?"

"I'm sorry to tell you, Mrs. Vanderlea, but Ms. Maplewood is dead. She was killed earlier tonight."

"That—that's just ridiculous. She's in bed."

The simplest, cleanest way, Eve knew, was not to argue. "You may want to check on that."

"It's nearly four in the morning. Of course she's in bed. Her suite is back here, off the kitchen."

She swept away, through the spacious living area, furnished in what Eve recognized as antiques. A lot of gleaming wood and curved lines, deep colors, complex patterns, and sparkling glassware. It flowed into a media room, with the wall screen recessed, and the game and communication center housed in some sort of cabinet. Armoire, she corrected. That's what Roarke called those big-ass cabinets.

A dining room angled off to the side, with the kitchen behind it.

"I'd like you to wait here, please."

Snippy now, Eve noted. Irritated and afraid.

Mrs. Vanderlea opened a set of wide pocket doors and walked into what Eve assumed was Elisa Maplewood's personal area.

"This place is *huge*," Peabody whispered.

"Yeah, lots of space, lots of stuff." She looked around the kitchen. Everything was silver and black. Dramatic, efficient, and so clean she doubted even a team of sweepers would come up with a single mote of dust.

It wasn't that different a setup than the one in Roarke's house. She didn't think of the kitchen as hers. That was Summerset's province, and she was more than happy to let him rule there.

"I've met her before."

Peabody glanced back from her ogling of the massive AutoChef. "You know Vanderlea?"

"Met them, don't know them. One of the 'dos' I got dragged to. Roarke knows them. I didn't place the name, who the hell can remember all those *people?* But her face clicked."

She turned as Mrs. Vanderlea hurried back into the room. "She's not there. I don't understand. She's not in her room, or anywhere in her suite. Vonnie's sleeping. Her daughter, her little girl. I don't understand."

"Does she often go out at night?"

"No, of course she—*Mignon!*" With this, she dashed back into Elisa's suite.

"Who the hell is Mignon?" Eve muttered.

"Maybe Maplewood switched to girls. Might have a lover."

"Mignon's not here." Deann was sheet-white now, and her fingers trembled as she held them to her throat.

"Who is—"

"Our dog." She spoke quickly, the words jumping out of her mouth. "Really Elisa's dog, emotionally. A little teacup poodle I bought a few months ago—for company, for the girls, but Mignon bonded with Elisa. She—she probably took her for a walk. She often does that the last thing at night. She took the dog for a walk. Oh God. Oh my God."

"Mrs. Vanderlea, why don't you sit down. Peabody, some water?"

"Was there an accident? Oh God, was there an accident?" There weren't tears, not yet, but Eve knew there would be.

"No, I'm sorry, it wasn't an accident. Ms. Maplewood was attacked, in the park."

"Attacked?" She said it slowly, as if the word were foreign. "Attacked?"

"She was murdered."

"No. No."

"Drink a little water, ma'am." Peabody pressed the glass she'd poured into Deann's hands. "Sip a little water."

"I can't. I can't. How can this be? We were just talking, a few hours ago. We were sitting right here. She told me to take a blocker and go to bed. And I did. We . . . the girls were tucked in for the night, and she made me tea and told me to go to bed. How did this happen? What happened?"

No, Eve thought. It wasn't the time to make it worse with details. "Drink some water." She noticed Peabody going over to close the pocket doors.

The kid, Eve remembered. This wasn't a conversation a child should hear, if she should wake.

When she did wake, Eve thought, her world would be changed, irrevocably.

The 25th novel in the *New York Times* bestselling series featuring Eve Dallas

Creation in Death

by Nora Roberts writing as J. D. Robb

New York City, 2060: Lieutenant Eve Dallas never forgets a corpse. Her new case will resurrect memories of the women she couldn't save—and the killer who slipped out of her grasp...

"She is a woman who just doesn't know how to tell a bad story...If you haven't read Robb, this is a great place to start." —STEPHEN KING

"All the elements of a terrific police procedural coupled with gut-searing emotional drama and in-your-face characters that only a writer of Nora Roberts's caliber can deliver." —DAVID BALDACCI

"There's no such thing as too much Nora Roberts... Wonderful!" —ROBERT B. PARKER

penguin.com

M188T0308

Everyone's reading
NORA ROBERTS
writing as
J. D. ROBB